P9-BUI-426

PRAISE FOR
Bernard Cornwell

"One of today's truly great storytellers."
—Kirkus Reviews

"The direct heir to Patrick O'Brian."
—The Economist

"Perhaps the greatest writer of historical adventure novels today."
—Washington Post

PRAISE FOR
Sharpe's Devil

"A rousing read."
—Booklist

"With a plot up to its neck in blood and guts, this is adventure naked and unashamed."
—Mail on Sunday (London)

PRAISE FOR
the Richard Sharpe Series

"Richard Sharpe has the most astounding knack for finding himself where the action is . . . and adding considerably to it."
—Wall Street Journal

"Excellently entertaining. If you love historical drama . . . then look no further."
—Boston Globe

"Cornwell's blending of the fictional Sharpe with historical figures and actual battles gives the narrative a stunning sense of realism. . . . If only all history lessons could be as vibrant."
—San Francisco Chronicle

"A hero in the mold of James Bond, although his weapons are a Baker carbine and a giant cavalry sword."
—Philadelphia Inquirer

"Eminently successful historical fiction."
—Booklist

"The Sharpe novels do for the early-nineteenth-century land campaigns what Patrick O'Brian's Aubrey-Maturin series does for the sea. . . . His books do what good historical fiction must do—bring the period to life, and teach the reader something without making him feel as if he is back in school. On both counts, Cornwell succeeds admirably."
—American Way

Kelly Campbell

About the Author

BERNARD CORNWELL is the author of the acclaimed and bestselling Richard Sharpe series; the Grail Quest series, featuring *The Archer's Tale*, *Vagabond*, and *Heretic*; the Nathaniel Starbuck Chronicles; the Warlord Trilogy; and many other novels, including *Redcoat, Stonehenge 2000 B.C.*, and *Gallows Thief*. Bernard Cornwell lives with his wife in Cape Cod.

BOOKS BY BERNARD CORNWELL

The Sharpe Novels (in chronological order)

SHARPE'S TIGER*
Richard Sharpe and the Siege of Seringapatam, 1799

SHARPE'S TRIUMPH*
Richard Sharpe and the Battle of Assaye, September 1803

SHARPE'S FORTRESS*
Richard Sharpe and the Siege of Gawilghur, December 1803

SHARPE'S TRAFALGAR*
Richard Sharpe and the Battle of Trafalgar, October 21, 1805

SHARPE'S PREY*
Richard Sharpe and the Expedition to Copenhagen, 1807

SHARPE'S RIFLES
Richard Sharpe and the French Invasion of Galicia, January 1809

SHARPE'S HAVOC*
Richard Sharpe and the Campaign in Northern Portugal, Spring 1809

SHARPE'S EAGLE
Richard Sharpe and the Talavera Campaign, July 1809

SHARPE'S GOLD
Richard Sharpe and the Destruction of Almeida, August 1810

SHARPE'S ESCAPE*
Richard Sharpe and the Bussaco Campaign, September to October 1810

SHARPE'S BATTLE*
Richard Sharpe and the Battle of Fuentes de Oñoro, May 1811

SHARPE'S COMPANY
Richard Sharpe and the Siege of Badajoz, January to April 1812

SHARPE'S SWORD
Richard Sharpe and the Salamanca Campaign, June and July 1812

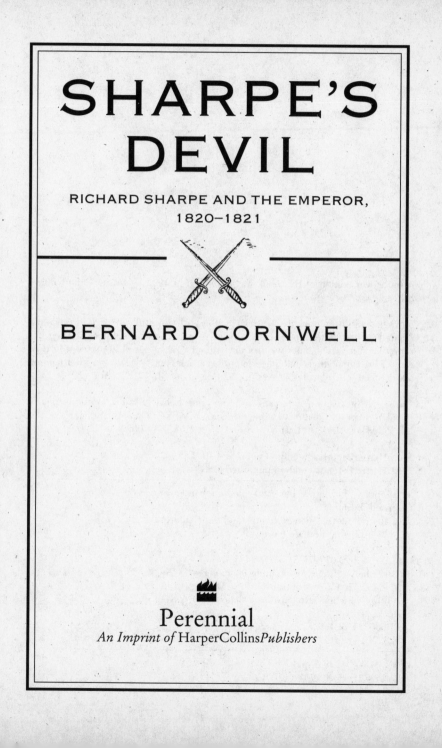

SHARPE'S DEVIL

RICHARD SHARPE AND THE EMPEROR,
1820–1821

BERNARD CORNWELL

Perennial
An Imprint of HarperCollinsPublishers

A hardcover edition of this book was published in 1992 by HarperCollins Publishers.

SHARPE'S DEVIL. Copyright © 1992 by Bernard Cornwell. All rights reserved. Printed in the United States of America. No part of this book may be used or reproduced in any manner whatsoever without written permission except in the case of brief quotations embodied in critical articles and reviews. For information address HarperCollins Publishers, Inc., 10 East 53rd Street, New York, NY 10022.

HarperCollins books may be purchased for educational, business, or sales promotional use. For information please write: Special Markets Department, HarperCollins Publishers, Inc., 10 East 53rd Street, New York, NY 10022.

First HarperPaperbacks edition published 1993.
First HarperPerennial edition published 1999.

The Library of Congress has catalogued the hardcover edition as follows:
Cornwell, Bernard.
    Sharpe's devil : Richard Sharpe and the Emperor,
1820–1821 / by Bernard Cornwell.
      p. cm.
   ISBN 0-06-017977-5
    1. Sharpe, Richard (Fictitious character)—
Fiction.   2. Great Britain—History, Military—19th
century—Fiction. 3. Historical fiction. 4. Adventure
stories. I. Title
PR6053.O75S495   1992
823'.914—dc20   91-58360

ISBN 0-06-093229-5 (pbk.)
   05 RRD H 20 19 18 17 16 15

Sharpe's Devil is affectionately
dedicated to Toby Eady,
my friend and agent,
who has endured Sharpe and me
these many years.

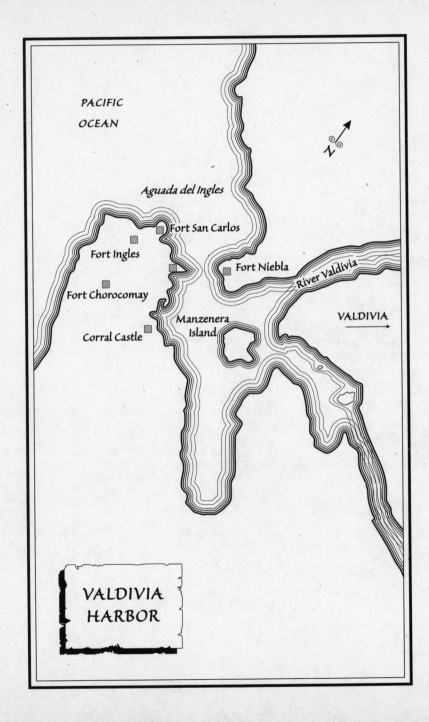

PACIFIC
OCEAN

Aguada del Ingles

Fort San Carlos

Fort Ingles

Fort Niebla

River Valdivia

Fort Chorocomay

VALDIVIA

Manzenera
Island

Corral Castle

N

VALDIVIA
HARBOR

PROLOGUE

There were sixteen men and only twelve mules. None of the men was willing to abandon the journey, so tempers were edgy and not made any better by the day's oppressive and steamy heat. The sixteen men were waiting by the shore, where the black basalt cliffs edged the small port and where there was no wind to relieve the humidity. Somewhere in the hills there sounded a grumble of thunder.

All but one of the sixteen men were uniformed. They stood sweltering and impatient in the shade of heavily branched evergreen trees while the twelve mules, attended by black slaves, drooped beside a briar hedge that was brilliant with small white roses. The sun, climbing toward noon, shimmered an atmosphere that smelled of roses, pomegranates, seaweed, myrtle and sewage.

Two warships, their square-cut sails turned dirty gray by the long usage of wind and rain, patroled far offshore. Closer, in the anchorage itself, a large Spanish frigate lay to twin anchors. It was not a good anchorage, for the ocean's swells were scarcely vitiated by the embracing shore, nor was the water at the quayside deep enough to allow a great ship to moor alongside, and so the sixteen men had come ashore in the Spanish frigate's longboats. Now they waited in the oppressive, windless heat. In one of the houses just beyond the rose-bright hedge a baby cried.

"More mules are being fetched. If you gentlemen will do

us the honor of patience? And accept our sincerest apologies." The speaker, a very young red-coated British Lieutenant whose face was running with sweat, displayed too much contrition. "We didn't expect sixteen gentlemen, you understand, only fourteen, though of course there would still have been insufficient transport, but I have spoken with the Adjutant, and he assures me that extra mules are being saddled, and we do apologize for the confusion." The Lieutenant had spoken in a rush of words, but now abruptly stopped as it dawned on him that most of the sixteen travelers would not have understood a word he had spoken. The Lieutenant blushed, then turned to a tall, scarred and dark-haired man who wore a faded uniform jacket of the British 95th Rifles. "Can you translate for me, sir?"

"More mules are coming," the Rifleman said in laconic, but fluent Spanish. It had been nearly six years since the Rifleman had last used the language regularly, yet thirty-eight days on a Spanish ship had brought his fluency back. He turned again to the Lieutenant. "Why can't we walk to the house?"

"It's all of five miles, sir, uphill, and very steep." The Lieutenant pointed to the hillside above the trees where a narrow road could just be seen zig-zagging perilously up the flax-covered slope. "You really are best advised to wait for the mules, sir."

The tall Rifle officer made a grunting noise, which the young Lieutenant took for acceptance of his wise advice. Emboldened, the Lieutenant took a step closer to the Rifleman. "Sir?"

"What?"

"I just wondered." The Lieutenant, overwhelmed by the Rifleman's scowl, stepped back. "Nothing, sir. It doesn't signify."

"For God's sake, boy, speak up! I won't bite you."

"It was my father, sir. He often spoke of you and I wondered if you might recall him? He was at Salamanca, sir. Hardacre? Captain Roland Hardacre?"

"No."

"He died at San Sebastian?" Lieutenant Hardacre added pathetically, as though that last detail might revive his father's image in the Rifleman's memory.

The Rifleman made another grunting noise that might have been translated as sympathy, but was in fact the inadequate sound of a man who never knew how to react properly to such revelations. So many men had died, so many widows still wept and so many children would be forever fatherless that the Rifleman doubted there was a sufficiency of pity for all the war's doings. "I didn't know him, Lieutenant, I'm sorry."

"It was truly an honor to meet you anyway, sir," Lieutenant Hardacre said, then stepped gingerly backward as though he might yet be attacked by the tall man whose black hair bore a badger streak of white and whose dark face was slashed by a jagged scar. The Rifleman, who was wishing he could respond more easily and sympathetically to such appeals to his memory, was Richard Sharpe. His uniform, which might have looked shabby on a beggar's back, bore the faded insignia of a Major, though at the war's end, when he had fought at the greatest widow-making field of all, he had been a Lieutenant Colonel. Now, despite his uniform and the sword that hung at his side, he was just plain mister and a farmer.

Sharpe turned away from the embarrassed Lieutenant to stare morosely across the sun-glinting sea at the far ships that guarded this lonely, godforsaken coast. Sharpe's scar gave him a sardonic and mocking look. His companion, on the other hand, had a cheerful and genial face. He was a very tall man, even taller than Sharpe himself, and was the only man among the sixteen travelers not wearing a uniform. Instead the man was dressed in a brown wool coat and black breeches that were far too thick for this tropical heat and, in consequence, the tall man, who was also hugely fat, was sweating profusely. The discomfort had evidently not affected his cheerfulness, for he gazed happily about at the dark cliffs, at the banyan trees, at the slave huts, at the rain clouds swelling above the black volcanic peaks, at the sea, at the small town, and at last delivered himself of his considered verdict. "A rare old shitheap of a place, wouldn't you say?" The fat man, who was called Mister Patrick Harper and was Sharpe's companion on this voyage, had expressed the exact same sentiment at dawn when, as their ship crept on a small wind to the island's anchorage, the first light had revealed the unappealing landscape.

"It's more than the bastard deserves," Sharpe replied, but without much conviction, merely in the tone of a man making conversation to pass the time.

"It's still a shitheap. How in Christ's name did they ever find the place? That's what I want to know. God's in his heaven, but we're a million miles from anywhere on earth, so we are!"

"I suppose a ship was off course and bumped into the bloody place."

Harper fanned his face with the brim of his broad hat. "I wish they'd bring the bloody mules. I'm dying of the bloody heat, so I am. It must be a fair bit cooler up in them hills."

"If you weren't so fat," Sharpe said mildly, "we could walk."

"Fat! I'm just well made, so I am." The response, immediate and indignant, was well practiced, so that if any man had been listening he would have instantly realized that this was an old and oft-repeated altercation between the two men. "And what's wrong with being properly made?" Harper continued. "Mother of Christ, just because a man lives well there's no need to make remarks about the evidence of his health! And look at yourself! The Holy Ghost has more beef on its bones than you do. If I boiled you down I wouldn't get so much as a pound of lard for my trouble. You should eat like I do!" Patrick Harper proudly thumped his chest, thus setting off a seismic quiver of his belly.

"It isn't the eating," Sharpe said. "It's the beer."

"Stout can't make you fat!" Patrick Harper was deeply offended. He had been Sharpe's sergeant for most of the French wars and then, as now, Sharpe could think of no one he would rather have beside him in a fight. But in the years since the wars the Irishman had run a hostelry in Dublin, "and a man has to be seen drinking his own wares," Harper would explain defensively, "because it gives folks a confidence in the quality of what a man sells, so it does. Besides, Isabella likes me to have a bit of flesh on my bones. It shows I'm healthy, she says."

"That must make you the healthiest bugger in Dublin!" Sharpe said, but without malice. He had not seen his friend for over three years and had been shocked when Harper had arrived in France with a belly wobbling like a sack of live eels, a face as round as the full moon and legs as thick as howitzer barrels. Sharpe himself, five years after the battle at Waterloo, could still wear his old uniform. Indeed, this very morning, taking the uniform from his sea chest, he had been forced to stab a new hole in the belt of his trousers to save them from collapsing around his ankles. He wore another belt over his jacket, but this one merely to support his sword. It felt very strange to have the weapon hanging at his side again. He had spent most of his life as a soldier, from the age of sixteen until he was thirty-eight, but in the last few years he had become accustomed to a farmer's life. From time to time he might carry a gun to scare the rooks out of Lucille's orchard or to take a hare for the pot, but he had long abandoned the big sword to its decorative place over the fireplace in the chateau's hall, where Sharpe had hoped it would stay forever.

Except now he was wearing the sword again, and the uniform, and he was again in the company of soldiers. And of sixteen mules, because four more animals had at last been found and led to the waiting men who, trying to keep their dignity, clumsily straddled the mangy beasts. The black slaves tried not to show their amusement as Patrick Harper clambered onto an animal that looked only half his own size, yet which somehow sustained his weight.

An English Major, a choleric-looking man mounted on a black mare, led the way out of the small town and onto the narrow mountain road which made its tortuous way up the towering mountainside toward the island's interior. The slopes on either side of the road were green with tall flax plants. A lizard, iridescent in the sunlight, darted across Sharpe's path and one of the slaves, who was following close behind the mounted men, darted after the animal.

"I thought slavery had been abolished?" commented Harper, who had evidently forgiven Sharpe for the remarks about his fatness.

"In Britain, yes," Sharpe said, "but this isn't British territory."

"It isn't? What the hell is it then?" Harper asked indignantly. And indeed, if the island did not belong to Britain then it seemed ridiculous for it to be so thickly inhabited with British troops. Off to their left was a barrack where three companies of redcoats were being drilled on the parade ground, to their right a group of scarlet-coated officers were exercising their horses on a hill slope, while ahead, where the valley climbed out of the thick flax into the bare uplands, a guardpost straddled the road beside an idle semaphore station. The flag above the guardpost was the British union flag. "Are you telling me this might be Irish land?" Harper asked with heavy sarcasm.

"It belongs to the East India Company," Sharpe explained patiently. "It's a place where they can supply their ships."

"It looks bloody English to me, so it does. Except for them black fellows. You remember that darkie we had in the grenadier company? Big fellow? Died at Toulouse?"

Sharpe nodded. The black fellow had been one of the battalion's few casualties at Toulouse, killed a week after the peace treaty had been signed, only no one at the time knew of it.

"I remember he got drunk at Burgos," Harper said. "We put him on a charge and he still couldn't stand up straight when we marched him in for punishment next morning. What the hell was his name? Tall fellow, he was. You must remember him. He married Corporal Roe's widow, and she got pregnant and Sergeant Finlayson was taking bets on whether the nipper would be white or black. What was his name, for Christ's sake?" Harper frowned in frustration. Ever since he had met Sharpe in France they had held conversations like this, trying to flesh out the ghosts of a past that was fast becoming attenuated.

"Bastable," the name suddenly shot into Sharpe's head, "Thomas Bastable."

"Bastable! That was him, right enough. He used to close his eyes whenever he fired a musket, and I never could get him out of the habit. He probably put more bullets into more angels than any soldier in history, God rest his soul. But he was a terror with the bayonet. Jesus, but he could be a terror with a spike!"

"What color was the baby?" Sharpe asked.

"Bit of both, far as I remember. Like milky tea. Finlayson wouldn't pay out till we had a quiet word with him behind the lines, but he was always a slippery bugger, Finlayson. I never did understand why you gave him the stripes." Harper fell silent as the small group of uniformed men approached a shuttered house that was surrounded by a neatly trimmed hedge. Bright flowers grew in a border on either side of a pathway made from crushed seashells. A gardener, who looked Chinese, was digging in the vegetable patch beside the house, while a young woman, fair-haired and white-dressed, sat reading under a gazebo close to the front hedge. She looked up, smiled a familiar greeting at the red-faced Major who led the convoy of mules, then stared with frank curiosity at the strangers. The Spanish officers bowed their heads gravely, Sharpe tipped his old-fashioned brown tri-corne hat, while Harper offered her a cheerful smile. "It's a fine morning, miss!"

"Too hot, I think." Her accent was English, her voice gen-tle. "We're going to have rain this afternoon."

"Better rain than cold. It's freezing back home, so it is."

The girl smiled, but did not respond again. She looked down at her book and slowly turned a page. Somewhere in the house a clock struck the tinkling chimes of midday. A cat slept on a windowsill.

The mules climbed slowly on toward the guardpost. They left the flax and the banyan trees and the myrtles behind, emerging onto a plateau where the grass was sparse and brown and the few trees stunted and wind-bent. Beyond the barren grassland were sudden saw-edged peaks, black and menacing, and on one of those rocky crags was a white-walled house which had the gaunt gallows of a semaphore station built on its roof. The semaphore house stood on the skyline and, because they were backed by the turbulent dark rain clouds, its white painted walls looked unnaturally bright. The semaphore machine beside the guardhouse on the road suddenly clattered into life, its twin black arms creaking as they jerked up and down.

"They'll be telling everyone that we're coming," Harper, who was finding every mundane event of this hot day exciting, said happily.

"Like as not," Sharpe said.

The redcoats on duty at the guardpost saluted as the Spanish officers rode past. Some smiled at the sight of the monstrous Harper overlapping the struggling mule, but their faces turned to stone when Sharpe glowered at them. Christ, Sharpe thought, but these men must be bored. Stuck four thousand miles from home with nothing to do but watch the sea and the mountains and to wonder about the small house five miles from the anchorage. "You do realize," Sharpe said to Harper suddenly, and with a sour expression, "that we're almost certainly wasting our time."

"Aye, maybe we are," Harper, accustomed to Sharpe's sudden dark moods, replied with great equanimity, "but we still thought it worth trying, didn't we? Or would you come all this way and stay locked up in your cabin? You can always turn back."

Sharpe rode on without answering. Dust drifted back from his mule's hooves. Behind him the telegraph gave a last clatter and was still. In a shallow valley to Sharpe's left was another English encampment, while to his right, a mile away, a group of uniformed men exercised their horses. When they saw the approaching party of Spaniards they spurred away toward a house that lay isolated at the center of the plateau and within a protective wall and a cordon of red-coated guards.

The horsemen, who were escorted by a single British officer, were not wearing the ubiquitous red coats of the island's garrison, but instead wore dark blue uniforms. It had been five years since Sharpe had seen such uniform jackets worn openly. The men who wore that blue had once ruled Europe from Moscow to Madrid, but now their bright star had fallen and their sovereignty was confined to the yellow stucco walls of the lonely house that lay at this road's end.

The yellow house was low and sprawling, and surrounded by dark, glossy-leaved trees and a rank garden. There was nothing cheerful about the place. It had been built as a cow-shed, extended to become a summer cottage for the island's Lieutenant Governor, but now, in the dying days of 1820, the house was home to fifty prisoners, ten horses and unnum-bered rats. The house was called Longwood, it lay in the very middle of the island of Saint Helena, and its most important prisoner had once been the Emperor of France.

Bonaparte.

They were not, after all, wasting their time.

It seemed that General Bonaparte had an avid appetite for visitors who could bring him news of the world beyond Saint Helena's seventy square miles. He received such visitors after luncheon, and as his luncheon was always at eleven in the morning, and it was now twenty minutes after noon, the Spanish officers were told that if they cared to walk in the gardens for a few moments, His Majesty would receive them when he was ready.

Not "General Bonaparte," which was the greatest dignity his British jailers would allow him, but "His Majesty," the Emperor, would receive the visitors, and any visitor unwilling to address His Majesty as *Votre Majesté* was invited to strad-dle his mule and take the winding hill road back to the port of Jamestown. The Captain of the Spanish frigate, a reclusive man called Ardiles, had bridled at the instruction, but had restrained his protest, while the other Spaniards, all of them army officers, had equably agreed to address His Majesty as majestically as he demanded. Now, as His Majesty finished luncheon, his compliant visitors walked in the gardens where toadstools grew thick on the lawn. Clouds, building in the west, were reflected in the murky surfaces of newly dug ponds. The English Major who had led the procession up to the plateau, and who evidently had no intention of paying any respects to General Bonaparte, had stepped in the deep mud of one of the pond banks, and now tried to scrape the muck off his boots with his riding crop. There was a grumble of thunder from the heavy clouds above the white-walled semaphore station.

"It's hard to believe, isn't it?" Harper was as excited as a child taken to a country fair. "You remember when we first saw him? Jesus! It was raining that day, so it was." That first glimpse had been at the battlefield of Quatre Bras, two days before Waterloo, when Sharpe and Harper had seen the Emperor, surrounded by lancers, in the watery distance. Two days later, before the bigger bloodletting began, they had watched Bonaparte ride a white horse along the French ranks. Now they had come to his prison and it was, as Harper had said, hard to believe that they were so close to the ogre, the tyrant, the scourge of Europe. And even stranger that Bonaparte was willing to receive them so that, for a few heart-stopping moments on this humid day, two old soldiers of Britain's army would stand in the same stuffy room as Bonaparte and would hear his voice and see his eyes and go away to tell their children and their grandchildren that they had met Europe's bogeyman face to face. They would be able to boast that they had not just fought against him for year after bitter year, but that they had stood, nervous as schoolboys, on a carpet in his prison house on an island in the middle of the South Atlantic.

Sharpe, even as he waited, found it hard to believe that Bonaparte would receive them. He had ridden all the way from Jamestown in the belief that this expedition would be

met with a scornful refusal, but had consoled himself that it
would be sufficient just to see the lair of the man who had
once terrified all of Europe, and whose name was still used
by women to frighten their children into obedience. But the
uniformed men who opened Longwood's gates had welcomed them, and a servant now brought them a tray of weak
lemonade. The servant apologized for such pale refreshment,
explaining that His Majesty would have liked to serve his dis-
tinguished visitors wine, but that his British jailers were too
mean to provide him with a sufficient supply, and so the lemonade must be enough. The Spanish officers turned dark,
reproving glances on Sharpe, who shrugged. Above the hills
the thunder growled. The English Major, disdaining to min-
gle with the Spanish visitors, slashed with his riding crop at a
glossy-leaved hedge.

After a half hour the sixteen visitors were ushered into the
house itself. It smelled dank and musty. The wallpaper of the
hallway and of the billiard room beyond was stained with
damp. The pictures on the wall were black and white etchings, soiled and fly-blown. The house reminded Sharpe of a
poor country rectory that desperately pretended to a higher
gentility than it could properly afford. The house was certainly a pathetically far cry from the great marble floors and
mirrored halls of Paris where Sharpe and Harper, after the
French surrender in 1815, had joined the soldiers of all
Europe to explore the palaces of a defeated and humiliated
empire. Then, in echoing halls of glory, Sharpe had climbed
massive staircases where glittering throngs had once courted
the ruler of France. Now Sharpe waited to see the same man
in an anteroom where three buckets betrayed that the house
roof leaked, and where the green baize surface of the billiard
table was as scuffed and faded as the Rifleman's jacket that
Sharpe had worn in special honor of this occasion.

They waited another twenty minutes. A clock ticked

loudly, then wheezed as it gathered its strength to strike the half hour. Just as the clock's bell chimed, two officers wearing French uniforms with badly tarnished gold braid came into the billiard room. One gave swift instructions in French which the other man translated into bad Spanish.

The visitors were welcome to meet the Emperor, but must remember to present themselves bareheaded to His Imperial Majesty.

The visitors must stand. The Emperor would sit, but no one else was allowed to sit in His Imperial Majesty's presence.

No man must speak unless invited to do so by His Imperial Majesty.

And, the visitors were told once again, if a man was invited to speak with His Imperial Majesty then he must address the Emperor as *Votre Majesté*. Failure to do so would lead to an immediate termination of the interview. Ardiles, the dark-faced Captain of the frigate, scowled at the reiterated command, but again made no protest. Sharpe was fascinated by the tall, whip-thin Ardiles, who took extraordinary precautions to avoid meeting his own passengers. Ardiles ate his meals alone, and was said to appear on deck only when the weather was appalling or during the darkest night watches when his passengers could be relied on to be either sick or asleep. Sharpe had met the Captain briefly when he had embarked on the *Espiritu Santo* in Cadiz, but to some of the Spanish army officers this visit to Longwood gave them their first glimpse of their frigate's mysterious Captain.

The French officer who had translated the etiquette instructions into clumsy Spanish now looked superciliously at Sharpe and Harper. "Did you understand anything at all?" he asked in badly accented English.

"We understood perfectly, thank you, and are happy to accept your instructions," Sharpe answered in colloquial

French. The officer seemed startled, then gave the smallest nod of acknowledgment.

"His Majesty will be ready soon," the first French officer said, and then the whole group waited in an awkward silence. The Spanish army officers, gorgeous in their uniforms, had taken off their bicorne hats in readiness for the imperial audience. Their boots creaked as they shifted their weight from foot to foot. A sword scabbard rapped against the bulbous leg of the billiard table. The sour Captain Ardiles, looking as malignant as a bishop caught in a whorehouse, stared sourly out of the window to where a rumble of ominous thunder cannoned about the black mountains. Harper rolled a billiard ball slowly down the table's length. It bounced off the far cushion and slowed to a stop.

Then the double doors at the far end of the room were snatched open and a servant dressed in green and gold livery stood in the entrance. "The Emperor will receive you now," he said, then stood aside.

And Sharpe, his heart beating as fearfully as if he again walked into battle, went to meet an old enemy.

It was all so utterly different from everything Sharpe had anticipated. Later, trying to reconcile reality with expectation, Sharpe wondered just what he had thought to find inside the yellow-walled house. The ogre of legend? A small toadlike man with smoke coming from his nostrils? A horned devil with bloody claws? But instead, standing on a hearth rug in front of an empty fireplace, Sharpe saw a short, stout man wearing a plain green riding coat with a velvet collar, black knee breeches and coarse white stockings. In the velvet lapel of the coat was a miniature medallion of the Légion d'honneur.

All those details Sharpe noticed later, as the interview progressed, but his very first impression as he went through the

door and shuffled awkwardly into line was the shock of famil-
iarity. This was the most famous face in the world, a face
repeated on a million pictures, a million etchings, a million
plates, a million coins. This was a face so familiar to Sharpe
that it was truly astonishing to see it in reality. He involun-
tarily gasped, causing Harper to push him onward. The
Emperor, recognizing Sharpe's reaction, seemed to smile.

Sharpe's second impression was of the Emperor's eyes.
They seemed full of amusement as though Bonaparte, alone
of all the men in the room, understood that a jest was being
played. The eyes belied the rest of Bonaparte's face, which
was plump and oddly petulant. That petulance surprised
Sharpe, as did the Emperor's hair which alone was unlike his
portraits. It was as fine and wispy as a child's. There was
something feminine and unsettling about that silky hair and
Sharpe perversely wished that Bonaparte would cover it with
the cocked hat he carried under his arm.

"You are welcome, gentlemen," the Emperor greeted the
Spanish officers, which pleasantry was translated into Spanish by a bored-looking aide. The greeting prompted a chorus
of polite responses from all but the disdainful Ardiles.

The Emperor, when all sixteen visitors had found somewhere to stand, sat in a delicate gilt chair. The room was
evidently a drawing room, and was full of pretty furniture,
but it was also as damp as the hallway and billiard room outside. The skirting boards, beneath the water-stained wallpaper, were disfigured by tin plates that had been nailed over
rat holes and, in the silence that followed the Emperor's
greeting, Sharpe could hear the dry scratching of rats' feet in
the cavities behind the tin patched wall. The house was evidently infested as badly as any ship.

"Tell me your business," the Emperor invited the senior
Spanish officer present. That worthy, an artillery Colonel
named Ruiz, explained in hushed tones how their vessel, the

Spanish frigate *Espiritu Santo,* was on passage from Cadiz, carrying passengers to the Spanish garrison at the Chilean port of Valdivia. Ruiz then presented the *Espiritu Santo*'s Captain, Ardiles, who, with scarcely concealed hostility, offered the Emperor a stiffly reluctant bow. The Emperor's aides, sensitive to the smallest sign of disrespect, shifted uneasily, but Bonaparte seemed not to notice or, if he did, not to care. Ardiles, asked by the Emperor how long he had been a seaman, answered as curtly as possible. Clearly the lure of seeing the exiled tyrant had overcome Ardiles's distaste for the company of his passengers, but he was at pains not to show any sense of being honored by the reception.

Bonaparte, never much interested in sailors, turned his attention back to Colonel Ruiz, who formally presented the officers of his regiment of artillery who, in turn, bowed elegantly to the small man in the gilded chair. Bonaparte had a kindly word for each man, then turned his attention back to Ruiz. He wanted to know what impulse had brought Ruiz to Saint Helena. The Colonel explained that the *Espiritu Santo,* thanks to the superior skills of the Spanish Navy, had made excellent time on its southward journey and, being within a few days sailing of Saint Helena, the officers on board the *Espiritu Santo* had thought it only proper to pay their respects to His Majesty the Emperor.

In other words, they could not resist making a detour to stare at the defanged beast chained to its rock, but Bonaparte took Ruiz's flowery compliment at its face value. "Then I trust you will also pay your respects to Sir Hudson Lowe," he said drily. "Sir Hudson is my jailer. He, with five thousand men, seven ships, eight batteries of artillery and the ocean which you gentlemen have crossed to do me this great honor."

While the Spanish-speaking Frenchman translated the Emperor's mixture of scorn for his jailers and insincere flattery for his visitors, Bonaparte's eyes turned toward Sharpe and Harper who, alone in the room, had not been introduced. For a second, Rifleman and Emperor stared into each other's eyes, then Bonaparte looked back to Colonel Ruiz. "So you are reinforcements for the Spanish army in Chile?"

"Indeed, Your Majesty," the Colonel replied.

"So your ship is also carrying your guns? And your gunners?" Bonaparte asked.

"Just the regiment's officers," Ruiz replied. "Captain Ardiles's vessel has been specially adapted to carry passengers, but alas she cannot accommodate a whole regiment. Especially of artillery."

"So the rest of your men are where?" The Emperor asked blithely.

"They're following on two transport ships," Ruiz said airily, "with their guns."

"Ah!" The Emperor's response was apparently a polite acknowledgment of the trivial answer, yet the silence that followed, and the fixity of his smile, were a sudden reproof to these Spaniards who had chosen the comfort of Ardiles's fast frigate while leaving their men to the stinking hulks that would take at least a month longer than the *Espiritu Santo* to make the long, savage voyage around South America to where Spanish troops were trying to reconquer Chile from the rebel government. "Let us hope the rest of your regiment doesn't decide to pay me their respects," Bonaparte broke the slightly uncomfortable mood that his unspoken criticism had caused, "or else Sir Hudson will fear they have come to rescue me!"

Ruiz laughed, the other army officers smiled, and Ardiles, perhaps hearing in the Emperor's voice an edge of longing that the other Spaniards had missed, scowled.

"So tell me," Bonaparte still spoke to Ruiz, "what are your expectations in Chile?"

Colonel Ruiz bristled with confidence as he expressed his eager conviction that the rebel Chilean forces and government would soon collapse, as would all the other insurgents in the Spanish colonies of South America, and that the rightful government of His Majesty King Ferdinand VII would thus be restored throughout Spain's American dominions. The coming of his own regiment, the Colonel asserted, could only hasten that royal victory.

"Indeed," the Emperor agreed politely, then moved the conversation to the subject of Europe, and specifically to the troubles of Spain. Bonaparte politely affected to believe the Colonel's assurance that the liberals would not dare to revolt openly against the King, and his denial that the army, sickened by the waste of blood in South America, was close to mutiny. Indeed, Colonel Ruiz expressed himself full of hope for Spain's future, relishing a monarchy growing ever more powerful, and fed ever more riches by its colonial possessions. The other artillery officers, keen to please their bombastic Colonel, nodded sycophantic agreement, though Captain Ardiles looked disgusted at Ruiz's bland optimism and showed his skepticism by pointedly staring out of the window as he fanned himself with a mildewed cocked hat.

Sharpe, like all the other visitors, was sweating foully. The room was steamy and close, and none of its windows was open. The rain had at last begun to fall and a zinc bucket, placed close to the Emperor's chair, suddenly rang as a drip fell from the leaking ceiling. The Emperor frowned at the noise, then returned his polite attention to Colonel Ruiz who had reverted to his favorite subject of how the rebels in Chile, Peru and Venezuela had overextended themselves and must inevitably collapse.

Sharpe, who had spent too many shipboard hours listening to the Colonel's boasting, studied the Emperor instead of paying any attention to Ruiz's long-winded bragging. By now

Sharpe had recovered his presence of mind, no longer feeling dizzy just to be in the same small room as Bonaparte, and so he made himself examine the seated figure as though he could commit the man to memory forever. Bonaparte was far fatter than Sharpe had expected. He was not as fat as Harper, who was fat like a bull or a prize boar is fat, but instead the Emperor was unhealthily bloated like a dead beast swollen with noxious vapors. His monstrous potbelly, waistcoated in white, rested on his spread thighs. His face was sallow and his fine hair was lank. Sweat pricked at his forehead. His nose was thin and straight, his chin dimpled, his mouth firm and his eyes extraordinary. Sharpe knew Bonaparte was fifty years old, yet the Emperor's face looked much younger than fifty. His body, though, was that of an old, sick man. It had to be the climate, Sharpe supposed, for surely no white man could keep healthy in such a steamy and oppressive heat. The rain was falling harder now, pattering on the yellow stucco wall and on the window, and dripping annoyingly into the zinc bucket. It would be a wet ride back to the harbor where the longboats waited to row the sixteen men back to Ardiles's ship.

Sharpe gazed attentively about the room, knowing that when he was back home Lucille would demand to hear a thousand details. He noted how low the ceiling was, and how the plaster of the ceiling was yellowed and sagging, as if, at any moment, the roof might fall in. He heard the scrabble of rats again, and marked other signs of decay like the mildew on the green velvet curtains, the tarnish in the silvering of a looking-glass, and the flaking of the gilt on the glass's frame. Under the mirror a pack of worn playing cards lay carelessly strewn on a small round table beside a silver-framed portrait of a child dressed in an elaborate uniform. A torn cloak, lined with a check pattern, hung from a hook on the door. "And you, *monsieur,* you are no Spaniard. What is your business here?"

The Emperor's question, in French, had been addressed to Sharpe who, taken aback and not concentrating, said nothing. The interpreter, assuming that Sharpe had misunderstood the Emperor's accent, began to translate, but then Sharpe, suddenly dry-mouthed and horribly nervous, found his tongue. "I am a passenger on the *Espiritu Santo,* Your Majesty. Traveling to Chile with my friend from Ireland, Mister Patrick Harper."

The Emperor smiled. "Your very substantial friend?"

"When he was my Regimental Sergeant Major he was somewhat less substantial, but just as impressive." Sharpe could feel his right leg twitching with fear. Why, for God's sake? Bonaparte was just another man, and a defeated one at that. Moreover, the Emperor was a man, Sharpe tried to convince himself, of no account anymore. The prefect of a small French *departement* had more power than Bonaparte now, yet still Sharpe felt dreadfully nervous.

"You are passengers?" the Emperor asked in wonderment. "Going to Chile?"

"We are traveling to Chile in the interests of an old friend. We go to search for her husband, who is missing in battle. It is a debt of honor, Your Majesty."

"And you, *monsieur?*" The question, in French, was addressed to Harper, "you travel for the same reason?"

Sharpe translated both the question and Harper's answer. "He says that he found life after the war tedious, Your Majesty, and thus welcomed this chance to accompany me."

"Ah! How well I understand tedium. Nothing to do but put on weight, eh?" The Emperor lightly patted his belly, then looked back to Sharpe. "You speak French well, for an Englishman."

"I have the honor to live in France, Your Majesty."

"You do?" The Emperor sounded hurt and, for the first time since the visitors had come into the room, an expression of genuine feeling crossed Bonaparte's face. Then he managed to cover his envy by a friendly smile. "You are accorded a privilege denied to me. Where in France?"

"In Normandy, Your Majesty."

"Why?"

Sharpe hesitated, then shrugged. "*Une femme.*"

The Emperor laughed so naturally that it seemed as though a great tension had snapped in the room. Even Bonaparte's supercilious aides smiled. "A good reason," the Emperor said, "an excellent reason! Indeed, the only reason, for a man usually has no control over women. Your name, *monsieur.*"

"Sharpe, Your Majesty." Sharpe paused, then decided to try his luck at a more intimate appeal to Bonaparte. "I was a friend of General Calvet, of Your Majesty's army. I did General Calvet some small service in Naples before—" Sharpe could not bring himself to say Waterloo, or even to refer to the Emperor's doomed escape from Elba which, by route of fifty thousand deaths, had led to this damp, rat-infested room in the middle of oblivion. "I did the service," Sharpe continued awkwardly, "in the summer of '14."

Bonaparte rested his chin on his right hand and stared for a long time at the Rifleman. The Spaniards, resenting that Sharpe had taken over their audience with the exiled tyrant, scowled. No one spoke. A rat scampered behind the wainscot, rain splashed in the bucket, and the wind gusted sudden and loud in the chimney.

"You will stay here, *monsieur,*" Bonaparte said abruptly to Sharpe, "and we will talk."

The Emperor, conscious of the Spaniards' disgruntlement, turned back to Ruiz and complimented his officers on their martial appearance, then commiserated with their Chilean enemies for the defeat they would suffer when Ruiz's guns finally arrived. The Spaniards, all except for the scowling Ardiles, bristled with gratified pride. Bonaparte thanked them all for visiting him, wished them well on their further voyage, then dismissed them. When they were gone, and when only Sharpe, Harper, an aide-de-camp and the liveried servant remained in the room, the Emperor pointed Sharpe toward a chair. "Sit. We shall talk."

Sharpe sat. Beyond the windows the rain smashed malevolently across the uplands and drowned the newly dug ponds in the garden. The Spanish officers waited in the billiard room, a servant brought wine to the audience room, and Bonaparte talked with a Rifleman.

The Emperor had nothing but scorn for Colonel Ruiz and his hopes of victory in Chile. "They've already lost that war, just as they've lost every other colony in South America, and the sooner they pull their troops out, the better. That man," this was accompanied by a dismissive wave of the hand toward the door through which Colonel Ruiz had disappeared, "is like a man whose house is on fire, but who is saving his piss to extinguish his pipe tobacco. From what I hear there'll be a revolution in Spain within the year." Bonaparte made another scornful gesture at the billiard-room door, then turned his dark eyes on Sharpe. "But who cares about Spain. Talk to me of France."

Sharpe, as best he could, described the nervous weariness of France; how the royalists hated the liberals, who in turn distrusted the republicans, who detested the ultra-royalists, who feared the remaining Bonapartistes, who despised the clergy, who preached against the Orleanists. In short, it was a *cocotte*, a stew pot.

The Emperor liked Sharpe's diagnosis. "Or perhaps it is a powder keg? Waiting for a spark?"

"The powder's damp," Sharpe said bluntly.

Napoleon shrugged. "The spark is feeble, too. I feel old. I am not old! But I feel old. You like the wine?"

"Indeed, sir." Sharpe had forgotten to call Bonaparte *Votre Majesté,* but His Imperial Majesty did not seem to mind.

"It is South African," the Emperor said in wonderment. "I would prefer French wine, but of course the bastards in London won't allow me any, and if my friends do send wine from France then that hog's turd down the hill confiscates it. But this African wine is surprisingly drinkable, is it not? It is called *Vin de Constance.* I suppose they give it a French name to suggest that it has superb quality." He turned the stemmed glass in his hand, then offered Sharpe a wry smile. "But I sometimes dream of drinking a glass of my Chambertin again. You know I made my armies salute those grapes when they marched past the vineyards?"

"So I have heard, sir."

Bonaparte quizzed Sharpe. Where was he born? What had been his regiments? His service? His promotions? The Emperor professed surprise that Sharpe had been promoted from the ranks, and seemed reluctant to credit the Rifleman's claim that one in every twenty British officers had been similarly promoted. "But in my army," Bonaparte said passionately, "you would have become a General! You know that?"

Your army lost, Sharpe thought, but was too polite to say as much, so instead he just smiled and thanked the Emperor for the implied compliment.

"Not that you'd have been a Rifleman in my army." The Emperor provoked Sharpe. "I never had time for rifles. Too delicate a weapon, too fussy, too temperamental. Just like a woman!"

"But soldiers like women, sir, don't they?"

The Emperor laughed. The aide-de-camp, disapproving that Sharpe so often forgot to use the royal honorific, scowled, but the Emperor seemed relaxed. He teased Harper about his belly, ordered another bottle of the South African wine, then asked Sharpe just who it was that he sought in South America.

"His name is Blas Vivar, sir. He is a Spanish officer, and a good one, but he has disappeared. I fought alongside him once, many years ago, and we became friends. His wife asked me to search for him," Sharpe paused, then shrugged. "She is paying me to search for him. She has received no help from her own government, and no news from the Spanish army."

"It was always a bad army. Too many officers, but good troops, if you could make them fight." The Emperor stood and walked stiffly to the window from where he stared glumly at the pelting rain. Sharpe stood as well, out of politeness, but Bonaparte waved him down. "So you know Calvet?" The Emperor turned at last from the rain.

"Yes, sir."

"Do you know his Christian name?"

Sharpe supposed the question was a test to determine if he was telling the truth. He nodded. "Jean."

"Jean!" The Emperor laughed. "He tells people his name is Jean, but in truth he was christened Jean-Baptiste! Ha! The belligerent Calvet is named for the original head-wetter!" Bonaparte gave a brief chuckle at the thought as he returned to his chair. "He's living in Louisiana now."

"Louisiana?" Sharpe could not imagine Calvet in America.

"Many of my soldiers live there." Bonaparte sounded wistful. "They cannot stomach that fat man who calls himself the King of France, so they live in the New World instead." The Emperor shivered suddenly, though the room was far from cold, then turned his eyes back to Sharpe. "Think of all the soldiers scattered throughout the world! Like embers kicked from a campfire. The lawyers and their panders who now rule Europe would like those embers to die down, but such fire is not so easily doused. The embers are men like our friend Calvet, and perhaps like you and your stout Irishman here. They are adventurers and combatants! They do not want peace; they crave excitement, and what the filthy lawyers fear, *monsieur*, is that one day a man might sweep those embers into a pile, for then they would feed on each other and they would burn so fiercely that they would scorch the whole world!" Bonaparte's voice had become suddenly fierce, but now it dropped again into weariness. "I do so hate lawyers. I do not think there was a single achievement of mine that a lawyer did not try to dessicate. Lawyers are not men. I know men, and I tell you I never met a lawyer who had real courage, a soldier's courage, a man's courage." The Emperor closed his eyes momentarily and, when he opened them, his expression was kindly again and his voice relaxed. "So you're going to Chile?"

"Yes, sir."

"Chile." He spoke the name tentatively, as though seeking a memory on the edge of consciousness. "I well recall the service you did me in Naples," the Emperor went on after a pause, "Calvet told me of it. Will you do me another service now?"

"Of course, sir." Sharpe would later be amazed that he had so readily agreed without even knowing what the favor was, but by that moment he was under the spell of a Corsican magician who had once bewitched whole continents; a magician, moreover, who loved soldiers better than he loved anything else in all the world, and the Emperor had known what Sharpe was the instant the British Rifleman had walked into the room. Sharpe was a soldier, one of the Emperor' beloved mongrels, a man able to march through shi' sleet and cold and hunger to fight like a devil at the end of the day, then fight again the next day and the next, and the Emperor could twist such soldiers about his little finger with the ease of a master.

"A man wrote to me. A settler in Chile. He is one of your countrymen, and was an officer in your army, but in the years since the wars he has come to hold some small admiration for myself." The Emperor smiled as though apologizing for such immodesty. "He asked that I would send him a keepsake, and I am minded to agree to his request. Would you deliver the gift for me?"

"Of course, sir." Sharpe felt a small relief that the favor was of such a trifling nature, though another part of him was so much under the thrall of the Emperor's genius that he might have agreed to hack a bloody path down Saint Helena's hillside to the sea and freedom. Harper, sitting beside Sharpe, had the same look of adoration on his face.

"I understand that this man, I can't recall his name, is presently living in the rebel part of the country," the Emperor elaborated on the favor he was asking, "but he tells me that packages given to the American consul in Valdivia always reach him. I gather they were friends. No one else in Valdivia, just the American consul. You do not mind helping me?"

"Of course not, sir."

The Emperor smiled his thanks. "The gift will take some time to choose, and to prepare, but if you can wait two hours, *monsieur?*" Sharpe said he could wait and there was a flurry of orders as an aide was dispatched to find the right gift. Then Napoleon turned to Sharpe again. "No doubt, *monsieur*, you were at Waterloo?"

"Yes, sir. I was."

"So tell me," the Emperor began, and thus they talked, while the Spaniards waited and the rain fell and the sun sank and the redcoat guards tightened their nighttime ring about the walls of Longwood, while inside those walls, as old soldiers do, old soldiers talked.

It was almost full dark as Sharpe and Harper, soaked to the skin, reached the quayside in Jamestown where the *Espiritu Santo*'s longboats waited to take the passengers back to Ardiles's ship.

At the quayside a British officer waited in the rain. "Mister Sharpe?" He stepped up to Sharpe as soon as the Rifleman dismounted from his mule.

"Lieutenant Colonel Sharpe," Sharpe answered, irritated by the man's tone.

"Of course, sir. And a moment of your time, if you would be so very kind?" The man, a tall and thin Major, smiled and guided Sharpe a few paces away from the curious Spanish officers. "Is it true, sir, that General Bonaparte favored you with a gift?"

"He favored each of us with a gift." Each of the Spaniards, except for Ardiles who had received nothing, had been given a silver teaspoon engraved with Napoleon's cipher, while Harper had received a silver thimble inscribed with Napoleon's symbol, a honeybee. Sharpe, having struck an evident note of affection in the Emperor, had been privileged with a silver locket containing a curl of the Emperor's hair.

"But you, sir, forgive me, have a particular gift?" the Major insisted.

"Do I?" Sharpe challenged the Major, and wondered which of the Emperor's servants was the spy.

"Sir Hudson Lowe, sir, would appreciate it mightily if you were to allow him to see the gift." Behind the Major stood an impassive file of redcoats.

Sharpe took the locket from out of his pocket and pressed the button that snapped open the silver lid. He showed the

Major the lock of hair. "Tell Sir Hudson Lowe, with my compliments, that his dog, his wife or his barber can provide him with an infinite supply of such gifts."

The Major glanced at the Spanish officers who, in turn, glowered back. Their displeasure was caused simply by the fact that the Major's presence delayed their departure, and every second's delay kept them from the comforts of the *Espiritu Santo*'s saloon, but the tall Major translated their enmity as something that might lead to an international incident. "You're carrying no other gifts from the General?" he asked Sharpe.

"No others," Sharpe lied. In his pocket he had a framed portrait of Bonaparte, which the Emperor had inscribed to his admirer, whose name was Lieutenant Colonel Charles, but that portrait, Sharpe decided, was none of Sir Hudson Lowe's business.

The Major bowed to Sharpe. "If you insist, sir."

"I do insist, Major."

The Major clearly did not believe Sharpe, but could do nothing about it. He stepped stiffly backward. "Then good day to you, sir."

The *Espiritu Santo* weighed anchor in the next day's dawn and, under a watery sun, headed southward. By midday the island of Saint Helena with its ring of warships was left far behind, as was the Emperor, chained to his rock.

And Sharpe, carrying Bonaparte's gift, sailed to a distant war.

PART
I

BAUTISTA

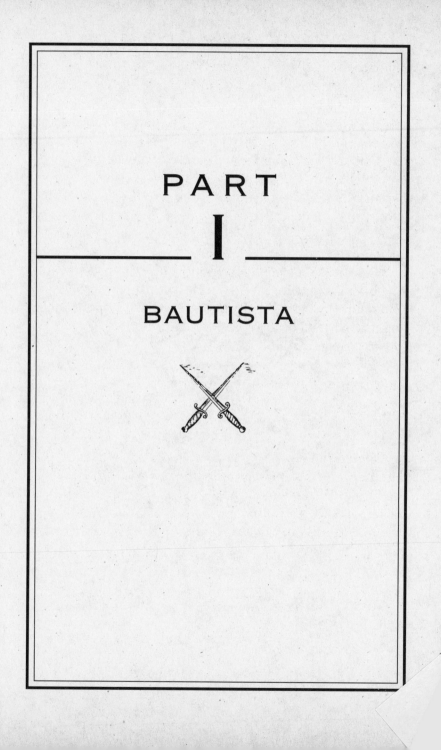

C apitan-General Blas Vivar's wife, the Countess of Mouromorto, had been born and raised in England, but
Sharpe had first met Miss Louisa Parker when, in 1809 and
with thousands of other refugees, she was fleeing from Napoleon's invasion of northern Spain. The Parker family, oblivious to the chaos that was engulfing a continent, could grieve
only for their lost Protestant Bibles with which they had for-
lornly hoped to convert Papist Spain. Somehow, in the wel-
tering chaos, Miss Louisa Parker had met Don Blas Vivar
who, later that same year, became the Count of Mouromorto.
Miss Parker had meanwhile become a Papist, and thereafter
Blas Vivar's wife. Sharpe saw neither of them again till, in
the late summer of 1819, Doña Louisa Vivar, Countess of
Mouromorto, arrived unannounced and unexpected in the
Normandy village where Sharpe farmed.

At first Sharpe did not recognize the tall, black-dressed
woman whose carriage, attended by postilions and outriders,
drew up under the chateau's crumbling arch. He had supposed the lavish carriage to belong to some rich person who,
traveling about Normandy, had become lost in the region's
green tangle of lanes and, it being late on a hot summer's
afternoon, had sought out the largest farmhouse of the village for directions and, doubtless, refreshments as well.
Sharpe, his face sour and unwelcoming, had been prepared
to turn the visitors away by directing them to the inn at Sel-

eglise, but then a dignified woman had stepped down from the carriage and pushed a veil back from her face. "Mister Sharpe?" she had said after a few awkward seconds, and suddenly Sharpe had recognized her, but even then he had found it hard to reconcile this woman's reserved and stately appearance with his memories of an adventurous English girl who had impulsively abandoned both her Protestant religion and the approval of her family to marry Don Blas Vivar, Count of Mouromorto, devout Catholic, and soldier of Spain.

Who, Doña Louisa now informed Sharpe, had disappeared. Blas Vivar had vanished.

Sharpe, overwhelmed by the suddenness of the information and by Louisa's arrival, gaped like a village idiot. Lucille insisted that Doña Louisa must stay for supper, which meant staying for the night, and Sharpe was peremptorily sent about making preparations. There was no spare stabling for Doña Louisa's valuable carriage horses, so Sharpe ordered a boy to unstall the plough horses and take them to a meadow while Lucille organized beds for Doña Louisa and her maids, and rugs for Doña Louisa's coachmen. Luggage had to be unstrapped from the varnished carriage and carried upstairs where the chateau's two maids laid new sheets on the beds. Wine was brought up from the damp cellar, and a fine cheese, which Lucille would otherwise have sent to the market in Caen, was taken from its nettle-leaf wrapping and pronounced fit for the visitor's supper. That supper would not be much different from any of the other peasant meals being eaten in the village for the chateau was pretentious only in its name. The building had once been a nobleman's fortified manor, but was now little more than an overgrown and moated farmhouse.

Doña Louisa, her mind too full of her troubles to notice the fuss her arrival had prompted, explained to Sharpe the immediate cause of her unexpected visit. "I have been in

England and I insisted the Horse Guards tell me where I might find you. I am sorry not to have sent you warning of my coming, but I need help." She spoke peremptorily, her voice that of a woman who was not used to deferring the gratification of her wishes.

She was nevertheless forced to wait while Sharpe's two children were introduced to her. Patrick, age five, offered her ladyship a sturdy bow while Dominique, age three, was more interested in the ducklings that splashed at the moat's edge. "Dominique looks like your wife," Louisa said.

Sharpe merely grunted a noncommittal reply, for he had no wish to explain that he and Lucille were not married, nor how he already had a bitch of a wife in London whom he could not afford to divorce and who would not decently crawl away and die. Nor did Lucille, coming to join Sharpe and their guest at the table in the courtyard, bother to correct Louisa's misapprehension, for Lucille claimed to take more pleasure in being mistaken for Madame Richard Sharpe than in using her ancient title, though Sharpe, much to Lucille's amusement, now insisted on introducing her to Louisa as the Vicomtesse de Seleglise, an honor which duly impressed the Countess of Mouromorto. Lucille, as ever, tried to disown the title by saying that such nonsenses had been abolished in the revolution and, besides, anyone connected to an ancient French family could drag out a title from somewhere. "Half the ploughmen in France are Viscounts," the Viscountess Seleglise said with self-deprecation, then politely asked whether the Countess of Mouromorto had any children.

"Three," Louisa replied, and then went on to explain how an additional two children had died in infancy. Sharpe, supposing that the two women would get down to the interminable and tedious feminine business of making mutual compliments about their respective children, let the conversation become a meaningless drone, but Louisa surprisingly brushed the subject of children aside, only wanting to talk of her missing husband. "He's somewhere in Chile," she said.

Sharpe had to think for a few seconds before he could place Chile, then he remembered a few scraps of information from the newspapers that he read in the inn beside Caen Abbey where he went for dinner on market days. "There's a war of independence going on in Chile, isn't there?"

"A rebellion!" Louisa corrected him sharply. Indeed, she went on, her husband had been sent to suppress the rebellion, though when Don Blas had reached Chile he had discovered a demoralized Spanish army, a defeatist squadron of naval ships, and a treasury bled white by corruption, yet within six months he had been full of hope and had even been promising Louisa that she and the children would soon join him in Valdivia's Citadel which served as Chile's official residence for its Captain-General.

"I thought Santiago was the capital of Chile?" Lucille, who had brought some sewing from the house, inquired gently.

"It was," Louisa admitted reluctantly, then added indignantly, "till the rebels captured it. They now call it the capital of the Chilean Republic. As if there could be such a thing!" And, Louisa claimed, if Don Blas had been given a chance, there would be no Chilean Republic, for her husband had begun to turn the tide of Royalist defeat. He had won a series of small victories over the rebels; such victories were nothing much to boast of, he had written to his wife, but they were the first in many years and they had been sufficient to persuade his soldiers that the rebels were not invincible fiends. Then, suddenly, there were no more letters from Don Blas, only an official dispatch which said that His Excellency Don Blas, Count of Mouromorto and Captain-General of the Spanish Forces in His Majesty's dominion of Chile, had disappeared.

Don Blas, Louisa said, had ridden to inspect the fortifications at the harbor town of Puerto Crucero, the southern-most garrison in Spanish Chile. He had ridden with a cavalry escort, and had been ambushed somewhere north of Puerto Crucero, in a region of steep hills and deep woods. At the time of the ambush Don Blas had been riding ahead of his escort, and he was last seen spurring forward to escape the closing jaws of the rebel trap. The escort, driven away by the fierceness of the ambushers, had not been able to search the valley where the trap had been sprung for another six hours, by which time Don Blas, and his ambushers, had long disappeared.

"He must have been captured by the rebels," Sharpe suggested mildly.

"If you were a rebel commander," Louisa observed icily, "and succeeded in capturing or killing the Spanish Captain-General, would you keep silent about your victory?"

"No," Sharpe admitted, for such a feat would encourage every rebel in South America and concomitantly depress all their Royalist opponents. He frowned. "Surely Don Blas had aides with him?"

"He had a small escort."

"Yet he was riding alone? In rebel country?" Sharpe's soldiering instincts, rusty as they were, rebelled at such a thought.

Louisa, who had rehearsed these questions and answers for weeks, shrugged. "They tell me that no rebels had been seen in those parts for many months. That Don Blas often rode ahead. He was impatient, you surely remember that?"

"But he wasn't foolhardy." A wasp crawled on the table and Sharpe slapped down hard. "The rebels have made no proclamations about Don Blas?"

"None!" There was despair in Louisa's voice. "And when I ask for information from our own army, I am told there is no information to be had. It seems that a Captain-General can disappear in Chile without a trace! I do not even know if I am a widow." She looked at Lucille. "I wanted to travel to Chile, but it would have meant leaving my children. Besides, what can a woman do against the intransigence of soldiers?"

Lucille shot an amused glance at Sharpe, then looked down again at her sewing.

"The army has told you nothing?" Sharpe asked in astonishment.

"They tell me Don Blas is dead. They cannot prove it, for they have never found his body, but they assure me he must be dead." Louisa said that the King had even paid for a Requiem Mass to be sung in Santiago de Compostela's great cathedral, though Louisa had shocked the royal authorities by refusing to attend such a Mass, claiming it to be indecently premature. Don Blas, Louisa insisted, was alive. Her instinct told her so. "He might be a prisoner. I am told there are tribes of heathen savages who are reputed to keep white men as slaves in the forest. And Chile is a terrible country," she explained to Lucille, "there are pygmies and giants in the mountains, while the rebel ranks are filled by rogues from Europe. Who knows what might have happened?"

Lucille made a sympathetic noise, but the mention of white slaves, pygmies, giants and rogues made Sharpe suspect that his visitor's hopes were mere fantasies. In the five years since Waterloo Sharpe had met scores of women who were convinced that a missing son or a lost husband or a vanished lover still lived. Many such women had received notification that their missing man had been killed, but they stubbornly clung to their beliefs; supposing that their loved one was trapped in Russia, or kept prisoner in some remote Spanish town, or perhaps had been carried abroad to some far raw colony. Invariably, Sharpe knew, such men had either settled with different women or, more likely, were long dead and buried, but it was impossible to convince their womenfolk of either harsh truth. Nor did he try to persuade Louisa now, but instead asked her whether Don Blas had been popular in Chile.

"He was too honest to be popular," Louisa said. "Of course he had his supporters, but he was constantly fighting corruption. Indeed, that was why he was traveling to Puerto Crucero. The Governor of the southern province was an enemy of Don Blas. They hated each other, and I heard that Don Blas had proof of the Governor's corruption and was traveling to confront him!"

Which meant, Sharpe wearily thought, that his friend Don Blas had been fighting two enemies: the entrenched Spanish interest as well as the rebels who had captured Santiago and driven the Royalists into the southern half of the country. Don Blas had doubtless been a good enough commander to beat the rebels, but was he a clever enough politician to beat his own side? Sharpe, who knew what an honest man Don Blas was, doubted it, and that doubt convinced him still further that his old friend must be dead. It took a cunning fox to cheat the hunt, while the brave beast that turned to fight the dogs always ended up torn into scraps. "So isn't it likely," Sharpe spoke as gently as he could, "that Don Blas was ambushed by his own side?"

"Indeed it's possible!" Louisa said. "In fact I believe that is precisely what happened. But I would like to be certain."

Sharpe sighed. "If Don Blas was ambushed by his own side, then they are not going to reveal what happened." Sharpe hated delivering such a hopeless opinion, but he knew it was true. "I'm sorry, my lady, but you're never going to know what happened."

But Louisa could not accept so bleak a verdict. Her instinct had convinced her that Don Blas was alive, and that conviction had brought her into the deep, private valley where Sharpe farmed Lucille's land. Sharpe wondered how he was going to rid himself of her. He suspected it would not be easy, for Doña Louisa was clearly obsessed by her husband's fate.

"Do you want me to write to the Spanish authorities?" he offered. "Or perhaps ask the Duke of Wellington to use his influence?"

"What good will that do?" Louisa challenged. "I've used every influence I can, till the authorities are sick of me. I don't need influence, I need the truth." Louisa paused, then took the plunge. "I want you to go to Chile and find me that truth."

Lucille's gray eyes widened in surprise, while Sharpe, equally astonished at the effrontery of Louisa's request, said nothing. Beyond the moat, in the elms that grew beside the orchard, rooks cawed loud and a house-martin sliced on saber wings between the dairy and the horse-chestnut tree. "There must be men in South America who are in a better position to search for your husband?" Lucille remarked very mildly.

"How do I trust them? Those officers who were friends of my husband have either been sent home or posted to remote garrisons. I sent money to other officers who claimed to be friends of Don Blas, but all I received in return are the same lies. They merely wish me to send more money, and thus they encourage me with hope but not with facts. Besides, such men cannot speak to the rebels."

"And I can?" Sharpe asked.

"You can find out whether they ambushed Don Blas, or whether someone else set the trap."

Sharpe, from all he had heard, doubted whether any rebels had been involved. "By someone else," he said diplomatically, "I assume you mean the man Don Blas was riding to confront? The Governor of, where was it?"

"Puerto Crucero, and the governor's name was Miguel

Bautista," Louisa spoke the name with utter loathing, "and Miguel Bautista is Chile's new Captain-General. That snake has replaced Don Blas! He writes me flowery letters of condolence, but the truth is that he hated Don Blas and has done nothing to help me."

"Why did he hate Don Blas?" Sharpe asked.

"Because Don Blas is honest, and Bautista is corrupt. Why else?"

"Corrupt enough to murder Don Blas?" Sharpe asked.

"My husband is not dead!" Louisa insisted in a voice full of pain, so much pain that Sharpe, who till now had been trying to pierce her armor of certainty, suddenly realized just what anguish lay behind that self-delusion. "He is hiding," Louisa insisted, "or perhaps he is wounded. Perhaps he is with the savages. Who knows? I only know, in my heart, that he is not dead. You will understand!" This passionate appeal was directed at Lucille, who smiled with sympathy, but said nothing. "Women know when their men die," Louisa went on, "they feel it. I know a woman who woke in her sleep, crying, and later we discovered that her husband's ship had sunk that very same night! I tell you, Don Blas is alive!" The cry was pathetic, yet full of vigor, tragic.

Sharpe turned to watch his son who, with little Dominique, was searching inside the open barn door for newly laid eggs. He did not want to go to Chile. These days he even resented having to travel much beyond Caen. Sharpe was a happy man, his only worries the usual concerns of a farmer— money and weather— and he wished Louisa had not come to the valley with her talk of cavalry and ambush and savages and corruption. Sharpe's more immediate concerns were the pike that decimated the millstream trout and the crumbling sill of the weir that threatened to collapse and inundate Lucille's water meadows, and he did not want to think of far-off countries and corrupt governments and missing soldiers.

Doña Louisa, seeing Sharpe stare at his children, must have understood what he was thinking. "I have asked for help everywhere," she made the appeal to Lucille as much as to Sharpe. "The Spanish authorities won't help me, which is why I went to London." Louisa, who perhaps had more faith in her English roots than she would have liked to admit, explained that she had sought the help of the British government because British interests were important in Chile. Merchants from London and Liverpool, in anticipation of new trading opportunities, were suspected of funding the rebel government, while the Royal Navy kept a squadron on the Chilean coast and Louisa believed that if the British authorities, thus well connected with both sides of the fighting parties, demanded news of Don Blas then neither the rebels nor the Royalists would dare refuse them.

"Yet the British say they cannot help!" Louisa complained indignantly. "They say Don Blas's disappearance is a military matter of concern only to the Spanish authorities!" So, in desperation, and while returning overland to Spain, Louisa had called on Sharpe. Her husband had once done Sharpe a great service, she tellingly reminded Sharpe, and now she wanted that favor returned.

Lucille spoke excellent English, but not quite well enough to have kept up with Louisa's indignant loquacity. Sharpe translated, and added a few facts of his own; how he did indeed owe Blas Vivar a great debt. "He helped me once, years ago," Sharpe said, deliberately vague, for Lucille never much liked to hear of Sharpe's exploits in fighting against her own people. "And he is a good man," Sharpe added, and knew the compliment was inadequate, for Don Blas was more than just a good man. He was, or had been, a generous man of rigorous honesty; a man of religion, of charity, and of ability. .

"I do not like asking this of you," Louisa said in an unnaturally timid voice, "but I know that whoever seeks Don Blas must treat with soldiers, and your name is respected everywhere among soldiers."

"Not here, it isn't," Lucille said robustly, though not without an affectionate smile at Sharpe, for she knew how proud he would be of the compliment just paid him.

"And, of course, I shall pay you for your trouble in going to Chile," Louisa added.

"Of course Richard will go," Lucille, understanding that promise, said quickly.

"Though I don't need any money," Sharpe said gallantly.

"Yes, you do," Lucille intervened calmly and, more pointedly, in English so that Louisa would understand. Lucille had already estimated the worth of Doña Louisa's black dress, and of her carriage, and of her postilions and outriders and horses and luggage, and Lucille knew only too well how desperately her chateau needed repairs and how badly her estate needed the investment of money. Lucille paused to bite through a thread, "But I don't want you to go alone. You need company. You've been wanting to see Patrick, so you should write to Dublin tonight, Richard."

"Patrick won't want to come," Sharpe said, not because he thought his friend would truly refuse such an invitation, but rather because he did not want to raise his own hopes that his oldest friend, Patrick Harper, would give up his comfortable existence as landlord of a Dublin tavern and instead travel to one of the remotest and evidently most troubled countries on earth.

"It would be better if you did take a companion," Louisa said firmly. "Chile is horribly corrupt. Don Blas believed that men like Bautista were simply extracting every last scrap of profit before the war was lost, and that they did not care about victory, but only for money. But money will open doors for you, so I plan to give you a sum of coin to use as bribes, and it might be sensible to have a strong man to help you protect such a fortune."

"And Patrick is certainly strong," Lucille said affectionately.

Thus the two women had made their decisions. Sharpe, with Harper, if his old friend agreed, would sail to Chile. Doña Louisa would provide Sharpe with two thousand gold English guineas, a coinage acceptable anywhere in the world, and a sum sufficient to buy Sharpe whatever information he needed, then she would wait for his news in her Palace of Mouromorto in Orense. Lucille, meanwhile, would hire an engineer from Caen to construct a new weir downstream of the old, the first repair to be done with the generous fee Louisa insisted on paying Sharpe.

Who, believing that he sailed to find a dead man, was now in mid-Atlantic, on a Spanish frigate, sailing to a corrupt colony, and bearing an Emperor's gift.

The talk on board the *Espiritu Santo* was of victories to come and of the vengeance that would be taken against the rebels once Colonel Ruiz's guns reached the battlefields. It was artillery, Ruiz declared to Sharpe, that won wars. "Napoleon understood that!"

"But Napoleon lost his wars," Sharpe interjected.

Ruiz flicked that objection aside. The advance in the science of artillery, he claimed, had made cavalry and infantry vulnerable to the massive destructive power of guns. There was no future, he said, in pursuing rebels around the Chilean wilderness; instead they must be lured under the massed guns of a fortress and there pulverized. Ruiz modestly disclaimed authorship of this strategy, instead praising the new Captain-General, Bautista, for the idea. "We'll take care of Cochrane in exactly the same way," Ruiz promised. "We'll lure him and his ships under the guns of Valdivia, then turn the so-called rebel Navy into firewood. Guns will mean the end of Cochrane!"

Cochrane. That was the name that haunted every Spaniard. Sharpe heard the name a score of times each day. Whenever two Spanish officers were talking, they spoke of Cochrane. They disliked Bernardo O'Higgins, the rebel Irish General and now Supreme Director of the independent Chilean Republic, but they hated Cochrane. Cochrane's victories were too flamboyant, too unlikely. They believed he was a devil, for there could be no other explanation for his success.

In truth Lord Thomas Cochrane was a Scotsman, a sailor, a jailbird, a politician and a rebel. He was also lucky. "He has the devil's own luck," Lieutenant Otero, the *Espiritu Santo*'s First Lieutenant, solemnly told Sharpe, "and when Cochrane is lucky, the rebellion thrives." Otero explained that it was Cochrane's naval victories that had made most of the rebellion's successes possible. "Chile is not a country in which armies can easily march, so the Generals need ships to transport their troops. That's what that devil Cochrane has given them—mobility!" Otero stared gloomily at the wild seas ahead, then shook his head sadly. "But in truth he is nothing but a pirate."

"A lucky pirate, it seems," Sharpe observed drily.

"I sometimes wonder if what we call luck is merely the will of God," Otero observed sadly, "and that therefore Cochrane has been sent to scourge Spain for a reason. But God will surely relent." Otero piously crossed himself and Sharpe reflected that if God did indeed want to punish Spain, then in Lord Cochrane He had found Himself a most lethal instrument. Cochrane, when master of a small Royal Naval sloop, and at the very beginnings of the French wars when Spain had still been allied with France, had captured a Spanish frigate that outgunned and outmanned him six to one. From that moment he had become a scourge of the seas, defying every Spanish or French attempt to thwart him. In the end his defeat had not come at the hands of Britain's enemies, but of its courts, which had imprisoned him for fraud. He had fled the country in disgrace, to become the Admiral of the Chilean Republic's Navy and such was Cochrane's reputation that, as even the *Espiritu Santo*'s officers were forced to admit, no Spanish ship dared sail alone north of Valdivia, and those ships that sailed the waters south of Valdivia, like the *Espiritu Santo* herself, had better be well armed.

"And we are well armed!" the frigate's officers liked to boast. Captain Ardiles exercised the *Espiritu Santo*'s gun crews incessantly so that the passengers became sick of the heavy guns' concussion that shook the very frame of the big ship. Ardiles, perhaps enjoying the passengers' discomfort, demanded ever faster service of the guns, and was willing to expend powder barrel after powder barrel and roundshot after roundshot in his search for the perfection that would let him destroy Cochrane in battle. The frigate's officers, enthused by their reclusive Captain's quest for efficiency, boasted that they would beat Cochrane's ships to pulp, capture Cochrane himself, then parade the devil through Madrid to expose him to the jeers of the citizens before he was garotted in slow agony.

Sharpe listened, smiled and made no attempt to mention that Lord Cochrane had fought scores of shipborne battles, while Ardiles, for all his gun practices, had never faced a real warship in a fight. Ardiles had merely skirmished with coastal brigs and pinnaces that were a fraction of the *Espiritu Santo*'s size. Captain Ardiles's dreams of victory were therefore wild, but not nearly so fantastic as the other stories that began to flourish among the *Espiritu Santo*'s nervous passengers as the ship sailed ever closer to the tip of South America.

Neither Colonel Ruiz nor any of his officers had been posted
to Chile before, yet they knew it to be a place of giants, of
one-legged men who could run faster than racehorses, of
birds larger than elephants, of serpents that could swallow a
whole herd of cattle, of fish that could tear the flesh from a
man's bones in seconds, and of forests that were home to
tribes of savages who could kill with a glance. In the mountains, so it was reliably said, were tribes of cannibals who
used women of an unearthly beauty to lure men to their
feasting pots. There were lakes of fire and rivers of blood. It
was a land of winged demons and daylight vampires. There
were deserts and glaciers, scorpions and unicorns, fanged
whales and poisonous sea serpents. Ruiz's regimental priest,
a fat syphilitic drunkard who wept when he thought of the
terrors awaiting him, knelt before the crucifix nailed to the
Espiritu Santo's mainmast and swore he would reform and
be good if only the mother of Christ would spare him from
the devils of Chile. No wonder Cochrane was so successful,
the priest told Harper, when he had such devilish magic on
his side.

The weather became as wild as the stories. It was supposed to be summer in these southern latitudes, yet more
than one dawn brought hissing sleet showers and a thick frost
which clung like icy mildew in the sheltered nooks of the
Espiritu Santo's upper decks. Huge seas, taller than the lanterns on the poop, thundered from astern. The tops of such
waves were maelstroms of churning white water which
seethed madly as they crashed and foamed under the frigate's stern.

Most of the Spanish artillery officers succumbed to seasickness. Few of the sick men had the energy to climb on
deck and, in front of the scornful sailors, lower their
breeches to perch on the beakhead, so instead the passengers voided their bellies and bowels into buckets that

slopped and spilled until the passenger accommodations stank like a cesspit. The food did not help the ship's well-being. At Saint Helena the *Espiritu Santo* had stocked up with yams which had by now liquefied into rancid bags, while most of the ship's meat, inadequately salted in Spain, was wriggling with maggots. The drinking water was fouled. There were weevils in the bread. Even the wine was sour.

Sharpe and Harper, crammed together in a tiny cabin scarcely big enough for a dog, were luckier than most passengers, for neither man was seasick, and both were so accustomed to soldiers' food that a return to half-rotted seamen's rations gave no offense. They ate what they could, which was not much, and Harper even lost weight so that, by the time the *Espiritu Santo* hammered into a sleety wind near Cape Horn, the Irishman could almost walk through the cabin door without touching the frame on either side.

"I'm shriveling away, so I am," he complained as the frigate quivered from the blow of a great sea. "I'll be glad when we reach land, devils or no devils, and there'll be some proper food to eat. Christ, but it's cold up there!"

"No mermaids in sight?"

"Only a three-horned sea serpent." The grotesque stories of the fearful Spanish army officers had become a joke between the two men. "It's bad up there," Harper warned more seriously. "Filthy bad."

Sharpe went on deck a few moments later to find that conditions were indeed bad. The ocean was a white shambles, blown ragged by a freezing wind that came slicing off the icesheets which lay to the south. The *Espiritu Santo*, its sails furled down to mere dark scraps, labored and thumped and staggered against the weather's malevolence. Sharpe, tired of being cooped up in the stinking 'tweendecks, and wanting some fresh air, steadied himself against the quarterdeck's starboard carronade. There were few other people on

deck, merely a handful of sailors who crouched in the lee
scuppers, two men who were draped in tarpaulin capes by
the wheel, and a solitary cloaked figure who clung to a
shroud on the weather side of the poop.

The cloaked man, seeing Sharpe, carefully negotiated a
passage across the wet and heaving deck, and Sharpe, to his
astonishment, saw that it was the reclusive Captain Ardiles,
who had not been seen by any of the passengers since the
Espiritu Santo had left Saint Helena.

"Cape Horn!" Ardiles shouted, pointing off to starboard.

Sharpe stared. For a long time he could see nothing, then
an explosion of shredded water betrayed where a black scrap
of rock resisted the pounding waves.

"That's the last scrap of good earth that many a sailorman
saw before he drowned!" Ardiles spoke with a gloomy relish,
then clutched at the tarred rigging as the *Espiritu Santo* fell
sideways into the green heart of a wave's trough. He waited
till the frigate had recovered and was laboring up a great
slope of savaged white sea. "So what did you think of Napoleon?" Ardiles asked Sharpe.

Sharpe hesitated, wanting his answer to be precise. "He
put me in mind of a man who has played a hugely successful
joke on people he despises."

Ardiles, who had flat, watchful eyes in a hungry, cadaver-
ous face, thought about Sharpe's answer, then shrugged.
"Maybe. But I think he should have been executed for his
joke."

Sharpe said nothing. He could see the waves breaking on
Cape Horn more clearly now, and could just make out the
loom of a black cliff beyond the battered water. God, he
thought, but this is a fearful place.

"They made me sick!" Ardiles said suddenly.

"Sick?" Sharpe had only half heard Ardiles's scathing

words and had assumed that the frigate's Captain was talking about the seasickness that afflicted most of the army officers.

"Ruiz and the others! Fawning over that man! Jesus! But Bonaparte was our enemy. He did enough damage to Spain! If it were not for Bonaparte you think there'd be any rebellion in South America? He encouraged it! And how many more Spaniards will die for that man's evil? Yet these bastards bowed and scraped to him. Given half a chance they'd have licked his bum cleaner than a nun's finger!"

Sharpe staggered as the ship rolled. A rattle of sleet and foam shot down the deck and slammed into the poop. "I can't say I wasn't impressed by meeting Bonaparte!" he shouted in defense of the Spanish army officers. "He's been my enemy long enough, but I felt privileged to be there. I even liked him!"

"That's because you're English! Your women weren't raped by those French bastards, and your children weren't killed by them!" Ardiles stared balefully into the trough of a scummy wave that roared under the *Espiritu Santo*'s counter. "So what did you talk about when you were alone with him?"

"Waterloo."

"Just Waterloo?" Ardiles seemed remarkably suspicious.

"Just that," Sharpe said, with an air of irritation, for it was none of Ardiles's business what he and a stricken Emperor had discussed.

Ardiles, sensing he had offended Sharpe, changed the subject by waving a hand toward the cabins where Ruiz's artillery officers sheltered from the storm in their vomit-rinsed misery. "What do you think of officers who don't share their men's discomforts?"

Sharpe believed that officers who abandoned their men were officers on their way to defeat, but tact kept him from saying as much to the sardonic Ardiles, so instead he made some harmless comment about being no expert on Spanish shipping arrangements.

"I think such officers are bastards!" Ardiles had to shout to be heard over the numbing sound of the huge seas. "The only reason they sailed on this ship is because the voyage will be six or eight weeks shorter! Which means they can reach the whorehouses of Valdivia ahead of their Sergeants," Ardiles spat into the scuppers. "They're good whorehouses, too. Too good for these bastards."

"You know Chile well?" Sharpe asked.

"Well enough! I've visited twice a year for three years. They use my ship as a passenger barge! Instead of letting me look for Cochrane and beating the shit out of him, they insist that I sail back and forth between Spain and Valdivia! Back and forth! Back and forth! It's a waste of a good ship! This is the largest and best frigate in the Spanish Navy and they waste it on ferrying shit like Ruiz!" Ardiles scowled down into the frigate's waist where the green water surged and broke ragged about the lashed guns, then he turned his saturnine gaze back to Sharpe. "You're looking for Captain-General Vivar, yes?"

"I am, yes." Sharpe was not surprised that Ardiles knew his business, for he had made no secret of his quest, yet he was taken aback by the abrupt and jeering manner of the Captain's asking and Sharpe's reply had consequently been guarded, almost hostile.

Ardiles leaned closer to Sharpe. "I knew Vivar! I even liked him! But he was not a tactful man. Most of the army officers in Chile thought he was too clever. They had their own ideas on how the war should be lost, but Vivar was proving them wrong, and they didn't like him for that."

"Are you saying that his own side killed him?"

Ardiles shook his head. "I think he was killed by the rebels. He was probably wounded in the ambush, his horse

galloped into deep timber, and he fell off. His body's probably still out there, ripped apart by animals and chewed by
birds. The oddest part of the whole thing, to my mind, is why
he was out there with such a small escort. There were only
fifteen men with him!"

"He was always a brave man," said Sharpe, who had not
heard just how small the escort had been and now hid his
surprise. Why would a Captain-General travel with such a
tiny detachment? Even in country he thought safe?

"Maybe more foolish than brave?" Ardiles suggested. "My
own belief is that he had an arrangement to meet the rebels,
and that they double-crossed him."

Sharpe, who had convinced himself that Don Blas had
been murdered by his own people, found this new idea grotesque. "Are you saying he was a traitor?"

"He was a patriot, but he was playing with fire." Ardiles
paused, as though debating whether to say more, then he
must have decided that his revelation could do no harm. "I
tell you a strange thing, Englishman. Two months after Vivar
arrived in Chile he ordered me to take him to Talcahuana.
That means nothing to you, so I shall explain.

"It is a peninsula, close to Concepción, and inside rebel
territory. His Excellency's staff told Don Blas it was not safe
to go there, but he scoffed at such timidity. I thought it was
my chance to fight against Cochrane, so I went gladly. But
two days north of Valdivia we struck bad weather. It was
awful! We could not go anywhere near land; instead we rode
out the storm at sea for four days. After that Don Blas still
insisted on going to Talcahuana. We anchored off Punta
Tombes and Don Blas went ashore on his own. On his own!
He refused an escort. He just took a fowling-piece! He said
he wanted to prove that a nobleman of Spain could hunt
freely wherever His Spanish Majesty ruled in this world. Six
hours later he came back with two brace of duck, and

ordered me back to Valdivia. So what? You are asking. I will tell you what! I myself thought it was merely bravado. After all, he had made me sail for a week through waters patroled by the rebel navy, but later I heard rumors that Don Blas had gone ashore to meet those rebels. To talk with them. I don't know if that is true, but on my voyage home with the news of Don Blas's disappearance, we captured a rebel pinnace with a dozen men aboard and two of them told me that the devil Cochrane himself had been waiting to meet Don Blas, but that after two days they decided he was not coming, and so Cochrane went away."

"You believed them?"

Ardiles shrugged. "Do dying men tell lies or truth? My belief, Englishman, is that they were telling the truth, and I think Don Blas died when he tried to resurrect the meeting with the rebels. But you believe Don Blas to be alive, yes?"

Sharpe hesitated, but Ardiles had favored him with a revelation, and Sharpe's truth was nowhere near so dangerous, so he told it. "No."

"So why are you here?"

"Because I've been paid to look for him. Maybe I shall find his dead body?" Because even that, Sharpe had decided, would give Louisa some small comfort. It would, at the very least, offer her certainty and if Sharpe could arrange to have the body carried home to Spain then Louisa could bury Don Blas in his family's vault in the great cathedral in Santiago de Compostela.

Ardiles scoffed at Sharpe's mild hopes. He waved northward through the spitting sleet and the spume and the wild waves' turmoil. "That's a whole continent up there! Not an English farmyard! You won't find a single body in a continent, Englishman, not if someone else has decided to hide it."

"Why would they do that?"

"Because if my tale of carrying Don Blas to meet the rebels is right, then Don Blas was not just a soldier, but a soldier playing politics, and that's a more dangerous pastime than fighting. Besides, if the Spanish high command decides not to help you, how will you achieve anything?"

"By bribes?" Sharpe suggested.

Ardiles laughed. "I wish you luck, Englishman, but if you're offering money they'll just tell you what you want to hear until you've no money left, then they'll clean their knife blades in your guts. Take my advice! Vivar's dead! Go home!"

Sharpe crouched against a sudden attack of wind-slathered foam that shrieked down the deck and smashed white against the helmsman and his companion. "What I don't understand," Sharpe shouted when the sea had sucked itself out of the scuppers, "is why the rebels haven't boasted about Don Blas's death! If you're a rebel and you kill or capture your enemy's commander, why keep it a secret? Why not trumpet your success?"

"You expect sense out of Chile?" Ardiles asked cynically.

Sharpe ducked again as the wind flailed more salt foam across the quarterdeck. "Don Blas's widow doesn't believe it was the rebels who attacked her husband. She thinks it was Captain-General Bautista."

Ardiles looked grimmer than ever. "Then Don Blas's widow had best keep her thoughts to herself. Bautista is not a man to antagonize. He has pride, a memory and a taste for cruelty."

"And for corruption?" Sharpe asked.

Ardiles paused, as though weighing the good sense of continuing this conversation, then he shrugged. "Miguel Bautista is the prince of thieves, but that doesn't mean he won't one day be the ruler of Spain. How else do men become great, except by extortion and fear? I will give you some advice, Englishman," Ardiles's voice had become fierce with intensity, "don't make an enemy of Bautista. You hear me?"

"Of course." The warning seemed extraordinary to Sharpe, a testimony to the real fear that Miguel Bautista, Vivar's erstwhile enemy, inspired.

Ardiles suddenly grinned, as though he wanted to erase the grimness of his last words. "The trouble with Don Blas, Englishman, was that he was very close to being a saint. He was an honorable man, and you know what happens to honorable men—they prove to be an embarrassment. This world isn't governed by honorable men, but by lawyers and politicians, and whenever such scum come across an honest man they have to kill him." The ship shuddered as a huge wave smashed ragged down the port gunwale. Ardiles laughed at the weather's malevolence, then looked again at Sharpe. "Take my advice, Englishman. Go home! I'll be sailing back to Spain in a week's time, which gives you just long enough to visit the *chingana* behind the church in Valdivia, after which you should sail home to your wife."

"The *chingana?*" Sharpe asked.

"A *chingana* is where you go for a *chingada*," Ardiles said unhelpfully. "A *chingana* is either a tavern that sells whores, or a whorehouse that sells liquor, and the *chingana* behind the church in Valdivia has half-breed girls who give *chingadas* that leave men gasping for life. It's the best whorehouse for miles. You know how you can tell which is the best whorehouse in a Spanish town?"

"Tell me."

"It's the one where all the priests go, and this one is where the Bishop goes! So visit the mestizo whores, then go home and tell Vivar's wife that her husband's body was eaten by wild pigs!"

But Sharpe had not been paid to go home and tell stories. He had taken Doña Louisa's money, and he was far from

home, and he would not go back defeated. He would find
Don Blas, no matter how deep the forest or high the hill. If
Don Blas still had form, then Sharpe would find it.

He had sworn as much, and he would keep his promise.
He would find Don Blas.

Albatrosses ghosted alongside the *Espiritu Santo*'s rigging.
The frigate, Cape Horn left far behind her, was sailing before
a friendly wind on a swirling current of icy water. Dolphins
followed her, while whales surfaced and rolled on either
flank.

"Christ, but there's some meat on those bloody fish!"
Harper said in admiration as a great whale plunged past the
Espiritu Santo. The ship was sailing north along the Chilean
coast, out of sight of land, though the proximity of the shore
was marked by the towering white clouds that heaped above
the Andes. Inshore, the sailors said, were yet stranger creatures—penguins and sea lions, mermaids and turtles—but
the frigate was staying well clear of the uncharted Chilean
coastline so that Harper, to his regret, was denied a chance
of glimpsing such monsters. Ardiles, still hoping to capture
his own monster, Lord Cochrane, continued to exercise his
guns even though his men were already as well trained as
any gunners Sharpe had ever seen.

Yet it seemed there was to be no victory over the devil
Cochrane on this voyage, for the *Espiritu Santo*'s lookouts
saw no other ships till the frigate at last closed on the land.
Then the lookouts glimpsed a harmless fleet of small fishing
vessels that dragged their nets through the cold offshore rollers. The men aboard the fishing boats claimed not to have
seen any rebel warships. "Though God only knows if they're
telling the truth," Lieutenant Otero told Sharpe. Land was
still out of sight, but everyone on board knew that the voyage
was ending. Seamen were repairing their clothes, sewing up

huge rents in breeches and darning their shirts in readiness
to meet the girls of Valdivia. "One day more, just one day
more," Lieutenant Otero told Sharpe after the noon sight,
and sure enough, next dawn, Sharpe woke to see the dark
streak of land filling the eastern horizon.

That afternoon, under a faltering wind, a friendly tide
helped the *Espiritu Santo* into Valdivia's harbor. Sharpe and
Harper stood on deck and stared at the massive fortifications
that guarded this last Spanish stronghold on the Chilean
coast. The headland that protected the harbor was crowned
by Fort Ingles, which in turn could lock its cannonfire with
the guns of Fort San Carlos. Both forts lay under the protection of the artillery in the Chorocomayo fort which had been
built on the headland's highest point. Beyond San Carlos,
and still on the headland that formed the harbor's western
side, lay Fort Amargos and Corral Castle. The *Espiritu Santo*'s First Lieutenant proudly pointed out each succeeding
stronghold as the frigate edged her way around the headland.
"In Chile," Otero explained yet again, "armies move by sea
because the roads are so bad, but no army could ever take
Valdivia unless they first capture this harbor, and I just wish
Cochrane would try to capture it! We'd destroy him!"

Sharpe believed him, for there were yet more defenses to
add their guns to the five forts of the western shore. Across
the harbor mouth, where the huge Pacific swells shattered
white on dark rocks, was the biggest fort of all, Fort Niebla,
while in the harbor's center, head on to any attacking ships,
lay the guns and ramparts of Manzanera Island. The harbor
would be a trap, sucking an attacker inside to where he
would be ringed with high guns hammering heated shot
down onto his wooden decks.

Only two of the forts, Corral Castle and Fort Niebla, were
modern stone-walled forts. The other forts were little more
than glorified gun emplacements protected by ditches and

timber walls, yet their cannons could make the harbor into a killing ground of overlapping gunnery zones. "If we were an enemy ship," Otero boasted of the ring of artillery, "we would be in hell by now."

"Where's the town?" Sharpe asked. Valdivia was supposed to be the major remaining Spanish garrison in Chile, yet to Sharpe's surprise, the great array of forts seemed to be protecting nothing but a stone quay, some tarred sheds and a row of fishermen's hovels.

"The town's upstream." Otero pointed to what Sharpe had taken for a bay just beside Fort Niebla. "That's the river mouth and the town's fifteen miles inland. You'll be dropped at the north quay where you find a boatman to take you upstream. They're dishonest people, and they'll try to charge you five dollars. You shouldn't pay more than one."

"The *Espiritu Santo* won't go upstream?"

"The river's too shallow." Lieutenant Otero, who had charge of the frigate, paused to listen to the leadsman who was calling the depth. "Sometimes the boatmen will take you halfway and then threaten to put you ashore in the wilderness if you won't pay more money. If that happens, the best thing to do is to shoot one of the Indian crew members. No one objects to the killing of a savage, and you'll find the death has a remarkably salutary effect on the other boatmen."

Otero turned away to tend to the ship. Fort Niebla was firing a salute which one of the long nine pounders at the frigate's bow returned. The gunfire echoed flatly from the steep hills where a few stunted trees were permanently windbent toward the north. Seamen were streaming aloft to furl the sails after their long passage. There was a crash as the starboard anchor was struck loose, then a grating rumble as fathoms of chain clattered through the hawse. The fragrant scents of the land vainly tried to defeat the noxious carapace of the *Espiritu Santo*'s cesspit-laced-with-powder stench. The frigate, her salute fired, checked as the anchor bit into the harbor's bottom, then turned as the tide pulled the fouled hull slowly around. The smoke of the gun salute writhed and drifted across the bay. "Welcome to Chile," Otero said.

"Can you believe it?" Harper said with amazement. "We're in the New World!"

An hour later, their seabags and money chest under the guard of two burly seamen, Sharpe and Harper stepped ashore onto the New World. They had reached their voyage's end in the quaking land of giants and pygmies, of unicorns and ghouls, in the rebellious land that lay under the volcanoes' fire and the devil's flail. They were in Chile.

George Blair, British Consul in Valdivia, blinked short-sightedly at Richard Sharpe. "Why the hell should I tell you lies? Of course he's dead!" Blair laughed mirthlessly. "He'd better bloody be dead. He's been buried long enough! The poor bugger must be in a bloody bad state if he's still alive; he's been underground these last three months. Are you sure you don't have any gin in your baggage?"

"I'm sure."

"People usually bring me gin from London." Blair was a plump, middle-aged man, wearing a stained white shirt and frayed breeches. He had greeted his visitors wearing a formal black tailcoat, but had long discarded the coat as too cumbersome in the day's warmth. "It's rather a common courtesy," he grumbled, "to bring gin from London."

Sharpe was in no state to notice either the Consul's clothes or his unhappiness; instead his thoughts were a whirlpool of disbelief and shock. Don Blas was not missing at all, but was dead and buried, which meant Sharpe's whole voyage was for nothing. At least, that was what Blair reckoned.

"He's under the paving slabs in the garrison church at Puerto Crucero," George Blair repeated in his hard, clipped accent. "Jesus Christ! I know a score of people who were at the damned funeral. I wasn't invited, and a good thing too. I have to put up with enough nonsense in this Goddamn place without watching a pack of pox-ridden priests mumbling bloody Latin in double-quick time so they can get back to their native whores."

"God in his heaven," Sharpe blasphemed, then paused to gather his scattered wits, "but Vivar's wife doesn't know! They can't bury a man without telling his wife!"

"They can do whatever they damn well like! But don't ask me to explain. I'm trying to run a business and a consulate, not explain the remnants of the Spanish bloody empire." Blair was a Liverpool merchant who dealt in hides, tallow, copper and timber. He was a bad-tempered, overworked and harassed man, yet, as Consul, he had little option but to welcome Sharpe and Harper into his house that stood in the main square of Valdivia, hard between the church and the outer ditch of the town's main fort, which was known simply as the Citadel. Blair had placed Louisa's bribe money, all eighteen hundred golden guineas, in his strong room which was protected by a massive iron door and by walls of dressed stone blocks a foot and a half thick. Louisa had given Sharpe two thousand guineas, but the customs officials at the wharf in Valdivia had insisted on a levy of ten percent. "Bastards," Blair had commented when he heard of the impost. "It's supposed to be just three percent."

"Should I complain?" Sharpe had already made an unholy fuss at the customs post, though it had done no good.

"To Captain-General Bautista?" Blair gave another mirthless laugh. "He's the bastard that pegs up the percentage. You were lucky it wasn't fifteen percent!" Then, over a plate of sugared cakes and glasses of wine brought by his Indian servants, Blair had welcomed Sharpe to Valdivia with the news that Vivar's death was no mystery at all. "The bugger was riding way ahead of his escort, was probably ambushed by rebels, and his horse bolted with him when the trap was sprung. Then three months later they found his body in a ravine. Not that there was much left of the poor bugger, but they knew it was him, right enough, because of his uniform. Mind you, it took them a hell of a long time to find his body, but the dagoes are bloody inefficient at everything except levying customs duties, and they can do that faster than anyone in history."

"Who buried him?" Sharpe asked,

The Consul frowned in irritated puzzlement. "A pack of bloody priests! I told you!"

"But who arranged it? The army?"

"Captain-General Bautista, of course. Nothing happens here without Bautista giving the nod."

Sharpe turned and stared through Blair's parlor window which looked onto the Citadel's outer ditch where two dogs were squabbling over what appeared to be a child's discarded doll, but then, as the doll's arm ripped away, Sharpe saw that the dogs' plaything was the body of an Indian toddler that must have been dumped in the ditch. "Why the hell weren't you invited to the funeral, Blair?" Sharpe turned back from the window. "You're an important man here, aren't you? Or doesn't the British Consul carry any weight in these parts?"

Blair shrugged. "The Spanish in Valdivia don't much like the British, Colonel. They're losing this fight, and they're blaming us. They reckon most of the rebellion's money comes from London, and they aren't far wrong in thinking that. But it's their own damned fault if they're losing. They're too bloody fond of lining their own pockets, and if it comes to a choice between fighting and profiteering, they'll take the money every time. Things were better when Vivar was in charge, but that's exactly why they couldn't stomach him. The bugger was too honest, you see, which is why I didn't see too many tears shed when they heard he'd been killed."

"The bugger," Sharpe said coldly, "was a friend of mine." He turned to stare again at the ditch where a flock of carrion birds edged close to the two dogs, hoping for a share of the child's corpse.

"Vivar was a friend of yours?" Blair sounded shocked.

"Yes."

The confirmation checked Blair, who suddenly had to reassess the importance of his visitors, or at least of Sharpe. Blair had already dismissed Harper as a genial Irishman who carried no political weight, but Sharpe, despite his rustic clothes and weathered face, was suddenly proving a much more difficult man to place. Sharpe had introduced himself as Lieutenant Colonel Sharpe, but the wars had left as many Colonels as they had bastards, so the rank hardly impressed Consul Blair, but if Lieutenant Colonel Sharpe had been a friend of Don Blas Vivar, who had been Count of Mouro-morto and Captain-General of Spain's Chilean Dominion, then such a friendship could also imply that Sharpe was a friend of the high London lords who, ultimately, gave Blair the privileges and honors that eased his existence in Valdivia. "A bad business," Blair muttered, vainly trying to make amends for his flippancy.

"Where was the body found?" Sharpe asked.

"Some miles northeast of Puerto Crucero. It's a wild area, nothing but woods and rocks." Blair was speaking in a much more respectful tone now. "The place isn't a usual haunt of the rebels, but once in a while they'll appear that far south. Government troops searched the valley after the ambush, of course, but no one thought to look in the actual ravine till a hunting party of Indians brought news that a white god was lying there. That's one of their names for us, you see. The white god, of course, turned out be Don Blas. They reckon that he and his horse must have fallen into the ravine while fleeing from his attackers."

"You're sure it was rebels?" Sharpe turned from the window to ask the question. "I've heard it might have been Bautista's doing."

Blair shook his head. "I've not heard those rumors. I'm not saying Bautista's not capable of murder, because he is. He's a cruel son of a whore, that one, but I never heard any tales of his having killed Captain-General Vivar, and believe me, Chile breeds rumor the way a nunnery breeds the pox."

Sharpe was unwilling to let the theory slip. "I heard Vivar had found out about Bautista's corruption, and was going to arrest him."

Blair mocked Sharpe's naiveté. "You don't arrest a man for breathing, do you? Everyone's corrupt here! If Vivar was going to arrest Bautista then it would have been for something far more serious than corruption. No, Colonel, that dog won't hunt."

Sharpe thumped a fist in angry protest. "But to be buried three months ago! That's long enough for someone to tell the authorities in Europe! Why the hell did no one think to tell his wife?"

It was hardly Blair's responsibility, though he tried to answer as best he could. "Maybe the ship carrying the news was captured? Or shipwrecked? Sometimes ships do take a God-horrible time to make the voyage. The last time I went home we spent over three weeks just trying to get round Ushant! Sick as a dog, I was!"

"Goddamn it." Sharpe turned back to the window. Was it all a misunderstanding? Was this whole benighted expedition merely the result of the time it sometimes took for news to cross between the old and new worlds? Had Don Blas been decently buried all this time? It was more than possible, of course. A ship could easily take two or three months to sail from Chile to Spain, and if Louisa had been in England when the news arrived in Galicia then it was no wonder that

Sharpe and Harper had come on a fool's errand. "Don't you bury the dead in this town?" he asked bad-temperedly.

Blair was understandably bemused by the sudden question, but then saw Sharpe was staring at the dead child in the Citadel's ditch. "We don't bury that sort of rubbish. Lord, no. It's probably just the bastard of some Indian girl who works in the fortress. Indians count for nothing here!" Blair chuckled. "A couple of Indian families won't fetch the price of a decent hunting dog, let alone the cost of a burial!"

Sharpe sipped the wine, which was surprisingly good. He had been astonished, while on the boat coming from the harbor to the town, to see lavish vineyards terraced across the riverside hills. Somehow, after the grotesque shipboard tales, he had expected a country full of mystery and horror, so the sight of placid vineyards and lavish villas had been unexpected, rather like finding everyday comforts in the pits of hell. "I'll need to go to Puerto Crucero," he now told Blair.

"That could be difficult," Blair sounded guarded, "very difficult."

"Why?" Sharpe bristled.

"Because it's a military area, and because Bautista doesn't like visitors going there, and because it's a port town, and the Spaniards have lost too many good harbors on this coast to let another one go, and because they think all Englishmen are spies. Besides, the Citadel at Puerto Crucero is the place where the Spanish ship their gold home."

"Gold?" Harper's interest sparked.

"There's one or two mines left; not many and they don't produce much, and most of what they do produce Bautista is probably thieving, but what little does go back to Madrid leaves through the wharf of Puerto Crucero's Citadel. It's the nearest harbor to the mines, you see, which is why the dagoes are touchy about it. If you ask to visit Puerto Crucero they might think you're spying for Cochrane. You know who Cochrane is?"

"I know," Sharpe said.

"He's a devil, that one," chuckled Blair, unable to resist admiration for a fellow Briton, "and they're all scared to hell of him. You want to see a dago piss in his breeches? Just mention Cochrane. They think he's got horns and a tail."

Sharpe dragged the conversation back to his purpose. "So how do I get permission to visit Puerto Crucero?"

"You have to get a travel permit from army headquarters."

"Which is where?"

"In the Citadel, of course." Blair nodded at the great fort which lay on the river's bend at the very heart of Valdivia.

"Who do I see there?"

"A young fellow called Captain Marquinez."

"Will Marquinez pay more attention to you than to me?" Sharpe asked.

"Oh, Christ, no! Marquinez is just an overgroomed puppy. He doesn't make the decision. Bautista's the one who'll say yea or nay." Blair jerked a thumb toward his padlocked strong room. "I hope there's plenty of money in that box you fetched here, or else you'll be wasting your time in Chile."

"My time is my own," Sharpe said acidly, "which is why I don't want to waste it." He frowned at Harper who was happily devouring Blair's sugar cakes. "If you can stop feeding yourself, Patrick, we might start work."

"Work?" Harper sounded alarmed, but hurriedly swilled down the last of his wine and snatched a final sugar cake before following Sharpe out of Blair's house. "So what work are we doing?" the Irishman asked.

"We're going to dig up Don Blas's body, of course," Sharpe said, "and arrange to have it shipped back to Spain." Sharpe's confident voice seemed to rouse Valdivia's town square from the torpor of siesta. A man who had been dozing on the church steps looked irritably toward the two tall strangers who strode so noisily toward the Citadel. A dozen Indians, their squat faces blank as carvings, sat in the shade of a mounted statue which stood in the very center of the square. The Indians, who were shackled together by a length of heavy chain manacled to their ankles, pretended not to notice Sharpe, but could not hide their astonishment at the sight of Harper, doubtless thinking that the tall Irishman was a giant. "They're admiring me, so they are!" Harper boasted happily.

"They're working out how many families they could feed off your carcass. If they boiled you down and salted the flesh there probably wouldn't be famine in this country for a century."

"You're just jealous." Harper, seeing new sights, was a happy man. The French wars had given him a taste for travel, and that taste was being well fed by Chile, and his only disappointment so far was the paucity of one-legged giants, unicorns or any other mythical beasts. "Look at that! Handsome, aren't they, now?" He nodded admiringly toward a group of women who, standing in the shade of the striped awnings that protected the shop fronts, returned Harper's curiosity and admiration. Harper and Sharpe were new faces in a small town, and thus a cause for excited speculation. The wind swirled dust devils across the square and flapped the ornate Spanish ensign that flew over the Citadel's gatehouse. A legless beggar, swinging along on his hands, followed Sharpe and pleaded for money. Another, who looked like a leper, made a meaningless noise and held out the stump of a wrist toward the two strangers. A Dominican monk, his white robes stained with the red dust that blew everywhere, was arguing with a carter who had evidently failed to deliver a shipment of wine.

"We're going to need a carter," Sharpe was thinking aloud

as he led Harper toward the Citadel's sentries, "or at least a cart. We're also going to want two riding horses, plus saddlery, and supplies for as long as it takes to get to Puerto Crucero and back. Unless we can sail home from Puerto Crucero? Or maybe we can sail down there! That'll be cheaper than buying a cart."

"What the hell do we want a cart for?" Harper was panting at the brisk pace set by Sharpe.

"We need a cart to carry the coffin to Puerto Crucero, unless, of course, we can go there by ship."

"Why the hell don't we have a coffin made in Puerto Crucero?" Harper asked. "The world's not so short of carpenters that you can't find a man to knock up a bloody box!"

"Because a box won't do the trick!" Sharpe said. "The thing has to be watertight, Patrick, not to keep the rain out but to keep the decay in. We're going to need a tinsmith, and I don't suppose Puerto Crucero has too many of those! So we'll have a watertight box made here before we go south."

"We could plop him in a vat of brandy?" Harper suggested helpfully. "There's a fellow who drinks in my place that was a gunner's mate on the *Victory* at Trafalgar, and he says that after the battle they brought Nelson back in a barrel of brandy. My fellow had a look at the body when they unstowed it, and he says the Admiral was as fresh as the day he died, so he was, with flesh soft as a baby, and the only change was that all the man's hair and nails had grown wild. He tasted the brandy too, so he did. He says it was a bit salty."

"I don't want to put Don Blas in brandy," Sharpe said irritably. "He'll be half-rotted as it is, and if we put him in a cask of bloody liquor he'll like as not dissolve altogether, and instead of burying the poor man in Spain we'll just be pouring him away. So we'll put him in a tin box, solder him up tight, and take him back that way."

"Whatever you say," Harper said grimly, the tone provoked by the unfriendly faces of the sentries at the fort's gate. The Citadel reminded Sharpe of the Spanish fortresses he had assaulted in the French wars. It had low walls over which the muzzles of the defenders' guns showed grimly, and a wide, dry moat designed to be a killing ground for any attackers who succeeded in crossing the earthen glacis which was banked to ricochet assaulting cannonfire safely up and over the defenders' heads. The only incongruity about Valdivia's formidable Citadel was an ancient-looking tower that stood like a medieval castle turret in the very center of the fortifications.

A Sergeant accosted Sharpe and Harper on the bridge, then reluctantly allowed them into the fort itself. They walked through the entrance tunnel, across a wide parade ground, then through a second gateway into a cramped and shadowed inner courtyard. One wall of the yard was made by the ancient lime-washed tower which was pockmarked by bullet holes. There were smears of dried blood near some of the bullet marks, suggesting that this cheerless place was where Valdivia's prisoners met their firing squads.

They enquired at the inner guardroom for Captain Marquinez who, arriving five minutes later, proved to be a tall, strikingly handsome and extraordinarily fashionable young man. His uniform seemed more appropriate for the jeweled halls of Madrid than for this far, squalid colony. He wore a Hussar jacket so frogged with gold braid that it was impossible to see the cloth beneath, a white kid-skin pelisse edged with black fur, and skin-tight sky-blue cavalry breeches decorated with gold embroidery and silver side-buttons. His epaulette chains, sword sling, spurs and scabbard furnishings were all of shining gold. His manners matched his uniform's tailoring. He apologized to have kept his visitors waiting, welcomed them to Chile on behalf of Captain-General Bautista, then invited Sharpe and Harper to his quarters where, in a wide, comfortable room, his servant brought cups of steaming chocolate, small gold beakers of a clear Chilean brandy and a plate of sugared grapes. Marquinez paused in front of a gilt-framed mirror to check that his wavy black hair was in place, then crossed to his wide-arched window to show off the view. "It really is a most beautiful country," the Captain spoke wistfully, as though he knew it was being lost.

The view was indeed spectacular. The window looked eastward across the town's thatched roofs, then beyond the shadowy foothills to the far snow-topped mountains. One of those distant peaks was pluming a stream of brown smoke to the south wind. "A volcano," Marquinez explained. "Chile has a number of them. It's a tumultuous place, I fear, with frequent earthquakes, but fascinating despite its dangers." Marquinez's servant brought cigars, and Marquinez hospitably offered a burning spill to Harper. "So you're staying with Mister Blair?" he asked when the cigars were well lit. "Poor Blair! His wife refused to travel here, thinking the place too full of dangers! Still, if you keep Blair filled with gin or brandy he's a happy enough man. Your Spanish is excellent, permit me to congratulate you. So few of your countrymen speak our language."

"We both served in Spain," Sharpe explained.

"You did! Then our debt to you is incalculable. Please, seat yourselves. You said you had a letter of introduction?"

Marquinez took and read Doña Louisa's letter which did not specifically describe Sharpe's errand, but merely asked any Spanish official to offer whatever help was possible. "Which of course we will offer gladly!" Marquinez spoke with what seemed to be a genuine warmth. "I never had the pleasure of meeting Don Blas's wife. He died, of course, before she could join him here. So very tragic, and such a waste. He was a good man, even perhaps a great man! There was something saintly about him, I always thought." The last compliment, uttered in a very bland voice, somehow suggested what an infernal nuisance saints could be. Marquinez carefully folded the letter's pendant seal into the paper, then handed it back to Sharpe with a courtly flourish. "And how, sir, might we help you?"

"We need a permit to visit Puerto Crucero where we want to exhume Don Blas's body, then ship it home." Sharpe, encouraged by Marquinez's friendliness, saw no need to be delicate about his needs.

Marquinez smiled, revealing teeth as white and regular as a small child's. "I see no extraordinary difficulties there. You will, of course, need a permit to travel to Puerto Crucero." He went to his table and riffled through his papers. "Did you sail out here on the *Espiritu Santo?*"

"Yes."

"She's due to sail back to Spain in a few days and I see that she's ordered to call at Puerto Crucero on her way. There's a gold shipment ready, and Ardiles's ship is the safest transport we have. I see no reason why you shouldn't travel down the coast in the *Espiritu Santo* and, if we're fortunate, you might even take the body back to Europe in her hold."

Sharpe, who had been prepared by Blair for every kind of official obstructiveness, dared not believe his good fortune. The *Espiritu Santo* could indeed solve all his problems, but Marquinez had qualified his optimism with one cautious word that Sharpe now echoed as a tentative query. "Fortunate?"

"Besides the permit to travel to Puerto Crucero," Marquinez explained, "you will need a permit to exhume Don Blas's body. That permit is issued by the church, of course, but I'm sure the Bishop will be eager to satisfy the Dowager Countess of Mouromorto. However, you should understand that sometimes the church is, how shall I say? Dilatory?"

"We came prepared for such difficulties," Sharpe said.

"How so?" The question was swift.

"The church must have charities dear to its heart?"

"How very thoughtful of you." Marquinez, relieved that Sharpe had so swiftly understood the obstacle, offered his guests a dazzling smile and Sharpe wondered how a man kept his teeth so white. Marquinez then held up a warning hand. "We mustn't forget the necessary license to export a body. There is a disease risk, you understand, and we have to satisfy ourselves that every precaution has been taken."

"We came well prepared," Sharpe said dourly. The requirements, so far as he could see, were two massive bribes. One to the church which, in Sharpe's experience, was always greedy for cash, and the other to the army authorities to secure the travel permit and for the license to export a body, which license, Sharpe suspected, had just been dreamed up by the inventive Marquinez. Doña Louisa, Sharpe thought, had understood Chile perfectly when she insisted on sending him with the big chest of coins. Sharpe smiled at the charming Marquinez. "So when, *señor,* may we expect a travel permit? Today?"

"Oh, dear me, no!" Marquinez frowned, as though Sharpe's suggestion of such haste was somehow unseemly.

"Soon?" Sharpe pressed.

"The decision is not mine," Marquinez said happily.

"Our affairs will surely not be of interest to Captain-General Bautista?" Sharpe said with what he hoped was a convincing innocence.

"The Captain-General is interested in all our visitors, especially those who have been notable soldiers," Marquinez bowed to Sharpe, whose fame had been described in Louisa's letter of introduction. "Tell me," Marquinez went on, "were you at Waterloo?"

"Yes."

"Then I am sure the Captain-General will want to meet

you. General Bautista is an afficionado of the Emperor. He would, I think, be delighted to hear of your experiences." Marquinez beamed delightedly, as if a mutual treat awaited his master and Sharpe. "Such a pleasure to meet you both!" Marquinez said, then ushered them back to the guardroom. "Such a pleasure," he said again.

"So how did it go?" Blair asked when they returned.

"Very well," Sharpe said. "All things considered, it couldn't have gone much better."

"That means you're in trouble," Blair said happily, "that means you're in trouble."

That night it rained so heavily that the town ditch flooded with earth-reddened water which, in the moonlight, looked like blood. Blair became drunk. He bemoaned that his wife was still in Liverpool and commiserated with Sharpe and Harper that their wives were, respectively, in France and Ireland. "You live in bloody France?" Blair kept asking the question as though to dilute the astonishment he evidently felt for Sharpe's choice of a home. "Bloody funny place to live, I mean if you've been fighting the buggers. It must be like a fox moving in with the rabbits!"

Sharpe tried to talk of more immediate matters, like Captain-General Bautista and his fascination for Napoleon, but Blair did not want to talk about the Spanish commander. "He's a bastard. A son-of-a-whore bastard, and that's all there is to say about him." It was clear that Blair, despite his privileged status as a diplomat, feared the Spanish commander.

"Are you saying he's illegitimate?" Sharpe asked disingenuously.

"Oh, Christ, no." Blair glanced at the servants as though fearing they had suddenly learned English and would report this conversation to Bautista's spies. "Bautista's a younger son, so he needs to make his own fortune. He got his posting here because his father is a Minister in Ferdinand VII's government, and he greased his son a commission in the artillery and an appointment in Chile, because this is where the money is. But the rest Bautista did for himself. He's capable! He's efficient and a hard worker. He's probably no soldier, but he's no weakling. And he's making himself rich."

"So he's corrupt?"

"Corrupt!" Blair mocked the word. "Of course he's corrupt. They're all corrupt. I'm corrupt! Everyone here knows the bloody war is lost. It's only a question of time before the Spaniards go and the Chileans can bugger up their own country instead of having someone else to do it for them, so what Bautista and his people are doing is making themselves rich before someone takes away the tray of baubles." Blair paused, sipped, then leaned closer to Sharpe. "Your friend Vivar wasn't corrupt, which is why he made enemies, but Bautista, he's a coming man! He'll make his money, then go home and use that money to buy himself office in Madrid. Mark my words, he'll be the power in Spain before he's fifty."

"How old is he now?"

"He's a youngster! Thirty, no more." Blair, clearly deciding he had said enough about the feared Bautista, pushed his glass to the end of the table for a servant girl to fill with a mixture of rum and wine. "If you want a whore, Colonel," Blair went on, "there's a *chingana* behind the church. Ask for the girl they call La Monja!" Blair rolled his eyes heavenward to indicate what exquisite joys awaited Sharpe and Harper if they followed his advice. "She's a mestizo."

"What's a mestizo?" Harper asked.

"Half-breed, and that one's half woman and half wildcat."

"I'd rather hear about Bautista," Sharpe said.

"I've told you, there's nothing to tell. Man's a bastard. Cross him and you get butchered. He's judge, jury and exe-

cutioner here. He's also horribly efficient. You want some
more rum?"

Sharpe glanced at the two Indian girls who, holding their
jugs of wine and rum, stood expressionless at the edge of the
room. "No."

"You can have them, too," Blair said hospitably. "Help
yourselves, both of you! I know they look like cows, but they
know their way up and down a bed. No point in employing
them otherwise. They can't cook and their idea of cleaning a
room is to rearrange the dirt, so what else are they good for?
And in the dark you don't know they're savages, do you?"

Sharpe again tried to turn the conversation back to his
own business. "I need to find the American Consul. Does he
live close?"

"What the hell do you want Fielding for?" Blair sounded
offended, as though Sharpe's question suggested that Fielding was a better Consul than Blair.

Sharpe had no intention of revealing that he possessed a
signed portrait of Napoleon which the American Consul was
supposed to smuggle to a British Colonel now living in the
rebel part of the country, so instead he made up a story about
doing business for an American expatriate living in Normandy.

"Well, you're out of luck," Blair said with evident satisfaction. "Fielding's away from Valdivia this week. One of his
precious whaling boats was impounded by the Spanish Navy,
so he's on Chiloe, trying to have the bribe reduced to something under a King's ransom."

"Chiloe?" Sharpe asked.

"Island down south. Long way away. But Fielding will be
back in a week or so."

Sharpe hid his disappointment. He had been hoping to
deliver the portrait quickly, then forget about the Emperor's
gift, but now, if he were to keep his promise to Bonaparte,

he would have to find some other way of reaching Fielding. "Have you ever heard of a Lieutenant Colonel Charles?" He asked Blair as casually as he could.

"Charles? Of course I've heard of Charles. He's one of O'Higgins's military advisers."

"So he's a rebel?"

"Of course he's a bloody rebel! Why else would he have come to Chile? He likes to fight, and Europe isn't providing any proper wars these days, so all the rascals come over here and complicate my life instead. What do you want with Charles?"

"Nothing," Sharpe said, then let the subject drop. An hour later he and Harper went to their beds and lay listening to the water sluice off the tiles. The mattresses were full of fleas. "Like old times," Harper grumbled when they woke early the next morning.

Blair was also up at first light. The rain in the night had been so heavy that part of the misted square was flooded, and the inundation had turned the rubbish-choked ditch into a moat in which foul things floated. "A horrid day to travel," Blair complained when he met them in his parlor where coffee waited on the table. "It'll be raining again within the hour, mark my words."

"Where are you going?"

"Downriver. To the port." Blair groaned and rubbed his temples with his fingertips. "I've got to supervise some cargo loading, and probably see the Captain of the *Charybdis*."

"What's the *Charybdis*?" Harper asked.

"Royal Navy frigate. We keep a squadron on the coast just to make sure the bloody dagoes don't shoot any of our people. They know that if they upset me, I'll arrange to have their toy boats blown out of the water." Blair shivered, then groaned with pain. "Breakfast!" he shouted toward the kitchen, then flinched as a muffled rattle of musketry sounded from the Citadel. "That's another rebel gone," Blair said thickly. There was a second ragged volley. "Business is good this morning."

"Rebels?" Sharpe asked.

"Or some poor bugger caught with a gun and no money to bribe the patrol. They shove them up against the Angel Tower, say a quick Hail Mary, then send the buggers into eternity."

"The Angel Tower?" Sharpe asked.

"It's that ancient lump of stone in the middle of the fort. The Spaniards built it when they first came here, way back in the dark ages. Bloody thing has survived earthquake, fire and rebellion. It used to be a prison, but it's empty now."

"Why is it called the Angel Tower?" Harper asked.

"Christ knows, but you know what the dagoes are like. Some drunken Spanish whore probably saw an angel on its top and the next thing you know they're all weeping and praying and the priests are carrying around the collection plate. Where's my Goddamned bloody breakfast?" he shouted toward the kitchen.

Blair, well breakfasted at last, left for the harbor an hour later. "Don't expect anything from Marquinez," he warned Sharpe. "They'll promise you anything, but deliver nothing. You'll not hear a word from that macaroni until you offer him a fat bribe."

Yet no sooner had Blair gone than a message arrived from the Citadel asking Colonel Sharpe and Mister Harper to do the honor of attending on Captain Marquinez at their earliest opportunity. So, moments later, Sharpe and Harper crossed the bridge, walked through the tunnel that pierced the glacis, crossed the outer parade courtyard and into the inner yard where two bodies lay like heaps of soiled rags against the bloodstained wall of the Angel Tower. Marquinez, greeting Sharpe in the courtyard, was embarrassed by the bodies. "A wagon is coming to take them to the cemetery. They were rebels, of course."

"Why don't you just dump them in the ditch like the Indian babies?" Sharpe asked Marquinez sourly.

"Because the rebels are Christians, of course," Marquinez replied, bemused that the question had even been asked.

"None of the Indians are Christian?"

"Some of them are, I suppose," Marquinez said airily, "though personally I don't know why the missionaries bother. One might as well offer the sacrament to a jabbering pack of monkeys. And they're treacherous creatures. Turn your back and they'll stab you. They've been rebelling against us for hundreds of years, and they never seem to learn that we always win in the end." Marquinez ushered Sharpe and Harper into a room with a high arched ceiling. "Will you be happy to wait here? The Captain-General would like to greet you."

"Bautista?" Sharpe was taken aback.

"Of course! We have only one Captain-General!" Marquinez was suddenly all charm. "The Captain-General would like to welcome you to Chile himself. Captain Ardiles told him how you had a private audience with Bonaparte and, as I mentioned, the Captain-General has a fascination with the Emperor. So, do you mind waiting? I'll have some coffee sent. Or would you prefer wine?"

"I'd prefer our travel permits," Sharpe said truculently.

"The matter is being considered, I do assure you. We must do whatever we can to look after the happiness of the Countess of Mouromorto. Now, if you will excuse me?" Marquinez, with a confiding and dazzling smile, left them in the room, which was furnished with a table, four chairs and a crucifix hanging from a bent horseshoe nail. A broken saddle tree was discarded in one corner, while a lizard watched Sharpe from the curved ceiling. The room's one window looked onto the execution yard. After an hour, during which no one came to fetch Sharpe and Harper, a wagon creaked into the yard and a detail of soldiers swung the two dead rebels onto the wagon's bed.

Another hour passed, noted by the chiming of a clock somewhere deep in the fort. Neither wine, coffee, nor a summons from the Captain-General arrived. Captain Marquinez had disappeared, and the only clerk in the office behind the guardroom did not know where the Captain might be found. The rain fell miserably, slowly diluting the bloodstains on the lime-washed wall of the Angel Tower.

The rain fell. Still no one came and, as the clock chimed another half hour, Sharpe's patience finally snapped. "Let's get the hell out of here."

"What about Bautista?"

"Bugger Bautista." It seemed that Blair was right about the myriad of delays that the Spanish imposed on even the simplest bureaucratic procedure, but Sharpe did not have the patience to be the victim of such nonsense. "Let's go."

It was raining much harder now. Sharpe ran across the Citadel's bridge, while Harper lumbered after him. They splashed across the square's cobbles, past the statue where the group of chained Indians still sat vacantly under the cloudburst, to where a heavy wagon, loaded with untanned hides, was standing in front of Blair's house. The untreated leather stank foully. A uniformed soldier was lounging under the Consul's arched porch, beside the drooping British flag, apparently guarding the wagon's stinking cargo. The daydreaming soldier straightened as Sharpe approached. "You can't go in there, *señor!*" He moved to block Sharpe's path. "*Señor!*"

"Shut up! Get out of my bloody way!" Sharpe, disgusted with all things Spanish, rammed his forearm onto the soldier's chest, piling him backward. Sharpe expected Blair's door to be locked, but unexpectedly it yielded to his thrust. He pushed it wide open as Harper ran into the porch's shelter. The dazed sentry took one look at the tall Irishman's size and decided not to make an issue of the confrontation. Sharpe stamped inside. "Damn Marquinez! Damn Bautista! Damn the bloody Spaniards!" He took off his wet greatcoat and shook the rain off it. "Bloody, bloody Spaniards! They never bloody change! You remember when we liberated their Goddamned bloody country and they wanted to charge customs duty on the powder and shot we used to do it? Goddamned bloody Spaniards!"

Harper, who was married to a Spaniard, smiled soothingly. "We need a cup of tea, that's what we need. That and some decent food, but I'll settle for dry clothes first." He started climbing the stairs, but halfway to the landing he suddenly checked, then swore. "Jesus!"

"What?"

"Thieves!" Harper was charging up to the landing. Sharpe followed.

"Get down!" Harper screamed, then threw himself sideways through an open doorway. Sharpe had a glimpse of two men in a second doorway, then the landing was filled with smoke as one of the men fired a gun. The noise was huge, echoing around the house. Bitter-smelling smoke churned in the corridor. Sharpe did not see where the bullet went. He only knew it had not hit him.

He scrambled to his feet and ran past the doorway where Harper had sheltered. He could hear the thieves running ahead of him. "We've got the buggers trapped!" He shouted the encouragement for Harper, then he saw that there was another staircase at the back of the house, presumably a stair for servants, and the two thieves were jumping its steps three at a time.

"Stop!" Sharpe bellowed. He had visited the Citadel in

civilian clothes, not bothering to wear any weapons. "Stop!"
he shouted again, but the two men were already scrambling
out into the stableyard. The mestizo cook was screaming.

Sharpe reached the kitchen door as the thieves tugged
open the stableyard gate. Sharpe ran into the rain, still shouting at the men to stop. Both thieves were carrying sacks of
plunder, and both were armed with short-barreled cavalry
carbines. One carbine had been fired, but now the second
man, fearing Sharpe's pursuit, turned and aimed his gun.
The man had black hair, a bushy moustache and a scar on his
cheek, then Sharpe realized the carbine was at point-blank
range and he hurled himself sideways, slithering through
puddles of rain and heaps of stable muck to thump against a
bale of straw. The gate was open now, but the moustached
gunman did not run; instead he carefully leveled the carbine
at Sharpe. He was holding the gun one-handed. There was a
pause of a heartbeat, then he smiled and pulled the trigger.

Nothing happened. For a second the man just gaped at
Sharpe, then, suddenly scared, he hurled the carbine like a
club and took off through the gate after his companion.

Sharpe was climbing to his feet, but had to drop flat again
as the gun flew over his head. He stood again, slipped as he
began running, found his balance, then clung to the gatepost
when he saw that the two men had disappeared into a
crowded alley. He swore.

He closed the gate, brushed the horse manure off his
jacket and breeches, picked up the thief's carbine and went
back to the kitchen. "Stop your noise, woman!" he snapped
at the cook, then stared up to where Harper had appeared at
the top of the back stairs. "What's the matter with you?"

"God save Ireland." Harper came slowly down the stairs.
He had gone pale as paper, and had a hand clapped to the
side of his head. Blood showed between his fingers. "Bugger
shot me!" Harper staggered against the wall, but managed to

keep his balance. "I went through the whole damned French wars, so I did, and never once did I take a bullet, and now a damned thief in a damned town at the end of the damned world hits me! Jesus sweet Christ!" He took his hand away and blood oozed from his sandy hair to trickle down his neck. "I'm feeling dizzy, so I am."

Sharpe helped Harper to a chair, sat him down, then probed the blood-soaked hair. The damage was slight. The bullet had seared across the scalp, breaking the skin, but not doing any other damage. "The bullet just grazed you," Sharpe said in relief.

"Grazed, indeed! I was hit, so I was!"

"Barely broke the skin."

"Lucky to be alive, I am. Sweet mother of God, but I could have been dead by now."

"Luckily you've got a skull like a bloody ox." Sharpe rapped Harper's temple. "It would take a twelve pounder to dent that skull."

"Would you listen to him! As near to death as a goose at Christmas, so I am, and all he can do is tap my skull!"

Sharpe went to the big water vat by the back door, soaked a piece of cloth, and tossed it to Harper. "Hold that against your head. It'll bring you back to life. I'm going to see what the bastards took."

Apart from their weapons and the chest with Louisa's gold, all of which had been locked in Blair's strong room, the thieves appeared to have taken everything. Sharpe, disconsolate, went downstairs to where Harper was dabbing his bloody head with the wet rag. "The lot," Sharpe said bitterly. "Your bag, my bags, our clothes, boots, razors. The lot."

"The Emperor's thimble?" Harper asked in disbelief.

"Everything," Sharpe said. "Bonaparte's portrait, and some stuff of Blair's as well. I can't tell what, but the candlesticks are gone and those small pictures that were on the shelf. Bastards!"

"What about your locket?"

"Around my neck."

"The guns?"

Sharpe shook his head. "The strong-room padlock wasn't touched." He picked up the thief's weapon. "The bastard tried to shoot me twice. It wouldn't fire."

"He forgot to prime it?"

Sharpe opened the pan and saw a sludge of wet powder there, then saw that the trigger was loose. He scraped the priming out of the pan and tapped the gun's butt on the floor. His guess was that the carbine's mainspring had jammed because the wood of the stock had swollen in the damp weather. It was a common enough problem with cheap guns. He tapped harder and this time the trapped spring jarred itself free and the flint snapped down on the emptied pan.

"Swollen wood?" Harper asked.

"Saved my life, too. Bugger had me lined up at five paces." He peered at the lockplate and saw the mark of the Cadiz Armory, which made this a Spanish army gun. There was nothing sinister in that. The world was awash with old army weapons; even Sharpe and Harper carried rifles with the British Government's Tower Armory mark on their plates.

Sharpe turned to the whimpering cook and accused her of letting the two thieves into the house, but the woman protested her innocence, claiming that the two men must have climbed across the church roof and jumped from there onto the half-roof at the side of Blair's house. "It has happened before, *señor*," she said resignedly, "which is why the master has his strong room."

"What do we do now?" Harper still held the rag against his head.

"I'll make a formal complaint," Sharpe said. "It won't

help, but I'll make it anyway." He went back to the Citadel where, in the guardroom, a surly clerk took down a list of the stolen property. Sharpe, as he dictated the missing items, knew that he wasted his time.

"You wasted your time," Blair said when he came home. "Place is full of bloody thieves. That clerk will already have thrown your list away. You'll have to buy more clothes tomorrow."

"Or look for the bloody thieves," Harper, his head sore and bandaged, growled threateningly.

"You'll never find them," Blair said. "They brand some of them on the forehead with a big *L,* but it doesn't do any good." Sharpe guessed the *L* stood for *ladron,* thief. "That's why I have a strong room," Blair went on, "it would take more than a couple of cutthroats to break in there." He had fetched a bottle of gin back from the H.M.S. *Charybdis* and in consequence was a happy man. By nightfall he was also a drunken man who once again offered Sharpe and Harper the run of his servants. "None of them are poxed. They'd better not be, God help them, or I'll have the skin off their backs."

"I'll manage without," Sharpe said.

"Your loss, Sharpe, your loss."

That night the clouds rolled back from the coastal plain so that the dawn brought a wondrous clean sky and a sharp, bright sun that rose to silhouette the jagged peaks of the Andes. There was something almost springlike in the air—something so cleansing and cheerful that Sharpe, waking, felt almost glad to be in Chile, then he suddenly remembered the events of the previous day, and knew that he must spoil this bright clean day by buying a new greatcoat, new breeches, a coat, shirts, small clothes and a razor. At least, he thought grimly, he had been wearing his good kerseymere coat for his abortive visit to Bautista, which had served to save the coat from the thieves and to save Sharpe from

Lucille's wrath. She was forever telling him he should dress more stylishly, and the dark green kerseymere coat had been the first success in her long and difficult campaign. The coat had become somewhat soiled with horse manure when Sharpe rolled in the stableyard, but he supposed that would brush out.

He pulled on shirt, breeches and boots, then carried the coat downstairs so that one of Blair's servants could attack it with a brush. Blair was already up, drinking bitter coffee in the parlor and with him, to Sharpe's utter surprise, was Captain Marquinez. The Captain had a gold-edged shako tucked under one arm. The shako had a tall white plume that shivered as Marquinez offered Sharpe a low bow. "Good morning, Colonel!"

"Got our travel permits, have you?" was Sharpe's surly greeting.

"What a lovely morning!" Marquinez smiled with delight. "Mister Blair has offered me coffee, but I cannot accept, for we are summoned to the Captain-General's audience."

"Summoned?" Sharpe asked. Blair clearly thought Sharpe's hostility was inappropriate, for he was making urgent signals that Sharpe should behave more gently.

Marquinez smiled. "Summoned indeed, Colonel."

Sharpe poured himself coffee. "I'm an Englishman, Captain. You don't summon me."

"What Colonel Sharpe means—" Blair began.

"Colonel Sharpe reproves me, and quite rightly." The plume nodded as Marquinez bowed again. "It would give Captain-General Bautista the most exquisite delight, Colonel, if you and Mister Harper would favor him with your attendance at this morning's audience."

"Bloody hell," Sharpe said. And wondered just what sort of man he would find when he at last met Vivar's enemy.

B autista's audience hall was a palatial room dominated by a carved and painted royal coat of arms that hung above the fireplace. Incongruously, for it was not cold, a small fire burned in a grate that was dwarfed by the huge stone hearth. The windows at either end of the hall were open; those at the east, where the early sun now dazzled, looked onto the Angel Tower and its execution yard, while the western windows offered a view across the defenses to the swirling waters of the Valdivia River. The whole room, with its blackened beams, lime-washed walls, bright escutcheon and stone pillars, was intended as a projection of Spanish royal power, a grandiose echo of the Escorial.

The room's real power, though, lay not in the monarch's coat of arms, nor in the royal portraits that hung on the high walls, but in the energetic figure that paced up and down, up and down, behind a long table that was set before the fireplace and at which four aides-de-camp sat and took dictation. Watching the pacing man, and listening to his every word, was an audience of seventy or eighty officers. This was evidently how Captain-General Bautista chose to do his business: openly, efficiently, crisply.

Miguel Bautista was a tall, thin man with black hair which was oiled and brushed back so that it clung like a sleek cap to his narrow skull. His face was thin and pale, dominated by a long nose and the dark eyes of a predator. There was,

Sharpe thought, a glint of quick intelligence in those eyes, but there was something else too, a carelessness, as though this young man had seen much of the world's wickedness and was amused by it. He wore a uniform that was new to Sharpe. It was an elegantly cut cavalry tunic of plain black cloth, but with no symbols of rank except for two modest epaulettes of silver chain. His breeches were black, as were his cavalry boots and even the cloth covering of his scabbard. It was a simple uniform, but one which stood in stark contrast to the colorful uniforms of the other officers in the room.

Some of those officers had evidently come as petitioners, others because they had information that Bautista needed, and yet more because they were on the Captain-General's staff. All were necessary to complete what Sharpe realized was a piece of theater. This was Bautista's demonstration, held at a deliberately inconvenient early hour, to show that he was the enthusiastic master of every detail that mattered in his royal province. He paced incessantly, casting off the matters of business one after the other with a swift efficiency. A Lieutenant of Cavalry was given permission to marry, while a Major of Artillery was refused leave to travel home to Spain. "Does Major Rodriguez think that no other officer ever had a dying mother?" There was laughter from the audience at that sally, and Sharpe saw Colonel Ruiz, the bombastic artilleryman who had sailed on the *Espiritu Santo,* laughing with the rest.

Bautista called various officers to make their reports. A tall, gray-haired Captain detailed the ammunition reserves in the Perrunque arsenal, then a Medical Officer reported on the number of men who had fallen sick in the previous month. Bautista listened keenly, noting that the Puerto Crucero garrison had shown a marked increase in fever cases. "Is there a contagion there?"

"We're not sure, Your Excellency."

"Then find out!" Bautista's voice was high and sharp. "Are the townspeople affected? Or just the garrison? Surely someone has thought to ask that simple question, have they not?"

"I don't know, Your Excellency," the hapless Medical Officer replied.

"Then find out! I want answers! Answers! Is it the food? The garrison's water supply? The air? Or just morale?" He stabbed a finger at the Medical Officer. "Answers! Get me answers!"

It was an impressive display, yet Sharpe felt unconvinced by it. It was almost as if Bautista was going through the motions of government merely so that no one could accuse him of dereliction when his province vanished from the maps of the Spanish Empire. He was, Sharpe thought, a young man full of self-importance, but so far Sharpe could see no evidence of anything worse—of, say, the cruelty that made Bautista's name so feared. The Captain-General had resumed pacing up and down before the small and redundant fire, stabbing more questions into his audience as he paced. How many cattle were in Valdivia's slaughteryards? Had the supply ships arrived from Chiloe? Was there any news of Ruiz's regiment? None? How many more weeks must they wait for those extra guns? Had the Puerto Crucero garrison test-fired their heated shot, and if so, what was their rate of fire? How long had it taken to heat the furnace from cold to operational heat? General Bautista suddenly whirled on Sharpe and pointed his finger, just as if Sharpe was one of the subservient officers who responded so meekly to each of Bautista's demands. "You were at Waterloo?" The question was rapped out in the same tone that the General had used to ask about the monthly sick returns.

"Yes, sir."

"Why did Napoleon lose there?"

The question took Sharpe somewhat by surprise, despite Marquinez having warned him that the Captain-General was fascinated by Napoleon and his battles. Did Bautista see himself as a new Napoleon, Sharpe wondered? It was possible. The Captain-General was still a young man and, like his hero, an artillery officer.

"Well?" Bautista chivied Sharpe.

"He underestimated the British infantry," Sharpe said.

"And you, of course, were a British infantryman?" Bautista asked in a sarcastic tone, provoking more sycophantic laughter from his audience. Bautista cut the laughter short with a swift chop of his hand. "I heard that he lost the battle because he waited too long before beginning to fight."

"If he'd have started earlier," Sharpe said, "we'd have beaten him sooner." That, Sharpe knew, was not true. If Bonaparte had opened the battle at dawn he would have ridden victorious into Brussels at dusk, but Sharpe would be damned before he gave Bautista the satisfaction of agreeing with him.

The Captain-General had walked close to Sharpe and was staring at the Englishman with what seemed a genuine curiosity. Sharpe was a tall man, but even so he had to look up to meet the dark eyes of the Captain-General. "What was it like?" Bautista asked.

"Waterloo?" Sharpe felt tongue-tied.

"Yes! Of course. What was it like to be there?"

"Jesus," Sharpe said helplessly. He did not know if he could describe such a day, certainly he had never done so to anyone except those, like Harper, who had shared the experience and who could therefore see beyond the tale's incoherence. Sharpe's fiercest memory of the day was simply one of terror; the terror of standing under the massive concussion of the French bombardment that, hour by hour, had ground down the British line till there were no reserves left. The remainder of the day had faded into unimportance. The opening of the battle had been full of excitement and motion, yet it was not those heart-stirring moments that Sharpe remembered when he woke sweating in the night, but rather that inhuman mincing machine of the French artillery; the lurid flickering of its massive cannon flames in the smoke bank, the pathetic cries of the dying, the thunder of the roundshot in the overheated air, the violence of the soil spewed up by the striking shots and the stomach-emptying terror of standing under the unending cannonade that had punched and crashed and pounded down the bravest man's endurance. Even the battle's ending, that astonishing triumph in which tired and seemingly beaten men had risen from the mud to rout the finest troops of France, had paled in Sharpe's memory beside the nightmarish flicker of those guns. "It was bad," Sharpe said at last.

"Bad!" Bautista laughed. "Is that all you can say?"

It was all Sharpe had said to the Emperor on Saint Helena, but Napoleon had not needed to hear more. Bonaparte had given Sharpe a look of such quick sympathy that Sharpe had been forced to laugh, and the Emperor had laughed with him. "It was supposed to be bad!" Bonaparte had said indignantly, "But it was evidently not bad enough, eh?" But now, because Sharpe spoke to a man who did not know how the heart shuddered with terror every time a shot punched the air with pressure, flame and death, he could only offer the inadequate explanation. "It was frightening. The guns, I mean."

"The guns?" Bautista asked with a sudden intensity.

"The French had a lot of artillery," Sharpe explained lamely, "and it was well handled."

"It was frightening?" Bautista wanted Sharpe's earlier assertion confirmed.

"Very."

"Frightening." Bautista repeated the word meaningfully,

letting it hang in the air as he walked back to his long table. "You hear that?" He shouted the question loudly, rounding on the startled audience. "Frightening! And that is how we will finish this rebellion. Not by marching men into the wilderness, but with guns, with guns, with guns, with guns!" With each repetition of the word he pounded his right fist into his left palm. "Guns! Where are your guns, Ruiz?"

"They're coming, Your Excellency," Ruiz said soothingly.

"I've told Madrid," Bautista went on, "time and again to send me guns! We'll break this rebellion by enticing its forces to attack our strongholds. Here! In Valdivia! We shall let O'Higgins bring his armies and Cochrane his ships into the range of our guns and then we shall destroy them! With guns! With guns! With guns! But if Madrid doesn't send me guns, how can we win?" He was rehearsing the arguments that would explain the loss of Chile. He would blame it on Madrid for not sending enough guns, yet guns, as any real soldier knew, could not win the war.

Because relying on guns and forts was a recipe for doing nothing. It was generalship by defense. Bautista did not want to risk marching an army into the field and suffering a horrific defeat, so instead he was justifying his inaction by pretending it was a strategy. Let Madrid send enough guns, Bautista claimed, and the enemy would be destroyed when they attacked the Royalist strongholds, yet even the dullest enemy would eventually realize it was both cheaper and more effective to starve a fortress into submission than to drown it in blood. Bautista's strategy was designed solely to transfer the blame for defeat onto other men's shoulders, while he became rich enough to challenge those men when he returned to Madrid. No wonder, Sharpe thought, Blas Vivar had hated this man. He was betraying his soldiers as well as his country.

"Why have you come here, Mister Sharpe?" Bautista had suddenly turned on Sharpe again.

Sharpe, noting that he had not been accorded the honorific of his rank, decided not to make an issue of it. "I'm here at the behest of the Countess of Mouromorto to carry her husband's remains home to Spain."

"She is evidently an extravagant woman? Why did she not simply ask me to send her husband home?"

Sharpe did not want to explain that Louisa had not heard of her husband's death or burial when he left, so he just shrugged. "I can't say, sir."

"You can't say. Well, it seems a small enough request. I shall consider my decision, though I must say that so far as most of us are concerned, the sooner General Vivar is out of Chile, the better." The quip provoked another outburst of laughter which this time Bautista allowed to continue. "You knew General Vivar?" he asked Sharpe when the sycophancy had subsided.

"We fought together in '09, at Santiago de Compostela."

Blas Vivar's fight at Santiago de Compostela had been one of the great events of the Spanish war, a miraculous victory which had proved to many Spaniards that the French were not invincible, and Sharpe's mention of the battle made many of the officers in the audience look at him with a new interest and respect, but to General Bautista the battle was mere history.

"Vivar was like many veterans of the French wars," Bautista said sarcastically, "in his belief that the experience of fighting against Bonaparte's armies prepared him for suppressing a rebellion in a country like Chile. But they are not the same kind of fighting! Would you say they were the same kind of fighting, Mister Sharpe?"

"No, sir." Sharpe replied in all honesty, but even so he felt that he was somehow betraying his dead friend by agreeing.

Bautista, pleased to have elicited the agreement from Sharpe, smiled, then glanced at Harper's bandaged head. "I hear you were sadly inconvenienced yesterday?"

Again Sharpe was surprised by the suddenness of the question, but he managed to nod. "Yes, sir."

The smile grew broader as Bautista snapped his fingers. "I would not like you to return to England with an unhappy memory of Chile, or convinced that my administration is incompetent to police Valdivia's alleys. So I am delighted to tell you, Mister Sharpe, that the thieves were apprehended and your effects recovered." The click of his fingers had summoned two orderlies who each carried a bag into the room. The bags were placed on the table. "Come!" Bautista ordered. "Come and examine them! I wish to be assured that everything has been recovered. Please!"

Astonished, Sharpe and Harper walked to the table and, in front of the audience, unpacked the bags. Everything seemed to be there, but not in the same condition. Their clothes, which had been soiled and crumpled from the long sea voyage, had all been laundered and pressed. Their boots had been polished, and Sharpe did not doubt that their razors had been stropped to a murderous edge. "It's all here," he said, and thinking he had not been gracious enough, he made a clumsy half-bow to Bautista. "Thank you, Your Excellency."

"Everything is there?" Bautista demanded. "Nothing is missing?"

It was then that Sharpe realized one thing was missing: the portrait of Napoleon. Harper's small silver thimble, duly polished, was in one of the bags, but not the silver-framed portrait of the Emperor. Sharpe opened his mouth to report the loss, then abruptly closed it as he considered that the portrait's absence could be a trap. Bautista was evidently obsessed with Napoleon, which made it very likely that the

Captain-General had himself purloined the signed portrait. Nor, Sharpe decided, was the loss of the portrait important. It was a mere *souvenir,* as the French said, and Lieutenant Colonel Charles could always write and request another such keepsake. Sharpe also had a strong suspicion that if he mentioned the missing picture, Bautista might refuse to issue the travel permits and so, without considering the matter further, Sharpe shook his head. "Nothing is missing, Your Excellency."

Bautista smiled as though Sharpe had said the right thing, then, still smiling, he clicked his fingers again, this time summoning a squad of infantrymen who escorted two prisoners. The prisoners, in drab brown clothes, had their wrists and ankles manacled. The chains scraped and jangled as the two men were forced to the room's center.

"These are the thieves," Bautista announced.

Sharpe stared at the two men. They were both black-haired, both had moustaches, and both were terrified. Sharpe tried to remember the face of the man who had aimed the carbine at him, and in his memory that man had sported a much bigger moustache than either of these prisoners, but he could not be certain.

"What do you do," Bautista asked, "with thieves in your country?"

"Imprison them," Sharpe said, "or maybe transport them to Australia."

"How merciful! No wonder you still have thieves. In Chile we have better ways to deter scum." Bautista turned to the fire, drew a big handkerchief from his uniform pocket, then wrapped the handkerchief around the metal handle of what Sharpe had supposed to be a long poker jammed into the basket grate. It was not a poker, but rather a branding iron. Bautista jerked it free of the coals and Sharpe saw the letter *L,* for *ladron,* glowing at its tip.

"No! *Señor!* No!" The nearest thief twisted back, but two soldiers gripped him hard by the arms, and a third stood behind the man to hold his head steady.

"The punishment for a first offense is a branding. For the second offense it is death," Bautista said, then he held the brand high and close to the thief's forehead, close enough for the man to feel its radiant heat. Bautista hesitated, smiling, and it seemed to Sharpe that the whole room held its breath. Colonel Ruiz turned away. The elegant Marquinez went pale.

"No!" the man screamed, then Bautista pushed the brand forward and the scream soared high and terrible. There was a sizzling sound, a flash of flame as the man's greasy hair briefly flared with fire, then the big room filled with the smell of burning flesh. Bautista held the brand on the man's skin even as the thief collapsed.

The iron was pushed back into the coals as the second man was hauled forward. That second man looked at Sharpe. "*Señor,* I beg you! It was not us! Not us!"

"Your Excellency!" Sharpe called.

"If I were in England," Bautista jiggled the iron in the fire, "would you think it proper for me to interfere with English justice? This is Chile, Mister Sharpe, not England. Justice here is what I say it is, and I treat thieves with the certain cure of pain. Exquisite pain!" He pulled the brand free, turned and aimed the bright letter at the second man.

"God save Ireland," Harper said softly beside Sharpe. Most of the audience looked shocked. One uniformed man had gone to a window and was leaning across the wide stone sill. Bautista, though, was enjoying himself. Sharpe could see it in the dark eyes. The second man screamed, and again there was the hiss of burning skin and the stink of flesh cooking, and then the second man, like the first, had the big *L* branded forever on his forehead.

"Take them away," Bautista commanded as he tossed the branding iron into the fireplace, then turned and stared defiantly at Sharpe. The Captain-General looked tired, as though all the joy of his morning had suddenly evaporated. "Your request to travel to Puerto Crucero and recover the body of Don Blas Vivar is granted. Captain Marquinez will issue you with the necessary permits, and you will leave Valdivia tomorrow. That finishes today's business. Good day."

The Captain-General, his morning display of efficiency and cruelty complete, turned on his heels and walked away.

"Who were they?" Sharpe challenged Marquinez.

"They?"

"Those two men."

"They were the thieves, of course."

"I don't believe it," Sharpe claimed angrily. "I didn't recognize either man."

"If they were not the thieves," Marquinez said very calmly, "then how do you explain their possession of your property?" He smiled as he waited for Sharpe's answer and, when none came, he opened a drawer of his desk and took out a sheaf of documents. "Your travel permits, Colonel. You will note they specify you must leave Valdivia tomorrow." He dealt the documents onto the desk one by one, as though they were playing cards. "Mister Harper's travel pass, which bears the same date restrictions as your own. This is your fortress pass, which gives you entry to the Citadel at Puerto Crucero, and finally, a letter from His Excellency giving you permission to exhume the body of General Vivar." Marquinez smiled. "Everything you wish!"

Sharpe, after his flash of anger, felt churlish. The papers were indeed everything he needed, even down to the letter authorizing the exhumation. "What about the church's permission?"

"I think you will find that no churchman will countermand the wishes of Captain-General Bautista," Marquinez said.

Sharpe picked up the papers. "You've been very helpful, Captain."

"It is our pleasure to be helpful."

"And at least we'll have fine weather for our voyage," Harper put in cheerfully.

"Your voyage?" Marquinez asked in evident puzzlement, then understood Harper's meaning. "Ah! You are assuming that you will be traveling on board the *Espiritu Santo*. Alas, she has no spare passenger cabins, at least not till she has dropped those passengers traveling to Puerto Crucero. Which means that you must travel overland. Which is good news, gentlemen! It will offer you a chance to see some of our lovely countryside."

"But if we don't have to catch the ship," Sharpe asked, "why do we have to leave tomorrow?"

"You surely want to have your business in Puerto Crucero finished by the time the *Espiritu Santo* arrives there, do you not? Else how will you be able to travel back to Europe in her? Besides, we always specify the dates for travel, Colonel, otherwise how do we know the permits have been properly used?"

"But I need a tin-lined coffin made!" Sharpe insisted, "and I can't do that and buy horses all in one day!"

Marquinez brushed the objections aside. "The armorers at Puerto Crucero will be pleased to make a coffin for you. And I'm sure Mister Blair will be happy to help you buy horses and saddles, as well as supplies for the journey."

Sharpe still protested the arrangement. "Why can't we sleep on the *Espiritu Santo*'s deck? We don't need cabins."

Marquinez tried to soothe Sharpe. "The fault is entirely ours. We insisted that Captain Ardiles carry reinforcements for the Puerto Crucero garrison, and he claims he cannot cram another soul on board his ship. Alas." Marquinez sounded genuinely sympathetic. "But even if you could change Ardiles's mind, then you would still need new travel permits because these, as you can plainly see, are good only for land travel and do not give you permission to journey by sea. It is the regulations, you understand." Marquinez offered Sharpe one of his dazzling white smiles. "But perhaps, Colonel, you will do me the honor of letting me escort you for the first few miles? I could bring some company!" Marquinez raised his eyebrows to indicate that the company would be enjoyable. "And perhaps you will do me the favor of allowing me to provide you with luncheon? It would provide me with an opportunity to show you some scenery that is truly spectacular. I beg you! Please!" Marquinez waited for Sharpe's assent, then sensed the Englishman's suspicions. "My dear Colonel," Marquinez hastened to reassure Sharpe, "bring Mister Blair if that will make you easier!"

It seemed churlish to refuse. So far Marquinez had exacted neither payment nor bribe for the travel permits, indeed he had produced everything Sharpe had wanted, and the elegant young Captain seemed genuinely enthusiastic about showing Sharpe and Harper some of Chile's most beautiful countryside, and so Sharpe accepted the invitation, and then, with the permits safe in his pocket, he went to seek Blair's urgent help in buying horses and supplies.

They had just one day before they rode south to rendez-vous with a corpse.

It was, Harper said, a countryside so lovely and so fertile that it seemed only fitting that he rode it on a horse of gold.

In truth the horse was nothing special, but the beast had cost more money than either Harper or Sharpe had ever paid for a horse, and Sharpe's horse had cost just as much, yet Blair had been at pains to convince them that the animals had been purchased at something close to a bargain price. "Horses are expensive here!" the Consul had pleaded, "and when you leave Chile you should be able to sell them at a profit. Or something close to a profit."

"At a loss, you mean?" Sharpe asked.

"You need horses!" Blair insisted, and so they had paid for the two most expensive lumps of horseflesh ever bred. Harper's was a big mare, gray with a wall left eye and a hard, bruising gait. She was not pretty, but she was stubborn and strong enough to cope with Harper's weight. Sharpe's horse was also a mare, a chestnut with a docked tail and gaunt ribs. "All she needs is a bit of feeding," Blair had said, then negotiated the price of a mule that was to carry their luggage as well as the box which, taken from Blair's strong room, was now even more depleted of its precious gold.

What was left in the box was still a small fortune, and one that seemed increasingly unnecessary. So far, to Sharpe's astonishment, everything had proved remarkably easy. "It must be your reputation," Blair had said. The Consul claimed to be too busy to accept Marquinez's invitation, but had assured Sharpe there could be no danger in Marquinez's company. "Or perhaps Bautista thinks you've got a deal of influence back in Spain. You're a lucky man."

The lucky man now rode south under a sky so pale and blue that it seemed to have been rinsed by the recent winds and rains. Sharpe and Harper rode with the exquisitely uniformed Captain Marquinez ahead of an ebullient pack of young officers and their ladyfriends. The girls rode sidesaddle, what they called "English-style," provoking laughter in their companions by their loud cries of alarm whenever the road was particularly steep or treacherous. At those moments the officers vied in their attentions to hold the ladies steady. "The girls are not used to riding," Marquinez confided to Sharpe. "They come from an establishment behind the church. You understand?" There was an odd tone of disapproval in Marquinez's voice. Occasionally, when a girl's laughter was particularly loud, Marquinez would wince with embarrassment, but on the whole he seemed happy to be free of Valdivia and riding into such lovely country. A dozen officers' servants brought up the rear of the convoy, carrying food and wine for an outdoor luncheon.

They rode through wide vineyards, past rich villas and through white-painted villages, yet always, beyond the vines or the orchards or the tobacco fields, or behind the churches with their twin towers and high-peaked roofs, there were the great sharp edged mountains and deep swooping valleys and rushing white streams that cut like knives down from the peaks, above which, staining the otherwise clear sky, the smoke of two volcanoes smeared the blue with their gray-brown plumes. At other times, staring to their right, Sharpe and Harper could see ragged fingers of rocky land jutting and clawing out to an island-wracked sea. A ship, her white sails bright in the sun, was racing southward from Valdivia.

Luncheon was served beside a waterfall. Hummingbirds darted into a bank of wildflowers. The wine was heady. One of the girls, a dark-skinned mestizo, waded in the waterfall's pool, urged by her friends ever farther into the deepening water until her skirt was hitched high about her thighs and the young officers cheered their glimpse of dark, tantalizing skin. Marquinez, sitting beside Sharpe, was more interested in a patrol of a dozen cavalrymen that idled southward on small, wiry horses. Marquinez raised a languid hand to acknowledge the patrol's presence, then looked back to Sharpe. "What did you think of the Captain-General?"

A dangerous question, and one that Sharpe parried easily. "He seemed very efficient."

"He's a man of genius," Marquinez said enthusiastically.

"Genius?" Sharpe could not hide his skepticism.

"Customs dues have increased threefold under his rule, so have tax revenues. We have firm government at last!" Sharpe glanced at his companion's handsome face, expecting to see cynicism there, but Marquinez clearly meant every word he said. "And once we have all the guns we need," Marquinez went on, "we'll reconquer the northern regions."

"You'd best be asking Madrid for some good infantry," Sharpe said.

Marquinez shook his head. "You don't understand Chile, Colonel. The rebels think they're invincible, so sooner or later they will come to our fortresses, and they will be slaughtered, and everyone will recognize the Captain-General's genius." Marquinez tossed pebbles into the pool. Sharpe was watching the mestizo girl who, her thighs and skirt soaking, climbed onto the bank. "You find her pretty?" Marquinez suddenly asked.

"Yes. Who wouldn't?"

"They're pretty when they're young. By the time they're twenty and have two children they look like cavalry mules." Marquinez fished a watch from his waistcoat pocket. "We must be leaving you, Colonel. You know your way from here?"

"Indeed." Sharpe had been well coached by Blair in the route he must take. He and Harper would climb into the hills where their travel permit dictated that they must spend the night at a high fortress. Tomorrow they would ride down into the wilder country that sprawled across the border of the southern province. It was in that unsettled country, close to the hell-dark forests where embittered Indian tribes lived, that Blas Vivar had died. Blair and Marquinez had both assured Sharpe that the border country had been tamed since Vivar's death, and that the highway could be used in perfect safety. "There have been no rebels there since Blas Vivar died," Marquinez said. "There have been some highway robberies, but nothing, I think, that should worry either you or Mister Harper."

"They're welcome to try, so they are," Harper had said, and indeed he and Sharpe fairly bristled with weapons. Sharpe wore his big butcher's blade of a sword, the sword with which he had fought through Portugal, Spain and France, and then at the field of Waterloo. It was no ordinary infantry officer's sword, but instead the killing blade of a trooper from Britain's Heavy Cavalry. Soldiers armed with just such big swords had carved a corps of veteran French infantry into bloody ruin at Waterloo, capturing two Eagles as they did it. The sword was reckoned a bad weapon by experts—unbalanced, ugly and too long in its blade—but Sharpe had used it to lethal effect often enough, and by now he had a sentimental attachment to it. He also had a loaded Baker rifle slung on one shoulder, and had two pistols in his belt.

Harper was even more fiercely armed. He too carried a rifle and two pistols, and had a saber at his waist, yet the Irishman also carried his own favorite weapon; a seven-barreled gun, made for Britain's navy, yet too powerful for any but the biggest and most robust men to fire. The navy, which had wanted a weapon that could be fired like an overweight shotgun from the rigging onto an enemy's deck, had abandoned the weapon because of its propensity to shatter the shoulders of the men pulling its trigger, but in Patrick Harper the seven-barreled gun had found a soldier capable of taming its brute ferocity. The gun was a cluster of seven half-inch barrels which were fired by a single lock, and was, in its effect, like a small cannon loaded with grapeshot. Sharpe was hoping that any highway robber, seeing the weapon, let alone the swords, rifles and pistols, would think twice before trying to steal the strongbox.

"Bloody odd, when you think about it," Harper broke

their companionable silence an hour after they had parted from Marquinez.

"What's odd?"

"That there wasn't any room on the frigate. It was a bloody big boat." Harper frowned. "You don't think the buggers want us on this road so they can do us some mischief, do you?"

Sharpe had been wondering the same thing, but unaware how best to prepare for such trouble, he had not thought to perturb Harper by talking about it. Yet there was something altogether too convenient about the ease with which Marquinez had given them all the necessary permits but then denied them the chance to travel on the *Espiritu Santo,* something which suggested that maybe Sharpe and Harper were not intended to reach Puerto Crucero after all. "But I think we're safe today," Sharpe said.

"Too many people about, eh?" Harper suggested.

"Exactly." They were riding through a plump and populated countryside on a road that was intermittently busy with other travelers; a friar walking barefoot, a farmer driving a wagon of tobacco leaves to Valdivia, a herdsman with a score of small bony cattle. This was not the place to commit murder and theft; that would come tomorrow in the wilder southern hills.

"So what do we do tomorrow?" Harper asked.

"We ride very carefully," Sharpe answered laconically. He was not as sanguine as he sounded, but he did not know how else to plan against a mere possibility of ambush and he was unwilling to think of just turning back. He had come to Chile to find Blas Vivar and, even if his old friend was dead, he would still do his best to carry him home.

That night, in obedience to their travel permits, they stopped at a timber-walled fort that had been built so high above the surrounding land that it had been nicknamed the

Celestial Fort. Its simple log ramparts stared east to the mountains and west to the sea. To the north of the Celestial Fort, at the foot of the steep ridge that gave the fort its commanding height, was a small ragged village that was inhabited by natives who worked a nearby tobacco plantation. To the south, like a sullen warning of the dangers to come, were line after line of dark, wooded ridges. "I trust you brought your own food?" the fort's commander, a cavalry Captain named Morillo, greeted Sharpe and Harper.

"Yes."

"I'd like to feed you, but rations are scarce." Morillo gave Sharpe back the travel permits while his men eyed the newcomers warily. Morillo was a tall young man with a weathered face. His eyes were cautious and watchful, the eyes of a soldier. His job was to lead his cavalrymen on long, aggressive patrols down the highway, deterring any rebels who might think of ambushing its traffic. "Not that we have rebels here now," Morillo said. "The last Captain-General swept these valleys clean. He was a cavalryman, so he knew how to attack." There was an unspoken criticism in the words, suggesting that the new Captain-General knew only how to defend.

"I knew Vivar well," Sharpe said. "I rode with him in Spain. At Santiago de Compostela."

Morillo stared at Sharpe with momentary disbelief. "You were at Santiago when the French attacked the cathedral?"

"I was in the cathedral when they broke the truce."

"I was a child then, but I remember the stories. My God, but what times they were." Morillo frowned in thought for a few seconds, then abruptly twisted to stare across the fort's parade ground, which was an expanse of smoothly trampled earth. "Do you know Sergeant Dregara?"

"Dregara? No."

"He rode in an hour ago, with a half troop. He was asking about you."

"About me? I don't know him," Sharpe said.

"He knows you, and your companion. They're across the parade ground, around an open fire. Dregara's got a striped blanket over his shoulders."

Sharpe half-turned and surreptitiously stared across the fort to where the group of cavalry troopers squatted about their fire. Sharpe suspected, but could not be sure, that it was the same patrol that had saluted Marquinez at lunchtime.

Morillo drew Sharpe away from the ears of his own men. "Sergeant Dregara tells me he proposes to escort you tomorrow."

"I don't need an escort."

"Maybe what you need and what you will receive are very different, Colonel Sharpe. Things often are in Chile. Do I need to explain more?"

Sharpe had walked with the tall Spanish Captain into the open gate of the fort. Both men stopped and stared toward the distant sea which, from this eyrie, looked like a wrinkled sheet of hammered silver. "I assume, Captain," Sharpe said, "that you regret the death of Don Blas?"

Morillo was tense as he skirted the betrayal of the present Captain-General with his admiration of the last. "Yes, sir, I do."

"It happened not far from here, am I right?"

"A half day's journey south, sir." Morillo turned and pointed across the misted valleys of the wild country. "It wasn't on the main road, but off to the east."

"Strange, isn't it," Sharpe said, "that Don Blas cleared the rebels out of this region, yet was ambushed here by those same rebels?"

"Things are often strange in Chile, sir." Morillo spoke very warily.

"Perhaps," Sharpe said pointedly, "you could patrol southward tomorrow? Along the main road?"

Morillo, understanding exactly what Sharpe was suggesting, shook his head. "Sergeant Dregara brought me orders. I'm to ride to Valdivia tomorrow. I'm to leave a dozen men on post here, and the rest are to go to the Citadel with me. We're to report to Captain Marquinez before two o'clock in the afternoon."

"Meaning an early start," Sharpe said, "that will leave my friend and I alone with Sergeant Dregara?"

"Yes, sir." Morillo stooped to light a cigar. The wind whipped the smoke northward. He snapped shut the glowing tinderbox and pushed it into his sabretache. "The orders are signed by Captain-General Bautista. I've never received orders direct from a General before." Morillo drew on his cigar and Sharpe felt a chill creep up his spine. "You should also understand, sir," Morillo spoke with an admirable understatement, "that General Bautista is not kind to men who disobey his orders."

"I do understand that, Captain."

"I'd like to help you, sir, truly I would. General Vivar was a good man." Morillo shook his head ruefully. "When he was in command we had a score of forts like this one. We were training native cavalry. We were aggressive! Now?" He shrugged. "Now the only patrols are to keep this road open. We don't really know what's happening fifty miles east."

Sharpe turned to look back into the fort. "These aren't built for defense."

"No, sir. They're just refuges where tired men can spend a few nights in comparative safety. General Vivar deliberately made them uncomfortable so that we wouldn't be tempted to live in them permanently. He believed our place was out there." Morillo waved toward the darkening hills.

The temporary nature of the fort's accommodation was suggesting an idea to Sharpe. There was only one walled and roofed structure, a log·cabin which Sharpe guessed was the officer's perquisite, while the other cavalrymen were sheltered beneath the overhang of the firestep. Essentially the fort was nothing more than a walled bivouac; there was not even a water supply inside the walls. The horses had to be watered at the stream at the ridge's foot, and any other drinking water had to be lugged up from the same place. Sharpe gestured at the log cabin. "Your quarters, Captain?"

"Yes, sir."

"Maybe Mister Harper and I can share them with you?"

Morillo frowned, not quite understanding the request, but he nodded anyway. "We'll be cramped, but you're welcome."

"What time do you rouse the men?" Sharpe asked.

"Usually at six. We'd expect to leave at seven."

"Could you leave earlier? While it was dark?"

Morillo nodded cautiously. "I could."

Sharpe smiled. "I'm thinking, Captain, that if Sergeant Dregara is convinced Mister Harper and I are still asleep, he won't disturb us. He may even wait till midmorning before he ventures to knock on the door of your quarters."

Morillo understood the ruse, but looked doubtful. "He'll surely see your horses are gone."

"He might not notice if the horses are missing. After all, his horses and a dozen of yours will still be here. But he'll notice if the mule is gone, so I'll just have to leave it here, won't I?"

Morillo drew on his cigar, then blew a stream of smoke toward the distant sea. "Captain-General Bautista's orders are addressed to me. They say nothing about you, sir, and if you choose to leave at three in the morning, then I can't stop you, can I?"

"No, Captain, you can't. And thank you."

But Morillo was not finished. "I'd still be unhappy about you using the main road, sir. Even if you get a six-hour start on Dregara, you'll be traveling slowly, while he knows the short cuts." Morillo smiled. "I'll give you Ferdinand."

"Ferdinand?"

"You'll meet him in the morning." Morillo seemed amused, but would not say more.

The two men went back into the fort where the cooking fires crackled and smoked. Sentries paced the firestep as darkness seeped up from the valleys to engulf the sky and the mountains. Sulphurous yellow clouds shredded off the Andean peaks to spill toward the seaward plains, patterning the stars and shadowing the moon. An hour after sundown, Sharpe and Harper accompanied Captain Morillo as he went around the cooking fires to announce that his Valdivia patrol would be leaving three hours before dawn. Men groaned at the news, but Sharpe heard the humor behind their reaction and knew that at least these men still had confidence in their cause. Not all Vivar's work had gone to waste.

"And you, *señor?*" Sergeant Dregara, who had been sitting at the fire with Morillo's sergeants, looked slyly up at Sharpe. "You will go early, too?"

"Good Lord, no!" Sharpe yawned. "I'm an English gentleman, Sergeant, and English gentlemen don't stir till at least an hour after dawn."

"And the Irish not for another hour after that," Harper put in happily.

Dregara was a middle-aged runt of a man with yellow teeth, a lined face, a scarred forehead and the eyes of a killer. He was holding a half-empty bottle of clear Chilean brandy that he now gestured toward Sharpe. "Maybe we can ride south together, *señor?* There is sometimes safety in numbers."

"Good idea," Sharpe said in his best approximation of the braying voice some British officers liked to use. "And one of your men can bring us hot shaving water at, say, ten o'clock? Just tell the fellow to knock on the door and leave the bowl on the step."

"Shaving water?" Dregara clearly hated being treated as a servant.

"Shaving water, Sergeant. Very hot. I can't bear shaving in tepid water."

Dregara managed to suppress his resentment. "*Si, señor.* At ten."

The troopers wrapped themselves in blankets and lay down under the meager shelter of the fort's firestep. The sentries paced overhead. Somewhere beyond the wall, in the forests that lapped against the ridge, a beast screamed. Sharpe, sleepless on the floor of Morillo's quarters, listened to Harper's snores. If Dregara was supposed to kill them, Sharpe thought, how would Bautista react when he heard they still lived? And why would Bautista kill them? It made no sense. Maybe Dregara meant no harm, but why would Morillo be ordered back to Valdivia? The questions flickered through Sharpe's mind, but no answers came. It made sense, he supposed, that Bautista should resent Doña Louisa's interest in her husband's fate, for that interest could bring the scrutiny of Madrid onto this far, doomed colony, but was killing Louisa's emissaries the way to avert such interest?

He slept at last, but it seemed he was woken almost immediately. Captain Morillo was shaking his shoulder. "You should go now, before the others stir. My Sergeant will open the gate. Wake up, sir!"

Sharpe groaned, turned over, groaned again. There had been a time when he could live on no sleep, but he felt too old for such tricks now. There was a pain in his back, and an ache in his right leg where a bullet had once lodged. "Oh, Jesus."

"Dregara's bound to be awake when my men leave, and he mustn't see you," Morillo hissed.

Sharpe and Harper pulled on their boots, strapped on their sword belts, slung their weapons, then carried their saddles, bags and the strongbox to the fort's gate where a Sergeant let them out into the chill night. A moment later Morillo, together with a much smaller man, brought their horses. The mule was left behind in the fort to lull any suspicions Dregara might have.

"This is Ferdinand," Morillo introduced the small man. "He's your guide. He'll take you across the hills and cut a good ten hours off your journey. He's a *picunche*. He speaks no Spanish, I'm afraid, nor any other Christian language, but he knows what to do."

"*Picunche?*" Sharpe asked.

He was given his answer as a cloud slid from the moon to reveal that Ferdinand, named for the King of Spain, was an Indian. He was a small, thin man, with a flat mask of a face, dressed in a tatter of a cast-off cavalry uniform decorated with bright feathers stuck into its loops and buttonholes. He wore no shoes and carried no weapon.

"*Picunche* is a kind of tribal name," Morillo explained as he helped saddle Harper's horse. "We use the Indians as scouts and guides. There aren't many savages who are friendly to us. Don Blas wanted to recruit more, but that idea died with him."

"Doesn't Ferdinand have a horse?" Harper asked.

Morillo laughed. "He'll outrun your horses over a day's marching. He'll also give you a fighting chance to stay well ahead of Sergeant Dregara." Morillo tightened a girth strap, then stepped away. "Ferdinand will find his way back to me when he's finished with you. Good luck, Colonel."

Sharpe thanked the cavalry Captain. "How can we repay you?"

"Mention my name to Vivar's widow. Say I was a true man to her husband." Morillo was hoping that Doña Louisa would still have some influence in Spain, influence that would help his career when he was posted home again..

"I shall tell her you deserve whatever is in her gift," Sharpe promised, then he pulled himself into the saddle and took the great strongbox onto his lap. "Good luck, Captain."

"God bless you, *señor*. Trust Ferdinand!"

The Indian reached up and took hold of both horses' bridles. The moon was flying in and out of ragged clouds, offering a bare light to the dark slope down which Ferdinand led their horses to where the trees closed over their heads. The main road went eastward, detouring about the thickly wooded country into which Ferdinand unerringly led them just as a bugle called its reveille up in the Celestial Fort. Sharpe laughed, pulled his hat over his eyes to protect them from the twigs and followed a savage to the south.

At dawn they rode through the forests of morning, hung with mists, spangled with a million beads of dew that were given light by the lancing, slanting rays of the rising sun. Drifts of vapor softened the great tree trunks among which a myriad of bright birds flew. The clouds had cleared, gone back to the mountains or blown out to the endless oceans. Ferdinand had relinquished the horses' bridles and was content simply to lead the way through the towering trees. "I wonder where the hell we are," Harper said.

"Ferdinand knows," Sharpe replied, and the mention of his royal name made the small Indian turn and smile with file-sharpened teeth.

"We could have done with a few hundred of him at Water-loo," Harper said. "They'd have frightened the buggers to death by just grinning at them."

They rode on. At times, when the path was especially steep or slippery, they dismounted and led the horses. Once they circled a hill on a narrow path above a chasm of pearl-bright mist. Strange birds screeched at them. The worst moment of the morning came when Ferdinand brought them to a great canyon that was crossed by a perilously frag-ile bridge made of leather, rope and green wood. The green wood slats were held in place by the twisted leather straps and the whole precarious roadway was suspended from the rope cables. Ferdinand made gestures at Sharpe and Harper, grunting the while in a strange language.

"I think," Harper said, "he wants us to cross one at a time. God save Ireland, but I think I'd rather not cross at all."

It was a terrifying crossing. Sharpe went first and the whole structure shivered and swayed with every step he took. Ferdinand followed Sharpe, leading his blindfolded horse. Despite its blindfold the horse was nervous and trembling. Once, when the mare missed her footing and plunged a hoof through the slats, she began to panic, but Ferdinand soothed and calmed the beast. Far beneath Sharpe the mist shredded to reveal a white thread which was a quick-flowing stream deep in the canyon's jungle.

Harper was white with terror when he finished the cross-ing. "I'd rather face the Imperial bloody Guard than do that again."

They remounted and rode on, taking it in turns to balance the great box of golden guineas on their saddles' pommels. Ferdinand loped tirelessly ahead. Harper, chewing a lump of hard bread, had begun to think of Bautista. "Why does that long-nosed bastard want to kill us?"

"God knows. I've been trying to make sense of it, and I can't."

Harper shook his head. "I mean if the man wants to be rid of us, then why the hell doesn't he just let us take Don Blas's body and be away? Why send those fellows to kill us?"

"If he did send them." Sharpe, as the morning unfolded into sun-drenched innocence, had again begun to doubt the fears that had crowded in on him during the night.

"He sent them, right enough," Harper said. "He's an evil bastard, that Bautista. You only had to look in his eye. If a man like that comes into the tavern I throw him out. I won't have him drinking my ale!"

"I don't know if he's evil," Sharpe said, "but he's certainly frightened."

"Bautista? Frightened?" Harper was scornful.

"He's like a man playing drumhead." Drumhead was a card game that had been popular in the army. It was a simple game, needing only a pack of cards, as many players as wanted to risk their money and a playing surface like a drumhead. Each player nominated a card and another man dealt the cards face up onto the drumhead. The man whose card appeared last won the game.

"Drumhead?" Harper was still unconvinced.

"Bautista's playing for very big stakes, Patrick. He's cheating left, right and center and he knows, if he's caught, that he'll face court martial, disgrace, maybe even imprisonment. But if he wins, then he wins very big indeed. He's watching the cards turn over and he's dreading that he'll lose. But he can't stop playing because the winnings are so huge."

"Then why the hell doesn't he fight the war properly?" Harper grunted as he settled the strongbox more comfortably on his pommel.

"Because he knows the war is lost," Sharpe said. "It would take an extraordinary soldier to win this war, and Bautista isn't an extraordinary soldier. Don Blas might have won it, but only if Madrid had sent him the ships to beat Cochrane, which they didn't. So Bautista knows he's going to lose, and that means he has to do two things. First, he needs to blame someone else for losing the war, and second, he has to grab as much of Chile's wealth as possible. Then he can go home rich and blameless, and he can use the money to gain power in Madrid."

"But why kill us? We're bugger all to do with his problems."

"We're the enemy," Sharpe said. "The closest Bautista came to losing was when Don Blas was here. Don Blas knew something that would destroy Bautista, and he was on the point of confronting Bautista when he died. We're on Don Blas's side, so we're enemies." It was the only answer that made sense to Sharpe, and though it was an answer full of gaps, it helped to explain the Captain-General's enmity.

"So he'll kill us?" Harper asked indignantly.

Sharpe nodded. "But not in public. If we can reach Puerto Crucero, we're safe. Bautista needs to blame our disappearance on the rebels. He won't dare attack us in a public place."

"I pray to God you're right," Harper said feelingly. "I mean there's no point in dying here, is there now?"

Sharpe felt a pang of guilt for having invited his friend. "You shouldn't have come."

"That's what Isabella said. But, Goddamn it, a man gets tired of children after a time. I'm glad to be away for a wee while, so I am." Harper had left four children in Dublin: Richard, Liam, Sean and the baby, Michael, whose real name was in a Gaelic form that Sharpe could not pronounce. "But I wouldn't want never to see the nippers again," Harper went on, "would I now?"

"There's not much to do now," Sharpe tried to reassure

him. "We just have to dig up Don Blas, seal him in a tin coffin, then take him home."

"I still think you should put him in brandy," Harper said, his fears forgotten.

"Whatever's quickest," Sharpe allowed, then he forgot that small problem, for Ferdinand had led them out from the trees and onto what had to be the main road from Valdivia to Puerto Crucero. The road stretched empty and inviting in either direction, and with no sign of any vengeful pursuers. Ferdinand was grinning, then said something in his own language.

"I think he means he's leaving us here," Harper said before pointing vigorously to the south.

Ferdinand nodded eagerly, intimating that they should indeed ride in that direction.

Sharpe opened the box, took out a guinea, and gave it to the Indian. Ferdinand tucked the coin into a pocket of his filthy uniform, offered a sharp-toothed grin of thanks, then turned back into the forest. Sharpe and Harper, brought safe to the road and far ahead of their pursuers, were out of danger. Ahead lay Puerto Crucero and a friend's grave, behind was a thwarted enemy, and Sharpe, almost for the first time since he had reached the New World, felt his hopes rise.

That evening, just before sunset, they reined their tired horses on the rocky crest above the natural harbor of Puerto Crucero. Sharpe, weary to his very bones, turned in his aching saddle and saw no sign of any pursuit. Dregara had been cheated. Sharpe and Harper, thanks to Captain Morillo and his Indian guide, had come safely to their haven where, like a sorcerer's castle perched on a crag, stood the Citadel of Puerto Crucero.

At the heart of the Citadel, and brilliant white in the day's last sunlight, stood the garrison church where Blas Vivar lay buried. Beside the church was a castle keep over which, streaming stiff in the sea's hard wind, the great royal banner of Spain flew colorful and proud. The dark, wild country where murder might have been committed was behind them and in front were witnesses and light. There was also the harbor from which, by God's grace, they would sail home with the body of a dead hero.

The harbor was not a massive refuge like Valdivia's magnificent haven, but instead lay within a wide hook of low, rocky land that stopped the surge of the Pacific swells, but allowed the insistent southern winds to tug and fret at the anchorage. Even now the harbor was flecked with white by the wind that streamed the royal banner at the fort's summit.

The town was built where an inner harbor had been made with a stone breakwater. The town itself was a huddle of warehouses, fishing shacks and small houses. Nothing could move in the town or harbor without being observed from the great high fortress. The road to the fort zig-zagged up the rock hill to disappear into a tunnel that pierced a wide stone wall studded with cannon embrasures. "A bastard of a fort to take," Harper said.

"Then thank God we don't need to." Sharpe flourished the pass which gave them entry to the citadel.

The pass, signed and sealed by Miguel Bautista, worked its charm. Sharpe and Harper were saluted at every guardpost, escorted through the fortress's entrance tunnel, and greeted effusively by the officer of the day, a Major Suarez, who seemed somewhat astonished by the pass. In all likelihood, Sharpe suspected, Suarez had never seen such a document, for Sharpe suspected it had been issued only to lull him into a false sense of security, but now, even if Bautista had not so intended, his signature was working a wonderful magic.

"You'll accept our hospitality?" Major Suarez was standing behind his desk, eager to show Sharpe and Harper due respect. "There is an inn beside the harbor, but I can't recommend it. You'll permit me to have two officers' rooms made ready for you?"

"And a meal?" Harper suggested.

"Of course!" Suarez, assuming that Bautista was their patron, could not do enough to help. "Perhaps you will wait in my quarters while the room and the food are made ready?"

"I'd rather see the church," Sharpe said.

"I'll send for you as soon as things are ready." Suarez snapped his fingers, summoning ostlers to take care of the tired horses, and orderlies to carry the travelers' bags for safekeeping into the officers' quarters. Sharpe and Harper kept only the strongbox which they carried between them into the welcome coolness of the garrison church, a building of stern beauty. The walls were painted white while the heavily beamed ceiling was of a shining wood that had been oiled almost to blackness. On the walls were marble slabs that commemorated officers who had died in this far colony. Some had been killed in skirmishes, some had drowned off the coast, some had died in earthquakes, and a few, very few, had died of old age. Other marble plaques remembered the officers' families: women who had died in childbirth, children who had been killed or captured by Indians and babies who had died of strange diseases and whose souls were now commended to God.

Sharpe and Harper put the strongbox down in the nave, then walked slowly through the choir to climb the steps to the altar, which was a magnificent confection of gold and silver. Crucifixes, candle holders and ewers graced the niches and shelves of the intricate altar screen on which painted panels depicted the torture and death of Christ.

Many of the flagstones close to the altar were gravestones. Some had ornate coats of arms carved above the names, and most of the inscriptions were in Latin, which meant Sharpe could not read them; yet even without Latin he could see that none of the stones bore the name of his friend. Then Harper moved aside a small rush mat that had covered a paving slab to the right of the altar and thus discovered Don Blas's grave. "Here," Harper said softly, then crossed himself. The stone bore two simple letters chiseled into its surface. *BV*.

"Poor bastard," Sharpe said gently. There were times when he found his lack of any religion a handicap. He supposed he should say a prayer, but the sight of his old friend's grave left him feeling inadequate. Don Blas himself would have known what to say, for he had always possessed a graceful sureness of touch, but Sharpe felt awkward in the hushed church.

"You want to start digging?" Harper asked.

"Now?" Sharpe sounded surprised.

"Why not?" Harper had spotted some tools in a side chapel where workmen had evidently been repairing a wall. He fetched a crowbar and worked it down beside the slab. "At least we can see what's under the stone."

Sharpe expected to find a vault under the gravestone, but they levered up the heavy slab to find instead a patch of flattened yellow shingle.

"Christ only knows how deep he is," Harper said, then drove the crowbar hard into the gravel. Sharpe went to the side chapel and came back with a trowel that he used to scrape aside the stones and sand that Harper had loosened with the crowbar. "We'll probably have to go down six feet," Harper grumbled, "and it'll take us bloody hours."

"I reckon Major Suarez will give us a work party tomorrow," Sharpe said, then moved aside to let Harper thrust down with the bar again.

Harper slammed the crowbar down. It crashed through the shingle, thumped on something hollow, then abruptly burst through into a space beneath.

"Jesus!" Harper could not resist the imprecation.

Sharpe twisted aside, a hand to his mouth. The crowbar had pierced a coffin that had been buried scarcely a foot beneath the floor, and now the shallow grave was giving off a stink so noxious that Sharpe could not help gagging. He stepped backward, out of range of the effluvia. Harper was gasping for clean air. "God save Ireland, but you'd think they'd bury the poor man a few feet farther down. Jesus!"

It was the smell of death—a sickly, clogging, strangely sweet and never-to-be-forgotten stench of rotting flesh. Sharpe had smelled such decay innumerable times, yet not lately, not in these last happy years in Normandy. Now the first slight hint of the smell brought back a tidal wave of memories. There had been a time in his life, and in Harper's life, when a man slept and woke and ate and lived with that reek of mortality. Sharpe had known places, like Waterloo, where even after the dead had all been buried the stench persisted, souring every tree and blade of grass and breath of air with its insinuating foulness. It was the smell that traced a soldier's passing, the grave smell, and now it pervaded the church where a friend was buried.

"Christ, but you're right about needing an airtight box to hold him." Harper had retreated to the edge of the choir. "We'll drink the brandy, and he can have the box."

Sharpe crept closer to the grave. The stench was appalling, much worse than he remembered it from the wars. He held his breath and scraped with his trowel at the hole Harper had made, but all he could see was a splinter of yellow wood in the gravel.

"I think we should wait and let a work party do this," Harper said fervently.

Sharpe scuttled back a few feet before taking a deep breath. "I think you're right." He shuddered at the thought of the body's corruption and tried to imagine his own death and decay. Where would he be buried? Somewhere in Normandy, he supposed, and beside Lucille, he hoped, perhaps under apple trees so the blossoms would drift like snow across their graves every spring.

Then the door at the back of the church crashed open, disrupting Sharpe's gloomy reverie, and suddenly a rush of heavy boots trampled on the nave's flagstones. Sharpe turned, half-dazzled by the sunlight which lanced low across the world's rim to slice clean through the church's door. He could not see much in the eye of that great brilliance, but he could see enough to understand that armed men were swarming into the church.

"Sweet Jesus," Harper swore.

"Stop where you are!" a voice shouted above the tramp and crash of boot nails.

It was Sergeant Dregara, his dark face furious, who led the rush. Behind him was Major Suarez carrying a cocked pistol and with a disappointed look on his face as though Sharpe and Harper had abused his friendly welcome. Dregara, like his travel-stained men, was carrying a cavalry carbine that he now raised so that its barrel gaped into Sharpe's face.

"No!" Suarez said.

"Easiest thing," Dregara said softly.

"No!" Major Suarez insisted. There were a score of infantrymen in the church who waited, appalled, for Dregara to blow Sharpe's brains across the altar. "They're under arrest," Suarez insisted nervously.

Dregara, plainly deciding that he could not get away with murder in the presence of so many witnesses, reluctantly lowered the carbine. He looked tired, and Sharpe guessed that he and his cavalrymen must have ridden like madmen in their pursuit. Now Dregara stared malevolently into the Englishman's face before turning away and striding back down the church's nave. "Lock them up." He snapped the order, even though he was a Sergeant and Suarez a Major. "Bring me their weapons, and that!" He gestured at the strongbox and two of his men, hurrying to obey, lifted the treasure.

Major Suarez climbed to the altar. "You're under arrest," he said nervously.

"For what?" Sharpe asked.

"General Bautista's orders," Suarez said, and he had gone quite pale, as though he could feel the cold threat of the Captain-General's displeasure reaching down from Valdivia. Dregara was plainly Bautista's man, known and feared as such. "You're under arrest," Suarez again said helplessly, then waved his men forward.

And Sharpe and Harper were marched away.

They were taken to a room high in the fortress, a room that looked across the harbor entrance to where the vast Pacific rollers pounded at the outer rocks to explode in great gouts of white water. Sharpe leaned through the bars of the high window and stared straight down to see that their prison room lay directly above a flight of rock-cut steps which led to the citadel's wharf. To the north of the wharf was a shingle beach where a handful of small fishing boats lay canted on their sides.

The window bars were each an inch thick and deeply rusted, but, when Harper tried to loosen them, they proved stubbornly solid. "Even if you managed to escape," Sharpe asked in a voice made acid by frustration, "and survived the eighty-foot drop to the quay, just where the hell do you think you'd go?"

"Somewhere they serve decent ale, of course," Harper gave the bars a last massive but impotent tug, "or maybe to that Jonathan out there." He pointed to a brigantine which had just anchored in the outer harbor. The boat was flying an outsize American flag, a splash of bright color in the twilight gloom. Sharpe assumed the flag was intentionally massive so that, should the dreaded Lord Cochrane make a raid on Puerto Crucero, he could not mistake the American ship for a Spanish merchantman.

Sharpe wished Cochrane would make a raid, for he could see no other route out of their predicament. He had tried hammering on their prison door, demanding to be given paper and ink so that he could send a message to George Blair, the Consul in Valdivia, but his shouting was ignored.

"Damn them," Sharpe growled, "damn them and damn them!"

"They won't dare punish us," Harper tried either to console Sharpe or to convince himself. "They're scared wicked of our navy, aren't they? Besides, if they meant us harm they wouldn't have put us in here. This isn't such a bad wee place," Harper looked around their prison. "I've been in worse."

The room was not, indeed, a bad wee place. The wall beside the window had been grievously cracked at some point, Sharpe assumed by one of the famous earthquakes that racked this coast, but otherwise the room was in fine repair and furnished comfortably enough. There were two straw-filled mattresses on the floor, a stool, a table and a lidded bucket. Such comforts suggested that Major Suarez, or his superiors, would deal very gingerly with two British citizens.

It was also plain to Sharpe that the Puerto Crucero authorities were waiting for instructions from Valdivia, for, once incarcerated, they were left alone for six days. No one interrogated them, no one brought them news, no one informed them of any charges. The only visitors to the high prison room were the orderlies who brought food and emptied the bucket. The food was good, and plentiful enough even for Harper's appetite. Each morning a barber came with a pile of hot towels, a bowl and a bucket of steaming water. The barber shook his head whenever Sharpe tried to persuade the man to bring paper, ink and a pen. "I am a barber, I know nothing of writing. Please to tilt your head back, *señor.*"

"I want to write to my Consul in Valdivia. He'll reward you if you bring me paper and ink."

"Please don't speak, *señor,* when I am shaving your neck."

On the fifth morning, under a sullen sky from which a

sour rain spat, the *Espiritu Santo* had appeared beyond the northern headland and, making hard work of the last few hundred yards, beat her way into the outer harbor where, with a great splash and a gigantic clanking of chain, she let go her two forward anchors. Captain Ardiles's frigate, like the American brigantine which still lay to her anchors in the roadstead, drew too much water to be safe in the shallow inner harbor, and so she was forced to fret and tug at her twin cables while, from the shore, a succession of lighters and longboats ferried goods and people back and forth.

The next morning, under the same drab sky, the *Espiritu Santo* raised her anchors and, very cautiously, approached the stone wharf which lay at the foot of the citadel's crag. It was clear to Sharpe that the big frigate could only lay alongside the wharf at the very top of the high tide, and that as a result Captain Ardiles was creeping his way in with extreme caution. The frigate was being towed by longboats, and had men casting lead lines from her bows. She finally nestled alongside the wharf and Harper, leaning as far out as the bars would allow him, described how the contents of a cart were being unloaded by soldiers and carried on board the frigate. "It's the gold!" Harper said excitedly. "They must be loading the gold! My God, there's enough gold there to buy a Pope!"

The frigate only stayed at the wharf long enough to take on board the boxes from the cart before she raised a foresail and slipped away from the dangerously shallow water to return to her deeper anchorage. "Lucky bastards," Harper said as the rattle of the anchor chains echoed across the harbor. "They'll be going home soon, won't they? Back to Europe, eh? She could take us to Cadiz, we'd have a week in a good tavern, then I'd catch a sherry boat north to Dublin. Christ, what wouldn't I give to be on board her?" He watched as a longboat pulled away from the frigate and was rowed back toward the citadel's steps, then he sighed. "One way or another we've made a mess of this job, haven't we?"

Sharpe, lying on one of the mattresses and staring at the cracks in the plastered ceiling, smiled. "Peace isn't like war. In wartime things were simpler." He turned his head toward the metal-studded door beyond which footsteps sounded loud in the passageway. "Bit early for food, isn't it?"

The door opened, but instead of the usual two servants carrying the midday trays, Major Suarez and a file of infantrymen now stood in the stone passageway. "Come," Suarez ordered. "Downstairs. The Captain-General wants you."

"Who?" Sharpe swung his legs off the cot.

"General Bautista is here. He came on the frigate." The terror in Suarez was palpable. "Please, hurry!"

They were taken downstairs to a long hall which had huge arched windows facing onto the harbor. The ceiling was painted white and decorated with an iron chandelier under which a throng of uniformed men awaited Sharpe's arrival. The crowd of officers reminded Sharpe of the audience that had watched Bautista attending to his duties in the Citadel at Valdivia.

Bautista, attended by Marquinez and his other aides, was again offering a display of public diligence. He was working at papers spread on a table on which rested Sharpe's sword and Harper's seven-barrel gun. The strongbox was also there. The sight of the weapons gave Sharpe a pulse of hope that perhaps they were to be released, even maybe allowed to travel home on the *Espiritu Santo,* for Captain Ardiles was among the nervously silent audience. Sharpe nodded at the frigate's Captain, but Ardiles turned frostily away, revealing, to Sharpe's astonishment, George Blair, the British Consul. Sharpe tried to cross the hall to speak with Blair, but a soldier pulled him back. "Blair!" Sharpe shouted, "I want to talk to you!"

Blair made urgent hushing motions as though Sharpe disturbed a sacred assembly. Captain Marquinez, as beautifully uniformed as a palace guard, frowned at Sharpe's temerity, though Bautista, at last looking up from his paperwork, seemed merely amused by Sharpe's loud voice. "Ah, Mister Sharpe! We meet again. I trust you have not been discommoded? You're comfortable here? You find the food adequate?"

Sharpe, suspicious of Bautista's affability, said nothing. The Captain-General, plainly enjoying himself, put down his quill pen and stood up. "This is yours?" Bautista put his hand on the strongbox.

Sharpe still said nothing, while the audience, relishing the contest that was about to begin, seemed to tense itself.

"I asked you a question, Mister Sharpe."

"It belongs to the Countess of Mouromorto."

"A rich woman! But why does she send her money on voyages around the world?"

"You know why," Sharpe said.

"Do I?" Bautista opened the strongbox's lid. "One thousand, six hundred and four guineas. Is that correct?"

"Yes," Sharpe said defiantly, and there was a murmur of astonishment from Bautista's audience as they translated the figure into Spanish dollars. A man could live comfortably for a whole lifetime on six and a half thousand dollars.

"Why were you carrying such a sum in gold?" Bautista demanded.

Sharpe saw the trap just in time. If he had admitted that the money had been given to him for use as bribes, then the Captain-General would accuse him of attempting to corrupt Chilean officials. Sharpe shrugged. "We didn't know what expenses we might have," he answered vaguely.

"Expenses?" Bautista sneered. "What expenses are involved in digging up a dead man? Shovels are so expensive

in Europe?" The audience murmured with laughter, and
Sharpe sensed a relief in the assembled officers. They were
like men who had come to a bullfight and they wanted to see
their champion draw blood from the bull, and the swift jest
about the price of shovels had pleased them. Now Bautista
took one of the coins from the strongbox, picked up a riding
crop from the table, and walked toward Sharpe. "Tell me,
Mister Sharpe, why you came to Chile?"

"To collect the body of Don Blas," Sharpe said, "as you
well know."

"I heard you were groveling in General Vivar's grave like
a dog," Bautista said. "But why carry so much gold?"

"I told you, expenses."

"Expenses." Bautista sneered the word, then tossed the
coin to Sharpe.

Sharpe, taken by surprise, just managed to snatch the
guinea coin out of the air.

"Look at it!" Bautista said. "Tell me what you see?"

"A guinea," Sharpe said.

"The cavalry of Saint George," Bautista still sneered. "Do
you see that, Mister Sharpe?"

Sharpe said nothing. The guinea coin had the head of the
King on one side, and on its obverse bore the mounted figure
of Saint George thrusting his lance into the dragon's flank.
The nickname for such coins was the Cavalry of Saint George
which, during the French wars and in the form of lavish sub-
sidies to foreign nations, had been sent to do battle against
Bonaparte.

"The British Government uses such golden cavalry to
foment trouble, isn't that so, Mister Sharpe?"

Again Sharpe said nothing, though he glanced toward
Blair to see if the Consul planned any protest, but Blair was
clearly cowed by the company and seemed oblivious of Bautista's jeering.

"Afraid to send their own men to fight wars," Bautista sneered, "the British pay others to do their fighting. How else did they beat Napoleon?"

He let the question hang. The audience smiled. Sharpe waited.

Bautista came close to Sharpe. "Why are you in Chile, Mister Sharpe?"

"I told you, to collect General Vivar's body."

"Nonsense! Nonsense! Why would the Countess of Mouromorto send a lackey to collect her husband's body? All she needed to do was ask the army headquarters in Madrid! They would have been happy to arrange an exhumation—"

"Doña Louisa did not know her husband was dead," Sharpe said, though it sounded horribly lame even as he said it.

"What kind of fool do you take me for?" Bautista stepped even closer to Sharpe, the riding crop twitching in his hand. His aides, not daring to move, stood frozen behind the table, while the audience watched wide-eyed. "I know why you came here," Bautista said softly.

"Tell me."

"To communicate with the rebels, of course. Who else was the money for? All the world knows that the English want to see Spain defeated here."

Sharpe sighed. "Why would I bring money to the rebels in a Royal ship?"

"Why indeed? So no one would suspect your intentions?" Bautista was enjoying tearing Sharpe's protests to shreds. "Who sent you, Sharpe? Your English merchant friends who think they can make more profit out of Chile if it's ruled by a rebel government?"

"The Countess of Mouromorto sent me," Sharpe insisted.

"She's English, is she not?" Bautista responded swiftly. "Do you find it noble to fight for trade, Sharpe? For cargoes

of hide and for barrels of tallow? For the profits of men like
Mister Blair?" He threw a scornful hand toward the Consul
who, seemingly pleased at being noticed, bobbed his head in
acknowledgment.

"I fought alongside Don Blas," Sharpe said, "and I fight
for the same things he wanted."

"Oh, do tell me! Please!" Bautista urged in a caustic voice.

"He hated corruption," Sharpe said.

"Don't we all?" Bautista said with wonderfully feigned
innocence.

"Don Blas believed men could live in freedom under fair
government." It was an inadequate statement of Vivar's
creed, but the best Sharpe could manage.

"You mean Vivar fought for liberty!" Bautista was
delighted with Sharpe's answer. "Any fool can claim liberty
as his cause. Look!" Bautista pointed at the hugely flagged
American brigantine in the outer harbor. "The Captain of
that ship is waiting for whalers to rendezvous with him so he
can take home their sperm oil and whalebone. He comes
every year, and every year he brings copies of his country's
declaration of independence, and he hands them out as
though they're the word of God! He tells the mestizos and
the criollos that they must fight for their liberty! Then, when
he's got his cargo, he sails home and who do you think emp-
ties that cargo in his precious land of liberty? Slaves do!
Slaves! So much for his vaunted liberty!" Bautista paused to
let a rustle of agreement sound in his audience. "Of course
Vivar believed in liberty!" Bautista interrupted the murmur-
ing. "Vivar believed in every impracticality! He wanted God
to rule the world! He believed in truth and love and pigs with
wings." The audience laughed delightedly. Captain Marquinez and one or two others even clapped at their Captain-
General's wit, while Bautista, delighted with himself, smiled
at Sharpe. "And you share Vivar's beliefs, Mister Sharpe?"

"I'm a soldier," Sharpe said stubbornly, as though that excused him from holding beliefs.

"A plain, bluff man, eh? Then so am I, so I will tell you very plainly that I believe you are telling lies. I believe you came to Chile to bring money and a message to the rebels."

"So you believe in pigs with wings too?"

Bautista ignored the sneer, striding instead to the table where he opened a writing box and took out an object which he tossed to Sharpe. "What is that?"

"Bloody hell," Harper murmured, for the object which Bautista had scornfully shied at Sharpe was the signed portrait of Napoleon that had been stolen in Valdivia.

"This was stolen from me," Sharpe said, "in Valdivia."

"At the time," Bautista jeered from the window, "you denied anything more was missing. Were you ashamed of carrying a message from Napoleon to a mercenary rebel?"

"It isn't a message!" Sharpe said scornfully. "It was a gift."

"Oh, Mister Sharpe!" Bautista's voice was full of disappointment, as though Sharpe was not proving a worthy opponent. "A man carries a gift to a rebel? How did you expect to deliver this gift if you were not to be in communication with the rebels? Tell me!"

Sharpe said nothing.

Bautista smiled pitifully. "What a bad conspirator you are, Mister Sharpe. And such a bad liar, too. Turn the portrait over. Go on! Do it!" Bautista waited till Sharpe had dutifully turned the picture over, then pointed with his riding crop. "That backing board comes off. Pull it."

Sharpe saw that the stiffening board behind the printed etching had been levered out of the frame. The board had been replaced, but now he prized it out again and thus revealed a piece of paper which had been folded to fit the exact space behind the board.

"Open it! Go on!" Bautista was enjoying the moment.

At first glance the folded paper might have been taken for a thickening sheet which merely served to stop the glass from rattling in the metal frame, but when Sharpe unfolded the sheet he saw that it bore a coded message. "Oh, Christ," Sharpe said softly when he realized what it was. The ink-written code was a jumble of letters and numerals and meant nothing to Sharpe, but it was clearly a message from Bonaparte to the mysterious Lieutenant Colonel Charles, and any such message could only mean trouble.

"You are pretending you did not know the message was there?" Bautista challenged Sharpe.

"Of course I didn't."

"Who wrote it? Napoleon? Or your English masters?"

The question revealed that Bautista's men had not succeeded in breaking the code. "Napoleon," Sharpe said, then tried to construct a feeble defense of the coded message. "It's nothing important. Charles is an admirer of the Emperor's."

"You expect me to believe that an unimportant letter would be written in code?" Bautista asked mockingly, then he calmly walked to Sharpe and held out his hand for the message. Sharpe paused a second, then surrendered the message and the framed portrait. Bautista glanced at the code. "I believe it is a message from your English masters, which you inserted into the portrait. What does the message say?"

"I don't know." Sharpe, conscious of all the eyes that watched him, straightened his back. "How could I know? You probably concocted that message yourself." Sharpe believed no such thing. The moment he had seen the folded and coded message he had known that he had been duped into being Napoleon's messenger boy, but he dared not surrender the initiative wholly to Bautista.

But Sharpe's counteraccusation was a clumsy riposte and Bautista scoffed at it. "If I planned to incriminate you by concocting a message, Mister Sharpe, I would hardly invent one that no one could read." His audience laughed at the easy parry, and Bautista, like a matador who had just made an elegant pass at his prey, smiled, then walked to one of the high arched windows which, unglazed, offered a view across the harbor and out to the Pacific. Bautista turned in the window and beckoned to his prisoners. "Come here! Both of you!"

Sharpe and Harper obediently walked to the window, which looked down onto a wide stone terrace that formed a gun battery. The guns were thirty-six-pound naval cannons that had been removed from their ship trolleys and placed on heavy garrison mounts. There were twelve of the massive guns, each capable of plunging a vicious fire down onto any ship that dared attack Puerto Crucero's harbor.

Yet Bautista had not invited Sharpe and Harper to see the guns, but rather the man who was shackled to a wooden post at the very edge of one of the embrasures. That man was Ferdinand, the Indian guide who had brought them through the misted mountains ahead of Dregara's pursuit. Now, stripped of his tattered uniform and dressed only in a short brown kilt, Ferdinand was manacled just seven or eight feet from the muzzle of one of the giant cannons. Dregara, who was clearly an intimate of Bautista's, stood holding a smoking linstock beside the loaded gun. Sharpe, understanding what he was about to see, turned in horror on Bautista. "What in Christ's name are you doing?"

"This is an execution," Bautista said in a tone of voice he might use to explain something to a small child, "a means of imposing order on an imperfect world."

"You can't do this!" Sharpe protested so strongly that one of the infantrymen stepped in front of him with a musket and bayonet.

"Of course I can do this!" Bautista mocked. "I am the

King's plenipotentiary. I can have men killed, I can have them imprisoned, I can even have them broken down to the ranks, like Private Morillo who is being sent to the mines to learn the virtues of loyalty."

"What has this man done?" Sharpe gestured at Ferdinand.

"He has displeased me, Mister Sharpe," Bautista said, then he beckoned the other men in the room forward so they could watch the execution from the other windows. Bautista's eyes were greedy. "Are you watching?" Bautista asked Sharpe.

"You bastard," Sharpe said.

"Why? This is a quick and painless death, though admittedly messy. You have to understand that the savages believe their souls will not reach paradise unless their bodies are intact for the funeral rites. They consequently have a morbid fear of dismemberment, which is why I devised this punishment as a means of discouraging rebellion among the Indian slaves. It works remarkably well."

"But this man has done nothing! Morillo did nothing!"

"They displeased me," Bautista hissed the words, then he looked down to the gun battery and held up a hand.

Ferdinand, his lips drawn back from his filed teeth, seemed to be praying. His eyes were closed. "God bless you!" Sharpe shouted, though the Indian showed no signs of hearing.

"You think God cares about scum?" Bautista chuckled, then dropped his hand.

Dregara reached forward and the linstock touched the firing hole. The sound of the cannon was tremendous; loud enough to rattle the iron chandelier and hurt the eardrums of the men crowded at the windows. Harper crossed himself. Bautista licked his lips, and Ferdinand died in a maelstrom of smoke, fire and blood. Sharpe glimpsed the Indian's shattered trunk whirling blood as it was blasted away from the parapet, then the smoke blew apart to reveal a splintered stake, a pair of bloody legs, and lumps and spatters of blood and flesh smeared across the cannon's embrasure. The rest of Ferdinand's body had been scattered into the outer harbor where screaming gulls, excited by this sudden largesse, dived and tore and fought for shreds of his flesh. Far out to sea, beyond the rocky spit of land, the cannonball crashed into the swell with a sudden white plume, while in the nearer waters, scraps of flesh and splinters of bone and drops of blood rained down to the frenzied gulls. Men had rushed to the rail of the American brigantine, fearful of what the gunfire meant, and now they stared in puzzlement at the blood-flecked water. Bautista sighed with pleasure, then turned away as the white-faced gun crew heaved the dead man's legs over the parapet.

There was a stunned silence in the hall. The stench of powder smoke and fresh blood was keen in the air as Bautista, half smiling, turned to his audience. "Mister Blair?"

"Your Excellency?" George Blair ducked an eager and frightened pace forward.

"You have heard my questions to Mister Sharpe today?"

"Indeed, Your Excellency."

"Do you confirm that I have treated the prisoners fairly? And with consideration?"

Blair smirked and nodded. "Indeed, Your Excellency."

Bautista went to the table and held up the signed portrait of Napoleon and the folded message. "You heard the prisoner's assertion that Napoleon wrote this message?"

"I did, Your Excellency, indeed I did."

"And you see it is addressed to a notorious rebel?"

"I do, Your Excellency, indeed I do."

Bautista's face twitched with amusement. "Tell me, Blair, how your government will respond to the news that Mister Sharpe was acting as an errand boy for Bonaparte?"

"They will doubtless regard any such message as treasonable correspondence, Your Excellency." Blair bobbed obsequiously.

Bautista smiled, and no wonder, for Sharpe's possession of the Emperor's message was enough to condemn Sharpe, not just with the Spanish, but with the British too. The British might possess the greatest navy and the strongest economy in the world, yet they were terrified of the small fat man cooped up in Saint Helena's Longwood, and maybe they were terrified enough to allow Bautista to tie two British subjects to wooden stakes and blow their souls into eternity at the mouths of loaded cannons. Sharpe, suddenly feeling very abandoned, also felt frightened.

Bautista sensed the fear and smiled. He had won now. He turned again to Blair. "Either Mister Sharpe was carrying a message from Napoleon, which makes him an enemy of his own country, or else this is a message from the British merchants who are my country's enemies, but either way, Mister Sharpe's possession of the message calls for punishment. Might I assume, Blair, that your government would not approve if I were to execute Mister Sharpe?"

Blair beamed as though Bautista had made a fine jest. "My government would be displeased, Your Excellency."

"But you do accept that Mister Sharpe deserves punishment?"

"Alas, Your Excellency, it appears so." Blair nodded obsequiously at the Captain-General, then snatched a sideways glance at Sharpe who wondered just how much of Doña Louisa's money the Consul was taking as a bribe.

Bautista strolled back to the table where he picked up Sharpe's heavy sword. "This was carried at Waterloo?" Sharpe said nothing, but Bautista did not need an answer. "I shall keep it as a trophy! Perhaps I shall have a plaque made for it. 'Taken from an English soldier who at last met his match'!"

"Fight for it now, you bastard," Sharpe called.

"I don't fight against lice, I just smoke them out." Bautista dropped the sword onto the table, then adopted a portentous tone of voice. "I declare your possessions are forfeited to the Spanish crown, and that the two of you are unwelcome in Chile. You are therefore expelled from these territories, and will embark on the next ship to leave this harbor." Bautista had already prepared the expulsion papers which now, with a theatrical flourish, he offered to Captain Ardiles of the *Espiritu Santo*. "That would be your frigate, Captain. You have no objections to carrying the prisoners home?"

"None," Ardiles, ready for the request, said flatly.

"Put them to work. No comforts! Sign them on to your crew and make them sweat."

"Indeed, Your Excellency." Ardiles took the papers and pushed them into the tail pocket of his uniform.

Bautista came close to Sharpe. "I would have preferred to put you to work in the mines, Englishman, so think yourself lucky."

"Frightened of the Royal Navy?" Sharpe taunted him.

"Be careful, Englishman," Bautista said softly.

"You're a thief," Sharpe said just as quietly. "And Vivar knew it, which is why you killed him."

At first Bautista looked astonished at the accusation, then it made him laugh. He clapped with delight at his amusement, then waved at Major Suarez. "Take them away! Now!" The audience, in ludicrous sycophancy, began to applaud wildly as the infantrymen who had escorted Sharpe and Harper from their prison now chivied the two men through an archway and onto a flight of wide stone steps that ran down beside the bloody gun battery. The steps, which were very steep and cut from the crag on which the citadel stood, led down to the fortress quay where a longboat from the *Espiritu Santo* waited.

Ardiles followed, his scabbard's metal tip clattering on the stone steps. "Into the boat!" he ordered Sharpe and Harper when they reached the quay.

"Make them sweat!" Bautista shouted from the gun battery's parapet. "Put them at the oars now! You hear me, Ardiles! Put them at the oars! I want to see them sweat!"

Ardiles nodded to the Bosun who made space for Sharpe and Harper on the bow thwarts. The other oarsmen grinned. Captain Ardiles, cloaked against the cold south wind, sat in the stern sheets where, it seemed to Sharpe, he carefully avoided his two captives' eyes. "Push off!" he ordered.

"Oars!" the Bosun shouted. From the high arched windows above the battery of heavy guns, a row of faces stared down at Sharpe's humiliation.

"Stroke!" the Bosun shouted, and Sharpe momentarily thought of rebelling, but knew that such mutiny would lead nowhere. Instead, like Harper, he pulled clumsily. Their oarblades splashed and clattered on the other oars as they dragged the heavy boat away through the blood-flecked water. A gull, disturbed by the longboat's proximity, flapped up from the water with a length of Ferdinand's intestines in its beak. Other gulls screamed as they fought for the delicacy.

"Pull!" the Bosun shouted, and Sharpe felt a pang of impotent anger. The rage was not directed at his tormentors, but at himself. He had been in the Americas little more than a week, yet now he would have to crawl back to Europe, confess his failure, and try to return Louisa her money. Which effort, he much feared, would mean bankruptcy. Except he knew that Louisa would forgive him, and that clemency hurt almost as much as bankruptcy. Goddamn and Goddamn and Goddamn! He had been rooked like a child wandering into a cutpurse's tavern! It was that knowledge that really hurt, that he had been treated like a fool, and deservedly so. And to have lost his sword! The sword was only a cheap Heavy Cavalry blade, ugly and ill-balanced, but it had been a gift from Harper and it had kept Sharpe alive in some grim battles. Now it would be a trophy on Bautista's wall. Christ! Sharpe stared at the fortress where Bautista ruled, and he felt the horrid impotence of failure, and the horrid certainty that he could never have his revenge. He was being taken away, across a world and back to ignominy, and he was helpless.

He was helpless, he was penniless, and he had just come ten thousand bloody miles for nothing.

The frigate, with its cargo of gold, sailed on that evening's tide. Sharpe and Harper were put to work on a capstan that raised one of the anchors, then sent down to the gundeck where they helped to stack nine- and twelve-pounder shots in the ready racks about the frigate's three masts. They worked till their muscles were sore and sweat was stinging their eyes, but they had no other choice. The dice had rolled badly, there was no other explanation, and the two men must knuckle under. Which did not mean they had to be subservient. A huge scarred beast of a man, a one-eyed seaman who was an evident leader of the forecastle, came to look them over, and such was the man's power that the Bosun's mates quietly edged back into the shadows when he gestured them away.

"My name's Balin," the huge man said, "and you're English."

"I'm English," Sharpe said, "he's Irish."

Balin jerked his head to order Harper aside. "I've no quarrel with the Irish," he said, "but I've no love for Englishmen. Though mind you," he took a step forward, ducking under the deck beams, "I like English clothes. That's a fine coat,

Englishman. I'll take it." He held out a broad hand. Two
score of seamen made a ring to hide what happened from
any officers who might come down to the deck. "Come on!"
Balin insisted.

"I don't want trouble," Sharpe spoke very humbly, "I just
want to get home safely."

"Give me your coat," Balin said, "and there's no trouble."

Sharpe glanced left and right at the unfriendly faces in the
gundeck's gloom. Night had fallen, and the only lights were
a few glass-shielded lanterns that hung above the guns, and
the flickering flames made the seamen's faces even more
grim than usual. "If I give you the coat," Sharpe asked,
"you'll keep me from trouble?"

"I'll cuddle you to sleep, diddums," Balin said, and the
men laughed.

Sharpe nodded. He took off the fine green coat and held
it out to the massive man. "I don't want trouble. My friend
and I just want to get home. We didn't ask to be here, we
don't want to be here, and we don't want to make enemies."

"Of course you don't," Balin said scornfully, reaching for
the good kerseymere coat, and the moment his hand took
hold of the material Sharpe brought up his right boot, hard
and straight, the kick hidden by the coat until the instant it
slammed into Balin's groin. The big man grunted, mouth
open, and Sharpe rammed his head forward, hearing and
feeling the teeth break under his forehead's blow. He had
his hands in Balin's crotch now, squeezing, and Balin began
to scream. Sharpe let go with one hand and used that hand
like an axe on the big man's neck. Once, twice, harder a third
time, and finally Balin went down, bleeding and senseless.
Sharpe kicked him, breaking a rib, then slammed the heel of
his right boot into the one-eyed face, thus breaking Balin's
nose. The seaman's hand fluttered on the deck, so for good
measure Sharpe stamped on the fingers, shattering them.

Then he stooped, plucked a good bone-handled knife from Balin's belt, picked his coat up from the deck and looked around. "Does anyone else want an English coat?"

Harper had stunned a man who tried to intervene, and now stooped and took that man's knife for himself. The other seamen backed away. Balin groaned horribly, and Sharpe felt a good deal better as well as a good deal safer. From now on, he knew, he and Harper would be treated with respect. They might have made enemies, but those enemies would be exceedingly cautious from now on.

That night, as the frigate's bows slathered into the great rollers and exploded spray past the galley and down to the guns in the ship's waist, Sharpe and Harper sat by the beakhead and watched the clouds shred past the stars. "Do you think that shithead Bautista invented the letter?" Harper asked.

"No."

"So it was Boney who wrote it?" Harper sounded disappointed.

"It had to be." Sharpe was fiddling with the locket of Napoleon's hair that still hung around his neck. "Strange."

"Being in code, you mean?"

Sharpe nodded. It probably made sense for Bautista to assume that the message had come from London, and had merely been hidden inside the Emperor's portrait, but Sharpe knew better. That coded message had come from Longwood, from the Emperor himself. Napoleon had claimed that Lieutenant Colonel Charles was a stranger, a mere admirer, but no one replied to such a man in code. The letter suggested a longstanding and sinister intrigue, but Sharpe could make no other sense of it. "Unless this Colonel Charles is supposed to organize a rescue?" he guessed.

And why not? Napoleon was a young man, scarcely fifty, and could expect to campaign for at least another twenty years. Twenty more years of battle and blood, of glory and horror. "God spare us," Sharpe murmured as he realized that the coded letter might mean that the Emperor would be loose again, rampaging about Europe. What had Bonaparte said? That all over the world there were embers, men like Charles, and Cochrane, even General Calvet in Louisiana, who only needed to be gathered together to cause a great searing blaze of heat and light. Was that what the coded message had been intended to achieve? Then maybe, Sharpe thought, it was just as well that Bautista had intercepted the hidden letter. "But why use us as messengers?" he wondered aloud.

"Boney can't meet that many people on their way to Chile," Harper observed sagely. "He'd have to use anyone he could find! Mind you, if I was him, I wouldn't rely on just one messenger getting through. I'd send as many copies of the letter as I could."

Dear God, Sharpe thought, but that could mean Charles already had his message and the escape could already be under way. He groaned at the thought of all that nonsense being repeated. The last time Bonaparte had escaped from an island it had driven Sharpe and Lucille from their Norman home. Their return had been difficult, for they had to live beside families whose sons and husbands had died at Waterloo, yet Sharpe had gone back and he had won his neighbors' trust again, but he could not bear to think that the whole horrid business would have to be endured a second time.

Except that now, in a ship which was being swallowed in the immensity of the Pacific under a sky of strange southern stars, there was nothing Sharpe could do. The Emperor's plot would unfold without Sharpe, Don Blas would rot in his stinking grave, and Sharpe, pressed as a seaman, would go home.

PART
II

COCHRANE

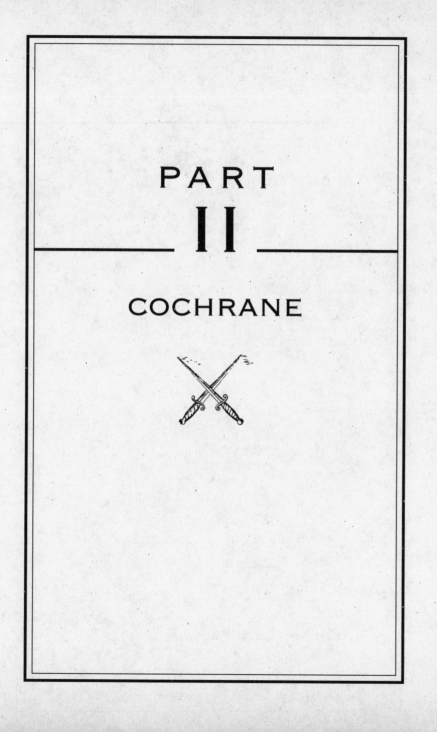

The *Espiritu Santo*'s crew, like their Captain, were eager to meet Lord Cochrane. They called him a devil, and crossed themselves when they spoke of him, yet they reckoned they could match this devil gun for gun and cutlass for cutlass and still beat him hollow. The crew might grumble when they were woken to an unexpected gun practice, or to rehearse repelling boarders, but they boasted of what their hardened skills would do to the devilish Cochrane if he dared attack the *Espiritu Santo*. They also boasted of the prize money they would win. Cochrane had captured his fifty-gun flagship, now called the *O'Higgins*, from the Spanish Navy which, stung by the defeat, had promised a fortune to whichever ship recaptured the lost vessel. Ardiles's men wanted that prize, and were willing to sweat as they practiced for it. Sharpe and Harper, deemed to be unskilled men, were allocated pikes and told that their job would be to stand on deck and be prepared to kill any man foolhardy enough to board the frigate. "Though perhaps it would be better if you did not carry weapons at all?" Captain Ardiles suggested when he heard that Sharpe and Harper were expected to be among the pikemen.

Ardiles, who was so reluctant to show himself to his passengers, proved to be a frequent visitor to the lower decks. He liked to inspect the guns and to smell the powder smoke which soured the ship with its stench after every practice session. He liked to talk with his men, who returned his interest with a genuine loyalty and devotion. Ardiles, the crew told Sharpe and Harper, was a proper seaman, not some gold-assed officer too high and mighty to duck his head under the beams of the lowest decks.

Ardiles, on one of his very first tours of inspection of the voyage, had taken Sharpe and Harper aside. "I hear you made your mark?" he asked drily.

"You mean Balin?" Sharpe asked.

"I do indeed; so watch your backs in a fight." Ardiles did not seem in the least upset that one of his prime seamen had been hammered, but he warned Sharpe and Harper that others on board might not be so sanguine. "Balin's a popular man, and he may have put a price on your heads." It was just after delivering that warning that Ardiles had wondered aloud whether Sharpe and Harper could be trusted to carry weapons in any fight against Lord Cochrane.

Sharpe ignored the question and Ardiles, who seemed amused at Sharpe's silent equivocation, perched himself on one of the tables that folded down between the guns. "Not that it's very likely your loyalty will be put to the test," Ardiles went on. "Cochrane doesn't usually sail this far south, so every hour makes it less likely that we'll meet him. Nevertheless, there's hope. We've assiduously spread rumors about gold, hoping to attract his attention."

"You mean there isn't gold on board?" Sharpe asked in astonishment.

"Sir," Ardiles chided Sharpe softly. So far the Spanish Captain had allowed Sharpe to treat him with a scant respect, but now he suddenly insisted on being addressed properly. Sharpe, prickly with hurt pride, did not instantly respond and Ardiles shrugged, as though the use of the honorific did not really matter to him personally, even though he was going to insist on it. "You've been a commanding officer, Sharpe,"

Ardiles spoke softly so that only Sharpe and Harper could hear him, "and you would have demanded the respect of your men, even those who were reluctant to be under your authority, and I demand the same. You might be a Lieutenant-Colonel on land, but here you're an unskilled seaman and I can have respect thrashed into you at a rope's end. Unlike General Bautista I'm not fond of witnessing punishment, so I'd rather you volunteered the word."

"Sir," Sharpe said.

Ardiles nodded acknowledgment of the reluctant courtesy. "No, there isn't gold on board. Any gold that we might have been taking home has probably been stolen by Bautista, but we went through the routine of loading boxes filled with rock from the citadel's wharf. I just hope that charade and the rumors it undoubtedly encouraged are sufficient to persuade Cochrane that we are stuffed with riches, for then he might come south and fight us. We hear that the rebel government owes him money. Much money! So perhaps he'll try to collect it from me. I'd like that. We'd all like that, wouldn't we?" Ardiles turned and asked the question of his crewmen who, hanging back in the gundeck's gloom, now cheered their Captain.

Ardiles, pleased with their enthusiasm, slid his rump off the table, then went back to his earlier question. "So can you be trusted, Sharpe?"

"What I was hoping for, sir," Sharpe did not reply directly, "was that you might put me aboard a fishing boat?" The *Espiritu Santo* had passed a score of boats that had come far out to sea to search for big tunny fish, and Sharpe had concocted the idea that perhaps one of the boats might carry him back to Chile where, in alliance with the rebels, he might yet retrieve Doña Louisa's money, exhume Blas Vivar's body and restore his own pride.

"No," Ardiles said calmly, "I won't. I have orders to take

you back to Europe, and I am a man who obeys orders. But are you? Whose side will you be on if we meet Cochrane?"

This time Sharpe did not hesitate. "Cochrane's side," he paused, "sir."

Ardiles was immediately and understandably hostile. "Then you must take the consequences if there's a fight, mustn't you?" He stalked away.

"What does that mean?" Harper said.

"It means that if we sight Lord Cochrane then he'll send Balin and his cronies to slit our throats."

Next day there were no more fishing boats, just an empty ocean and a succession of thrashing squalls. Sharpe, under the immense vacancy of sea and sky, felt all hope slide away. He had lost his uniform and sword; things of no value except to himself, but their loss galled him. He had lost Louisa's money. He had been humiliated and there was nothing he could do about it. He had been fleeced, then ignominiously kicked out of a country with only the clothes on his back. He felt heartsick. He was not used to failure.

But at least he was accustomed to hardship, and had no fears about surviving on board the *Espiritu Santo*. The hard bread, salted meat, dried fish and rancid wine that were the seamen's rations would have been counted luxuries in Sharpe's army. The worst part of the life, apart from the damp which permeated every stitch of clothing and bedding, were the Bosun's mates who, knowing that Sharpe had been a senior army officer, seemed to find a particular pleasure in finding him the dirtiest and most menial jobs on board. Sharpe and Harper mucked out the sheep and pigs that would be slaughtered for fresh meat during the voyage, they scrubbed the poopdeck each morning, they ground the rust off the blades of the boarding pikes that were racked on deck, and each afternoon they collected the latrine buckets from the passenger cabins and scoured them clean. Among

the score of passengers aboard the frigate were seven Spanish army officers, two of whom were sailing with their families, and those army officers, knowing Sharpe's history, stared
at him with frank curiosity. It was, Sharpe thought, going to
be a long voyage home.

Yet, like most ordeals, it abated swiftly. The humiliated
Balin might bear a grudge, but Harper inevitably discovered
a score of fellow Irishmen aboard the *Espiritu Santo*, all of
them exiles from British justice, and all of them eager to hear
Harper's news of home, and Sharpe, given temporary and
flattering status as an honorary Irishman, felt a good deal
safer from the Balin faction. One of the Bosun's mates was
from Donegal and his presence took much of the sting out
of Sharpe's treatment. A week into the voyage and Sharpe
was even beginning to enjoy the experience.

The next dawn brought proof that the sea could throw up
hardships far worse than anything yet inflicted on Sharpe and
Harper. They were scrubbing the poopdeck when the forward lookout hailed the quarterdeck with a cry that a boat
was in sight. Ardiles ran on deck and seized the watch officer's telescope, while the First Lieutenant, Otero, who
remembered Sharpe and Harper well from the outward voyage, and who was excruciatingly embarrassed by their change
of fortune, climbed to the lookout's post on the foremast
from where he trained his own telescope forward.

"What is she?" Ardiles called.

"A wreck, sir! A dismasted whaler, by the look of her."

"Goddamn." Ardiles had been hoping it would prove to
be the *O'Higgins*. "Change course to take a look at her, then
call me when we're closer!" Ardiles muttered the instruction
to the officer on watch, then, before taking refuge in his
cabin, he glowered at the handful of passengers who had
come on deck to see what had caused the sudden alarm.

Among the spectators were two army officers' wives who

were standing at the weather rail to stare at the stricken whaler. Their excited children ran from one side of the deck to the other, playing an involved game of tag. One of the small girls slipped on the wet patch left by Sharpe's holystone. "Move back! Give the ladies room!" the Bosun ordered Sharpe and Harper. "Just wait forrard! Wait till the passengers have gone below."

Sharpe and Harper went to the beakhead where, concealed by the forecastle, they could hide from authority and thus stretch their temporary unemployment. They joined a small group of curious men who gazed at the wrecked whaler. She was a small ship, scarcely a third the size of the *Espiritu Santo,* with an ugly squared-off stern and, even uglier, three splintered stumps where her masts had stood. A spar, perhaps a yardarm, had been erected in place of the foremast, and a small sail lashed to that makeshift mast. Despite the jury rig she seemed to be unmanned, but then, in answer to a hail from the Spanish frigate's masthead, two survivors appeared on the whaler's deck and began waving frantically toward the *Espiritu Santo.* One of the two unfolded a flag that he held aloft to the wind. "She's an American," the First Lieutenant shouted down to the forecastle where a midshipman was deputed to carry the news back to the Captain's cabin.

Ardiles, though, was not in his cabin, but had instead come forward. He had avoided the inquisitive passengers by using a lower deck, but now he suddenly appeared out of the low door which led to the beakhead. He nodded affably to the men who were perched on the ship's lavatory bench, then trained his telescope on the whaler.

"She isn't too badly damaged," Ardiles spoke to himself, but as Sharpe and Harper were the closest men, they grunted an acknowledgment of his words. "Hardly damaged at all!" Ardiles continued his assessment of the beleaguered American whaler.

"She looks buggered to me, sir," Sharpe said.

"She's floating upright," Ardiles pointed out, "so, as they say in the Cadiz boatyards, her hull must be as watertight as a duck's backside. Mind you, the hulls of whaling ships are as strong as anything afloat." He paused as he stared through the glass. "They've lost their rudder, by the look of it. They're using a steering oar instead."

"What could have happened to her, sir?" Harper asked.

"A storm? Perhaps she rolled over? That can snap the sticks out of a boat as quick as you like. And she's lost all her whaleboats, so I suspect her topsides were swept clean when she rolled. That would explain the rudder, too. And I'll warrant she lost a few souls drowned too, God rest them." Ardiles crossed himself.

Three men were now visible on the whaler's deck. Lieutenant Otero, still high on the foremast, read the whaler's name through his telescope and shouted it down to Captain Ardiles. "She's called the *Mary Starbuck!*"

"Probably the owner's wife," Ardiles guessed. "I hope the poor man has got insurance, or else Mary Starbuck will be making do with last year's frocks."

Lieutenant Otero, now that the *Espiritu Santo* was nearing the hulk, slid down the ratlines to leave tar smeared on his white trousers. "Do we rig a towing bridle?" he asked Ardiles.

Ardiles shook his head. "We haven't time to take them in tow. But prepare to heave to. And fetch me a speaking trumpet from the quarterdeck." Ardiles still stared at the whaler, his fingers drumming on the beakhead's low rail. "Perhaps, Sharpe, you'll find out what the Americans need? I doubt they want us to rescue them. Their hull isn't broached, and under that jury rig they could sail from here to the Californias."

The speaking trumpet was brought to the bows. Ten minutes later the frigate heaved to, backing her square sails so that she rolled and wallowed in the great swells. Sharpe, standing beside one of the long-barreled nine-pounder bow guns that were the frigate's pursuit weapons, could clearly read the whaler's name that was painted in gold letters on a black quarterboard across her stern. Beneath that name was written her hailing port, Nantucket. "Tell them who we are," Ardiles ordered, "then ask them what they want."

Sharpe raised the trumpet to his mouth. "This is the Spanish frigate *Espiritu Santo*," he shouted, "What do you want?"

"Water, mister!" One of the Americans cupped his hands. "We lost all our fresh water barrels!"

"Ask what happened." Ardiles, who spoke reasonable English, had not needed to have the American's request for water translated.

"What happened?" Sharpe shouted.

"She rolled over! We were close to the ice when a berg broke off!"

Sharpe translated as best he could, for the answer made little sense to him, but Ardiles both understood and explained. "The fools take any risk to chase whales. They got caught by an iceberg calving off the ice mass. The sea churns like a tidal wave when that happens. Still, they're good seamen to have brought their boat this far. Ask where they're heading."

"Valdivia!" came the reply. The whaler was close now, close enough for Sharpe and Ardiles to see how gaunt and bearded were the faces of the three survivors.

"Ask how many there are on board," Ardiles commanded.

"Four of us, mister! The rest drowned!"

"Tell them to keep away," Ardiles was worried that the

heavily built whaler might stove in the *Espiritu Santo*'s ribs. "And tell them I'll float a couple of water barrels to them." Ardiles saw Sharpe's puzzlement, and explained. "Barrels of fresh water float in salt water."

Sharpe leaned over the rail. "Keep away from our side! We're going to float water barrels to you!"

"We hear you, mister!" One of the Americans dutifully leaned on the makeshift steering oar, though his efforts seemed to have little effect for the clumsy whaler kept heaving herself ever closer to the frigate.

Ardiles had ordered two barrels of water brought onto deck and a sling rove to heave them overboard. Now, while he waited for the barrels to arrive, he frowned at the *Mary Starbuck*'s wallowing hulk. "Ask them where Nantucket is," he ordered suddenly.

Sharpe obeyed. "Off Cape Cod, mister!" Came back the answer.

Ardiles nodded, but some instinct was still troubling him. "Tell them to sheer away!" he snapped, then, perhaps not trusting Sharpe to deliver the order with sufficient force, he seized the speaking trumpet. "Keep clear! Keep clear!" he shouted in English.

"We're trying, mister! We're trying!" The man on the steering oar was desperately pushing against the whaler's weight.

"Trying?" Ardiles repeated the word, then, still in English, he swore. "The devil! They didn't lose their tryworks when they rolled!" He turned to shout toward the quarterdeck, but already events were accelerating to combat pace and Ardiles's warning shout was lost in the sudden chaos.

For just as Ardiles turned, so a massive wave lifted the whaler's square stern and an officer on the *Espiritu Santo*'s quarterdeck saw that the *Mary Starbuck*'s rudder was not shorn away after all, but was in place and being steered from a tiller concealed beneath the whaler's deck. The rudder was bringing the heavy boat toward the Spanish frigate, which meant the steering oar was faked, which meant the ship-wreck was faked, a fact that Ardiles had simultaneously guessed when he saw that the whaler's tryworks, a brick fur-nace built amidships in which the whale blubber was ren-dered down into the precious oil, had survived the apparent rolling of a ship that had destroyed three solid masts.

The Spaniards were shouting in warning, but the *Mary Starbuck* was already within ten feet of the frigate. A man aboard the whaler suddenly cut free the American flag and, in its place, unfurled a red, white and blue flag which was unfamiliar to Sharpe, but all too familiar to Ardiles. It was the flag of the Chilean rebel government. "Beat to quarters!" Ardiles shouted, and as he called the order aloud, so the hatch covers on the whaler's deck were thrust aside and Sharpe, astonished, saw that a huge gun was mounted in the hold. It was a carronade: a squat, wide-mouthed, short-range killer designed to shred men rather then smash the timbers or rigging of a ship. Sharpe also saw, before he and Harper dropped for cover behind the nine-pounder cannon, that a mass of men was seething up onto the whaler's deck. The men were armed with muskets, pikes, cutlasses, pistols and grapnels.

"Fire!" The order was shouted on board the *Mary Star-buck,* and the carronade belched a bellyful of iron scraps and links of rusted chain up at the *Espiritu Santo*'s waist. Most of the missiles struck the starboard gunwale, but a few Spanish crewmen, helping to lower the first water barrel over the side, were thrown back in a sudden spray of blood. The bar-rel, holed in a hundred places, sprayed drinking water into the bloody scuppers.

Grapnels came soaring across the narrowing gap of water. The metal hooks snagged on rigging or thumped into the decks. The *Espiritu Santo*'s crew, trained to just such an emergency, reacted fast. Some men started slashing at the ropes attached to the grapnels, while others ran to seize pikes or muskets. "Gun crews! Gun crews!" Ardiles had left the frigate's bows and was striding back to the quarterdeck where the children were screaming in terror. "Passengers down to the orlop deck!" Ardiles was astonishingly calm. "Quick now! Below!"

Musket balls whiplashed up from the whaler, which suddenly struck the frigate's side, so hard that some of the *Espiritu Santo*'s crew were knocked down by the force of the collision. The first boarders were already swarming up their ropes. Sharpe, snatching a glance from the beakhead, saw two of the invaders fall back as their rope was cut free. Another, gaining the gunwale, screamed as a pike slammed into his face to blind him and hurl him back to the *Mary Starbuck*'s crowded deck. The attackers, jostling at the ropes, were screaming a war cry that at first sounded jumbled and indistinct to Sharpe, but which now became clear. "Cochrane! Cochrane!" Ardiles, it seemed, was having his dearest wish granted.

A grapnel soared high over the *Espiritu Santo*'s bows to fall and catch on the beakhead. For the moment Sharpe and Harper were alone on the small hidden platform of the beakhead, and neither man moved to cut the rope free. "We're joining the fight then, are we?" Harper asked.

"I like Ardiles," Sharpe said, "but I'm damned if I'll fight for a man on the same side as Bautista."

"Ah, well. Back to the wars." Harper grinned, then instinctively ducked as another carronade fired, this one from the forecastle above them. The *Espiritu Santo*'s forecastle carronade, unable to depress its muzzle sufficiently, had not done great damage to the attackers, but its noise alone seemed to encourage the Spaniards who now began to shout their own war cry, *"Espiritu Santo! Espiritu Santo!"*

"So what do we do?" Harper asked.

"We start with that big bugger up there." Sharpe jerked his chin up toward the forecastle carronade. He had to shout, for more big guns were firing, these new ones from down below on the gundeck where the Spanish were evidently firing straight into the *Mary Starbuck*'s upper deck. Sharpe could hear the screams of men being disemboweled and flensed by the close-range horror of the big guns. Sharpe jumped, caught the edge of the forecastle's deck, and hauled himself up to where three men were serving the carronade. One of them, the gun captain, snapped at Sharpe to fetch some quoins so that the breech of the carronade could be elevated.

"I'm not on your side!" Sharpe yelled at the man. Behind Sharpe, Harper was struggling to haul his huge weight up the sheer face of the forecastle which, though only eight feet high, was too much for a man as heavy as Harper, which meant that Sharpe, for the moment, was alone. He grabbed one of the carronade's heavy spikes: a six-foot shaft of hardwood tipped with an iron point. The spike was used to aim the heavy gun by levering its trail around, and the wooden deck under the carronade's tail was pitted with holes left by the sharp iron point. Sharpe now lunged with the spike as though it was a bayonet. He did not want to kill, for his attack was unexpected and unfair, but the gun's Captain suddenly pulled a pistol from under his coat and Sharpe had no choice but to ram the spike forward with sudden and savage force so that the iron point punctured the man's belly. The gun Captain dropped his pistol to grip the spike's shaft. He was moaning sadly. Sharpe, still lunging forward, slammed the wounded man against the rail and, still pushing, heaved him overboard. Sharpe let go the spike so that the gun Captain, blood cartwheeling away from his wound, fell to the sea with the spike's shaft still rammed into his belly.

Sharpe turned. He ducked to retrieve the gun Captain's pistol and the carronade's rammer, swung with terrible force by one of the two remaining crewmen, slashed just above his head. Sharpe's right hand closed on the pistol just as he charged forward to ram his left shoulder into the Spaniard's belly. He heard the man's breath gasp out, then he brought the heavy pistol up and hammered it onto his attacker's skull. The third crew member had backed to the inboard edge of the forecastle where he was uselessly shouting for help. Harper, abandoning his attempt to climb the forward face of the forecastle, had ducked through the galley and was now climbing the companionway steps which led from the main-deck. The third crewmember, thinking that help was at last arriving, leaned down to give Harper a helping hand. Harper grabbed the offered hand, tugged, and the crewman tumbled down into the churning mass of men who fought in the ship's waist.

That larger fight was a gutter brawl of close-quarter horror. Cochrane's invaders had succeeded in capturing a third of the *Espiritu Santo*'s main deck, but were now faced by a disciplined and spirited crew that fiercely defended their ship. Cochrane's men, screaming like demons, had achieved an initial surprise, but Ardiles's hours of practice were beginning to pay dividends as his men forced the invaders back.

Sharpe, seeing his very first sea fight, was horrified by it. The killing was done in the confining space of a ship's deck which gave neither side room to retreat. On land, when faced by a determined bayonet attack, most soldiers gave ground, but here there was no ground to give, and so the dead and dying were trampled underfoot. The heaving ocean added a horrid air of chance to death. A man might parry a thrust efficiently and be on the point of killing his opponent when a wave surge might unsteady him and, as he flailed for balance, his belly would be exposed to a steel thrust. One of the Bosun's mates who had made Sharpe's first days aboard such misery had been so wounded and was now dying in the scuppers. The man writhed in brief spasms, his hands fluttering and clawing at the broken sword blade that was embedded in his belly. A midshipman was bleeding to death, calling for his mother, which pathetic cry swelled into a shriek of terror as a rebel stepped back on the boy's sliced belly. That rebel then died with a pistol bullet in his brain, hurled back in a spray of bright blood to slide down beside the Bosun's mate.

"God save Ireland," Harper muttered.

"Is the gun loaded?" Sharpe slapped the carronade, then ducked as a stray musket bullet slapped over his head.

"Looks like it!"

Sharpe found another spike which he used to lever the gun's trail around so that the carronade faced straight down the *Espiritu Santo*'s length to menace the quarterdeck, where Ardiles was assembling a group of seamen. Those seamen were undoubtedly intended to be the counterattack that would finish off Cochrane's assault. Sharpe hammered a quoin out from under the carronade's breech, thus raising the muzzle so that the dreadful weapon was pointing straight at the quarterdeck. The carronade was a pot of a gun, not a long, elegant and accurate cannon, but a squat cauldron to be charged with powder and metal scraps that flayed out like buckshot. A carronade's range was short, but inside that brief range it was foully lethal.

The whole ship quivered as another broadside slammed from the frigate's gundeck to shatter the heavy timbers of the whaler. Most of Cochrane's men were off the whaler now and crammed onto the Spaniard's deck where they were hemmed in by bloody pikes and bayonets. Ardiles, preparing his reserves to slam into the left flank of the invaders, was making things worse for Cochrane by destroying his only chance of escape by pounding the whaler into matchwood. Smoke was sifting from the open hold of the *Mary Starbuck*. Presumably some of the wadding from one of the *Espiritu Santo*'s cannons had set fire to a splintered timber inside the attacking ship.

Harper cocked the flintlock that was soldered onto the carronade's touchhole. Naval guns did not use linstocks, for the spluttering sparks of an open match were too dangerous on board a wooden ship crammed with gunpowder. Instead, just like a musket, the gun was fired by a spring-tensioned flint that was released by a lanyard. "Are you ready?" Sharpe gripped the lanyard and scuttled to one side of the gun to escape its recoil.

"Get down!" Harper shouted. Ardiles's men on the quarterdeck had at last seen the threat of the forecastle carronade and a dozen muskets were leveled. Sharpe dropped just as the volley fired. The sound of a musket volley, so achingly familiar, crackled about the ship as the balls whipsawed overhead. Sharpe answered the volley by yanking the carronade's lanyard.

The world hammered apart in thunder, in an explosion so close and hot and violent that Sharpe thought he was surely dead as the frigate shivered and dust spurted out of the cracks between her deck planks. Sharpe's second and more realistic thought was that the barrel of the carronade had burst, but then he saw that the gun, recoiling on its huge carriage, was undamaged.

The explosion had been aboard the *Mary Starbuck*. A store of gunpowder in the whaler's hull had ripped itself apart in a moment's blinding horror, tearing her deck into shards and exploding the wounded into the sea. Now what remained of the whaler was ablaze. The dark red flames leaped voraciously from her oil-soaked planks to flare as high as the *Espiritu Santo*'s topmasts.

"Mary, Mother of God," Harper said in awe, not at the incandescent whaler, but rather because the *Espiritu Santo*'s mainmast was toppling. The explosion had ripped out the frigate's chainplates and now the great mast swayed. Some men, now recovering their wits after being stunned by the concussion of the explosion, shouted in warning, while others, from both sides of the fight, were desperately slashing at the remaining grapnels so that the roaring blaze on the whaler would not leap across to destroy the frigate. Beyond that chaos Sharpe could see a red horror on the poop- and quarterdecks where the blast of his carronade had taken a terrible toll among Ardiles's men.

A rebel officer shouted a piercing warning. The swaying mainmast splintered and cracked. Canvas billowed down onto the deck and into the sea. The collapsing mast dragged in its wake the fore topmast and a nightmarish tangle of yards, halyards, lines and sails.

"Come on, Patrick!" Sharpe cocked the pistol and jumped down from the forecastle. A Spanish sailor, groggy from the explosion, tried to stand in Sharpe's way so he thumped the man on the side of his head with the pistol's heavy barrel. A Spanish army officer lunged at Sharpe with a long, narrow sword. Sharpe turned, straightened his right arm and pulled the trigger. The officer seemed to be snatched backward with a halo of exploding blood about his face. Smoke from the burning whaler whirled thick and black and choking across the deck. Sharpe hurled the pistol away and snatched up a fallen cutlass. "Cochrane!" he shouted, "Cochrane!" A mass of Cochrane's men were swarming toward the frigate's stern. The explosion and the subsequent fall of the mast had torn the heart out of the frigate's defenders, though a stubborn rear guard, under an unwounded Ardiles, gathered for a last stand on the quarterdeck.

To Sharpe's left was a tall man with red hair who carried a long and heavy-bladed sword. "To me! To me!" The red-haired man was wearing a green naval coat with two gold epaulettes and was the man the rebels were looking to for orders and inspiration. The man had to be Lord Cochrane. Sharpe turned away as a swarm of Spanish fighters came streaming up from the gundeck below. These new attackers were the frigate's guncrews who, their target destroyed, had come to recapture their maindeck.

Sharpe fought hand to hand, without room to swing a blade, only to stab it forward in short, hard strokes. He was close enough to see the fear in the eyes of the men he killed, or to smell the garlic and tobacco on their breath. He knew some of the men, but he felt no compunction about killing them. He had declared his allegiance to Ardiles, and Ardiles could have no complaint that Sharpe had changed sides without warning. Nor could Sharpe complain if, this fight lost, he was hung from whatever yardarm was left of the Spanish frigate. Which made it important not to lose, but instead to beat the Spaniards back in blood and terror.

Harper climbed the fallen trunk of the mainmast. He carried a boarding pike that he swung in a huge and terrifying arc. One of the Irish crew members, having decided to change sides, was fighting alongside Harper. Both men were screaming in Gaelic, inviting their enemies to come and be killed. A musket crashed near Sharpe, who flinched aside from its flame. He ripped the cutlass blade up to throw back an enemy. The cutlass was a clumsy weapon, but sea fighting was hardly a fine art. It was more like a gutter brawl, and Sharpe had grown up with such fighting. He slipped, fell hard on his right knee, then clawed himself up to ram the blade forward again. Blood whipped across a fallen sail. A sailor trapped beneath a fallen yard shrieked as a wave surge shifted the timber balk across his crushed ribs. Balin, his face and hand still bandaged, lay dead in the portside scuppers which now ran with the blood from his crushed skull. A group of rebels had found room to use their pikes. They lunged forward, hooking men with the crooked blade on the pike's reverse, then pulling their victims out of the *Espiritu Santo*'s ranks so that another pikeman, using the weapon's broad axe-head, could slash down hard. The pikemen were driving the frigate's guncrews back to the poopdeck where a rear guard waited with Ardiles and Lieutenant Otero.

The ship lurched on the swell, staggering Sharpe sideways. A bleeding man screamed and fell into the sea. It seemed that the *Espiritu Santo* must have taken on water for she did not come fully upright, but stayed listed to starboard. A volley of musket fire from Ardiles's group on the quarterdeck punched a hole in the rebels' ranks, but Cochrane, seeing the danger, had led a rampaging attack up to the poopdeck and now his men clawed and scrabbled up the last companionway to attack Ardiles and his men on the quarterdeck. Royalist Captain faced rebel Admiral. Their two swords clashed and scraped. More rebels were running past their leader, swarming up to the quarterdeck where a final, fanatic group of Spaniards, including most of the army officers, stood to protect their royal ensign.

A few despairing men still fought on the main deck. Sharpe kicked a man in the ankle, then hammered down the cutlass hilt as the man fell. Two men slashed at him, but Sharpe stepped back from their clumsy blades, then sliced his own forward. A rebel joined him, stabbing forward with a bayonet, and suddenly the portside steps to the poopdeck were open. Sharpe ran up. Above him, on the quarterdeck, Ardiles was pressed back by the man Sharpe supposed was Cochrane. Ardiles was no mean swordsman, but he was no

match for the red-haired rebel who was taller, heavier and
quicker. Ardiles lunged, missed, retreated and was toppled
over the railing by a sudden thrust of his opponent's sword.
The Spanish Captain fell onto the poopdeck at Sharpe's feet.
Sharpe stooped and took his sword.

"You," Ardiles said bleakly.

"I'm sorry," Sharpe said.

"Who the hell are you?" the red-haired man asked from
above Sharpe.

"A friend! Are you Cochrane?"

"I am, friend, indeed I am." Cochrane sketched a salute
with his sword, then turned to lead the attack on the desperate group that waited to defend their flag. On the poop and
main decks the victorious rebels disarmed Spaniards, but
about the great gaudy ensign a terrible battle still waged.
Pistols flared, muskets crashed smoke. A rebel squirmed in
awful pain in the scuppers. Other rebels, trying to fire down
at the stubborn stern guard, climbed the mizzen rigging, but
Lieutenant Otero, seeing the danger, ordered a group of the
frigate's marines to fire upward. One of the rebels screamed
as a bullet thudded into his belly. For a second he hung from
the ratlines, his blood spraying bright across the driver-sail,
then he fell to crash down into the sea. Another rebel, losing
his nerve, leaped after his dying colleague. The horror was
not all visited on the attackers. One of the *Espiritu Santo's*
midshipmen, no more than eleven years old, was clutching
his groin from which blood seeped to spread along a seam
between two scrubbed planks of the quarterdeck. The boy
was weeping and on his face was a look of utter astonishment. The *Mary Starbuck,* her fire roaring like a blast fur-
nace, had drifted away from the frigate. The sea between the
two ships was littered with wreckage and dead and drowning
men.

Lieutenant Otero ordered a final quixotic charge, perhaps

hoping to kill Lord Cochrane, but his men would not obey. A rebel officer shouted at the stern guard to surrender. Sharpe, the handle of his cutlass slippery with blood, climbed to thicken the ranks of the rebels who now made a threatening semicircle about the frigate's last defenders.

"Surrender, sir!" Lord Cochrane called. "You've done well! I salute you! Now, I beg you, no more killing!"

Lieutenant Otero crossed himself then, bitterly, threw down his sword. There was a clatter of falling guns and blades as his men followed his example. An army officer, disgusted, hurled his own sword overboard so he would not have to surrender it to rebels. A ship's boy wept, not because he was wounded, but because of the shame of losing the fight. A rebel slashed at the ensign's halyard and the bright flag of Spain fluttered down.

"Where are the pumps?" Cochrane shouted in urgent and execrable Spanish. It seemed an odd way to celebrate victory, but then the frigate lurched, and Sharpe, to his horror, realized that the *Espiritu Santo,* just like the burning *Mary Starbuck,* was sinking. "The pumps!" Cochrane shouted.

"This way!" Sharpe jumped down to the poop, then to the waist. From there he slithered down a rope to the gundeck where the main pumps were situated. He saw that the explosion of the *Mary Starbuck* had made a terrible slaughter on the gundeck. Until the moment the whaler blew up, the frigate's gunners had been firing point-blank through open hatches into the wooden hull that had been grinding against the Spanish warship, but the explosion had speared flame and debris through the open gun hatches to fan slaughter through the low-beamed deck. Two of the frigate's guns had been blown clean off their carriages. One dismounted gun was lying atop a dying, screaming man. Cochrane killed the man with an efficient slice of his sword, then shouted at his men to start the pumps working.

"Chippy! Find me the chippy!" Cochrane roared. The carpenter was fetched and ordered to discover the extent of the damage to the frigate's hull, then to start immediate repairs. The wounded Spanish gunners moaned. The frigate was already listing so far over that roundshot were rolling across her deck. "Can't talk now, bloody boat's sinking," Cochrane said to Sharpe. "We'll all be dead if we don't watch it. Pump, you bastards! Pump! Put the prisoners to work! Pump! Well done, Jorge! Well fought, Liam! But start pumping or we'll all be sucking the devil's tits before this day's done!" Cochrane, ducking under the gundeck's beams, scattered praise and humor among his victorious men. He set the rear pump working and peered down into the orlop deck where the women and children cowered. "Not flooded yet, good! Maybe there's hope. Christ, but that bugger should never have exploded. Are you Spanish?" This last question was addressed to Sharpe, shouted as Cochrane climbed nimbly back up to the bloody and wreckage-strewn main deck.

"English."

"Are you now?" Cochrane brushed ineffectively at the powder stains on his green uniform coat. "I suppose I've got to take the proper surrender from their poor bastard of a Captain. Rotten luck for him. He fought well. Ardiles, isn't it?"

"Yes," Sharpe said, "he's a good man," then took a pace backward as Captain Ardiles, his face stricken, walked with fragile dignity toward Lord Cochrane. The Spanish Captain had retrieved his sword, but only so that he could offer it in surrender to his victor. Ardiles held the sword hilt forward, the gesture of surrender, but he could not bring himself to speak the proper words.

Cochrane touched the hilt, his gesture of acceptance, then pushed the weapon back to Ardiles. "Keep it, Captain. Your men fought well, damned well." His Spanish was enthusias-

tic, but clumsy. "I also need your help if we're to save the
ship. I've sent a carpenter down to the bilge, but your man
will know the timbers better than he will. The pumps are
going. That damned explosion must have sprung some of the
timbers! Would you fetch your ladies up? They'll not be
harmed, I give you my word. And where's the gold?"

"There is no gold," Ardiles said very stiffly.

Cochrane, who had been speaking and moving with a fre-
netic energy, now stopped still as a statue and stared open-
mouthed at Ardiles. Then, a second later, he looked
quizzically at Sharpe who confirmed the bad news with a
nod. "Goddamn!" Cochrane said, though without any real
bitterness. "No gold? You mean I just blunted a sword for
nothing!" He gave a great billow of laughter that turned into
a whoop of alarm as the *Espiritu Santo* gave another creaking
jolt to starboard. A cutlass slid down the canted deck to clash
into the scuppers. "Help me!" Cochrane said to Ardiles, and
suddenly the two men disappeared, lost in technical discussion, while beneath Sharpe's feet the pumps clattered to
pulse puny jets of water over the side.

Somehow they stopped the ship from sinking, though it
took the best part of that day to do it. Cochrane's men salvaged the mainsail that had fallen overboard when the mainmast fell and from it cut great squares of canvas. They sewed
the squares together to make a huge pad that was then
dragged under the ship by means of cables which were first
looped under the frigate's bows, then dragged back under
her hull till the huge pad of material was fothered up against
the sprung timbers. The explosion on board the whaler had
driven in a section of the frigate's hull, but once the canvas
fother was in place the pumps at last could begin to win the
battle. Behind them, on an ocean scattered with the flotsam
of battle, the *Mary Starbuck* gave a last hiss of steam as she
sank.

On board the captured *Espiritu Santo* the wounded were treated. The surgeon worked on deck, tossing the amputated limbs overboard. A step behind the surgeon was the *Espiritu Santo*'s Chaplain, who gave the final unction to dying seamen. To those who were dying in too much pain the Chaplain gave a quietus with a narrow blade. Once dead, the shriven sailors were sewn into hammocks weighted with roundshot. The last stitch, by custom, was forced through the corpse's nose to make certain he was truly dead. None of the corpses twitched in protest. Instead, after a muttered prayer, they were all slid down to the sea's bed.

"What a resurrection there'll be on the Day of Judgment!" Cochrane, his emergency work done, had asked Sharpe and Harper to join him on the frigate's quarterdeck from where they watched the miserable procession of dead splashing over the side. "Just think of Judgment Day," Cochrane said exuberantly, "when the sea gives up its dead and all those sailormen pop out of the waves and start hollering for a tot of rum and a heavenly whore." His Lordship had protuberant eyes, a strong nose, full lips and an excited, energetic manner. "Christ," he hit Sharpe on the back, "but that was a close thing! They're the best fighters I've ever seen on a Spanish ship!"

"Ardiles's great ambition was to fight you," Sharpe explained. "He trained his men for years. All he wanted to do was to fight and beat you."

"Poor bastard. I sneak up on him like a rat, and he was dreaming of an honest broadside-to-broadside battle, eh?" Cochrane seemed genuinely sympathetic, "but a broadside pounding match was exactly what I wanted to avoid! I thought that sneaking up like a rat would do less damage to this ship, now look at it! No mainmast and half a bottom blown away!" He sounded remarkably cheerful despite the appalling damage. "You didn't give me the honor of your name, sir," he said to Sharpe, whereas the truth was that he had not given Sharpe a moment of time to make any kind of introduction.

"Lieutenant Colonel Richard Sharpe." Sharpe decided to go full fig with his introduction. "And this is my particular friend, Regimental Sergeant Major Patrick Harper."

Cochrane stared at both men with a moment's disbelief that vanished as he decided Sharpe must be telling the truth. "Are you, by God?" Cochrane, flatteringly, had evidently heard of the Rifleman. "You are?"

"Yes, my Lord, I am."

"And I'm Thomas, Tommy, or Cochrane, and not 'my Lord.' I was once a Knight Commander of the Order of the Bath, till the buggers couldn't stand my company so they turfed me out. I also had the honor of being held prisoner in the Fleet prison, and I was once a member of Parliament, and let me tell you, Sharpe, that the company in prison is a damned sight more rewarding than that available in His Fat Majesty's House of Commons which is packed full of farting lawyers. I also once had the honor of being a Rear Admiral in His Fat Majesty's Navy, but they didn't like my opinions any more than the Order of the Bath liked my company, so they threw me out of the navy too, so now I have the signal honor to be Supreme Admiral, Great Lord, and chief trou-blemaker of the Navy of the Independent Republic of Chile." He gave Sharpe and Harper an elaborate bow. "Pity about the *Mary Starbuck*. I bought her off a couple of Nan-tucket Yankees with the very last cash I possessed. I thought I'd get my money back by capturing the *Holy Spirit*. Awful damned name for a ship. Why do the dagoes choose such names? You might as well call a ship Angel-Fart. They should give their boats real names, like *Revenge* or *Arse-Kicker* or *Victory*. Are you really Richard Sharpe?"

"I truly am," Sharpe confessed.

"Then just what the hell are the two of you doing on this ship?"

"We were thrown out of Chile. By a man called Bautista."

"Oh, well done!" Cochrane said happily. "First class! Well done! You must be on the side of the angels if that piece of half-digested gristle doesn't like you. But what about that sniveling turd Blair? Didn't he try to protect you?"

"He seemed to be on Bautista's side."

"Blair's a greedy bastard," Cochrane observed gloomily. "If we ever get off this ship alive you should look him up and give him a damned good thrashing." His Lordship's gloom seemed justified for, despite the fothering and the pumping, the condition of the damaged frigate seemed to be suddenly worsening. The wind was rising and the seas were steeper, conditions that made the damaged hull pound ever harder into the waves. "The fother's shifting," Cochrane guessed. He had turned the *Espiritu Santo* northward and the captured frigate was running before the wind and current, yet even so her progress was painfully slow because of the damaged hull and the amount of wreckage that still trailed overboard.

Cochrane's sailing master, an elderly and lugubrious Scot named Fraser, threw a trailing log overboard. The log was attached to a long piece of twine which was knotted at regular intervals. Fraser let the twine run through his hands and counted the knots as they whipped past his fingers, timing them all the while on a big pocket watch. He finally snapped the watch shut and began hauling the log back. "Three knots, my Lord, that's all."

"Christ help us," Cochrane said. He frowned at the sea, then at the rigging. "But we'll speed up as we get the damage cleared. Eight days, say?"

"Ten," the sailing master said doubtfully, "maybe twelve,

but more probably never, my Lord, because she's taking water like a colander."

"Five guineas says we'll make it in eight days," Cochrane said cheerfully.

"Eight days to what?" Sharpe asked.

"To Valdivia, of course," Cochrane exclaimed.

"Valdivia?" Sharpe was astonished that Cochrane was trying to reach an enemy haven. "You mean there isn't a harbor closer than that?"

"There are hundreds of closer harbors," Cochrane said blithely, "thousands of harbors. Millions! There are some of the best natural harbors in the world on this coast, Sharpe, and they're all closer than Valdivia. The damned coast is thick with harbors. There are more harbors here than a man could wish for in a thousand storms! Isn't that so, Fraser?"

"Aye, it is, my Lord."

"Then why go to an enemy harbor?" Sharpe asked.

"To capture it, of course, why else?" Cochrane looked at Sharpe as though the Rifleman was mad. "We've got a ship, we've got men, we've got weapons, so what the hell else should we be doing?"

"But the ship's sinking!"

"Then the bloody ship might as well do something useful before it vanishes." Cochrane, delighted with having surprised Sharpe, whooped with laughter. "Enjoy yourself, Sharpe. If we take Valdivia, all Chile is ours! We're launched for death or victory, we're sailing for glory, and may the Devil take the hindmost!" He rattled off the old clichés of the French wars in a mocking tone, but there was a genuine enthusiasm on his face as he spoke. Here was a man, Sharpe thought, who had never tired of battle, but reveled in it, and perhaps only felt truly alive when the powder was stinking and the swords were clashing. "We're sailing for glory!"

Cochrane whooped again, and Sharpe knew he was under the command of a genial maniac who planned to capture a whole country with nothing but a broken ship and a wounded crew.

Sharpe had met Spain's devil, and his name was Cochrane.

The wind rose the next day. It shrieked in the broken rigging so that the torn shrouds and halyards streamed horizontally ahead of the laboring frigate as she thumped in slow agony through the big green seas. Both rebel and royalist seamen manned the pumps continually, and even the officers took their turns at the blistering handles. Sharpe and Harper, restored to grace as passengers, nevertheless worked the sodden handles for three muscle-torturing hours during the night. Besides the women and children, only Cochrane and Captain Ardiles were spared the agony of the endless pumps. Ardiles, suffering the pangs of defeat, had closeted himself in his old cabin which Cochrane, with a generosity that seemed typical of the man, had surrendered to his beaten opponent.

In the gray morning, when the wind was whistling to blow the wavetops ragged, Lord Cochrane edged the broken frigate nearer to land so that, at times, a dark sliver on the eastern horizon betrayed high ground. He had not wanted to close the coast, for fear that the captured *Espiritu Santo* might be seen by a Spanish pinnace or fishing boat that could warn Valdivia of his approach, but now he sacrificed that caution for the security of land. "If worse comes to worst," he explained, "then perhaps we might be able to beach this wreck in the channels. Though God knows if we'd survive them."

"Channels?" Sharpe asked.

Cochrane showed Sharpe a chart which revealed that the
Chilean coast, so far as it was known, was a nightmare tangle
of islands and hidden seaways. "There are thousands of natural harbors if you can get into the channels," Cochrane
explained, "but the channel entrances are as wicked as any
in the world. As dreadful as the western coast of Scotland!
There are cliffs on this coast that are as tall as mountains!
And God only knows what's waiting inside the channels. This
is unexplored country. The old maps said that monsters lived
here, and maybe they do, for no one's ever explored this
coast. Except the savages, of course, and they don't count.
Still, maybe the *O'Higgins* will find us first."

"Is she close?"

"Christ only knows where she is, though she's supposed to
rendezvous with us off Valdivia. I've left a good man in
charge of her, so perhaps he'll have the wits to come south
and look for us if we're late, and if he does, and finds us
sinking, then he can take us off." He stared bleakly at the
chart which he had draped over the *Espiritu Santo*'s shot-
torn binnacle. "It's a devil of a long way to Valdivia," he said
under his breath.

Sharpe heard a sigh of despair in Cochrane's voice.
"You're not serious about Valdivia, are you?" Sharpe asked.

"Of course I am."

"You're going to attack with this broken ship?"

"This and the *O'Higgins*."

"For God's sake," Sharpe protested, "Valdivia Harbor has
more fortresses than London!"

"Aye, I know. Fort Ingles, Fort San Carlos, Fort Amargos,
Corral Castle, Fort Chorocomayo, Fort Niebla, the Manzanera Island batteries and the quay guns," Cochrane rattled off
the list of fortifications with an irritating insouciance, as
though such defenses were flimsy obstacles that were bound

to fall before his reputation. "Say two thousand defenders in all? Maybe more."

"Then why, for God's sake?" Sharpe gestured at the exhausted men who stared dull-eyed at the threatening seas that roared up astern of the damaged frigate, hissed down her flanks, then rushed ahead in great gouts of wind-blown chaos.

"I have to attack Valdivia, Sharpe, because my lords and masters of the independent Chilean government, whom God preserve, have ordered me to attack Valdivia." Cochrane suddenly sounded glum, but offered Sharpe a rueful grin. "I know that doesn't make sense, at least not till you understand that the government owes me a pile of money that they desperately don't want to pay me."

"That still doesn't make sense," Sharpe said.

"Ah," Cochrane frowned. "Try it this way. The government promised me hard cash for every Spanish ship I captured, and I've taken sixteen so far, and the buggers don't want to honor the contract! They don't even want to pay my crews their ordinary wages, let alone the prize money. So instead of paying up they've ordered me to attack Valdivia. Now do you understand?"

"They want you to be killed?" Sharpe could only suppose that with Cochrane's death the debt due to him would be canceled.

"They probably wouldn't overmuch object to my death," Cochrane confessed, "except that it might encourage the damned Spaniards, so I suspect that the reasoning behind their order is slightly more subtle. They don't want to pay me, so they have issued me an impossible order. Now, if I refuse to obey the order they'll send me packing for disobedience, and refuse to give me my cash as a punishment for that disobedience, but if, on the other hand, I dutifully attack and fail, they'll accuse me of incompetence and punish me by confiscating the money they owe me. Either way they win and I am royally buggered. Unless, of course," Cochrane paused, and an impudent, wonderful grin crossed his face.

"Unless you win," Sharpe continued the thought.

"Oh, aye, that's the joy of it!" Cochrane slapped the rail of the quarterdeck. "My God, Sharpe, but that would be something! To win!" He paused, frowning. "Why was there no gold on this boat?"

"Because its presence was merely a rumor to lure you into making an attack."

"It damn well worked, too!" Cochrane barked with laughter. "But think of it, Sharpe! If the gold isn't here, then it has to be in Valdivia! Bautista's as greedy as any Presbyterian! He's been thieving for years, and now he's Captain-General there's been nothing to stop his mischief. Imagine it, Sharpe! The man has chests of money! Pots of gold! Rooms full of silver! Not a piddling little pile of coins, but enough treasure to make a man drool!" Cochrane laughed in relish of such plunder, and Sharpe saw in the Scottish nobleman a wonderful relic of an older, more glorious and more sordid age. Cochrane was a fighting sailor of the Elizabethan breed—a Drake or a Raleigh or a Hawkins—and he would fight like the devil the Spanish thought he was for gold, glory or just plain excitement.

"No wonder they turfed you out of Parliament," Sharpe said.

Cochrane bowed, acknowledging the compliment, but then qualified his acknowledgment. "I went into the Commons to achieve something, and it was a cruel shame I failed."

"What did you want to achieve?"

"Liberty, of course!" The answer was swift, but followed immediately by a deprecating smile. "Except I've learned there's no such thing."

"There isn't?"

"You can't have freedom and lawyers, Sharpe, and I've discovered that lawyers are as ubiquitous to human society as rats are to a ship." Cochrane paused as the frigate thumped her bluff bows into a wave trough. The ship seemed to take a long time to recover from the downward plunge, but gradually, painfully, the bows rose again. "You build a new ship," Cochrane went on, "you smoke out its bilges, you put rat poison down, you know the ship's clean when you launch it, but your first night out you hear the scratch of claws and you know the little bastards are there! And short of sinking the ship they'll stay there forever." He scowled savagely. "That's why I came out here. I dreamed it would be possible to make a new country that was truly free, a country without lawyers, and look what happened! We captured the capital, we drove the Spaniards to Valdivia, and is Santiago filled with happy people celebrating their liberty? No. It's filled with Goddamned lawyers making new laws."

"Bad laws?" Sharpe asked.

"What the hell do they care? It doesn't worry a rat if a law is good or bad. All they care is that they can make money enforcing it. That's what lawyers do. They make laws that no one wants, then make money disagreeing with each other what the damned law means, and the more they disagree the more money they make, but still they go on making laws, and they make them ever more complicated so that they can get paid for arguing ever more intricately with one another! I grant you they're clever buggers, but God, how I hate lawyers." Cochrane shouted the despairing cry to the cold, ship-breaking wind.

"In all history," he went on, "can you name one great deed or one noble achievement ever done by a lawyer? Can you think of any single thing that any lawyer has ever done to increase human happiness by so much as a smile? Can you think of even one lawyer who could stand with the heroes? Who could stand with the great and the daring and the saintly and the imaginative and the wondrous and the good? Of course not! Can a rat fly with eagles?" Cochrane had talked himself into a bitter mood. "It's the lawyers, of course, who refuse to honor the contract the government made with me. It's the lawyers who ordered me to capture Valdivia, knowing full well that it can't be done. But that doesn't mean we shouldn't try." He paused again, and looked down at the chart. "Except I doubt this broken ship will ever sail as far as Valdivia. Perhaps I'll have to console myself by capturing Puerto Crucero instead."

Sharpe felt his heart give a small leap of hope. "That's where I want to go," he said.

"Why in God's name would you want to go to a shit-stinking hole like Puerto Crucero?" Cochrane asked.

"Because Blas Vivar is buried there," Sharpe said.

Cochrane stared at Sharpe with a sudden and astonishing incredulity. "He's what?"

"Blas Vivar is buried in the garrison church at Puerto Crucero."

Cochrane seemed flabbergasted. He opened his mouth to speak, but for once could find nothing to say.

"I've seen his grave," Sharpe explained. "That's why I was in Chile, you see."

"You crossed the world to see a grave?"

"I was a friend of Vivar. And we came here to take his body home to Spain."

"Good God Almighty," Cochrane said, then turned to look up at the foremast where a group of his men were retrieving the halyards that had been severed when the mainmast fell. "Oh, well," he said in a suddenly uninterested voice, "I suppose they had to bury the poor fellow somewhere."

It was Sharpe's turn to be puzzled. Cochrane's first reaction to Don Blas's burial had been an intrigued astonishment, but now His Lordship was feigning an utter carelessness. And suddenly, standing on the same quarterdeck where Captain Ardiles had told him the story, Sharpe remembered how Blas Vivar had been carried north in the *Espiritu Santo* for a secret rendezvous with Lord Cochrane. It was a story that had seemed utterly fantastic when Sharpe had first heard it, but that now seemed to make more sense. "I was told that Don Blas once tried to meet you, but was prevented by bad weather. Is that true?" he asked Cochrane.

Cochrane paused for an instant, then shook his head. "It's nonsense. Why would a man like Vivar want to meet me?"

Sharpe persisted, despite His Lordship's glib denial. "Ardiles told me this ship carried Vivar north, but that a storm kept him from the rendezvous."

Cochrane scorned the tale with a hoot of laughter. "You've been at the wine, Sharpe. Why the hell would Vivar want to meet me? He was the only decent soldier Madrid ever sent here, and he didn't want to talk to the likes of me, he wanted to kill me! Good God, man, we were enemies! Would Wellington have hobnobbed with Napoleon? Does a hound bark with the fox?" Cochrane paused as the frigate wallowed in a trough between two huge waves, then held his breath as she labored up the slope to where the wind was blowing the crest wild. The pumps clattered below decks to spurt their feeble jets of splashing water overboard. "You said you were a friend of Blas Vivar?" Cochrane asked when he was sure that the frigate had endured.

"It was a long time ago." Sharpe said. "We met during the Corunna campaign."

"Did you now?" Cochrane responded blithely, as though he did not really care one way or another how Sharpe and Vivar had met, yet despite the assumed carelessness Sharpe detected something strangely alert in the tall, red-haired

man's demeanor. "I heard something very odd about Vivar,"
Cochrane went on, though with a studied tone of indiffer-
ence, "something about his having an elder brother who
fought for the French?"

"He did, yes." Sharpe wondered from where Cochrane
had dragged up that ancient story, a story so old that Sharpe
himself had half forgotten about it. "The brother was a passionate supporter of Napoleon, so naturally wanted a French
victory in Spain. Don Blas killed him."

"And the brother had the same name as Don Blas?" Cochrane asked with an interest which, however he tried to disguise it, struck Sharpe as increasingly acute.

"I can't remember what the brother was called," Sharpe
said, then he realized exactly how such a confusion might
have arisen. "Don Blas inherited his brother's title, so in that
sense they shared the same name, yes."

"The brother was the Count of Mouromorto?" Cochrane
asked eagerly.

"Yes."

"And the brother had no children?" Cochrane continued
the explanation, "So Blas Vivar inherited the title. Is that how
it happened?"

Sharpe nodded. "Exactly."

"Ah!" Cochrane said, as though something which had
been puzzling him for a long time abruptly made good sense,
but then he deliberately tried to pretend that the new sense
did not matter by dismissing it with a flippant comment. "It's
a rum world, eh?"

"Is it?" Sharpe asked, but Cochrane had abruptly lost
interest in the coincidence of Blas Vivar and his brother sharing a title and had started to pace his quarterdeck. He
touched his hat to one of the two Spanish wives. The other,
who had abruptly been translated into a widow the previous
day, was in her cabin where her maid was trying to staunch

her mistress's grief with unripe Chilean wine while her husband, a waxed thread stitched through his nose, was moldering at the Pacific's bottom.

Cochrane suddenly stopped his pacing and turned on Sharpe. "Did you sail in this ship from Valdivia?"

"No, from Puerto Crucero."

"So how did you get from Valdivia to Puerto Crucero? By road?"

Sharpe nodded. "Yes."

"Aha!" Cochrane's enthusiasm was back. "Is it a road on which troops can march?"

"They can march," Sharpe said dubiously, "but they'll never drag cannons all that way, and two companies of infantry could hold an army at bay for a week."

"You think so, do you?" Cochrane's enthusiasm faded as quickly as it had erupted. Cochrane had clearly been fantasizing about a land attack on Valdivia, but such an attack would be an impossibility without a corps of good infantry and several batteries of artillery, and even then Sharpe would not have wagered on its success. Siege warfare was the cruelest variety of battle, and the most deadly for the attacker.

"Surely," Sharpe said, "O'Higgins can't blame you if you fail to capture Valdivia?"

"Bernardo knows which way his breeches button," Cochrane allowed, "but you have to understand that he's been seduced by the vision of becoming a respectable, responsible, sensible, reliable, boring, dull and pious national leader. By which I mean that he listens to the bloody lawyers! They've told him he mustn't risk his own reputation by attacking Valdivia, and persuaded him that it's better for me to do the dirty work. Naturally they haven't given me any extra soldiers, because I just might succeed if they had. I'm just supposed to work a miracle!" He glowered unhappily, then folded up the chart. "No doubt we'll all be at the sea's bottom before the week's out," he said gloomily. "Valdivia or Puerto Crucero? We probably won't reach either."

The frigate creaked and rolled, and the pumps spewed their feeble splashes of water over the side. The motion of the stricken *Espiritu Santo* seemed ever more sluggish and ever more threatening. Sharpe, glancing up at the skies which glowered with clouds run ragged by the endless wind, sensed the hopelessness of the struggle, but even when there was no hope, men had to keep on fighting.

And so they did, northward, toward the great citadels of Spain.

They pumped. By God, how they pumped. The leather pump hoses, snaking down into the *Espiritu Santo*'s bilges, thrashed and spurted with the efforts of the men on the big oak handles. A man's spell at the handles was cut to just fifteen minutes, not because that was the extent of anyone's endurance, but rather because that was as long as any man could pump at full exertion, and if the pumps slackened by so much as an ounce a minute Cochrane swore the ship would be lost. Cochrane took turns himself now. He stripped to his waist and attacked the pump as though it was a lawyer whose head he pounded in with the big handles. Up and down, grunting and snarling, and the water spilled and slurped feebly over the side and still the frigate seemed to settle lower in the water and wallow ever more sluggishly.

The carpenters sounded the bilges again and reported that the hull timbers had been rotten. The frigate had been the pride of the Spanish navy, yet some of her protective copper must have been lost at sea, and the teredoes and gribble worms had attacked her bottom starboard timbers. The wood had been turned into riddled pulp which, compressed by the explosion of the *Mary Starbuck*, had shattered into rotted fragments.

capture the far more formidable Corral Castle before they marched around the southern side of the harbor to lay siege to Fort Niebla.

Cochrane rejected Sharpe's halfhearted ideas. "Good God, man, but think of the time you're taking! An hour to land our men, that's if we can land them at all, which we can't if the surf's high, then another half hour to form up, and what are the Spaniards going to be doing? You think they'll sit waiting for us? Christ, no! They'll meet us on the beach with a Hail Mary of musket balls. We'll be lucky if ten men survive! No. We'll risk the gunfire, hoist the ensigns, and run straight for the defense's heart!"

"If we make a land attack at night," Sharpe persisted in his less risky plan, "then the Spanish will be confused."

"Have you ever tried landing men on an exposed beach at night?" Cochrane demanded. "We'll all be drowned! No, Sharpe! To the devil with caution. We'll go for their heart!" He spoke enthusiastically but detected that others besides Sharpe doubted that the thing could be done. "Don't you understand," Cochrane cried passionately, "that the only reason we'll succeed is because the Spanish know this can't be done? They know Valdivia is impregnable, so they don't expect anyone to be mad enough to attack. Our very chance of victory comes from their strength, because their strength is so great that they believe themselves to be unbeatable! And that belief is lulling them to sleep. Gentlemen! We shall lance their pride and bring their great forts down to dust!" He picked up one of the bottles of brandy and eased out its cork. "I give you Valdivia, gentlemen, and victory!"

Men raised the bottles and drank to the toast, but Sharpe, alone in the room, could not bring himself to respond to Cochrane's toast. He was thinking of three hundred men ranged against the greatest fortress complex on the Pacific coast. The result would be slaughter.

"There was a time" —Harper had seen Sharpe's reluctance and now spoke very softly— "when you would have done the impossible, because nothing else would have worked."

Sharpe heard the reproof, accepted it, and reached for a bottle. He pulled the cork and, like Harper, drank to the impossible victory. "Valdivia," he said, "and triumph."

Fraser, Cochrane's sailing master, opined that the repaired *Kitty* might stay afloat long enough to reach Valdivia, but he did not sound optimistic. "Not that it matters," the old Scotsman told Cochrane, "for you'll all be dead bones once the dagoes start their guns on you."

The two ships, both clumsily disguised as unloved transport hulks, had sailed four days after Cochrane's council of war. Cochrane had left just thirty men in Puerto Crucero, most of them walking wounded and barely sufficient to guard the prisoners and hold the fort against a possible Spanish patrol. Every other man sailed on board the *Kitty* and the *O'Higgins*. The two warships stood well out to sea, traveling far from land so that no stray Spanish vessel might spot them.

The *Kitty*'s pumps clattered ceaselessly. She was repaired, but the new wood in her hull had yet to swell and close her seams, and so, from the moment the frigate was refloated, the pumps had been manned. Despite her repairs she was proving a desperately slow ship. Some of the men in Cochrane's expedition had declared her an unlucky ship and had been reluctant to sail in her, a superstition that Cochrane had lanced by choosing to sail in the fragile *Kitty* himself. Sharpe and Harper also sailed on the erstwhile *Espiritu Santo*, while Miller and his marines were on the *O'Higgins*. "I'll salute as you sink," had been Miller's cheerful farewell to Sharpe.

"If we don't sink, we'll die under the guns," Fraser opined, and the nearer the two ships came to Valdivia, the gloomier the old man became, though his gloom was always shot through with an affectionate admiration for Cochrane. "If any man can do the impossible, it's Cochrane," Fraser told Sharpe and Harper. They were five nights out of Puerto Crucero, on the last night before they reached Valdivia, and the ships were sailing without lights, except for one shielded lantern that burned on the faster *O'Higgins*'s stern. If the *O'Higgins* looked like it was going too far ahead in the darkness, a signal gun would be fired from one of the *Kitty*'s two stern guns which were still the only heavy armament that the frigate possessed. "I was with Cochrane when he took the *Gamo*," Fraser, who was steering the *Kitty*, said proudly. "Did you ever hear how he did that?"

"No."

"It was in '01, off Barcelona. His Lordship had a brig, called the *Speedy*. The smallest seagoing thing in the Royal Navy, she was, with just fifty-two men aboard and fourteen guns—seven guns a side and none of them more than four-pounders—and the mad devil used her to capture the *Gamo*. She was a Spanish frigate of thirty-two guns and three hundred men. You'd have said it couldn't be done, but he did it. He disguised us with an American flag, ran in close under her side, then held her up against the frigate as he blasted his seven popguns up through her decks. He held her there for an hour and a half, then boarded her. She surrendered." Fraser shrugged. "The trouble with Cochrane is that every time he does something insane, he gets away with it. One day he'll lose, and that'll be the end of him. Mind you, whenever he tangles with the lawyers, he loses. His enemies accused him of defrauding the stock exchange, which he didn't do, but they hired the best lawyers in London and His Lordship was so sure of his own innocence that he didn't even bother to turn up in court, which made it much easier for the bastards to find him guilty and put him in prison."

"And they hurled me out of the most noble Order of the Bath." Cochrane himself, who had crept up behind them, intervened. "Do you know what they do when they expel a man from the Order of the Bath, Sharpe?"

"No, my Lord."

Cochrane, who clearly relished the story, chuckled. "The ceremony happens at dead of night in Westminster Abbey. In the chapel of Henry VII. It's dark. At first you hear nothing but the rustle of robes and the scratching of shoes. It sounds like a convocation of rats, but it's merely the lawyers and lords and pimps and bum-suckers gathering together. Then, on the stroke of midnight, they tear the disgraced man's banner from above the choir stalls, and afterward they take a nameless man, who stands in for the villain, and they strap a pair of spurs on his heels and then, with an axe, they chop the spurs off! At night! In the Abbey! And all the rats and pimps applaud as they kick the man and the spurs and the banner down the steps, and down the choir, and down the nave, and out into the darkness of Westminster." Cochrane laughed. "They did that to me! Can you believe it? We're in the nineteenth century, yet still the bastards are playing children's games at midnight. But one day, by Christ, I'll go back to England and I'll sail up the Thames and I'll make those bastards wish their mothers had never given birth. I'll hang those dry bastards from the roofbeams of the Abbey, then play pell-mell with their balls in the nave."

"They're lawyers, Cochrane," Fraser said sourly, "they don't have balls."

Cochrane chuckled, then cocked his face to the night. "The wind's piping up, Fraser. We'll have a blow before tomorrow night."

"Aye, we will."

"So do you still think we're doomed, Sharpe?" Cochrane demanded fiercely.

"I think, my Lord, that tomorrow we shall need a miracle."

"It'll be easy," Cochrane said dismissively. "We'll arrive an hour before nightfall, at the very moment when the garrisons will be wanting to go off duty and put their feet up. They'll think we're transports, they'll ignore us, and as soon as it's dark we'll be swarming up the ramparts of Fort Niebla. By this time tomorrow night, Sharpe, you and I will have our feet under the commandant's table, drinking his wine, eating his supper, and choosing between his whores. And the day after that we'll go downriver and take Valdivia. Two days, Sharpe, just two days, and all Chile is ours. We will have won."

It all sounded so easy. Two days, six forts, two hundred guns, two thousand men, and all Chile as the prize.

In the darkness a glimmer of light showed from the stern lantern of the *O'Higgins*. The sea hissed and roared, lifting the sluggish hull of the *Kitty*, then dropping her down into the cold heart of the wave troughs. Beyond the one small glimmer of light there was no other sign of life in all the universe, neither a star nor moon nor landward light. The ships were in an immensity of darkness, commanded by a devil, sailing under a night sky of thick cloud, and traveling toward death.

They sighted land an hour after dawn. By midday they could see the signal tower that stood atop Fort Chorocomayo, the highest stronghold in Valdivia's defenses. The signal tower held a vast semaphore mast that reported the presence of the two strange ships, then fell into stillness.

Three hours before sunset Sharpe could see the Spanish flag atop Fort Ingles and he could hear the surf crashing on the rocks beside the *Aguada del Ingles*. No ships had come from the harbor to enquire about their business. "You see," Cochrane crowed, "they're fools!"

Two hours later, in the light of the dying sun, the *O'Higgins* and the *Kitty* trimmed their sails as they turned east about the rocky peninsula that protected Valdivia's harbor. They had arrived at the killing place.

The great clouds had gone, torn ragged by a morning gale that had gentled throughout the day until, in this evening of battle, the wind blew steady and firm, but without malice. Yet the sea was still ferocious. The huge Pacific rollers, completing their great journey across an ocean, heaved the *Kitty* up and down in a giant swooping motion, while to Sharpe's right the great waves shattered in shredding explosions of foam off the black rocks. "You would not, I think, want to make a landing on the *Aguada del Ingles* in these conditions," Cochrane said as he searched the shore with his telescope. Suddenly he stiffened. "There!"

"My Lord?" Sharpe asked.

"See for yourself, Sharpe!"

Sharpe took the glass. Dim in the gauzy light and through the shredding plumes of foam that obscured the sea's edge like a fog he could just see the first of the harbor's forts. "That's Fort Ingles!" Cochrane said. "The beach is just below it."

Sharpe moved the glass down to where the massive waves thundered up the *Aguada del Ingles*. He edged the glass back to the fortress which looked much as he remembered it from his earlier visit—a makeshift defense work with an earthen ditch and bank, wooden palisades, and embrasures for cannon. "They're signaling us!" he said to Cochrane as a string of flags suddenly broke above the fort's silhouette.

"Reply, Mister Almante!" Cochrane snapped, and a Chilean midshipman ran a string of flags up to the *Kitty*'s mizzen yard. The flags that Cochrane was showing formed no coherent message, but were instead a nonsense combination. "In the first place," Cochrane explained, "the sun's behind us, so

they can't see the flags well, and even if they could see the
flags they'd assume we're using a new Spanish code which
hasn't reached them yet. It'll make the buggers nervous, and
that, after all, is a good way to begin a battle." At the *Kitty*'s
stern the Spanish ensign rippled in the wind, while below
her decks the pumps sucked and spat, sucked and spat.

The gaunt arms of the telegraph atop Fort Ingles began to
rise and fall. "They're telling the other forts where we are,"
Cochrane said. He glanced down at the waist of the ship
where a crowd of men lined the starboard gunwale. Cochrane had permitted such sight-seeing, reckoning that if the
Kitty were indeed a Spanish transport ship, the men would
be allowed on deck to catch this first glimpse of their new
station. Also on deck were four nine-pounder field guns that
had been manhandled on board from Puerto Crucero's citadel. The guns were not there for their firepower, but rather
to make it look as if the *Kitty* was indeed carrying artillery
from Spain. Cochrane, unable to hide his excitement, beat a
swift tattoo on the quarterdeck rail with his hands. "How
long?" he snapped to Fraser.

"We'll make the entrance in one more hour," Fraser spoke
from the helm. "And an hour after that we'll have moonlight."

"The tide?" Cochrane asked.

"We're on the flood, my Lord, otherwise we'd never make
her past the harbor entrance. Say two and a half hours?"

"Two and a half hours to what?" Sharpe asked.

"One hour to clear the point," Cochrane explained, "and
another hour to work our way south across the harbor, then
half an hour to beat in against the river's current. It'll be dark
when we reach Fort Niebla, so I'll have to use a lantern to
illuminate our ensign. A night attack, eh!" He rubbed his big
hands in anticipation. "Ladders by moonlight! It sounds like
an elopement!" Below the *Kitty*'s decks were a score of

newly made ladders which would be taken ashore and used to assault Niebla's walls.

"There's a new signal, my Lord!" The midshipman called aloud in English, the language commonly used on the quarterdeck of Cochrane's ship.

"In Spanish from now on, Mister Almante, in Spanish!" If the Spaniards did send a guard ship then Cochrane wanted no one using English by mistake. "Reply with a signal that urgently requests a whore for the Captain," Cochrane gave the order in his execrable Spanish, "then draw attention to the signal with a gun."

The grinning Midshipman Almante began plucking signal flags from the locker. The new message, gaudily spelled out in a string of fluttering flags, ran quickly to the *Kitty*'s mizzen yard and, just a second later, one of the stern guns crashed a blank charge to echo across the sea.

"We are spreading confusion!" Cochrane happily explained to Sharpe. "We're pretending to be annoyed because they're not responding to our signal!"

"Another shot, my Lord?" Midshipman Almante, who was not a day over thirteen, asked eagerly.

"We must not overegg the pudding, Mister Almante. Let the enemy worry for a few moments."

The smoke from the stern gun drifted across the wildly heaving swell. The two ships were close to land now, close enough for great drifting mats of rust-brown weed to be thick in the water. Gulls screamed about the rigging. Two horsemen suddenly appeared on the headland's skyline, evidently galloping to get a closer look at the two approaching boats.

"Nelson was always seasick until battle was imminent," Cochrane said suddenly.

"You knew Nelson?" Sharpe asked.

"I met him several times. In the Mediterranean." Cochrane paused to train his telescope on the two riders. "They're worried about us, but they can't be seeing much. The sun's almost dead behind us. A strange little man."

"Nelson?"

"'Go for them,' he told me, 'just go for them! Damn the niceties, Cochrane, just go and fight!' And he was right! It always works. Oh, damn." The curse, spoken mildly, was provoked by the appearance of a small boat that was sailing out of the harbor and was clearly intending to intercept the *Kitty* and *O'Higgins*. Cochrane had half-expected such a guard boat, but plainly his disguise would have been easier to preserve if none had been despatched. "They are nervous, aren't they," he said to no one in particular, then walked to the quarterdeck's rail and picked up a speaking trumpet. "No one is to speak in any language but Spanish. You will not shout a greeting to the guard boat. You may wave at them, but that is all!" He turned sharply. "Spanish naval dress, gentlemen!"

Blue coats, cocked hats and long swords were fetched up from Cochrane's cabin and issued to every man on the quarterdeck. Harper, pleased to have a coat with epaulettes, strutted up and down. Fraser, dwarfed by his naval coat, scowled at the helm while Cochrane, his cocked hat looking oddly piratical, lit a cigar and pretended to feel no qualms about the imminent confrontation. The third Lieutenant, a man called Cabral who, though a fierce Chilean patriot, had been born in Spain, was deputed to be the *Kitty*'s spokesman. "Though remember, Lieutenant," Cochrane admonished him, "we're called the *Niño*, and the *O'Higgins* is now the *Cristoforo*." Cochrane glowered at the approaching boat which, under a bellying red sail, contained a dozen uniformed men. "We'll all be buggered," he muttered to Sharpe in his first betrayal of nerves, "if those two transport ships arrived last week."

The guard boat hove to under the *Kitty*'s quarter, presumably because she was the ship showing the signal flags, and was therefore deemed to be the ship in command of the small convoy. A man with a speaking trumpet demanded to know the *Kitty*'s identity.

"We're the *Niño* and *Cristoforo* out of Cadiz!" Cabral called back. "We're bringing Colonel Ruiz's guns and men."

"Where's your escort?"

"What escort?" Cochrane asked under his breath, then, almost at once, he hissed an answer to Cabral. "Parted company off Cape Horn."

"We lost them off Cape Horn!"

"What ship was escorting you?"

"Christ Almighty!" Cochrane blasphemed. "The *San Isidro*." He plucked the name at random.

"The *San Isidro, señor*," Cabral obediently parroted the answer.

"Did you meet the *Espiritu Santo?*" The guard boat asked.

"No!"

The interrogating officer, a black-bearded man in a naval Captain's uniform, stared at the sullen faces that lined the *Niño*'s rails. The man was clearly unhappy, but also nervous. "I'm coming aboard!" he shouted.

"We've got sickness!" Cabral, prepared for the demand, had his answer ready and, as if on cue, Midshipman Almante hoisted the yellow fever flag.

"Then you're ordered to anchor off the harbor entrance!" the bearded man shouted up. "We'll send doctors to you in the morning! You understand?"

"Tell them we don't trust the holding here, we want to anchor inside the harbor!" Cochrane hissed.

Cabral repeated the demand, but the bearded man shook his head. "You've got your orders! The holding's good enough for this wind. Anchor a half mile off the beach, use two anchors on fifteen fathoms of chain apiece, and sleep well! We'll have doctors on board at first light!" He signaled to his helmsman who bore away from the *Kitty*'s side and turned toward the harbor.

"Goddamn it!" Cochrane said.

"Why don't you just ignore the bugger?" Sharpe asked.

"Because if we try to run the entrance without permission they'll open fire."

"So we wait for dark?" Sharpe, who until now had been dead set against any such attack, was now the one trying to force Cochrane past the obstacle.

"There'll be a gibbous moon," Fraser said pessimistically, "and that will serve as well as broad sunlight to light their gunners' aim."

"Damn, damn, damn." Cochrane, usually so voluble, was suddenly enervated. He stared at the retreating guard boat and seemed bereft of ideas. Fraser and the other officers waited for his orders, but Cochrane had none to give. Sharpe felt a sudden pang of sympathy for the tall Scotsman. All plans were nothing but predictions, and like all predictions they were likely to be transformed by their first collision with reality, but the art of war was to prepare for such collisions and have a second or a third or a fourth option ready. Cochrane suddenly had no such options on hand. He had pinned his hopes on the Spanish supinely accepting his ruse, then feebly collapsing before his attack. Was this how Napoleon had been on the day of Waterloo? Sharpe wondered. He watched Cochrane and saw a man in emptiness, a clever man drained of invention who seemed helpless to stop the tide of disaster flooding across him.

"We've two hours of fair water, my Lord." Fraser, recognizing the moment of crisis, had adopted a respectful formality.

Cochrane did not respond. He was staring toward the harbor entrance. Was he thinking of making a dash for it? But how could two slow ships dash? Their speed, even with the tide's help, was scarcely above that of a man walking.

"We'll not get through, my Lord." Fraser, reading His Lordship's mind, growled the warning.

"No," Cochrane said, but said nothing more.

Fraser shot a beseeching look at Sharpe. Sharpe, more than any other man in the expedition, had counseled against this attack, and now, Fraser's look seemed to be saying, was the time for Sharpe to urge withdrawal. There was just one chance of avoiding disaster, and that was for the two ships to turn and slip away southward.

Sharpe said nothing.

Fraser, desperate to end the indecision, challenged Sharpe directly. "So what would you do, Sharpe?"

Cochrane frowned at Sharpe, but did not countermand Fraser's invitation.

"Well?" Fraser insisted. The ship was still creeping toward the harbor mouth. In another half mile she would open the entrance and be under the guns of Fort San Carlos.

Cochrane was a devil, Sharpe thought, and suddenly he felt a smaller imp rise in himself. Goddamn it, but a man did not come this far just to be challenged by a toy boat and then turn back! "If we anchor off the beach," Sharpe said, "they'll think we're obeying their orders. We wait till it's dark, then we send a boat or two ashore. We can say we're looking for fresh water if anyone questions us. Then we'll attack the nearest fort. We may only capture a few kegs of powder, but at least we'll have let the bastards know that we're still dangerous."

"Magnificent!" shouted Cochrane, released from his torpor. He slapped Sharpe's back. "Goddamn it, man, but magnificent! I like it! Mister Almante! A signal to the *O'Higgins*, if you please, ordering them to ready anchors!" Cochrane was suddenly seething with energy and enthusiasm. "But bugger snatching a few kegs of powder! Let's go for the whole pot! We'll capture the western forts, then use their guns to bombard Niebla while our ships work their way inside. That'll be at dawn, Mister Fraser, so perhaps you will work out the time of the morning's flood tide for me? I don't know why I didn't think to do it this way from the very start! Mister Cabral? Order a meal served below decks. Tell the men they've got two hours rest before we begin landing troops."

"Now you've done it," Fraser grumbled to Sharpe.

"You spoke, Mister Fraser?" Cochrane demanded.

"Nothing, my Lord."

"As soon as we're at anchor," Cochrane went on, "you'll lower boats, but do it on the side facing away from the land! We don't want the enemy to see we're launching boats, do we?"

"A hole in each end, my Lord?" Fraser asked.

"Then suck the damned egg dry!" Cochrane, knowing he had given Fraser an unnecessary order, gave a brief guffaw of laughter.

Behind the *Kitty* the sky was a glorious blaze of gold touched scarlet, in which a few ragged clouds floated silver gray. The sea had turned molten, slashed with shivering bands of black. The great Spanish ensign, given an even richer color by the sun's flaming gold, slapped and floated in the fitful wind.

The two ships crept toward the shore. Sharpe could hear the breakers now and see where they foamed white as they hissed and roared toward the sand. Then, just when it seemed that the *Kitty* must inevitably be caught up in that rush of foam and be swept inexorably to her doom, Fraser ordered both anchors let go. A seaman swung a sledgeham-mer, knocking a peg loose from the cathead, and the starboard anchor crashed down through the golden sea. The port anchor followed a second after, the twin chains rattling loud in the dusk. Then, with a jerk, the *Kitty* rounded up and lay with her bows pointing toward the setting sun and her stern toward the mainland. The headland, on which Fort Ingles stood, was now on her port side.

The *O'Higgins* anchored a hundred yards further out. Both ships jerked and snubbed angrily, but Fraser reported that the anchors were holding. "Not that it will help us," he added to Sharpe, "for the boats will never land on that beach." He jerked an unshaven chin toward the *Aguada del Ingles* where, in the last slanting light, the foam was shredding spray like smoke. Cochrane might believe a landing to be possible, but Sharpe suspected that Fraser was right and that any boat that tried to land through that boiling surf would be swamped.

Cochrane stared up to where his topmen were efficiently gathering in the *Kitty*'s sails. "The wind's backing, Fraser?"

"Aye, my Lord, it is."

Cochrane fidgeted a second. "We might leave the spanker rigged for mending, Mr. Fraser. It will hide your boats as they're launched."

Fraser did not like the idea. "The wind could veer, my Lord."

"Let's do it! Hurry now!"

The orders were given. Fraser offered Sharpe an explanation. The wind, he said, had been southerly all day, but had now gone into the west. By leaving the aftermost sail half hoisted he turned the ship into a giant weather vane. The wind would then keep the ship parallel to the beach, leaving the starboard side safely hidden from the fort. Cochrane could then launch his boats in the last of the daylight, safe from enemy gaze.

"Why not rig the sail full?" Sharpe asked. The sail was only half raised.

"Because that would look unnatural when you're at anchor. But half rig is how you'd hoist her for mending, and a half-collapsed sail hides the far side of the quarterdeck a deal better than a fully hoisted sail. Not that I suppose anyone up there understands seamanship."

Fraser had jerked a derisive thumb toward Fort Ingles above the beach. From Sharpe's position on the quarterdeck, the fort's ramparts formed the skyline, clearly showing six embrasures in its grim silhouette. The guns were less than a half mile from the *Kitty*. If the Spanish did suddenly discover that the two anchored ships were hostile, the guns would wreak havoc in the crowded lower decks. Sharpe shuddered and turned away. Harper, seeing the shudder, surreptitiously crossed himself.

The sun was now a bloated ball of fire on the horizon. Ashore the shadows were lengthening and coalescing into a gray darkness. On the *Kitty*'s quarterdeck, behind the concealing folds of heavy canvas, the ship's four longboats and two jolly boats were being lowered overboard. The Captain's barge was the last boat to be launched. Each boat held a single seaman whose job was to keep his craft from being crushed as the frigate heaved up and down on the swells. "Another hour," Cochrane spoke to Sharpe and Harper, "and it'll be dark enough to land troops. Why don't you get something to eat?"

Harper brightened at the thought and went below to the gundeck where the cooks were serving a stew of goat meat to the waiting men. Sharpe wanted to stay on deck. "Bring me something," he asked as Harper swung off the quarterdeck.

Sharpe, left alone, leaned on the rail and gazed at the fort. A sudden gust of wind came off the land, ruffling the sea and forcing Sharpe to snatch at his old-fashioned tricorne hat. The wind gust billowed the loosely rigged spanker, driving the canvas across the deck and occasioning a shout of alarm from Lieutenant Cabral who was almost thrown overboard by the gusting sail. "Stow that sail now!" Fraser ordered. The longboats were safely overboard and the spanker no longer hid any suspicious activity.

A dozen topmen scrambled up the ratlines and edged out on the mizzen yard to haul in the spanker. The wind was still pushing the sail, driving the stern of the *Kitty* away from the beach.

The wind gusted again, sighing in the rigging and making the boat lean seaward. Some of the men in the longboats feared being trapped under the hull and pushed off from the threatening *Kitty* with their long oars. The boats were all tethered to the frigate with lines, but now, as the heavy warship with its clanking pumps continued to blow toward them, the boat-minders pushed themselves as far from her tarred hull as their tethers would allow.

The *Kitty* kept turning so that her bows were pointing almost directly at Fort Ingles. Fraser knew that the fort's garrison must be able to see the longboats and even the dullest Spanish officer would realize what such a sight portended. Innocent ships waiting for medical attention did not launch a fleet of longboats. "Close up, damn you, close up!" Fraser shouted at the boat-minders. The topmen had furled the sail and the *Kitty* was swinging back again.

Cochrane came running up from his cabin where he had been eating an early supper. "What the hell is happening?"

"Wind veered." Fraser decently did not add that he had warned of just such a danger. "It drove us around."

"Sweet Jesus!" Cochrane, a leg of chicken in his hand, stared at the fort. The longboats were hidden again. "Did they see?" He asked the question of no one, merely articulating a worry.

The fort's silhouette betrayed nothing. No one moved there, no one waved from the ramparts. The gaunt semaphore gallows stayed unmoving.

Cochrane bit into the chicken. "They're asleep."

"Thank God for that," Fraser said.

"Thank God indeed," Cochrane said fervently, for the only thing that had kept the *Kitty* safe from a murderous bombardment was the Spaniards' inattention. Cochrane bit the last meat off the chicken leg. "No harm done, eh? The silly buggers are all dozing!" He hurled the chicken bone toward the high fortress as a derisory gesture.

And the fortress replied.

For the sentries on the ramparts of Fort Ingles had seen the longboats after all. The garrison had not been dozing, and now the gunners opened fire. Sharpe saw the smoke, heard the scream of a cannonball, then felt the shuddering crashes as the first two shots slammed into the *Kitty*'s weakened hull.

The Spaniards had been ready, and Cochrane's men were trapped.

S creams sounded from the gundeck. The Spanish shots had hit with a wicked exactness, slicing through the *Kitty*'s disguised gunports and into the crowded deck where Cochrane's assault force had been snatching its hasty meal.

Two more guns fired. One cannonball smacked into the sea, then bounced up into the frigate. The other slammed into the hull, lodging in a main timber.

"The boats! Into the boats!" Cochrane was shouting. "Assault force! Into the boats!" The sun was a flattened bar of melting light on the horizon, the moon a pale semicircle in the cloud-ridden sky above. Powder smoke drifted from the fort with the land wind. A signal rocket suddenly flared up from the fort's ramparts, its feather of flame shivering up into the darkling sky before a white light burst to drown the first pale stars.

"Into the boats! We're going to attack! Into the boats!"

More shots, more screams. Sharpe leapt off the quarterdeck just as a cannonball screeched across the poopdeck, gouging a splintered trench in the scrubbed wood. He twisted aside from the roundshot's impact, scrambled for the officers' companionway where, disdaining to use the ladder with its rope handles, he slithered down to the gundeck. "Patrick! Patrick!"

It was dark below. The lanterns had been extinguished as soon as the first shots struck the *Kitty* and the only illumination was the day's dying light that seeped into the carnage through the ragged holes ripped by the incoming roundshot. Those roundshot had ripped across the deck, flinging men aside like bloody rags. The wounded screamed, while the living trampled over the bodies in their desperate attempts to reach the open air.

"Patrick!"

Another roundshot banged into the deck. It cannoned off a ship's timber to slash slantwise through the struggling men. Splinters felled three men close to where the shot struck, while the shot itself sliced down a half dozen more. A spray of blood drops fogged the light for a foul instance, then the screams sounded terribly. Another ball cracked into the tier below. The pumps had stopped, and Sharpe could hear the gurgle of water slopping into the bilges. "Patrick!"

"I'm here!" the voice shouted from the deck's far end.

"I'll see you ashore!" There was no chance of struggling through the demented pack of panicking men. Harper and Sharpe must get themselves ashore as best they could and hope that in the sudden chaos they would meet on land.

Sharpe turned and hauled himself up to the poopdeck. Men were scrambling down the starboard side into the longboats. The O'Higgins was returning the fort's fire, but Sharpe could see the warship's roundshot were falling short. Gouts of black earth were erupting from the slope in front of Fort Ingles, and though some of the balls were ricocheting up toward the defenders, Sharpe doubted that the naval gunnery was doing the slightest good. The O'Higgins herself was wreathed in cannon smoke so that, in the day's death light, she looked like a set of black spidery masts protruding from a yellow-white, red-tinged bank of churning smoke. The fort had turned two guns on the O'Higgins. A great splash of water showed where a shot fell short inside the bank of smoke, then Sharpe was at the rail, a rope was in his hands and he shimmied desperately down to a longboat already crammed with sailors. The sailors had cutlasses, muskets, swords, pikes and clubs. "Bastards," one man said again and again, as if, somehow, the Spanish defenders had broken a rule of war by opening fire on the two anchored ships.

"Fast as you can! Fast as you can!" Cochrane was in another longboat and shouting at his oarsmen to make the journey to land as swiftly as possible. For the moment, shielded by the great bulk of the *Kitty,* the longboats were safe from the fort's gunfire, but the moment they appeared on the open sea the cannon would surely change their aim.

"Let go!" yelled Lieutenant Cabral, who had taken charge of Sharpe's boat. "Row!" The oarsmen strained at the long oars. Sharpe could see Harper in another boat. A cannonball whipped overhead, making a sizzling noise as it slanted down to slam into a green wave.

"Row!" Cabral shouted, and the longboat shot out from behind the *Kitty*'s protection. The coxswain turned the rudder so the boat was aimed for the shore. "Row!" Cabral screamed again, and the men bent the long oar shafts in their desperate urgency to close on the beach. A roundshot slapped the sea ten yards to the left, bounced once, then hammered into the *Kitty*'s stern where it sprang a six-foot splinter of bright wood. Sharpe glanced back at the frigate to see a bloody body, dripping intestines, heaved out of a half-opened gunport. Gulls screamed and slashed down to feed. Then Sharpe looked back to the beach because a new sound had caught his ear.

Muskets.

The Spaniards had sent a company of infantry down to the beach where the blue-coated soldiers were now drawn up at the high-tide line. Sharpe saw the ramrods flicker, then the muskets came up into the company's shoulders, and he instinctively ducked. The splintering sound of the volley came clear above the greater sounds of guns and booming surf. Sharpe saw a spatter of small splashes on the face of a wave and knew that the volley had gone wide.

"Row!" Cabral shouted, but the port-side oars had become entangled in a mat of floating weed and the boat broached. Behind Sharpe the *O'Higgins* fired a broadside and one of the balls whipped through the Spanish company, slinging two men aside and fountaining blood and sand up from the beach behind the soldiers. Sharpe stood, his balance precarious as he aimed his pistol. He fired. Muskets flamed bright from the beach. He heard the whistle of a ball near his head as he sat down hard.

"Row, row, row!" Cabral, standing beside Sharpe in the stern sheets, shouted at his oarsmen. "Row!" The oars were free of the weed again. There were a dozen men rowing and a score of men crouching between the thwarts. The oarsmen, their backs to the land and the muskets and the surf and the cannon, had wide, frightened eyes. One man was gabbling a prayer as he tugged at his oar.

"Bayonets!" Sharpe shouted at the men crouched on the bottom boards. "Fix bayonets!" He said it again in Spanish and watched as a dozen men, those who had bayonets, twisted their blades onto their muskets. "When we land," he called to the crouching men, "we don't wait to give the bastards a volley, we just charge!"

Off to the left were a dozen other longboats. Some had come from the *O'Higgins* and were carrying marines. The attacking boats were scattered across the sea. Sharpe flinched as he saw a great gout of exploding water betray where a cannonball had slapped home beside one of the laboring longboats, and he was certain that the roundshot's strike had been close enough to swamp the fragile-looking boat, but when the spray fell away he saw the boat was still afloat and its oarsmen still rowing.

The Spanish infantrymen fired again, but just like the fort's gunners, their own powder smoke was now obscuring their aim. Nor were they being intelligently led, for their officer was just telling the men to fire at the boats. If they had concentrated their fire on one boat at a time they could have reduced each longboat into a screaming horror of blood and splinters, but instead their musketry was flying wild and wide. Yet the Spaniards held the advantage, for the longboats still had to negotiate the murderous tumbling of the breaking surf. If a boat broached in the breaking waves and spilled its cargo, the waiting infantrymen would be presented with a bout of twilight bayonet practice.

The sun was gone, but there was still light in the sky. Sharpe crouched in the stern sheets and made sure his borrowed sword was loose in its scabbard. A broadside from the *O'Higgins* crashed overhead, twitching a skein of powder smoke as it slammed above the Spanish infantry to shatter the further slope into gouts of soil and grass. A gull screeched in protest. Another signal rocket whooshed into the sky to splinter into a fountain of light. It was too dark to use the semaphore arms, so Fort Ingles's defenders were rousing Valdivia Harbor's garrisons with the bright rockets.

"Row!" Cabral shouted, and the oarsmen grunted as they laid their full weight into the oars, but another great mat of floating weed impeded the boat, slewing it round. A man in the bows leaned overboard and hacked at the weed with a cutlass. "Back your oars!" Cabral screamed, "Back!" A bullet smacked into the gunwale, while another shattered an oar blade. Cochrane was shouting off to Sharpe's left, screaming at his men to be the first ashore. Cabral beat at the side of the boat in his frustration. One of the oarsmen shouted that it was too dangerous, that they would all drown in the surf, and Cabral drew his sword and threatened to skewer the man's guts if he did not row, and row hard! Then the longboat was free of the clinging weed and the oars could pull again. One or two of the rowers looked nervous, but any thoughts of mutiny were quelled by the sight of Cabral's drawn sword. "Row!" he shouted and the crest of a wave lifted the boat, driving it fast, and one of the rowers jerked forward and collapsed, blood slopping out of his mouth.

"Overboard!" Cabral shouted. "Heave him over! Juan, take his place! Row!" They rowed. Another wave took them, hissing them forward, driving them up to its white crest, then the wave was past and they slid down into a scummy, weedy trough, and the oarsmen pulled again, and the sky echoed with the thunder of guns and the crackle of musketry and the beach was close now, close enough for Sharpe to hear the sucking roar as the waves slid back toward the foam, then another breaker plucked them, bubbled them about with surf and hurled them fast toward the beach, and suddenly Sharpe could see the whole expanse of sand and the dark, smoke-fogged shapes of the waiting Spaniards at the top of the beach, then those dark shapes blossomed with pink flames as the muskets flared, but the strike of the musket balls was drowned in the sound and fury of the shattering surf's maelstrom that was now all around the shivering boat. Cabral was screaming orders, and somehow the coxswain was holding the bow straight on to the beach as the oarsmen gave a last desperate pull and then the bow dropped, bounced on the sand and drove on up. Cabral shouted at the men to jump out and kill the bastard sons of poxed whores, yet still the longboat was sliding up the beach, driven by the wave, while ten yards to the left another boat had turned sideways and rolled so that the welter of white water was littered with men, weapons and oars. Cabral's boat jarred to a halt. Sharpe leaped off the gunwale and found himself up to his knees in freezing water and churning sand.

He drew the borrowed sword. "Charge!" He knew he

must not give these enemy infantrymen a chance. The Spaniards, if they did but know it, could have calmly shot each landing boat to hell, then advanced in good order with outstretched bayonets to finish off the poor wet devils at the sea's edge, but Sharpe guessed the infantrymen were scared witless. The devil Cochrane was coming from the sea to kill them, and now was the time to add blood to their fears. "Charge!" he shouted. His boots were full of water and heavy with sand. He floundered up the beach, screaming at the men to follow him.

The rest of Cochrane's assault force scrambled ashore. The boats landed within seconds of each other and the men shook themselves free of the sucking breakers to charge the enemy in the maddened rush of men who wanted to revenge themselves for the terrors of the recent moments. The last of the light gleamed dully on the steel of swords and cutlasses and bayonets and boarding pikes. One man carried a great axe that was designed to cut away the wreckage of fallen rigging, but which now, like some ancient Viking berserker, he whirled over his head as he ran toward the Spanish company.

The Spaniards, seeing Cochrane's devils erupt from the sea like avenging fiends, turned and fled. God, Sharpe thought, but this was how pirates had assaulted the Spanish dominions for centuries; desperate men, armed with steel and stripped of scruples, erupting from small ships to shatter the perilous crust of civilized discipline that Madrid had imposed on the new world's golden lands.

"Form here! Form here!" Cochrane, tall and huge in the dusk, stood at the edge of the sand dunes behind the beach. "Let them go! Let them go!" Sharpe would have kept pursuing the fleeing Spaniards, but Cochrane wanted to make order out of the chaos. "Form here! Major Miller! You'll make the left of the line if you please!" As if in answer, one of Miller's drummers gave a rattle, then a flute sounded feebly in the twilight.

Harper, safely ashore and carrying a cutlass, ran behind the attackers to join Sharpe. "This is a rare business, so it is!" But the big Irishman seemed pleased, as though all the uncertainties of the last few weeks had dropped away.

Cannons roared from the fortress above them. Sharpe saw the flames stab pale across the sandy slope, then writhe and shrivel away inside the smoke. The roundshot crashed past Cochrane's men to spew sand up from the beach. The abandoned longboats and their clumsy oars rolled and jerked at the surf's edge, while out to sea the skeleton crews left aboard the two warships had abandoned the boats' anchors and, with just their foresails set, were taking the two boats out of range of the fort's guns.

"Down!" Cochrane would shelter his men behind the dunes while he organized his assault. "Get down!" He paced along the front of his ragged attackers. "Did anyone bring ladders? Did anyone bring ladders?"

No one had brought ladders. Three hundred wet and frightened men clung to a beach beneath a fort and all they had to fight with were their hand weapons: muskets, pistols, swords, pikes and cutlasses.

"Did you bring a ladder?" Cochrane asked Sharpe.

"No."

Cochrane slashed his sword at the dune grass. "We're rather buggered. Damn!"

The gunfire from the fort changed sound. Instead of the short percussive crack that denoted roundshot, there was suddenly the more muffled sound betraying that the defenders were loaded with canister or grape. Now each of the fort's cannons was like a giant shotgun, spraying a lethal and expanding fan of musket balls toward the attackers. Cochrane, as the rain of shot whistled overhead, ducked down.

"Shit!" He peered over the sand dune. Even through the smoke, and in the last of the daylight, it was plain that the earthen and wooden facade of Fort Ingles could not be assaulted without ladders, and even with ladders it would be suicidal for men to rise and walk into that gale of grapeshot. "Shit!" Cochrane said again, even more angrily.

"They'll only have guns on this face of the fort!" Sharpe shouted.

Cochrane nodded confirmation. "Facing the sea, yes!"

"We'll flank them! Give me some men!"

"Take the starboard Kittys," Cochrane ordered. The 'Kittys' were the men from the *Kitty* who were divided into two companies, port and starboard.

"Keep them busy here!" Sharpe told Cochrane. "Fire at them, make a noise, let them see you here. And when I shout for you, charge like hell!"

Sharpe called for the starboard Kittys, then ran right, along the beach, under cover of the dunes. Fifty men followed him. Harper was there, Lieutenant Cabral was there. The rest of Cochrane's attackers fired a volley up toward the fort as Sharpe, safely out of the cannons' line of fire, turned uphill. The moon was bright on the sand, bleaching it to look like heaped snow. The sea was crashing loud behind.

"Jesus, we're mad," Harper said.

Sharpe saved his breath. The hillside was steep and the tough grass stems slippery. He was working his way to his right, trying to stay well out of sight of the fort's defenders. With any luck the Spaniards would be mesmerized by the shrieking crowd of men crammed with Cochrane on the beach. Why had the Spaniards not charged down with more infantry? That question made Sharpe wonder whether the signal rockets were intended to summon infantry from the other forts. Behind him the defenders' cannons crashed their loads of canister and the attackers' muskets crackled a feeble reply. More muskets fired from the fort and Sharpe tried to gauge how many infantrymen were defending its ramparts from the noise of those muskets. He reckoned two hundred men, say three thin companies? That was more than enough to finish Cochrane's two hundred fifty invaders, many of whom had damp powder and whose muskets were therefore useless for anything except clubbing men to death. One good bayonet charge by three companies of Spanish infantry would finish Cochrane. The whole affair could be over in fifteen minutes, and the Chilean rebels would be bereft of their Admiral, and probably of their navy. Valdivia would be safe, Cochrane could be carried back to Madrid for a humiliating trial and a public execution, the Royalist provinces in Chile could be reinforced, the Spanish Navy would blockade the northern ports to starve out O'Higgins, and in two years, maybe less, the whole of Chile, and probably Peru as well, would be Spanish again. For Captain-General Bautista it would be total triumph, a vindication of all his theories of defensive warfare, and for Blas Vivar, if indeed he still lived and was a prisoner in the Angel Tower, it would mean death, for no one in Madrid would dare punish Bautista for a mere murder if, in exchange, he won them back their God-given empire. And all it would take for all those things to happen— for Vivar to die, for Bautista to triumph, for Cochrane to be humiliated, for Spain to win this war and for the whole history of the world to be nudged into a new course—was three companies of infantry. Just three! And surely, Sharpe thought, those three companies, and more, were being assembled for the charge at this very minute.

"Jesus, look at that!" Harper, panting beside Sharpe, was staring at a wooden fence that had been built across the headland and which now lay between Sharpe's small force and Fort Ingles. The fence was as tall as a man and made of split palings that formed a solid barrier, but what purpose such a fence served Sharpe could not understand. It hardly seemed defensive, for he could see no loopholes and no embrasures.

"Come on!" Sharpe said. There was nothing to be gained by gaping at the fence. It had to be approached, and a reconnaissance made of the ground beyond.

The strange fence lay on the far side of a crude ditch. It seemed to have been built to stop a flanking attack like the one Sharpe was making, but as no defenders manned the fence it had been a waste of effort constructing it. Sharpe's men rested at the bottom of the ditch while he peered through a chink between two palings. The fort lay two hundred yards away across open ground. There were no cannon embrasures on this western wall of the fort, though there was a deep ditch and the wall itself was steep enough to require ladders. A sentry was visible in the moonlight, standing on the wall's flat top.

Sharpe slid down to the ditch's bottom and stared up at the fence. It seemed to have been prefabricated in sections twenty feet long which had been fastened to thick posts sunk into the turf. Each section of fence would make, if not a ladder, at least a ramp. "Patrick? When I give the word I want you to knock out two sections of fence. They'll be our assault ladders." Sharpe was speaking in Spanish, loud enough for all the fifty men to hear him. "There's just one sentry on this side, everyone else is looking at the beach. The Spanish are scared. They're terrified of Cochrane and terrified of you because you're Cochrane's men. They think you're demons from hell! If we attack them hard and fast, they're going to crumple! They're going to run! We can take this fort! Your war cry is Cochrane! Cochrane! Now get your breath, make sure your guns are loaded, and be ready."

The men whose powder had been soaked when their boats overturned at the sea's edge were denoted to carry the fence sections. Those men would lead the charge. The rest would follow behind and, once the twin makeshift bridges were in place, stream across to bring terror to a fort. It would be a desperate throw, but better than being trapped on the beach by three companies of infantry. And, despite Cochrane's avowed intention to carry every fort tonight, Sharpe knew that just this single strong point would save the expedition. If Cochrane possessed just one fort then he would have guns and walls with which to defeat a Spanish counterattack, and so make a stand till the men left on the ships could arrange a rescue. Lord Cochrane might yet live, if this one fort would fall.

The fence sections had been nailed to their posts, and each nail needed nothing more than a strong wrench with a bayonet to be wrested free. Sharpe experimented on a couple of nails, then, satisfied, he slid down into the ditch's bottom where he reloaded the pistol he had fired from the boat. He checked that his other pistol was primed, then nodded at the men standing by the posts. "Go!" he said.

The men ripped the fence nails free. There was a splintering sound, the wavering of two great sections of wood, then the fence was falling. "Take hold of it!" Harper shouted. "Together now! Lift it, turn! Now go!"

"Charge!" Sharpe shouted, and he stumbled up the ditch side into the moonlight. Behind him the sea was a flicker of silver and black, while ahead of him the fortress walls were shadowed dark. The two pistols were in his belt, the sword in his hand. "Cochrane!" he shouted, "Cochrane!"

The men carrying the fence sections were lumbering across the tangle of ferns and grasses. The charge was slow, much slower than Sharpe had anticipated, made so by the weight of the cumbersome timber ramps. The carrying parties were advancing at scarcely more than a walking pace, but without the ramps the attack must fail, and so Sharpe knew he must hold his patience.

The single sentry on the fort's western wall gaped for a second, unslung his musket, decided that there were too many attackers for his single cartridge to destroy, and so turned to shout for help. His cry was drowned as the cannons cracked the night apart, slitting the moonlit darkness with their sharp stabs of flame. The wind carried the smoke toward Cochrane, away from Sharpe. The sentry shouted again, and this time he was heard.

"Cochrane!" Sharpe shouted, "Cochrane!" And suddenly men began to appear at the wall ahead. "Spread out!" Sharpe called. The first stabs of flame showed dark red on the ramparts. A ball fluttered near Sharpe, another flicked through the grass, a third cracked off one of the fence sections. The men carrying the makeshift ramps were running faster now, but the other men, unencumbered with the heavy burdens, were outstripping them, sprinting across the headland as though there would be security in the deep black shadows of the fort's ditch.

Sharpe ran with them. There were just fifty yards to go. The muskets crashed from the wall ahead. A man fell cursing to Sharpe's left, his hands clutching at his thigh. Sharpe could smell blood in the night—blood and powder smoke, the old and too familiar smells. Thirty yards, twenty, and another volley whipped overhead. The Spanish were firing high—the error of all inexperienced troops. The first of Sharpe's men were at the ditch. "Take aim!" Sharpe shouted at them, "Aim for their bellies!"

He put his sword into his left hand as he dragged one of his two pistols free. He cocked it, dropped to one knee beside the ditch, and took aim. The defenders were silhouetted against the moonlit sky while the attackers were dark shapes against the darker ground. Sharpe found a target, lowered the muzzle to the man's belly, fired. Sparks jetted bright and the recoil jarred up Sharpe's arm. The smoke blossomed, but when it was snatched away by the wind the man was gone, plucked off the fort's ramparts. Those ramparts were ten feet above Sharpe and twelve feet away. Then the first of the fence sections arrived and Harper was yelling at the men to plant its leading edge at the side of the ditch, then to lever the whole thing up and over, like a giant trapdoor that swung in the night to crash sickeningly against the sloping earth wall. The makeshift ramp lodged some three feet below the parapet, but that was close enough. "Come on!" Sharpe shouted. "Follow me!"

He ran across the makeshift bridge. The wooden palings bounced under Sharpe's boots. A musket flamed ahead, then with men on either side of him, he leaped for the rampart's top and the Spaniards were backing away, terrified of this sudden assault. Sharpe was screaming like a wild thing, his sword chopping down hard, and a defender was at his feet, squirming and screaming. Harper swung his cutlass like a bullock-killer, almost decapitating a man. The second bridge thumped into place and yet more men swarmed up its palings. Sharpe was leading the assault toward the cannon. An infantryman lunged with his bayonet, and Sharpe knocked it aside and rammed the hilt of his sword into the man's face. The rest of the defenders, terrified by this horror that had sprung from their flank, were running away, leaving the ramparts open for Sharpe and his assault party to reach the fort's northern bastions where the guns faced out to sea.

"Cochrane! Cochrane!" the attackers shouted, and to Sharpe their ragged chorus of voices sounded desperately thin, but it was enough to terrify the gunners who turned and bolted from their embrasures. The defending infantry, swept off the wall's top, were milling uncertainly in the courtyard beneath, and now the gunners added to the panic.

Sharpe dragged his second pistol free, aimed it down into the melee, and pulled the trigger.

"Cochrane!" He turned and bellowed the name into the darkness, down toward the white-fretted beach where the abandoned longboats still rolled and crashed in the tumbling surf. "Cochrane!"

"Sharpe?" Cochrane's voice sounded from the dark dunes.

"It's ours! Come on!" Christ, Sharpe thought, but they had done it! They had done it! His men were flooding into the first embrasure, hitting the captured gun with their cutlasses so that its barrel rang like a bell. "Come on, Cochrane! We've won!"

"Reload!" Harper was bellowing. "Reload!" He jumped down into the gunpit beside Sharpe. "Those bastards will counterattack." He nodded toward the fort's courtyard.

"Let's go for them!" Sharpe said.

Behind him the slope was suddenly swarming with Cochrane's men. Sharpe did not wait for them to reach the fort, but instead shouted at his men to attack the panicked Spaniards in the fort's courtyard. An officer was trying to rally the fugitives, and if he succeeded, and if the gunners recaptured their weapons, then Cochrane's men would be cut down in swaths. Sharpe had less than fifty men, and there were at least two hundred in the courtyard, but they were demoralized and they must not be allowed to recover their wits. "Come on!" Sharpe screamed. "Finish them off!" He charged.

Harper and a flood of maddened men came with him. Cutlasses chopped down, swords stabbed, pikes ripped at frightened men, but suddenly the enemy was melting away, running, because the panicked Spaniards had thrown open the fort's gate and were fleeing across the moonlit heath of the headland. They had left the Spanish flag flying on its staff beside the semaphore gallows, had abandoned their guns and were now running toward another fort that was visible from the ramparts of the captured Fort Ingles.

"After them!" Sharpe screamed, "After them!"

This was an added madness. One fort had fallen, and one captured fort was enough to guarantee Cochrane's survival. A hundred determined men could hold this fort by manhandling the guns to the land-facing ramparts and blasting away the Spanish counterattacks while Cochrane ferried his men off the beach to the waiting frigates, but suddenly Sharpe saw a chance to take a second fortress and so he took it.

He took the mad chance because he remembered a horror from long ago, a horror he had witnessed in Spain when, riding with German horsemen, he had seen a French square broken.

The survivors of that broken square had fled toward a second square which, opening its ranks to let in their fellow Frenchmen, had also opened themselves to the crazed horses and blood-spattered swords of the King's German Legion. The big horsemen had been riding among the fugitives and had broken that second square. The survivors of the second square, together with the few men who still lived from the first, had run for a third square which, rather than let itself be turned into a slaughterhouse, had opened fire on their own men. They had still gone down, ridden into hell by big horses and screaming cavalrymen.

Now Sharpe reckoned he could work a similar effect. The demoralized fugitives from Fort Ingles were running toward Fort San Carlos which, not more than four hundred yards away, was opening its gates to receive them. In the moonlight, and in the confusion, he reckoned his men would be indistinguishable from the fugitives. "On!" he shouted at his fifty men, "On!"

They ran with him. A broad beaten track led from Fort Ingles to Fort San Carlos which, unlike the north-facing Fort

Ingles, looked east across the neck of the harbor. Sharpe pushed a running Spaniard in the back, driving the man down into a ditch beside the road. He was among the Spaniards now, but they took no notice of him, nor of any of the other panting seamen who had infiltrated their ranks. The Spanish infantrymen cared only about reaching the safety of Fort San Carlos. The defenders of that second fort were standing on their ramparts, staring into the moonlight and trying to make sense of the confusion that had erupted on the headland's tip.

Some of the fleeing Spaniards at last understood their danger. An officer shouted and lashed his sword at a seaman who calmly rammed his pike into the man's ribs. Some of the running infantrymen broke off the road, running south toward the headland's farther fortresses. Cochrane had reached the first fort and, understanding what was happening, had already launched his men along the path behind Sharpe. The defenders of Fort San Carlos, seeing that second wave of attackers, assumed them to be their only threat. Muskets stabbed flame into the gathering darkness and the balls whipped over the heads of Sharpe's men.

Sharpe reached the bridge over the ditch of Fort San Carlos. The gateway was crammed with desperate men. Some, trying to escape their pursuers, clambered up the sides of the ramparts and Sharpe joined them, pulling himself up the steep earth slope. The defenses facing inland were negligible, designed to deter rather than hold off any real assault, perhaps because the fort's builders had never really expected an enemy to attack from the land. These forts were designed to pour a destructive cannonade down onto attacking ships, not to repel a madcap assault from the land. Corral Castle, the southernmost fort on the headland, had been built to resist such an assault, and Chorocomayo Castle, high on the headland's spine, was equipped with field artillery designed to keep a land attack from reaching the headland's neck, but no one had expected a landing on the Aguada del Ingles and then a crazy shrieking assault in the blood-sodden darkness.

Sharpe's boots flailed for a grip on the earth slope, and a Spanish defender, assuming him to be a refugee from Fort Ingles, reached down to help. Sharpe let the man pull him to the summit, thanked him, then tipped him down into the ditch. He swung his sword back, slicing at another man who wriggled desperately away. Two sailors from the *Kitty* ran past Sharpe, driving forward with fixed bayonets. The Spanish defenders did not wait for the challenge, but just fled. "Cochrane!" Sharpe shouted, "Cochrane!" He drove his attackers toward the men firing at Fort Ingles who, nervous of being trapped, were already abandoning the ramparts and edging backward. Harper was in the gateway, slashing and screaming at the men who blocked the entrance.

Then, with a suddenness that bespoke their desperate and fragile morale, the defenders of Fort San Carlos shattered just as the garrison of Fort Ingles had broken. The gunners, who were in their embrasures overlooking the moon-washed waters of the harbor, turned to see a churning mass of fighting men silhouetted on their western ramparts. They saw more men scramble onto the walls and they feared that the flood of men would wash down to swamp the courtyard and bring bayonets to the gunpits, and so the gunners fled. They leaped from their embrasures, scrambled up the ditch's far side and ran south toward the third fort, Amargos, that lay a half mile away and, like San Carlos, faced east onto the harbor.

The Spanish infantry, seeing the gunners go and realizing that there was nothing left to defend, broke as well. Sharpe, still on the western ramparts, cupped his hands and screamed toward Cochrane's men. "They're running! Go south! South!" he shouted in English. "Do you hear me, Cochrane?"

"I hear you!" the voice came back.

"They're running for the next fort!"

"Tally-ho! Tally-ho!" And Cochrane, throwing all caution to the wind, turned his men off the track to charge south toward Fort Amargos. The headland echoed with the yelps and cheers of the hunting rebels. Miller's drummers were trying to beat a quick tattoo, but the pace of the advance was too swift for such formal encouragement. The defenders of Fort San Carlos, denied the use of their gate, spilled over their earthen walls to flee toward safety. Now two sets of men were running for Fort Amargos whose defenders, thinking they were all loyal Spanish forces, opened its wooden gates to receive them.

Sharpe, his men disorganized and exhausted by their attacks on the first two forts, did not join the assault on Fort Amargos. Instead he jumped down to the courtyard and crossed to the flagpole that was nothing but a thin tree trunk skinned of its bark. He sawed with his sword till the flag fluttered free. Lieutenant Cabral, foraging through the fort's buildings, found a thin horse shivering in a stable. He offered to ride after Cochrane and bring back news of the night, an offer Sharpe gratefully accepted. Then, when picquets had been set on the captured ramparts and search parties sent to find the wounded, Sharpe sheathed his sword and walked to the gun embrasures.

Harper joined him. Most of the *Kitty*'s sailors were ransacking the fort, hurling bedding out of the log huts and hunting for coins in abandoned valises and rucksacks. A Midshipman, deputed by Sharpe to bring a butcher's bill, reported that he had found just three dead Spaniards and one dead rebel.

"God save Ireland," Harper said in amazement, "but that wasn't a battle, it was more like herding cattle!"

"They think we're devils," the Midshipman said. "I spoke to a wounded man and he said their bullets can't kill us. We're charmed, you see. We're protected by magic."

"No wonder the poor sods ran," Harper made the sign of the cross, then gave a huge yawn.

Sharpe sent the Midshipman to find Cochrane's surgeon, MacAuley. There were six men badly wounded, all Spaniards. Some of the *Kitty*'s men had sword cuts, and one had a bullet in his thigh, but otherwise the injuries were paltry. Sharpe had never known a victory to come so cheap. "Cochrane was right," he said to Harper. Or perhaps it had been the Spaniards who had defeated themselves, for men who believe in demons can be defeated easily.

Sharpe leaned on a gun embrasure and stared at the moon-glossed water of Valdivia Harbor. A score of ships, their cabin lights like cottage windows bright in the night, lay in the great bay, while across the water, perhaps a thousand yards away, a blaze of torches shone in Fort Niebla. Beside the fort was the entrance to the River Valdivia, leading to the town where supposedly Blas Vivar was a prisoner.

"We could give those bastards a shot or two?" Harper nodded toward the lights of Fort Niebla.

"They're out of musket range," Sharpe said idly.

"Not with muskets. With these buggers!" Harper slapped the nearest cannon. It was a massive thirty-six pounder, a ship-killing lump of artillery that had a depressed barrel in expectation of enemy ships coming through the harbor's entrance channel. The gun's roundshot would be held in place by a rope ring rammed against the ball to stop it rolling down the inclined barrel. A quill filled with a finely mealed powder stuck from the cannon's touchhole, and a portfire smoked and fizzed inside a protective barrel at the back of the gunpit. All the gun needed was to be re-aimed, then fired.

"Why not?" Sharpe said, then turned the cannon's elevating screw until it pointed to a spot just above the far Fort Niebla. Harper had already levered the trail around. Sharpe plucked the portfire from its barrel and blew on its burning tip till the fuse glowed a brilliant red. "Would you like to do the honors?"

"You do this one," Harper said, "and I'll do the next."

Sharpe stood to one side, reached over, and touched the glowing match to the quill in the touchhole. The fire flashed down to the charge, the gun crashed back on its carriage and a cloud of smoke billowed to hide the harbor. Men cheered as the ball screamed away across the water. Burning scraps of wad floated down the hillside and started small fires in the grass.

Harper fired the next gun, and so they went down the embrasures, sending the heavy shots toward the distant fort. Sharpe doubted that the cannonfire would do any damage, for he had no training in aiming such big guns, yet the shots were an expression of relief, even of joy. The defenders at Fort Niebla, doubtless confused by the noises and alarms of the night, did not fire back.

As the sound of the last shot echoed around the confining hills of the harbor, Sharpe looked south and saw that Cochrane's men were swarming across the ramparts of Fort Amargos. The fort's Spanish defenders were a fleeing rabble, the gate gaped open, and its flag was captured. Others of Cochrane's men, diverted from the newly captured Fort Amargos, were scrambling up the headland's central ridge to attack the gun emplacements of Fort Chorocomayo. Musket fire splintered the night as the attackers climbed. Cheers sounded from the ridge, a bugle called, and out in the harbor the nervous crews of neutral ships displayed bright lanterns in their rigging, advertizing to any attackers that they had no part in this night's fighting.

The fighting was ending. High on the ridge, under the bright sparks of the stars, musket flashes and cannon flames showed where Fort Chorocomayo briefly resisted Cochrane's assault. Chorocomayo had been constructed to stop an attack from the south, not the north, and the firing flared for only a few minutes before there was a sudden silence and, through the moonlit mist of powder smoke, Sharpe saw the silhouetted flag drop. Chorocomayo, like Amargos and San Carlos and Fort Ingles, had fallen. Three hundred wet and frightened men, coming from the sea, had ripped Valdivia's outer defenses into tatters. "Bloody amazing, is what it is!" Harper said.

"It surely is," Sharpe agreed, though he knew the worst was yet to come, for the most formidable of the Spanish defense works, Corral Castle, Fort Niebla, Manzanera Island and Valdivia's Citadel, were still in enemy hands, and all those strongholds, save only the gun batteries on Manzanera Island, were stone-walled and properly supplied with glacis, ditches and revetments. Yet those more taxing defenses would have to wait for daylight. Lieutenant Cabral, coming back on his horse, confirmed that Cochrane had called a halt for the night. The attack would continue in the morning, and till then the rebel forces were to stay where they were—to eat, sleep and rejoice.

Sharpe washed his sword blade clean in a trough of water, then joined Harper by a brazier where they ate Spanish sausages and a great loaf of bread, all washed down by a skin of harsh red wine. Harper had also found a basket of apples, and their smell reminded Sharpe of Normandy, for an instant, the homesickness was acute as a bullet's strike. He shook it away. The smell of the battle, of powder smoke and blood, was already gone, blown southward by the salty sea wind.

Major Miller, excited and proud, brought a further message from Cochrane. In the morning, Cochrane said, they would bombard the stone forts while the *Kitty* and the *O'Higgins* came into the harbor. Once Fort Niebla had surrendered the rebels would make the fourteen-mile journey upriver to attack Valdivia itself. Cochrane clearly had no doubts that the forts would surrender. "They're rotten!" Miller spoke of the defenders. "They've no heart, Sharpe, no belly for a fight!"

"They're badly led." Sharpe felt sorry for the Spaniards. In the French wars he had seen Spaniards fight with fantastic bravery and enviable skill, yet here, with only a corrupted regime to defend, they had collapsed. "They think we're devils," Sharpe said, "and that we can't be touched by bullets or blades. It isn't fair to a man to have to fight demons."

Miller laughed and touched the spiky tips of his moustache. "I always wanted a forked tail. Sleep well, Sharpe. Tomorrow will bring victory!"

"So it will," Sharpe said, "so it will," and he hoped the morrow would bring so much more besides. For tomorrow he would reach Valdivia where his sword and his money and his friend all lay captive. But all that must wait for the morning and the new day's battle. Until then, Sharpe slept.

The morning brought clouds and a thin mist through which, in an uncanny silence, Cochrane's two ships slipped like ghosts into Valdivia Harbor. The wounded *Kitty* was low in the water with a list to starboard and her pumps spitting water. She kept close to the western shore and to the protection of the captured guns of Fort San Carlos, while the *O'Higgins*, larger and more threatening, sailed boldly up the center of the channel. The *O'Higgins*'s gunports were open, but Fort Niebla did not respond to the challenge. Cochrane had ordered the fifty-gun ship to hold her fire, daring to hope that the Spanish would thereby be lulled into quiescence, and now, astonishingly, the harbor's remaining defenders simply stared as the enemy ships passed through the lethal entrance. It was almost as though the Spanish, stunned by the night's events, had become mere spectators to their empire's fall.

It was falling with hardly a shot, collapsing like a rotten tree in a brisk wind. Corral Castle was the first stronghold to surrender. Cochrane ordered one shot fired from Fort Chorocomayo, and within seconds of the roundshot thumping harmlessly into the fort's earthen glacis, the gates were dragged open, the flag was hurried down, and an artillery Major rode out under a flag of truce. The castle's commander, the Major told Cochrane, was drunk, the men were mutinous and the castle belonged to the rebellion. The artillery Major surrendered his sword with indecent haste. "Just send us home to Spain," he told Cochrane.

With the fall of Corral Castle every gun on the western side of the harbor was aimed at either Fort Niebla or at the batteries on Manzanera Island. The *Kitty* had been run aground to stop her from sinking, while the *O'Higgins* had anchored so that her formidable broadside was aimed at the guns on Manzanera.

Cochrane had summoned Sharpe to Fort Amargos, the stronghold that was closest to Fort Niebla, where His Lordship was dividing his attention between a tripod-mounted telescope aimed at the enemy fort and Fort Amargos's drunken commander's collection of pornographic etchings. "What I plan to do," he said, "is demand Niebla's surrender. Do you think it's possible for two women to do that? I wondered if you would be willing to go to Fort Niebla and talk to the commander? Oh, my word. That would give a man backache, would it not? Look at this, Miller! I'll bet your mother never did that with your father!"

Miller, who was shaving from a bowl set on a parapet, chuckled at the picture. "Very supple, my Lord. Good morning, Sharpe!"

"The commander's name is Herrera," Cochrane said to Sharpe. "I'm assuming he has command of Manzanera Island as well, but you'd better check when you see him. That's if you're willing to go."

"Of course I'll go," Sharpe said, "but why me?"

"Because Herrera's a proud man. Good God! I think I'll keep these for Kitty. Herrera hates me, and he'd find it demeaning to surrender to a Chilean, but he'll find nothing dishonorable in receiving an English soldier." Cochrane reluctantly abandoned the portfolio of pictures to pull an expensive watch from his waistcoat pocket. "Tell Herrera that his troops must leave their fortifications before nine

o'clock this morning. Officers can wear side-arms, but all
other weapons must be . . ." His Lordship's voice tailed away
to nothing. He was no longer looking at his watch, nor even
at the salacious pictures, but was instead staring incredu-
lously across the misted harbor. Then, recovering himself, he
managed a feeble blasphemy. "Good God."

"Bloody hell," Sharpe said.

"I don't believe it!" Major Miller, his chin lathered, stared
across the water.

"Good God," Cochrane said again, for the Spaniards,
without waiting for an envoy, or for any kind of attack, were
simply abandoning their remaining defenses. Three boats
were rowing hard away from Manzanera Island, while the
flag had rippled down over Fort Niebla and Sharpe could
see its garrison marching to the quay where a whole fleet of
longboats waited. The Spanish were withdrawing up the
river, going the fourteen miles to the Citadel itself. "Christ
on a donkey!" Cochrane blasphemed obscurely. "But it
rather looks like complete victory, does it not?"

"Congratulations, my Lord," Sharpe said.

"I never thanked you for last night, did I? Allow me to, my
dear Sharpe." Cochrane offered Sharpe a hand, but continued to gape in disbelief at the Spanish evacuation. "Good
God almighty!"

"We still have to take Valdivia," Sharpe said cautiously.

"So we do! So we do!" Cochrane turned away. "Boats! I
want boats! We're in a rowing race, my boys! We don't want
those bastards adding their muskets to the town's defenses!
Let's have some boats here! Mister Almante! Signal the
O'Higgins! Tell them we need boats! Boats!"

In the first pearly light of dawn Sharpe had seen a Spanish
longboat beached beneath the ramparts of Fort San Carlos.
He presumed the boat had served to provision the fort from
the main Spanish commissary in Fort Niebla, but now it

would help Cochrane complete his victory. Sharpe, knowing it would take time to fetch boats from the *O'Higgins,* ran back to the smaller Fort San Carlos where, shouting at Harper and the seamen to bring their weapons, he scrambled down the steep cliff path which led to a small shingle beach. A dozen startled seals flopped into the water as his hurried progress triggered a score of small avalanches, then his boots grated on the shingle and he began heaving the boat toward the sea.

The first thirty men to reach the shingle gained places in the boat. Sixteen seamen took the oars, the rest crouched between the thwarts. They carried muskets and cutlasses. Sharpe told them their task was to overtake the fleeing Spaniards and stop them from reinforcing Valdivia, then he encouraged the oarsmen by saying that the fugitives were bound to be carrying Fort Niebla's valuables in their boats.

The boat, fueled by greed, fairly leaped ahead. Cochrane, still waiting at Fort Amargos for his own boats to come from the *O'Higgins,* bellowed at Sharpe to pick him up, but Sharpe just waved, then urged his oarsmen on.

They passed the *O'Higgins.* What was left of the warship's crew gave a cheer. The coxswain of Sharpe's boat, a gray-haired Spaniard, was muttering that the sequestered Spanish longboat was a pig, with a buckled keelson and sprung planks, and that Cochrane would soon catch them in his superior boats. "Row, you bastards!" the coxswain shouted at the oarsmen. It was a race now, a race to snatch the plunder from the demoralized enemy.

Far off to Sharpe's right a warship had raised the Royal Navy's white ensign. The name *Charybdis* was inscribed in gold at her stern. A nearby merchant ship flew the Stars and Stripes. The two crews watched the odd race and some waved what Sharpe took to be encouragement. "Nice to see the navy here," Harper shouted from the bows. "Maybe they can give us a ride home!"

The longboat reached the strait between Manzanera Island and Fort Niebla. The gun barrels that should have kept Valdivia safe now stared emptily from abandoned embrasures. The gates of Fort Niebla hung open, while the remains of a cooking fire dribbled a trickle of smoke from a hut on Manzanera Island. A small, rough-haired dog yelped at the passing boat from the beach beneath the earthworks that protected the island's guns, but there were no other signs of life. The Spanish had deserted a position as strong as any Sharpe had ever seen. A man could have died of old age before he would have needed to yield Niebla or Manzanera, yet the Spanish had vanished into the morning mist without firing a shot.

The oarsmen grunted as the boat slammed into the turgid current of the outflowing Valdivia River. Harper, in the boat's bows, was watching for the fugitives, but Sharpe, in the stern, was looking for Cochrane. Some of the men in Sharpe's boat were bailing with their caps. The old boat had gaping seams and was leaking at an alarming rate, but the men were coping and the oarsmen had found a good, steady rhythm. Sharpe could see Cochrane's boats striking out from the far shore, but they were still a long way behind.

"What do we do if we catch up with the bastards?" the coxswain asked Sharpe.

"Say boo to them. They'll surrender."

The coxswain laughed. They were rowing past the quays at the river's mouth. A group of bemused families had come from the fishermen's cottages to stare at the morning's events. Sharpe wondered what difference any of this would make to such pitiably poor people. Bautista's rule could not be easy, but would O'Higgins make life better? Sharpe doubted it. He had talked once with an old man in the village of Seleglise, a man ancient enough to remember the old French king and to remember all the other Paris governments that had come through bloody revolution or *coup d'état,* and the old man had reckoned that not one of those governments had made the slightest difference to his life. His cows had still needed milking, his vegetables had needed weeding, his corn had needed cutting, his cherries needed picking, his taxes needed paying, the church had needed his money and no one, neither priest, politician, taxman nor prefect, had ever given him a penny or a thank-you for any of it. No doubt the Chilean peasantry would feel the same. All this morning's excitement meant was that a different set of politicians would become rich at the country's expense.

The boat was in the river valley now. The hills on either side were thick with trees. Two herons flapped lazily down one bank. The oarsmen had slowed, settling to the long haul. A fisherman, casting a hand net from a small leather boat, abandoned his tackle and paddled furiously for the safety of land as the strange boat full of armed men appeared. Harper had cocked a musket in case the Spaniards had set an ambush beyond the river's first bend.

The coxswain hugged the right bank, cutting the corner and risking the shallows to make the bend swiftly. The oars brushed reeds, then the river straightened and Sharpe, standing to get a clear view ahead, felt a pang, for there were no boats in sight. For a second he thought the Spaniards must have such superior boats that they had somehow converted a two-mile lead into four or five miles, but then he saw that the Spanish longboats had stopped altogether and were huddled on the southern riverbank. There must have been twenty boats there, all crammed with men and none of them moving. "There!" he pointed for Harper.

Then Sharpe saw horsemen on the river's bank. Cavalry? Had Bautista sent reinforcements upriver? For a second

Sharpe was tempted to turn the boat and seize Fort Niebla before the Spaniards, realizing how hugely they outnumbered Cochrane's puny forces, made their counterattack, but Harper suddenly shouted that the dagoes on the riverbank were flying a white flag.

"Bloody hell," Sharpe said, for there was indeed a white flag of truce or surrender.

The oarsmen, sensing Sharpe's momentary indecision, and needing a rest, had stopped rowing and the boat was beginning to drift back downstream. "A trap?" the coxswain asked.

"God knows," Sharpe said. Cochrane was forever using flags as a trick to get himself close to the enemy, and were the Spaniards now learning to use the same ruse? "Put me ashore," he told the coxswain.

The oars dipped again, took the strain, and drove hard for the southern bank. The bow touched, and Sharpe clambered over the thwarts, then jumped up onto tussocky grass. Harper followed him. Sharpe loosened the sword in its scabbard, checked that his pistols were primed, and walked slowly toward the horsemen who were a half mile away.

There were not many horsemen, perhaps twenty, and none was in uniform, suggesting that this was not a cavalry unit. The men carried two flags—one the white flag of truce, and the other a complicated ensign bearing a coat of arms. "They look like civilians," Harper commented.

The horsemen were cantering toward Sharpe and Harper. One of the leading riders had a large black hat and a scarlet sash. He stood in his stirrups and waved, as if to signify that he meant no harm. Sharpe checked that the longboat with its cargo of armed sailors was close enough to offer him support, then waited.

"There's that bastard Blair!" Harper exclaimed.

"Where?"

"White horse, six or seven back."

"So it is," Sharpe said grimly. The merchant and British Consul was among the horsemen who, like himself, were mostly middle-aged and prosperous-looking men. Their leader, the man wearing the scarlet sash, slowed as he neared Sharpe.

"Are you Cochrane?" he called in Spanish.

"Admiral Cochrane is following. He'll be here soon," Sharpe replied.

"We've come to surrender the town to you." The man reined in his horse, took off his hat, and offered Sharpe a bow. "My name is Manuel Ferrara, I have the honor to be the *alcalde* of Valdivia, and these gentlemen are senior and respected citizens of our town. We want no trouble, *senor*. We are merely merchants who struggle to make a poor living. As you know, our sympathies have always been with the Republic, and we beg that you will treat us with the respect due to civilians who have taken no part in the fighting."

"Shut up," Sharpe said. He pushed past the offended and astonished Mayor to reach Blair. "You bastard."

"Mister Sharpe?" Blair touched a nervous hand to his hat.

"You're supposed to look after British interests, you bugger, not suck Bautista's tits because you're frightened of him!"

"Now, Mister Sharpe, be careful what you say!"

"You shit-faced son of a whore." Sharpe took hold of Blair's right boot and heaved up, chucking the Consul bodily out of his saddle. Blair gave a yelp of astonishment, then collapsed into the mud on the far side of the horse. Sharpe steadied the beast, then mounted it himself. "You!" he said to the Mayor, who was still protesting his undying loyalty to the ideals of liberty and republicanism.

"Me, *señor?*"

"I told you to shut up. I don't give a fart for your republics.

I'm a monarchist. And get off your damned horse. My friend needs it."

"My horse? But this is a valuable beast, *señor*, and—"

"Get off," Sharpe said, "or I'll blow you off it." He drew one of his two pistols and cocked it.

The Mayor hastily slid off his horse. Harper, grinning, heaved himself into the vacated saddle. "Where's Bautista?" Sharpe asked the Mayor.

"The Captain-General is in the Citadel. But his men don't want to fight."

"But Bautista wants to fight?"

"Yes, *señor*. But the men think you are devils. They say you can't be killed!" The Mayor crossed himself, then turned fearfully as a shout from the river announced the arrival of Lord Cochrane and his boats.

"All of you!" Sharpe shouted at the Mayor's nervous deputation. "Off your horses! All of you! Now!" He kicked his heels to urge Blair's white horse forward. "What's this flag?" He gestured at the ornate coat of arms.

"The flag of the town of Valdivia, *señor*," the Mayor answered.

"Hold on to it, Patrick!"

Cochrane jumped ashore, roaring with questions. What was happening? Who were these men? Why had Sharpe tried to race ahead?

"Bautista's holed up in the Citadel," Sharpe explained. "Everyone else in Valdivia wants to surrender, but Bautista doesn't. That means he's waiting for your boats and he'll fire on you. But if a small group of us go ahead on horseback we might just fool them into opening the gates."

Cochrane seized a horse and shouted for others of his men to find themselves mounts. The remainder of his piratical force was to row upriver as fast as it could. The Mayor tried to make another speech about liberty and the Republic, but

Cochrane pushed him aside and dragged himself up into his saddle. He grinned at Sharpe. "Christ, but this is joy! What would we do for happiness if peace came?" He turned his horse clumsily, rammed his heels back, and whooped as the horse took off. "Let's go get the whores!"

His men cheered. Hooves thumped mud into the faces of the Mayor's delegation as Sharpe and Harper raced after Cochrane. The rebellion was down to a spearhead of just twenty men, but with a whole country as their prize.

They rode hard, following the river road east toward the town. On the horsemen's left the river flowed placidly toward the sea, while to their right was a succession of terraced vineyards, tobacco fields and orchards. There were no military posts, no soldiers and nothing untoward in the landscape. Bautista had put no pickets on the harbor road, and had set no ambushes in the trees. Cochrane and his men rode untroubled through two villages and past white-painted churches and plump farmhouses. Cochrane waved at villagers who, terrified of strangers, crouched inside their cottages till the armed horsemen had passed. Cochrane was in understandably high spirits. "It was impossible, you see! Impossible!"

"What was?" Sharpe asked.

"To capture the harbor with just three hundred men! That's why it worked. They couldn't believe there were so few of us. My God!" Cochrane pounded the pommel of his saddle in his exuberant enthusiasm, "I'm going to capture the Spanish treasury and those prickless legal bastards in Santiago will have to grovel at my feet to get the money!"

"You have to capture the Citadel first," Sharpe reminded him.

"Simplicity itself." In his present mood Cochrane would have attacked the Rock of Gibraltar with just a boat's crew.

He whooped with delirious joy, making his horse prick its ears back. The horses were tired, breathing hard on the slopes and sweating beneath their saddlecloths, but Cochrane ruthlessly pressed them on. What did it matter if he lost horses, so long as he gained a country?

Then, two hours after they had encountered the Mayor's delegation on the riverbank, the road breasted a low ridge and there, hazed with the smoke of its fires and dominated by the great Citadel within the river's bend, lay Valdivia.

Sharpe was about to ask just how Cochrane wanted to approach the Citadel, but His Lordship, seeing the prize so close, had already scraped back his heels and was shouting at Harper to hold the flag high. "We'll go straight for them! Straight for them! The devil take us if we fail! Go! Go! Go!"

"God save Ireland!" Harper shouted the words like a war cry, then he too raked back his heels.

"Jesus wept," Sharpe said, and followed. This was not war, it was madness, a race, an idiocy. An Admiral, a Dublin publican, an English farmer and sixteen rebels were attacking the biggest fort in Chile, and doing it as though it were a child's game. Harper, his horse pounding alongside Cochrane, held the flag high so that its fringed symbol streamed in the wind. Cochrane had drawn his sword and Sharpe now struggled to do the same, but pulling a long blade free when trying to stay aboard a galloping horse was not the easiest task. He managed it just as the horsemen funneled into the town itself, clattering onto a narrow street which led to the main square. A woman carrying a tray of bread tripped in her frantic effort to get out of their way. Fresh loaves spilled across the roadway. Sparks chipped off the cobbles from the horses' hooves. A priest shrank into a doorway, a child screamed, then the horsemen were in the main square and Cochrane was shouting at the fortress to open its gates.

"Open! Open!" he shouted in Spanish, and maybe it was

the sight of the flag, or perhaps the urgency of the horsemen that suggested they were fugitives from the disasters that were known to have occurred in the harbor, but magically, just as every other Spanish fortress had opened its gates, so this one threw open its entrance.

The horses crashed across the bridge. Cochrane and Harper were in the lead. Cochrane had a drawn sword, and the sight of the bare blade made the officer in the gateway shout in alarm, but it was too late. Harper dropped the tip of the flag and, at full gallop and with all his huge weight behind the flag's staff, he drove the tip of the pole into the officer's chest. There was an explosion of blood, a crunch of bone, then the officer went down with a shattered chest and a blood-soaked flag impaled in his ribs, while Harper, letting the staff go, was through the archway and into the outer courtyard.

"Surrender! Surrender!" Cochrane was screaming the word in a demented voice, flailing at panicked soldiers with the flat of his drawn sword. "Drop your muskets! Surrender!"

A musket fired from an upper window and the bullet flattened itself on the cobbles, but no other resistance was offered. The gate to the inner courtyard, hard by the Angel Tower, was closed. All around Sharpe the Spanish soldiers were throwing down their muskets. Cochrane was already out of his saddle, hurling men aside to reach a door into the main buildings where, he supposed, the treasury of a defeated empire would be found. His sailors followed him, abandoning their horses in the yard and screaming their leader's name as a war shout. It was the sound of that name that did the most damage. The Spanish soldiers, hearing that the devil Cochrane was among them, dropped to their knees rather than fight.

Sharpe threw himself out of the saddle. He knew the geography of the fort better than Cochrane and, with Harper beside him, he ran into the corridor that led to the inner guardroom. Footsteps thumped on floorboards above as men tried to escape the invaders. A pistol fired somewhere. A woman screamed.

Sharpe pushed open the door that led to the inner courtyard. A nine-pounder cannon stood there, facing the gate, and with it was a crew of four men who clearly had orders to fire the gun as soon as the gate was opened. "Leave it alone!" Sharpe shouted. The gun's crew turned and Sharpe saw that Captain Marquinez was its commander. Marquinez, as exquisitely uniformed as ever, saw Sharpe and foolishly yelped that his men should slew the gun around to face Sharpe.

There was no time to complete such a clumsy maneuver. Sharpe charged the gun.

A second man turned. It was Dregara. The Sergeant was holding a linstock to fire the cannon, but now dropped the burning match and fumbled to unsling the carbine from his shoulder.

"Stop him!" Marquinez screamed, then fled to the door of the Angel Tower. Sergeant Dregara raised the carbine, but too late, for Sharpe was already on him. The cavalryman backed away, tripped on the gun's trail, and fell. Sharpe slashed down with the sword, driving the carbine aside. Dregara tried to seize the sword blade, but Sharpe whipped the steel hard away, ripping off two of the cavalryman's fingers. Dregara hissed with pain, then lashed up with his boot, trying to kick Sharpe's groin. Sharpe swatted the kick aside with his left hand, then drove the sword with his right. He plunged it into Dregara's belly, then sliced it upward, using all his strength, so that the blade tore through the muscles and cartilage to pierce the cavalryman's chest cavity. The ribs stopped the slashing cut so Sharpe rammed the blade down, twisted it, then pulled it free. Dregara gave a weird, almost feminine, scream. Blood welled to fill his belly's cavity, then spilled bright onto the cobbles of the yard where so many rebels had been executed. The other two men of the gun's makeshift crew had tried to flee, but Harper had caught them both. He felled one with a fist, the other with a cutlass stroke.

The dying Dregara twitched like a landed fish. Sharpe stepped across the cannon's trail, around the puddling blood, then ran at the door of the Angel Tower.

He hit the door with his shoulder, gasped in pain and bounced off. Marquinez, safe inside the tower, had locked its door.

Behind Sharpe, Dregara gave a last gasp and died. The inner courtyard gate scraped open and Cochrane stood there, triumphant. "It's ours! They've surrendered!"

"Bautista?"

"God knows where he is! Come and help yourselves to the plunder!"

"We've got business in here."

Harper had seized a spike and now, with Sharpe's help, he turned the heavy cannon. It was a British gun, decorated with the British royal cipher, evidently one of the many cannons given by Britain to help Spain defeat Napoleon. The trail scraped on the cobbles and the ungreased axle protested, but finally they succeeded in swiveling the gun around until its bronze barrel, which Sharpe suspected was charged with canister, faced directly at the door of the Angel Tower. The door was only ten paces away. According to Marcos, the soldier who had told Vivar's story at Puerto Crucero, this door was the only way into the mysterious Angel Tower which, like a castle turret, was a fortress within a fortress. This ancient stone tower had withstood rebellion, war, earthquake and fire. Now it would meet Sharpe.

He plucked the fallen linstock from beside the disemboweled body of Sergeant Dregara, told Harper to stand aside, then touched the linstock to the quill.

The gun's sound echoed in the courtyard like the clap of doom. The gun had been double-shotted. A canister had been rammed down on top of a roundshot, and both projectiles now cracked in smoke and flame from the gun's barrel. The gun recoiled across the yard, crushing Dregara's body before it smacked brutally hard against the guardroom wall.

The door to the Angel Tower, struck by the exploding load of canister, simply vanished. One moment there had been a heavy wooden door reinforced with iron, and the next there were empty hinges and charred splinters of wood. The cannonball whipped through the smoke and wreckage to ricochet around the downstairs chamber of the tower.

When the noise and smoke subsided Sharpe stepped cautiously through the wreckage. He had the bloody sword blade in his hand. He expected to encounter the fetid stench of ancient dungeons and recent death, but there was only the acrid smell of the cannon's smoke inside the tower. The lowest story of the tower was a single room that was disappointingly commonplace: no barred cells, no racks or whips or manacles, nothing but a round whitewashed room that held a table, two chairs and a stone staircase that circled around the wall to disappear through a hole in the ceiling. That ceiling was made of thick timber planks that had been laid across huge crossbeams.

Harper had scooped up Dregara's carbine. He cocked the gun and edged up the stairs, keeping his broad back against the tower's outer wall. No noise came from the upper floors of the tower.

Sharpe drew a pistol and followed. Halfway to the gaping hole in the ceiling he reached out, held Harper back, and stepped past him. "My bird," he said softly.

"Careful, now," Harper whispered unnecessarily.

Sharpe crept up the stair. He carried his sword in his left hand, the heavy pistol in his right. "Marquinez!" he called.

There was no answer. There was no sound at all from the upper floors.

"Marquinez!" Sharpe called again, but still no answer. Sharpe's boots grated on the stone stairs. Each step took an immense effort of will. The butt of the pistol was cold in his hand. He could hear himself breathing. Every second he expected to see the blaze of a gun from the trapdoorlike hole that gaped at the stair's head.

He took another step, then another. "Marquinez!"

A gun fired. The sound was thunderous, like a small cannon.

Sharpe swore and ducked. Harper held his breath. Then, slowly, both men realized that no bullet had come near either of them. It was the sound of the gun, loud and echoing, that had stunned them.

"Marquinez!" Sharpe called.

There was a click, like a gun being cocked.

"For God's sake," Sharpe said, "there are hundreds of us! You think you can fight us all?"

"Oh, by Jesus, look at that, will you?" Harper was staring at a patch of the timber ceiling not far from the stairway. Blood was oozing between the planks to form bright droplets which coalesced, quivered, then splashed down to the floor beneath.

Sharpe ran up the stairs, no longer caring what noise he made. He pounded through the open trapdoor to find himself in another, slightly smaller, but perfectly circular room that took up all the rest of the space inside the tower. There had once been another floor, but it had long fallen in and its wreckage removed, and all that was left was a truncated stair which stopped halfway around the wall.

But the rest of the room was an astonishment. It was a

sybaritic cell, a celebration of comfort. It was no prison, unless a prison would be warmed with a big stone fireplace and lit by candles mounted in a lantern which hung from the apex of the stone roof. The walls, which should have been of cheerless stone, were draped with rugs and scraps of tapestry to make a soft, warm chamber. The wooden floor was scattered with more rugs, some of them fur pelts, while another pelt was draped on the bed, which stood in the very center of the circular room and on which lay the remains of Captain-General Miguel Bautista. Or rather what Sharpe supposed had been Captain-General Miguel Bautista, for all that was left of the Captain-General was a headless body dressed in the simple black and white uniform that Sharpe remembered well.

Bautista's head had disappeared. It had been blown away by Harper's seven-barreled gun with which Bautista had committed suicide. The gun lay on his trunk that had spilled so much blood onto the floorboards. Some blood had matted in the fur of the bed's coverlet, but most had puddled on the floor and run through the cracks between the ancient boards.

All around the room's outer edge were boxes. Plain wooden boxes. Between the boxes was a corridor which led to an open door. Sharpe had been told there was only the one entrance to the tower, but he had found a second. The stone around this second door had a raw, new appearance, as though it had only recently been laid. Sharpe, still holding his weapons, walked between the boxes and through the new doorway, and found himself in Captain Marquinez's quarters—the very same rooms in which the handsome Captain had received them on their first day in Valdivia.

Marquinez was sitting on his bed, holding a pistol to his head. He was shaking with fear.

"Put the gun down," Sharpe said quietly.

"He made me promise! He said he couldn't live without me!"

Sharpe opened his mouth, did not know what to say, so closed it again. Harper, who had stepped into the room behind Sharpe, said something under his breath.

"I loved him!" Marquinez wailed the declaration.

"Oh, Jesus," Sharpe said, then he crossed the room and lifted the pistol from Marquinez's nerveless fingers. "Where's Blas Vivar?"

"I don't know, *señor*, I don't know." Marquinez was in tears now. He had begun to shake, then slid down to his knees so that he was at Sharpe's feet where he wrapped his arms around Sharpe's legs like a slave beseeching for life. "I don't know!"

Sharpe reached down and disengaged the arms, then gestured toward the tower. "What's in the boxes, Marquinez?"

"Gold, plate, pearls, coin. We were going to take it back to Spain. We were going to live in Madrid and be great men." He was weeping again. "It was all going to be so wonderful!"

Sharpe gripped Marquinez's black hair and tipped the man's tearful face back. "Is Blas Vivar here?"

"No, *señor*, I swear it!"

"Did your lover ambush Vivar?"

"No, *señor!*"

"So where is he?"

"We don't know! No one knows!"

Sharpe twisted his grip, tugging Marquinez's hair painfully. "But you were the one who took the dog to Puerto Crucero and buried it?"

"Yes, *señor*, yes!"

"Why?"

"Because he ordered me to. Because it was embarrassing that we could not find the Captain-General's body. Because Madrid was demanding to know what had happened to General Vivar! We didn't know, but we thought he must be dead, so I found a dead dog and put that in a box instead. At least the box would smell right!" Marquinez paused. "I don't know where he is! Please! We would have killed him, if we could, because General Vivar had found out about us, and he was threatening to tell the church of our sin, but then he vanished! Miguel said it had to be the rebels, but we never found out! It wasn't our doing! It wasn't!"

Sharpe released Marquinez's hair. "Bugger," he said. He released the flint on his pistol and pushed the weapon back into his belt. "Bugger!"

"But look, *señor!*" Marquinez had climbed to his feet and, eager as a puppy for approval, edged into the tower room which had been his secret trysting place. "Look, *señor,* gold! And we have your sword, see?" He ran to a box, opened it, and drew out Sharpe's sword. Harper was opening other boxes and whistling with astonishment, though he was not so astonished to forget to fill his pockets with coins. "Here, *señor.*" Marquinez held out Sharpe's sword.

Sharpe took it, unbuckled the borrowed scabbard, and strapped his own sword in its place. He drew the familiar blade. It looked very dull in the dim lantern light.

"No, *señor!*" Marquinez thought Sharpe was going to kill him.

"I'm not going to kill you, Marquinez. I might kill someone else, but not you. Tell me where Bautista's quarters are."

Sharpe left Harper in his Aladdin's cave, went through Marquinez's rooms, across a landing, down a long corridor, and into a stark, severe chamber. The walls were white, the furniture functional, the bed nothing but a campaign cot covered with thin blankets. This was how Bautista wanted the world to see him, while the tower had been his secret and his fantasy. Now Lord Cochrane sat at Bautista's plain table with two pieces of paper in front of him. Three of Cochrane's sailors were searching the room's cupboards, but were evidently finding nothing of great value. Cochrane grinned as Sharpe came through the door. "You found me! Well done. Any news of Bautista?"

"He's dead. Blew his own head off."

"Cowardly way out. Found any treasure?"

"A whole room full of it. Top of the tower."

"Splendid! Go fetch, lads!" Cochrane snapped his fingers and his three men ran out into the corridor.

Sharpe walked to the table and leaned over Cochrane's two pieces of paper. One he had never seen before, but he recognized the other as the coded message that had been concealed in Bonaparte's portrait. Bautista must have kept the coded message, and Cochrane had found it. Sharpe suspected that the message was the most important thing in all the Citadel for Cochrane. The Scotsman talked of whores and gold, but really he had come for this scrap of paper that he was now translating by using the code that was written on the other sheet of paper. "Is there a Colonel Charles?" Sharpe asked.

"Oh, yes, but it wouldn't have done for anyone to think that Boney was writing to me, would it? So Charles was our go-between." Cochrane smiled happily, then copied another letter from the code's key.

"Where's Vivar?" Sharpe asked.

"He's safe. He's not a happy man, but he's safe."

"You made a bloody fool of me, didn't you?"

Cochrane heard the dangerous bite in Sharpe's voice, and leaned back. "No, I didn't. I don't think anyone could make a fool of you, Sharpe. I deceived you, yes, but I had to. I've deceived most people here. That doesn't make them fools."

"And Marcos? The soldier who told the story of Vivar being a prisoner in the Angel Tower? You put him up to it?"

Cochrane grinned. "Yes. Sorry. But it worked! I rather wanted your help during the assault."

Sharpe turned the coded message around so that it faced him. "So this was meant for you, then?"

"Yes."

Cochrane had only unlocked the first sentence of the Emperor's message. The words were in French, but Sharpe translated them into English as he read them aloud. "'I agree to your proposal, and urge haste.' What proposal?"

Cochrane stood. An excited Major Miller had come to the door, but Cochrane waved him away. His Lordship lit a cigar, then walked to a window that looked down into the main courtyard where two hundred Spaniards had surrendered to a handful of rebels. "It was all the Emperor's fault," Cochrane said. "He thought Captain-General Vivar was the same Count of Mouromorto who had fought for him at the war's beginning. We didn't know Mouromorto had a brother."

"'We'?" Sharpe asked.

Cochrane made a dismissive gesture with the cigar. "A handful of us, Sharpe. Men who believe the world should not be handed over to dull lawyers and avaricious politicians and fat merchants. Men who believe that glory should be undimmed and brilliant!" He smiled. "Men like you!"

"Just go on," Sharpe shrugged the compliment away, if indeed it was a compliment.

Cochrane smiled. "The Emperor doesn't like being cooped up on Saint Helena. Why should he? He's looking for allies, Sharpe, so he ordered me to arrange a meeting with the Count of Mouromorto, which I did, but the weather was shit-terrible, and Mouromorto couldn't get to Talcahuana. So we made a second rendezvous and, of course, he arrived and he heard me out, and then he told me I was thinking of his brother, not him, and, one way or another, it turned out that I was fumbling up the wrong set of skirts. So, of course, I had to take him prisoner. Which was a pity, because we'd met under a flag of truce." Cochrane laughed ruefully. "It would have been easier to kill Vivar, but not under a flag of truce, so I took him to sea, and we stranded him with a score of guards, six pigs and a tribe of goats on one of the Juan Fernandez islands." Cochrane drew on the cigar and watched its smoke drift out the window. "The islands are three hundred fifty miles off the coast, in the middle of nothing! They're where Robinson Crusoe was marooned, or rather where Alexander Selkirk, who was the original of Crusoe, spent four not uncomfortable years. I last saw Vivar eight weeks ago, and he was well and as comfortable as a man could be. He tried to escape a couple of times in this last year, but it's very hard to get off an island if you're not a seaman."

Sharpe tried to make sense of all the information. "What did Napoleon want of Don Blas, for God's sake?"

"Valdivia, of course. But not just Valdivia. Once it was secure we'd have marched north and taken over Chile, but the Emperor insisted that we provide him with a secure fortress before he'd join us, and this place is as fine a stronghold as any in the Americas. The Emperor thought Vivar was his man and would have just handed the fortress over!"

"To Napoleon?"

"Yes," Cochrane said, as though that was the most normal thing in all the world. "And why not? You think I fought these last months to watch more Goddamned lawyers form a government? For Christ's sake, Sharpe, the world needs Napoleon! It needs a man with his vision!" Cochrane was suddenly enthusiastic, full of the contagious vigor that made him such a formidable leader of men. "South America is rotten, Sharpe. You've seen that for yourself! It's an old empire, full of decay. But there's gold here, and silver, and iron, and copper, and fields as rich as any in Scotland's lowlands, and orchards and vines, and cattle! There are riches here! If we can make a new country here, a United States of South America, we can make a power like the world has never seen! We just need a place to start! And a genius to make it work. I'm not that genius. I'm a good Admiral, but I don't have the patience for government, but there is a man who does, and that man's willing!" Cochrane strode back to the table and snatched up the coded letter. "And Bonaparte can make this whole continent into a magical country, a place of gold and liberty and opportunity! All that the Emperor demanded of us was that we provide him with a secure base, and the beginnings of an army." Cochrane swept an arm around in a lavish gesture that encompassed all of Valdivia's Citadel, its town and its far harbor. "And this is it. This is the kernel of Napoleon's new empire, and it will be a greater and a better empire than any he has ever had before."

"You're mad!" Sharpe said without rancor.

"But it's a glorious madness!" Cochrane laughed. "You want to be dull? You want to live under the rule of pen-pushers? You want the world to lose its fire? You want old, jealous men to be cutting off your spurs with a butcher's axe at midnight just because you dare to live? Napoleon's only fifty! He's got twenty years to make this new world great. We'll bring his Guardsmen from Louisiana and ship volunteers from France! We'll bring together the best fighters of the European wars, from both sides, and we'll give them a cause worth the sharpening of any man's sword." Cochrane stabbed a finger toward Sharpe. "Join us, Sharpe! My God, you're the kind of man we need! We're going to fight our way north. Chile first, then Peru, then up to the Portuguese territories, and right up to Mexico, and God knows why we need to stop there! You'll be a General! No, a Marshal! Marshal Richard Sharpe, Duke of Valdivia, whatever you want! Name your reward, take whatever title you want, but join us!

If you want your family here, tell me! I'll send a ship for them. My God, Sharpe, it could be such joy! You and I, one on land, one on sea, making a new country, a new world!"

Sharpe let the madness flow around him. "What about O'Higgins?"

"Bernardo will have to make up his mind." Cochrane was pacing the room restlessly. "If he doesn't want to join us, then he'll go down with his precious lawyers. But you, Sharpe? You'll join us?"

"I'm going home," Sharpe said.

"Home?"

"Normandy. To my woman and children. I've fought long enough, Cochrane. I don't want more."

Cochrane stared at Sharpe, as though testing the words he had just heard, then he abruptly nodded his acceptance of Sharpe's decision. "I'm sending the *O'Higgins* for Bonaparte. If you won't join me, then I'll have to keep you from betraying me, at least till he gets here or until I can find you another ship to take you home. I'll bring Vivar here, and you and he can sail back to Europe together. There's nothing you or he can do to stop us now. It's too late! We have our fortress, and we just have to fetch Bonaparte from his prison, then march to glory!"

"You'll never get Bonaparte out of Saint Helena," Sharpe said.

"If I can take Valdivia's harbor and Citadel with three hundred men," Cochrane said, "I can get Bonaparte off an island. It won't be difficult! Colonel Charles has found a man who looks something like the Emperor. He'll pay a courtesy visit, just like you did, and leave the wrong man inside Longwood. Simple. The simple things always work best." Lord Cochrane mused for a moment, then barked a joyous yelp of laughter. "What joy you are going to miss," he said to Sharpe, "what joy you will miss."

Cochrane was unchaining Bonaparte. The devil, bored with peace, would open the vials of war. The Corsican ogre was to be loosed to mischief, to conquest and to battle without end. Bonaparte, who had drenched Europe in blood, would now soak the Americas, and Sharpe, who was trapped in Valdivia, could do nothing about it.

Except watch as all the horror started again.

EPILOGUE

As a child walking down that one-lane gravel road, I thought I understood the word *whore*. I had heard it before, growing up in a home with few attempts to censor the vulgarities of the world. I had probably already heard it screamed at my mother, who never denied any curse but who seemed to think her motherly arms would somehow protect her face and her *self* from what rained down. Somehow, I knew it was a word for women, and I knew it was something to be ashamed of. It was also a word for girls—girls who had been molested or maybe wore short shorts, as I was to discover soon enough. I was scared to call my granny such an ugly name.

It was not my word, but it came to be mine before many others. It was roughly akin to *little slut*, which I learned around the age of nine, when I was wearing a floral shirt that tied at the bottom. I thought it was fashionable, though I had no way to know such things. It came from a real clothing store—not a Big Lots or a consignment shop—so I prized it above my other shirts and felt just the faintest hint of being pretty when I wore it. But my dad caught a glimpse of skin between the bottom of the shirt and the top of my shorts. When he first told me I should cover up, I laughed, thinking it was a joke—after all, I was nine, and who sees a nine-year-old's stomach and thinks *little slut?*

You think that's funny? You want to walk around looking like a little slut? Don't you ever laugh at me again.

The smile stole from my face as I began to learn that if I felt *pretty* or *stylish*, something was wrong. That if I wanted to look cute—like everyone else always seemed to look with their nice clothes and nice hair and nice smiles—shame would follow.

I walked down to my granny's house—it was always *down*, since we were closer to the head of the holler—knowing that what I was about to do was wrong, maybe even a sin, though it was not specifically mentioned in the Bible, as far as I knew. I walked without seeing the blackberry brambles I searched through at other times, when I was on my way to ask Granny for some eggs, onions, or tomatoes. I didn't see the creek I spent countless hours poring through, catching crawdads whose pincers I feared, watching always for copperheads that might be aroused by my presence, ready to strike.

When I walked through the kitchen door, she looked up and asked right away what was wrong. I burst into tears and told her that I was supposed to tell her she was a whore, knowing I was taking a risk by not actually calling her that name but hoping it was close enough. Granny wrapped her arms around me, telling me everything was going to be all right and not to worry. Through my hot tears, I told her I was so sorry, and she pulled me to her and *shushed* my cries. I was relieved that there was no anger on her face, grateful that she knew this wasn't my idea.

I wonder now how she sorted through that heartache, the grieving for her broken granddaughter, for her broken son, for her own fractured dream of family and answered prayers. Maybe she saw God's will at work, some infallible plan that played out while I wept. Did she have faith that this, too, had its divine purpose and that obedient children would inherit the earth some fine day? She had faith, to be sure. But that's not what I saw on her face that day.

Before long, that same look would cross my own face more than once, as tragedies piled onto one another and I slowly came to realize I could not change that grim reality. I grew familiar with a feeling of dread that was nearly eclipsed by weariness. A heartache that could no longer cry out. But before I ever felt the same pain that Granny must have felt that day, I knew that she ached for me and for what was unfolding. I knew that this hurt her, too, and that we grieved together.

In that moment, perhaps like me, she wondered what else would be lost that day, what punishment would come for us all. Maybe she feared my father and what had come from her birthing bed. Maybe there was a story I didn't know, a history of transgression that rested in her memory in which this day was just another turning page. Maybe she clung to the love we had, the desperate devotion I felt for her, the need that only she could fill.

Maybe she didn't know what to think. How to feel. What she did know was that the child in front of her needed her, and that her own grief would have to wait.

She drove me home and responded to his insult while I stood there. *You leave her alone,* she said. *Don't you do that to my little girl again.* I was scared for her and awed as she spoke without fear, not knowing what he might do. It was the first time I had ever heard anyone defy him. It was the first and last time I ever heard anyone tell him not to hurt me.

It made sense to me then that he needed someone to tell him that, because in fact even I didn't understand that it wasn't okay to hurt me, whether it was my heart or my mind or my body at stake. I would spend much of my childhood quietly enduring whatever there was to endure, keeping my face still so my rage and fear did not betray me, so whoever it was would not punish me further.

When a teenage boy took me to an empty classroom in the basement of our church, I sat quietly on his lap like he told me to. I said nothing as he pulled my shirt out from under the waistband of my skirt. I stayed silent while his hands moved around my five-year-old body. When he was done, I went into the bathroom just like he said and fixed my clothes without a word. I never told Granny or Papaw Conn what the boy had done in the basement at church. I never told my parents. I don't know what he said to me to keep our little secret safe, but it didn't matter—I already knew how important it was for girls to keep our mouths shut.

No one thought to tell me when I became an adult, *It's okay now, you're allowed to say no.* I went from being a child who did not speak up, to being an adult who did not. Before I knew how to protect myself, I had to watch best friends turn away in disdain when I answered yes, the bruise on my neck was probably from my boyfriend. I had to hear a lover say things like, *How could you let those men do that, I don't know any other women who would let that happen.* I had to watch my friends become my ex-husband's friends and feel their affection for me diminish. Since I hadn't told stories about him, they believed all the stories he raced to tell.

I had to unlearn the most important lesson I had learned as a child, the most important rule of survival—to *be quiet.*

I asked my mom once whether she had ever told her father—kind, gentle Papaw Wright, who lived on the road we took to town—what my dad did to her. *Lord no, your dad wouldn't be able to drive past their house if I did.* It made sense at the time—we don't inconvenience a man who terrorizes his wife and children. We don't bother a kind, protective father with the knowledge of what his son-in-law has done and maybe watch that good father reveal a violence of his own. We don't want any trouble.

And besides, *You knew he was like this when you married him.*

CHAPTER 2

Gravel

It took a long time for me to understand that most people couldn't relate to the things I took for granted as a child. Things like how we had a cup of copperhead venom in the refrigerator for several years, how I watched my father tease and taunt the caged snake until it struck the Saran Wrap he had stretched over a plastic cup, how that cup sat beside our hot dogs and mustard and lifeless iceberg lettuce. For a while, whenever I looked through the refrigerator for something to eat, I thought to myself, *Better not drink the venom.*

What did he even want it for? There was probably a plan to use it against someone, or maybe he wanted to have it on hand just in case. I don't remember my parents ever warning us not to touch it. But we knew—we knew well that to get ourselves hurt by doing something stupid would only lead to a whipping.

We were tucked so far away in our holler, our own small, unbothered wilderness that the outside world could hardly reach, for better or for worse. My brother and I occupied ourselves in the ways that children of our sort did. We ran through the woods, we waded through creeks and climbed around on barbed-wire fences, we picked up empty corncobs that had been gnawed clean by the rats who lived in the corncrib long after my dad gave up on raising hogs. We knocked wasp nests down and picked up odd mushrooms we found growing. We used hammers and nails and climbed into the loft of the barn by scaling the uneven boards that jutted out along the corner, scraps of wood and dusty wood planers waiting to break our fall. In some ways, we were so very free.

But we were not free to speak our minds—our voices did not belong to us. There was no room to say, *I don't deserve this,* or *You are hurting me,* or *Please, no more.* Only one person had the power of language in our home, and words were just as potent as his other acts of violence.

Worse than being cussed at or belittled, though, was how he forced us to say cruel things and laughed at the spectacle: *Tell your mother to lay down and let her pups suck.* It made my stomach quiver to say it, though I did not know what it meant. He would tell me to say that to her, and I was too scared to say no, though I could sense it was wrong and somehow dirty. It was his way to shut her up, putting his words in our mouths, where they tasted like sawdust and liquor and muddy water. I didn't even wonder how my own words would feel when they rose up from within my quivering belly and came charging out.

Our father played strange games with us, all of us. He would grab my mother's hand and pull one of her fingers back, forcing it into an unnatural bend while she would cry out, *Please stop, no, you're hurting me, come on this isn't funny,* and he would grin and look at us kids, standing there with confusion and alarm on our faces, and then he would chuckle. He might let go long enough for her to sigh with relief, and I would think everything was okay until he bent her fingers in the wrong direction again. Sometimes he would do that until she buckled to the floor, begging on her knees for him to stop, almost crying, with my brother and me not knowing what was happening—could it really hurt when our father was smiling and laughing? Those two things did not make sense together, and I thought everything had to make sense, somehow.

At some point, I stopped trusting myself to know the difference between what made sense and what did not. I learned that when things looked wrong, felt wrong, there had to be something I didn't understand. I learned I should trust the man telling me to trust him, to accept whatever he was doing, no matter what my own good sense had to say. I learned to ignore my own judgment, and for a good long time, I had no idea that I could trust myself.

We used to go out to this man's house, an old man out in the country—Earl. Earl did not have indoor plumbing or electricity, but he did have a lot of empty metal Prince Albert Tobacco cans. Sometimes he would give one to my brother, and I wished he would give me one because they seemed precious and rare. Earl's skin was brown and wrinkled, and one of his eyes was smaller than the other. It looked like his face had been injured long ago, maybe in a war. The man raised hogs with my dad. We used to have hogs in our yard, and at one point, they stayed across the creek at the corncrib, but now the hogs were at Earl's place, where the hills were too steep to play on, and there were no woods in sight.

During one of our visits, my father called for me to come to him while I was walking around the fields, looking at the cows and trying to find a way to have fun. I went to him, and standing beside Earl, my father held out a long, thin red pepper to me.

Eat this, he said.

I told him I didn't like hot peppers.

The red ones aren't hot, he said. And though he was smiling, I knew I did not have a choice in the matter. I wanted to believe him and thought maybe this was a different kind of pepper than what I had tried before. I bit off the end, and instantly, my mouth was on fire. My father laughed at the joke as I rubbed my shirt on my tongue over and over, desperate to cool it down. I was embarrassed that he had made a joke of me in front of Earl, who I don't believe laughed, but I was in too much pain to care about much else. It was still burning when we left, and on the ride home, sitting in the back of the pickup truck, I wondered how long some pain could last.

I couldn't accept that my father would hurt me for fun, humiliate me for his pleasure and maybe the amusement of another grown man. All the things that I heard and saw and felt fell onto and into one another, clanging in a relentless, deafening echo that demanded my constant vigilance.

He talked about the bank and how they were going to take the house. He told our mother he would burn it down with all of us in it before the *goddamn bankers got their hands on it*. He talked about the Social Security office, the settlement that he deserved, the paperwork that needed to be done, and the appointments he had to go to. I heard the state attorney's name over and over, and I heard about the crooked doctors who wouldn't refill his prescriptions. I knew in my child's heart that when those people finally left him alone, his back injury would get better, and we could keep our house, and the settlement money would make up for him not working.

It was the lawyers, the bankers, the system—they were working against him, against *us*, and keeping me from having a dad who loved me and who could go fishing and grow a garden and put corn out for the wild turkeys in the hills behind our house, a dad who could just be happy to have us and our beautiful holler and the Daniel Boone National Forest all around us, bathing us in beauty each day, all day long, instead of a dad who sometimes turned to rage for no reason at all and left bruises on us or called us *little piece of shit* or woke us at night while he did awful things to our mother.

At the time, he was also still a drinker, and Dad liked to give me beer starting from a young age. I think I was around five when I stumbled into the corner of the refrigerator, off balance, and I heard him laughing. Much later, rummaging through the thousands of pictures my parents took—why did they take so many pictures?—I found one of myself in nothing but a diaper, sitting on a yellow lounge chair in front of our trailer that we lived in before they built the house, grasping a cold Stroh's with both hands. A can of lighter fluid completes that composition, the picture of white trash.

Mom told me later that the picture was staged, but she also told me in complete seriousness that they used to put beer in my bottle to make me sleep. Either way, I drank beer whenever they let me and liked it until I was nine years old and my Sunday school teacher said alcohol was bad for the liver. The next time my father offered me a drink of his beer, I told him, *I don't want any*, even though I was scared to death I would get into trouble for saying no. It turns out that the only thing I feared more than my father was going to Hell, because the God I learned about didn't take sin lightly.

It is a wonder we had so many pictures lying around, just like it is a wonder we were able to afford a Nintendo at some point. Just that one system—nothing fancier—and I don't remember us getting any games besides the first Super Mario Bros. and Duck Hunt. But why would such poor people spend their money like that? The time would inevitably come when we really needed that money for food, for the electric bill. They could have taken us to the dentist or saved up for the next disaster they surely knew was coming. But we lived the poverty boom-and-bust lifestyle. In a landscape littered with disappointment, immediate gratification seems to make sense. In a region defined by broken promises, you might as well take the safe bet, the pleasure of a moment that might never return. There is no promise of tomorrow, and there's a damn good chance tomorrow will be worse than today. Most of these crises can't be fixed with $300 anyway. Let's have some fun while we can.

Considering how little love there was to go around in our house, and how keenly I felt the shortage, I blamed my little brother in some way for the pain that set in at an early age. I took out all of my hostility and aggression on him, and if I had not been able to do that, I probably would have turned it all inward even more fervently than I did. We were Irish twins—he was born one year and four days later than I was. I was named after our mom's father, and my brother was named after our paternal grandfather. Junior was my playmate, my victim, and my witness, someone who shared my fear and my anger, at least until he found a way out of all that *feeling*.

The one and only time I ever heard my brother defy our father was during dinner, when he was about six years old. We were eating, and suddenly, my brother was crying. My father had either ridiculed him or harassed him for some little thing, but, still, he demanded to know why Junior was crying. I was proud and horrified when my brother responded, *Sometimes I just get so sick of you.* We all sat in perfect silence for a moment, which my father ended with a sweep of his arm, sending his plate full of food and glass full of milk into a kitchen cabinet and onto the floor. My brother sobbed over his plate, and my father thundered out of the kitchen, ordering our mother to clean up the mess.

Part of me was thrilled that Junior felt brave and confident enough to say those words—words I would have never said. As much as I resented him for seeming to be so much more lovable than I was, I felt a deep need to protect him as well. The other part of me wanted him to keep his mouth shut and not make our father angry, because Dad's anger never stayed contained. I just sat there, fear knotting itself inside me as I waited for Dad to come back into the kitchen, and watched Mom clean up the mess on her hands and knees.

Those were the kinds of scenes that could happen in the solitude of our holler. The slow realization that we were poor and sure did look it became entwined with stories about the needy I sometimes read or heard at school. I began to understand that things were different at our house, but I was smart enough not to tell my teachers or the police officer who came to school to teach us the names of all the drugs and how bad they are. I always knew we didn't have money, but it wasn't a lack of money that made me feel poor, worthless, *dirty*. I didn't know the word *poverty* yet, but there was a poverty that made our home feel so different from our granny's.

Poverty was the cheap meat we ate with boxed macaroni and cheese, but it was also the food my dad flung to the floor. It was the picture I found of my father's handiwork, a picture he took after he tore the kitchen faucet loose and hurled it through the kitchen window. It was the dentist appointments we never had, the coal stove spewing fine black soot onto our clothes, into our hair and our noses; it was the fire dying in the coal stove; it was my mother slammed into the coal stove. It was the ear infections that kept me from hearing every first insult, every first command. It was the electric going out during every storm, but it was also my father turning the meter upside down so it would run backward and we could pay the bill. It was the creek water we weren't supposed to drink, the same water we mixed into Kool-Aid. It was watching my dad shoot his gun at a dog by the creek. Watching him whip a dog with his belt. Watching him dump a dog's body in the woods. It was riding in his truck to another man's house, where he left me sitting as he took his rifle to the man's front door. It was the truck getting repossessed and the bank's men loading the truck with our trash at gunpoint before they could drive it away.

It was complicated. It refuses to be defined.

In my childhood fairy-tale world, my father was misunderstood. Not even he understood himself like I did. I hurt for him—his pain, the oppression of living poor and being a man who felt too small. I grew up in fear of this man I loved, ready to forget his transgressions in an instant. There were so many, it seems he killed the part of himself that might have claimed redemption.

I waited for the moment when we would wake up and realize that it was all a bad dream, that my father loved us and was there to protect us, that my mom was strong and worthy of his adoration. We would share a laugh at the odd dream that seemed so real and then go about being our true selves—selves that smiled because we weren't afraid, and our teeth weren't rotting, and no one would whip you because they thought maybe you were mocking them.

That moment never came, though I was *so sure* it would—I had faith that the father I loved would someday see himself as the good man I wanted him to be. I told myself it was only a matter of time, just around the corner. But those fairy tales don't end when you turn eighteen. You become a woman looking for another man who just needs your love, your devotion, your endless forgiveness. You keep stubbornly trying, waiting for dictators to become benevolent kings.

We didn't have central air-conditioning in the house and only had a window air conditioner in the living room when I was older. We kept the doors open when it was warm, the screen doors almost keeping the bugs out. There was a door at the side of the house, in the corner of the kitchen. Sitting at the kitchen table, you could see out the door to the creek and our trash bin beside it, an open, rusted metal container where we put bags of garbage until they started to pile up, and then we would burn them, plastic and all. Junior and I usually got to burn the trash, and it was especially fun when there was a Styrofoam plate in there. We would twirl the melting Styrofoam around a stick and watch it drip, like a liquid that didn't know what it was.

One morning while we were eating breakfast, Junior and I heard screams from outside. We jumped up from the kitchen table and went to the back door, where we stared through the screen. Our father had our mother's hair in one hand, and he was using it to pull her down the road toward Granny's house—they were at least to the first post of Granny's fence that marked the boundary and kept her cows in. We watched as he used his other fist to hit our mother over and over on her head, face, whatever he could get to. It was mostly her screams that we were hearing, though his were mixed in, too. For some reason, far away as they were, he suddenly noticed us, though he didn't stop dragging her.

Time stood still. The sound of his rage and her cries tore the leaves from the trees. His fist beat her head and her back and the sun beat down the gravel road and lit our faces and their bodies, and the water glittered in the creek just steps away from where we stood, motionless. My mother hit the gravel and the gravel hit back, both of them giving up something along the way. The sun shining hard, the air still, everything coming apart then—cells, neurons, shafts of light, all broken and breaking. Something was breaking inside of me, too, something I didn't even know I needed yet.

CHAPTER 3

Leaving Now

I was twenty-five when I asked my mom why she had stayed with my father for so long. *For you kids.* I asked whether maybe it would have been better for us if she hadn't stayed with him so long. *Yeah, I can see that now,* she said.

What is it that convinces so many women—and men as well—to endure destructive relationships *for the sake of the children?* My mother must have performed some painful mental calculations to measure the devil she knew against the one she did not. How could the fear and uncertainty of what *might* happen to her children compare to what *was happening* to her children? Of course, most parents don't want to deprive their child of the other parent. But maybe the other parent is cruel every once in a while—how does that weigh against every kindness that came before it? Maybe there are certain things within a person that only come out when they are responsible for a baby or arguing with a teenager, they're out of a job, or the burden of survival is just too much. Sometimes it feels impossible to weigh the potential loss of a parent against the pain that parent might inflict. And then there are the good times—those fleeting moments when you let yourself relax, when things suddenly seem to slide into place, when you finally think, *Things are getting better.* Maybe you do that for years.

I think now that my mother believed she was staying for us kids, but where would she have gone if she *had* tried to leave? She didn't have a full-time job for most of the eighties, and no safety net of friends or family who were ready to take her—*us*—in. My father habitually recorded phone conversations and rigged doors so he would know whether they had been opened. It didn't seem like any secret was safe from him, and there would have been no mercy if he had caught her planning to leave. We weren't living in the digital age—the only technology she had to work with was whatever dilapidated car she was driving at the time. And before she could overcome those challenges, she first had to escape the mental prison that he had built around her with every insult, every threat, every beating. Somehow, she had to convince herself that despite all evidence to the contrary, she was not powerless.

But why was she there with him in the first place? Why did she endure so much, sacrifice so much? Maybe she didn't know any better. Maybe she didn't like herself enough to demand better. Maybe she told herself things were going to be okay and one day woke up to find they certainly were not but that she had nowhere to go. Does it matter?

When I was around five, my uncle showed up at our house one day, and my dad accused my mom of flirting with him. I remember my uncle had a strange look on his face, and I didn't know why he looked so calm when my dad seemed to be on the verge of wanting to fight him. Maybe it was because they were both up for a good fight. But all of a sudden, my dad rode off in my uncle's truck with him, and Mom grabbed us kids and took us through the barbed-wire and electric fences into Granny's cow field. We ran to the creek that cut through the field and got down in it to hide when my uncle's truck drove back to our house and then left again. We waited until Mom said to run, and then we ran through the creek, trying to stay low and hidden, until we were close to Granny's house.

We got there and Papaw Conn loaded us into his pickup truck, where we all bent over as far as we could so nobody could see us through the windows. On the way out of the holler, we met my uncle and dad on their way back to the house. They hadn't stayed gone long, so they must have gone about halfway up the holler, to a neighbor who sometimes grew weed with my dad. Papaw stopped to talk to them, as you always do on country roads, and we stayed crouched down and quiet. Granny sat on the far end of the truck cab, her face betraying nothing. I learned so much from watching her but never stopped to wonder where and why she had learned to show so little emotion. I was just trying to survive, and maybe she was, too.

We finally drove on to Papaw and Grandma Wright's house. We may have been there a night—it's hard to keep all that leaving straight.

I think that was the time when Mom finally told my dad he needed *help* and she wasn't coming back until he got it. The next day, he went to the sixth floor of St. Claire Regional Medical Center—the psychiatric ward—and stayed there for two weeks. We visited him, and he introduced us to a woman with dark hair and wide eyes who would trade him cigarettes for pills. He showed us what he worked on while there, plaster-of-Paris fruits that he had painted with circus hues and cartoon smiles that didn't stay in their neat lines. The orange was my favorite, with its soft peach color, but the banana was too yellow and the apple too red, their smiles too white. When he came home, he hung them up above the kitchen stove, where they stayed until the house burned down. Looking at them always unsettled me, a constant reminder of his time on the *crazy floor*, when people started using the phrase *mildly schizophrenic*, whatever that meant.

It seems like we left a lot, but the worst time for me began at the IGA grocery store in town. We often brought Ale-8 bottles there to return for ten cents apiece, which added up to quite a bit when we hauled in cases at a time, all covered in the tiny ants that invaded our kitchen whenever it was warm, forming a marching line toward the trash can. We would store the Ale-8 bottles on the front porch, where the ants had all the access they could hope for to the sweet residue in the bottom of each bottle. I have pictures of me, three years old or so, holding a Pepsi bottle up to send the last of the pop into my mouth. I have a lot of pictures of myself from that age and onward to when my two front teeth visibly decayed. For the rest of my life, the sugar and the phosphoric acid from those pops changed the way I smiled.

It was usually my mom and us kids who hauled the bottles to the window in the corner of the store, where some man would take them to the back and give Mom the voucher for the cash. I watched, wondering whether the man minded all those ants and what happened to them once they were taken to the back of the store. Did they escape? Did they settle there, in the mysterious dark room in the back of the IGA, to live a comfortable life? Or did the man kill them, angry that we had brought them out of the holler?

For a few years, Mom would drive Junior and me everywhere in our brown Chevette. It often wouldn't start right away, and Mom would have us kids push it for a bit, and then she could pop the clutch to get it running. Junior and I would run to the car and hop in with it still moving. It was usually easy for us to push the car when we started at our driveway, since the road from our house to Granny's traveled on a slight downward slope. It was a little tricky to open the doors and hop in with the car moving, but we learned. As an adult, I learned to pop a clutch myself, even pushing a pickup truck while alone and pregnant, with the driver-side door open, until I had enough momentum to jump in and roll downhill with the clutch down and to hit the gas at just the right moment. As a kid, though, it was not so easy when the county roads department laid fresh gravel, since the thick, loose rocks were difficult to run on and we slipped more often. Much of the time, the road was worn smooth where the car and truck tires rolled over it, and a narrow path of rough gravel marked the center of the road.

One time in the IGA parking lot, a man noticed us, my brother and I still in grade school, trying to push the car fast enough for Mom to get it started. It was harder in the flat parking lot, without gravity on our side. The stranger came and helped, which struck me as odd at the time, and the look on his face told me he thought something was odd, too. As a kid, I couldn't push as fast as he could, so when he told us to get in the car and let him push, I did, and we rolled away. I'm sure Papaw Wright could have fixed the car with no problem. He owned and ran a successful garage all my life, and most of my mother's life, too. I imagine he would have wanted to fix it, knowing she was driving around with us children. I imagine it was my father who liked the car that way, always leaving my mother uncertain and with the threat of being stranded looming over her.

But once, there was a glimmer of something else in her when we arrived at the IGA. We didn't make it out of the car. Instead of opening her door, Mom stopped us with a strange look on her face. *Do you all just want to leave?*

I didn't know what she meant. I knew we were there for groceries, maybe some macaroni and cheese, and I didn't quite like the idea of whatever she was saying. She added, *I've saved up some money. We could just leave your dad. We don't have to go back.* I was the last to say *okay.* We went to the Super 8 Motel by the interstate, which was pretty nice because it had two beds and a color TV. Soon, we were on the phone with Dad, telling him we weren't coming back. He talked to Mom first and then to my brother, neither of them showing any emotion. They handed the phone to me and Dad was crying, begging me to come home, he would be different, everything would be different. He claimed he needed us, and that's all I needed to hear. I couldn't believe how callous my mom and brother had been, knowing Dad was *so sorry* for everything. Mom asked what I thought we should do, and I told her we should go back, Dad *promised* things would be better, and how could we leave him like this? We went back that night.

I had learned by then that his feelings were the most important in the family, that his moments of regret—authentic or not—were more important than whatever we felt at any time. I needed to forgive him like God forgave me for being such a sinner. None of us deserved forgiveness from our *heavenly father*, so who was I to withhold it from my *earthly father*? Who was allowed to be vengeful? Who was allowed to be angry?

I knew later that it was my fault, that Mom and Junior were ready for it to end, but I had dragged us back. The next time he beat her or made us cower or threatened someone, I knew I had let that happen. I had fallen for it, foolishly, when Mom and Junior knew better. But I wanted him to love us, and so when he cried, I thought it was the moment I had been waiting for—the moment he finally wanted us and knew how important we were to him.

I wanted to please, to avoid wrath. It was a devastating alchemy of abuse and religious fear, and I accepted my constant inner hell as punishment for how unworthy I was. Desperate to earn God's love, my father's love—anyone's love—I forgave in an instant, full of hope for some imaginary future. Like so many women before me and since, I learned that you go back, you stick it out, you love the man until he is saved by your sacrifice. It's the kind of thing you can always see going so badly in someone else's life, but not in your own.

~

Each time we went back, things were good for a few days, and sometimes for as long as a week. There were roses one time, and I told Mom, *That was nice of him.* She snorted a laugh and replied, *Sure, I'm the one who will have to pay for them.* My guess is that we all paid for them, in one way or another.

I thought my mom would leave us all only once. I was about six. My brother and I were playing outside and ran into the house when we heard her screams. I thought Dad was killing her, it was so much louder than the normal screaming. Instead, I found them squared off on either side of the kitchen table, and she was armed with a heavy antique kitchen scale. She was raging. I had never seen her so angry. She usually only looked scared when they fought. When he noticed us, my dad took the opportunity to mock her. *Look, kids—look at your mother. She's crazy, she's fucked up.*

His laughter was derisive and shook me. I didn't know what to think, how to make sense of her rage, her impending violence. Then he said the most shocking thing of all: *You'd better straighten up, or I'm going to take these kids and leave.* He had never threatened to take us before, and I implicitly knew he didn't want us. I was begging *please no* in my mind when she screamed, *Take them! Take them and get out of here, just leave me alone! I don't care anymore!*

I wondered in horror what would happen to us if he took us away. He might kill us, he might whip us, we might never see anyone we love again. I was more frightened then than ever, thinking she would sacrifice us for good, one last time, and we would be lost to the world. It didn't happen, of course. My father sent us to the car and we waited there for about fifteen minutes, but it was my mother who came and told us to get out, that we weren't leaving. I searched her face for some explanation, but it wasn't there. I never asked her what had happened, how it was that she was ready to watch us leave. I don't know who backed down first, but I imagine it was her. And I imagine that it was not my father's love that made her change her mind but that he spelled out the consequences for her if she didn't *put that fucking scale down right now*, and she started seeing things his way.

There was another time when she talked back to him, and I watched him grow more agitated. I wasn't even ten, but I asked her, *Why don't you just go along with what he says, make him happy?* It wasn't really a question—I was agitated, too. I knew that she knew what to do, how to survive—we all did. What was the point of fighting back? There would only be hell to pay. Some part of me knew that he was still in the wrong, of course, and that my mother had every right to stand up for herself. But I didn't care. I didn't have the emotional resources to always care about what was wrong or right or fair—I just wanted things to be bearable. I didn't want to wonder again what he was going to do to her, to us, to anyone we loved.

All that time, I was going to church every Sunday morning with Granny. Between church and God and all the uncensored reading I did, I developed my own superstitious faith in the unseen. Grandma Wright didn't go to church but chain-smoked and gave me grocery bags full of her tabloids—usually *Star*, which I would read cover to cover, intrigued by the lovers and wives, the breakups, and the scandalous red-carpet outfits. One time, there was a *Sun* in a bag she gave me, and I read it thinking it would be like *Star*. I found out pretty quickly it was more like the *National Enquirer* that sometimes appeared at Grandma's house but that I usually saw at the grocery checkout lines.

But in that issue of *Sun*, there was a set of instructions on how to make your deepest wish come true. In the lower right-hand corner of one of the pages, the tabloid gave directions to fold a new one-dollar bill in a particular order, place it in a new white handkerchief, put the handkerchief under one's pillow, and imagine what it was one longed for the most. And then, the instructions claimed—*abracadabra*—the wish would be granted.

It seemed so simple, but I wondered what exactly they meant by a *new* dollar bill. I could not find one in our house that was less than a few years old, but I thought I would give it a try anyway. My father had lots of handkerchiefs that he carried with him. None of them were in new condition, though. I went into my parents' bedroom as nonchalantly as I could and picked one that looked the whitest, thinking it would have to do. Back in my bedroom, I followed the directions for folding the dollar bill and handkerchief exactly so and looked forward to lying down that night.

I was not sure what I would wish for, but as I thought about it in the dark, I quickly started dreaming. *I am sleeping in a large white bed, covered by a pristine white comforter. My bedroom has beautiful wooden walls. My father walks in and I sit up, propping myself with the thick, soft pillows behind me. He is wearing a white suit and looks strong, healthy. He sits on my bed and says,* I just want to say thank you—thank you for showing me the light. *And I am relieved, proud, knowing I have finally saved him.*

Many years later, a boyfriend would tell me that it was *dark magic,* that my father's white suit marked him as a deceiver, that Lucifer was the *light bearer,* and that it was a spirit trying to trick me. For years, I just waited to see whether it would come true.

I didn't know yet that his cruelty and coldness never had anything to do with us, with how lovable we were, how good or bad we had been. As an adult, I could intellectualize it. I could talk about his own self-loathing, about projection, about abuse and cycles and emptiness, etc., ad infinitum. Eventually, I came to have a little more compassion for myself and for my life, which always seemed to be more difficult and a little more ugly than other people's lives. I realized how hard it is to manage a bank account and bills, and not smoke cigarettes or drink or some other form of self-medicating, when you still carry that feeling from childhood that tells you death is near, and you very well might die at the hands of someone you love, someone you need. And besides, I was reminded every Sunday in church that the world would end in decidedly unpleasant ways—probably any minute now—and that I was most likely going to Hell. It is hard to get your act together when you are waiting for the Apocalypse.

But inside, even at twenty, thirty, thirty-five years old, after becoming a mother myself and finding pity for my father who could not love us nor be loved, I still found myself hoping that before he died, I would know how it felt to have a father who loved me.

CHAPTER 4

Sunday Morning

Everyone knows, of course, that the only father you really need to worry about is the one in Heaven. He's the one whose judgment really matters, the one who can make Hell last forever. Half the time in church, that's what I thought about, full of fear and trembling—that some pain is endless, that some things burn relentlessly. That my heavenly father could hate me, despise me, revile me no matter what I did, because I was born into sin, and damn if nothing seemed to help, no matter how hard I prayed.

That's the only thing that made sense after I had learned so many Bible verses and cleaned my room and even made the teachers at school proud, but still felt like something was tearing me apart from within. All the awful things I felt inside must have been because I was such a sinner, even though I wasn't sure exactly what I had done wrong. I just *knew* that something was terribly wrong inside me. The hell I was in was just a promise of what was yet to come, if I didn't fix myself. If I didn't make it right.

But half the time, there was Jesus and the New Testament with its relative gentleness. I read most of the Bible alone, sometimes fervently preparing for Sunday school so I could win a mini-Snickers candy bar for memorizing my verses—which I was particularly good at—but mostly so I could go to Heaven, or at least have a fighting chance.

We read only from the King James Version of the Bible, which was so full of poetic language, so many *thou*s and *breadth*s, I was fully prepared to study philosophy and poetry in college but didn't know that yet.

Learning Bible stories from soft, old women with white hair made it easy to believe in Heaven. But then that older boy took me downstairs to a Sunday school classroom while everyone else listened to the sermon upstairs. He took me to the room I was supposed to go to after kindergarten and sat me on his lap as he pulled my shirt out from my skirt.

The skirt was dark blue, with a red hippopotamus embroidered on it. My shirt was light blue, a button-up, and had a scalloped collar. It's the same outfit I am wearing in a picture taken of my brother and me, a picture that hung in my granny's house for as long as I can remember.

The boy's grandparents were friends of my grandparents, and they called each other *Brother* and *Sister* in church. His grandfather had worked with my papaw Conn. The grandmother sang in the choir, and I loved the way she stood in front of the whole church sometimes, singing in a trembly voice: *Amazing grace, how sweet the sound, that saved a wretch like me.*

I saw the boy again when I was seventeen and attending church with my granny in a rare effort to please her with my potential to go to Heaven. He sat by his pretty wife in church; she held their baby. I watched them, wondering whether he remembered that day and recognized me. I prayed that whatever had led him to touch me had faded long ago, was forever extinguished, that his baby was safe.

I don't know that he didn't do more on that Sunday morning. I don't remember any physical pain or exactly what I felt other than a great, uneasy fear. I avoided that church classroom afterward, going so far as to stay in the younger Sunday school class for a year, rather than sit with the other kids my age in that room. My granny tried to convince me to go to the next class, but I claimed I just loved my Sunday school teacher too much and didn't want to leave her, which everyone eventually accepted. I wouldn't attend activities in that room and instead lingered elsewhere, around other Sunday school teachers, whenever all the other young children were gathered there. At the time, I didn't consciously think about what had happened, but I knew I didn't like the way I felt in that room. I still remember the way the tables looked, where the door was situated, the coolness of the air around us when he pulled me to him.

My parents didn't go to church with my granny except sometimes on Easter, and they encouraged us to pray in only one situation. They would tell us to go to one of our beds—mine or my brother's—and, in the dark, put our faces down to the bed and close our eyes. Then, as sincerely and excitedly as possible, we were to pray for Reese's Cups. We obeyed, and you know how God is good and if you ask, you will receive? Well, within just a few minutes of our praying, Reese's Cups would suddenly come raining down from above, and we would gather them up and take them to the living room. Our parents would ask, *Did God answer your prayers?* And we would say, *Yes, look at our Reese's Cups!* I didn't know whether they realized we knew they threw the candy in through the open door, and I never began to understand why they wanted us to pray for such a thing. Maybe there was some satisfaction in watching us ask for something they could deliver. I was embarrassed by the whole charade but kept it up, just like they told us to.

Despite my parents' lack of interest, I still wanted to be a good Christian. When I was nine, I decided to get baptized—I had been saved countless times at the altar, and I thought maybe going a step further with baptism would make the good feeling last longer. I wore a flowery dress, and in front of the whole church, our preacher, who looked a little like someone from *The Munsters*, dunked me backward into what was basically a large bathtub with a nature scene behind us.

Granny was waiting for me when I walked out sopping wet into the back room, and she asked me how I felt. I answered her, *Perfect,* and she assured me, *You are.*

But even after being baptized, I couldn't shake the feeling that something was terribly wrong. After a couple of weeks, I found myself listening intently to the sermon, straining to hear God's voice. All that happened, though, was that at the end of each service, the preacher would beseech all the sinners to *give it up, walk down that aisle, and give yourselves to God.* He was waiting for us, waiting to welcome us into the Kingdom of Heaven, and all we had to do was ask.

I thought he was talking to me because we both knew I was so awful inside, something wasn't right. Maybe the devil had gotten me, or I had committed so much sin without even meaning to. So again and again, I asked. I walked down the aisle, sick with fear, and cried at the altar beside my granny, who knelt and cried there every Sunday. Sometimes we prayed together. Sometimes she gave me her wet tissues to blow my nose into. I begged to be forgiven for my sins, for all the impurities that must have been making me feel like I was being torn apart nearly all the time. Sometimes the preacher came over and laid his hand on our shoulders and prayed with us, and I thought that might help. Sometimes he didn't, and we made our way back to the pews at the end of the service, but nothing felt different. After a while, I realized that the preacher knew my granny didn't need to be saved. Somehow, he knew she was there for the people she loved.

I wonder now whether anyone was puzzled by my weekly trek to the front of the church—there certainly weren't any other children up there. Did they think I was a zealot? That I was a child of God and able to hear him so clearly? Or perhaps, like my friends' mothers and some doting teachers, they simply thought that despite their concern, there was nothing they could do for me.

Growing up in a holler as we did in the 1980s and in eastern Kentucky, it was perfectly normal to get whipped as punishment. Dad often used his leather belt, but both our parents would sometimes make us go pick our own switches, and the only ones nearby were from those thorny black locust trees. The sting of the switch was accompanied by thorns tearing the skin of our legs or bare bottoms, so my brother and I were both pretty set on avoiding switchings and whippings as much as possible.

Sometimes I would stare out the kitchen window at the big black locust tree that grew there, thinking how uninviting it was with its thorns and hardness. Not the weeping willows of my fantasies, where I imagined that one day I would live with the tree spirits, despite never having been told a story about tree spirits or, at that point, having seen an actual weeping willow.

We ate like poor people in that kitchen. Lots of baloney sandwiches, lots of Kool-Aid. Sometimes, when Dad wasn't home and we had very little, my mom, brother, and I would share a can of beans for dinner. When Dad was there, we ate cautiously, hoping not to arouse his ire. That took some finesse, though, since there really was no predicting his anger.

But I use the word *poor* as if it were a simple word, as if you should understand. Being poor will always be married in my mind to the other, intangible sorts of poverty that infused my childhood. One night, the large black locust tree became a site for my knowledge of poverty when my mother, my brother, and I crushed aluminum cans beneath it. I started to stomp them onto one of the cinder blocks that formed our back steps, since that was easier than crushing them on the wet ground. My mother corrected me and had me move my cans back to the ground, saying we needed to mash them where some of the mud would get into them. That way, she said, they would weigh more when we took them to the aluminum recycling place.

I didn't know exactly what that meant about us, but I remember feeling ashamed when the large, dirty-looking man weighed our bags of cans. Surely he knew that part of the weight was from something other than aluminum. I avoided looking at my mother's face, hoping she wouldn't also have to feel the shame if she didn't see it in me. After all, we needed the money to buy milk.

We always knew someone poorer than we were, though. A family who lived in a bus. A little girl who had worms coming out of her nose, she was so infested with parasites. A man who liked to burn his son's arms with a lighter and then pull the scabs off and cover them with shaving cream. There was always something worse.

Ten years after my last whipping, a friend came to my house before we went to a party. We cooked steaks—she was on her period and craving meat. I watched them sizzle in the pan as my thoughts drifted, until I heard the zipping sound of her belt as she pulled it from her belt loops, frustrated with the constriction around her stomach. The look on my face when I wheeled around, still flinching, told her everything.

Easy, girl, she said. *I'm not your daddy.*

It was nice, in a way, to have someone who in that moment knew what had happened inside me, without me having to explain. Most people would have responded with a blank look, and then some sympathy after I explained my reaction with nervous laughter. If you don't know how it feels, there is no understanding that kind of fear. She was also the first person who knew, before I even said it, that it was hard to date a man with money, someone from a different class.

The day I agreed to call my granny a whore, I didn't get a switching, but I knew I had traded on something precious to save my *self,* my skin, my body. It was an impossible choice, at that age: to face my father's rage with no one to defend me, wondering how far he would go, or to insult my grandmother, the one person who made me feel safe and loved and seen. There was shame at either end, and a great question about who I was, who I could be in such a world. About why everything was so pretty around me, yet I felt so ugly inside.

CHAPTER 5

Gifted

One day in first grade, I shuffled to the balance beam in dejection. My best friend was playing with another girl who was younger and seemed to smile and laugh a lot. Even then, I had a sense that I wasn't as happy as other children, and most of them had a carefree air that I couldn't quite understand. Like they weren't always watching, on alert and taking note of the world around them.

My friend came to me and asked me what was wrong, and I told her how sad I was that she had another friend. She comforted me but told me that she could have other friends and still like me. That didn't make sense to me, though—I knew the world as a place where there is only so much love to go around, a finite amount of attention and care that any one person can give. My friend had dimples and a sweet smile, and her blue eyes lit up easily. I had felt lucky that she liked me, and it seemed that this was the end of my good fortune.

In fact, she did continue to be a friend, but I never again felt sure that any friend was there for good. It would take years—decades, even—to understand that all my relationships perfectly met my low expectations. That it was not bad luck or a curse that doomed me to feel constant loss, but that my beliefs about the world would shape everything around me, that my childhood trauma would render it all as if *through a glass, darkly*.

Still, as a child, I loved being at school, and when I look back to those early years, I remember laughing with my classmates and feeling like we were all friends. In second grade, a boy in my class and I came up with nicknames for ourselves by spelling our names backward. His worked out to something that sounded like *Carrie*, and mine was pronounced *E-bob*.

Almost twenty-five years later, I looked at the county jail website and saw that he was there, still in our hometown. He probably did not do as well in school as I did and likely had a hard time finding a decent job. His parents may have abused him, or he may have been raised by grandparents, or he may still live with his parents when he's not in jail. Whenever I look up inmates in the county jail, I inevitably see former classmates in there for burglary, robbery, methamphetamine manufacturing, narcotics trafficking, driving while intoxicated, and so on. I see grown boys I had crushes on, and I search their faces, looking for their stories.

This particular boy was a quiet, good-natured friend who had slightly chubby cheeks and a matter-of-fact air about him. In his mug shot, he stands in front of a cinder-block wall and stares straight into the camera, revealing nothing in his gaze. I search his eyes for some detail, some betrayal that will tell me how he got there. I wonder whether he is still kind or if he has come to hate the adults who failed him and now hates everyone else and himself in turn. I wonder whether he will find his way out or trudge along in a cycle of incarceration, joblessness, desperation, drug abuse, and, finally, a lonely death.

Or, I wonder, could he become a brilliant engineer or poet? Where does his passion lie? What is the spark inside him that gives him hope life is worth living and, even more, life still holds a promise of happiness in some unwritten future? I think about touching his soft cheeks and reminding him how we sat in the hallway in our elementary school, how I was studying spelling bee words, how we didn't think of ourselves as being any different from anyone else. How laughter came so easily, how we enjoyed that moment, no matter what else was haunting us from home and no matter the nightmares that would not stay put in the darkness, where they belonged.

In fourth grade, I entered the county school system's *gifted* program and was the only person from my school to do so at the time. I rode the bus alone from our little school, which sat near the same creek that flowed by my house, to the combined elementary and middle school in town. For one day a week, I went to this new place, meeting strangers and suddenly surrounded by throngs of people. I had no idea how to do anything I was supposed to do—I was constantly afraid I would get on the wrong bus and end up in another town, or I would go to the wrong room and be lost forever.

There were about fifteen other kids in the program, all from various schools in the county, and we would have our weekly gifted school day in a room adjacent to the basement library of the elementary wing. I thought all the other kids knew each other, though they probably did not. Almost everyone, though, seemed to possess a sort of ease, a self-assurance that they knew what to do and they were certain that what they were doing was good. We had Spanish lessons, and we learned about current events. It was the first I ever heard of the Soviet Union and the man with the strange red birthmark on his forehead. We learned about other cultures and had international food days, where our teacher made a Japanese chicken dish and we all said *konnichiwa*.

Early in the school year, we were given "About Me" sheets to fill out so we could get to know each other. It was a list of our favorites—favorite song, favorite television show, favorite food, etc. At that time, I had never heard any music except what played on the one country music station that reached our holler, and a few of the records my parents owned—a lot of country, a little Janis Joplin. My favorite musician

41

was Ricky Skaggs or George Jones—people my classmates had never heard of.

When I took that sheet home from my gifted class to try to tell my classmates "About Me," I sat in my father's recliner and read the sentences and thought about the blanks we were supposed to fill in. *Tell them about me.*

One of the questions asked, "If you could be any other person, who would you be?" My immediate thought was that I didn't want to be anyone else, because if I was someone else, someone else would have to be me, and nobody else could do it. I was nine, and I gave it no further thought. I don't remember whether I filled in the blanks so my teacher would be happy with my effort, but in that moment, it seemed imperative that I be *me*, and accept being *me*, so I could do whatever it was I needed to do. So it would all make sense in the end, this unbearable life I had.

Though I tried my best to figure out what I was supposed to do in my gifted class and did well in my work, I did not have what it took to succeed socially with the other students. I continued the program in the fifth grade—we all rode a bus to the board of education building, where we held our weekly class in a large conference room. Like dogs, wolves, and flocks of chickens, the kids had figured out a pecking order where I was at the bottom. They particularly enjoyed calling me *Boobie*, which tormented me to the point that my mother wrote our teacher a letter and told her I wanted to quit the program. The teacher took a few of the kids aside and told them to stop, and for a while it seemed they gave up that particular way of taunting me.

At one point, I told them about my nickname from grade school, *E-bob*, thinking it would be a preferable nickname to hear from them. I didn't realize, though, that anything they did or said would take on a hurtful edge, and the silly nickname that I had helped create and laughed about with my friend became the subject of songs, chants, and endless cruel jokes in my weekly gifted class. They seemed to take a lot of pleasure in provoking me, though most of the time I either glowered silently or cried with frustration and exhaustion.

Once, as we waited for the bus to take us to the board of education building, I sat on the front steps of the elementary school in town with my *science project*. We were given pretty loose parameters for constructing a science project, and I had no idea how to do one. My mother bought me a figure of the Statue of Liberty from the dollar store that, when placed in water, would expand over several days. I had never seen such a thing, and though I had a nagging doubt that it did not qualify as a scientific experiment, I did my best to make it work. I carefully cleaned an empty glass Tang jar from Grandma Wright's house and peeled the label off, then placed the figure in it and measured the amount of water I could add. I also measured the figure as it expanded, but before long, it outgrew the jar and sat contorted, the substance all soft and grotesque and Miss Liberty looking anything but regal. But I had nothing else to use, so I took it to school and hoped it would be acceptable to my teacher.

My fears about my misshapen Statue of Liberty were quickly confirmed by the other students, who began making fun of me in earnest while we waited for the bus to take us to class. I felt my face grow hot, and I tried to ignore them for a few minutes, but they were standing in front of me as I sat on a step at one side of the school entrance. They didn't seem likely to grow tired of their game that particular morning. I couldn't think of anything else to do, so I moved from one side of the school door to the other, desperate to get away from them and their mockery. When I sat back down on the steps, I slammed my Tang jar onto the concrete in rage, and the glass shattered while I was still holding on to it. Pieces of the jar flew away from me, and my swollen Statue of Liberty fell out, all her water lost around us. My classmates were suddenly silent and stared at me with wide eyes, and I ran into the school toward the bathroom, afraid of what I had done but relieved that they were finally quiet.

The tears fell hot down my face, and a man in the hallway looked at me, asking, *How are you doing today?* I didn't recognize him and assumed he was a teacher. I paused for a second and responded, *If I was any better, I would be dead.* He gave a concerned, *Aw, don't say that,* but I was already walking again. I rinsed my red face in the bathroom and ignored the girls who came in, too angry to feel embarrassed in that moment. When I went back outside to catch our bus, my classmates had gathered my things together, picked up the broken glass, and salvaged what was left of Miss Liberty. I was surprised by their rare kindness but got on the bus silently and did not acknowledge it. When my anger subsided, we were right back to the same roles.

I understand now that there were, in fact, other children like me—though they weren't likely to be in the gifted classes with me. The gifted program was full of kids whose parents liked them, or at least signed them up for gymnastics lessons and took them to get their teeth cleaned and all the things that were foreign to me. On normal school days, I was around other kids whose parents drank too much or did pills, who hit them with belts and mostly just didn't want to hear the kid make any noise. Not all of them were like that, but because we were in a poor part of the county, I didn't stick out like a sore thumb. There were plenty of other kids with their own personal hell burning inside them as we tried to memorize capital cities and the names of all our presidents and multiplication tables.

My little elementary school was mostly a haven, where my teachers liked me and I didn't stand out too much. Some days, though, after I turned in my work and was drawing or reading while the other kids finished, in my head I would hear my mother screaming like she was in two worlds at once, being beaten by my father some two miles away and coming to me at the same time, reminding me that something was always wrong. I didn't stop to think about it, but I somehow knew that the other kids weren't torn apart by what came from finishing their work and sitting in stillness, no longer distracted from their mothers' distant screams. I knew I wasn't like them.

CHAPTER 6

The Dark of Night

Growing up, I learned that although holidays were the best thing ever, there was also a very real chance that something would go wrong anytime we gathered for a family meal or opened presents. We went to Grandma Wright's on Christmas Eve, but we went to Granny Conn's house for most other holidays. Granny cooked all the food you could ever want in eastern Kentucky: turkey, ham, chicken and dumplings, mashed potatoes, corn bread, Stove Top stuffing, green beans from her garden, corn that she grew, and macaroni and tomatoes (made with her own canned tomatoes).

She insisted on giving me her canned vegetables long after I stopped appreciating them, and then after I started again. I remember the day I opened the last Mason jar of tomatoes she ever canned and gave to me. I held on to it like the treasure it was and still thank whoever is listening that I had sense enough to know its value.

On Christmas Eve, Grandma Wright usually baked a ham with pineapple rings—we didn't have pineapple anywhere else—but there was pizza, too. Nobody would deliver up in our holler, so we usually had pizza only at Grandma's. They got normal television, so Papaw Wright would be watching racing, wrestling, or *The Andy Griffith Show*. I always gave Grandma chocolate-covered cherries and gave Papaw a tin of cashews or walnuts still in the shell. I wrapped them with care, each time so proud I could give them something they loved.

I walked to my bedroom door one day not long before Christmas to find that my bed and floor were covered with plants, drying and sending off a scent that reminded me of the smell that came from my parents' bedroom sometimes.

My dad told me not to go in—*That's your Christmas*. And he laughed often about the way Christmas came for us, a good harvest that was quickly spent on the things we couldn't afford the rest of the year. Tax returns were like that sometimes, too—we got the Nintendo that one year, and my brother and I played Duck Hunt as much as we could stand it but played Super Mario Bros. until we beat it. Every time we went to a grocery store, I searched the magazine aisle for a cheat book and could usually memorize one cheat to use once we got back to the looming violence of our home.

When I was around six years old, Christmas Eve came, and my brother was eager to open a gift—*Just one*, he said—and my mother said we could. Dad wasn't home. I admonished them: *How could you all think of opening presents while our dad is out there working to make money for us on Christmas Eve?* My mother was as disgusted with me as I was with her: *Your dad's not working—he's drinking with his friends. Do you want to open a present or not?*

I opened the gift she handed me, but I was too young to pretend I wasn't crushed. That night, I slept on the couch until he stumbled through the door. He went to wake up my mother while I pretended to sleep in case he started hitting her.

My brother and I would get up in the mornings and check with each other. *Did you hear it?* I'd ask him. *Yeah. Did you?* We didn't really discuss the details. One night, I awoke to her cries, and I heard the sound of his fists. Then, *If you wake those goddamn kids up, I swear I will kill your fucking parents, you hear me?* He threw open my bedroom door, flipped the light on, and stood above me, looking for a flicker of awareness to betray me. After a minute—a few minutes? a lifetime?—he turned off my light, shut the door, and went to do the same thing in my brother's room. I knew Junior must be pretending to be asleep, too, fearing for our lives, her life, our grandma's and papaw's lives.

It is remarkable how good I became at hiding my feelings. I learned to keep my face blank, hold back tears, lower my eyes, and to lie when it really mattered. You would think this kind of skill would come in handy later in life—I could be an expert poker player, or an actress, or maybe even a politician. But still, I felt things too deeply—the hiding never lessened the intensity of all that *feeling*. As I grew older, I hid my emotions and pushed down my feelings in all my relationships, which was actually somewhat beneficial since I kept finding myself surrounded by people who reminded me of my father in some way. But all that hiding, all that silence, makes you vulnerable in a different way.

My six-year-old Christmas Eve, though, ended up being less violent than those kinds of occasions often were. Dad told us all to wake up, and as he fell to the floor and into the coffee table, as he cussed and pushed and threatened, we got our coats on. He wanted to go to the little country store owned by a woman named Birdie. That little country store should be on a calendar somewhere, one that depicts the simplicity of quiet country living. There was room for only two or three cars to park at one time, and you walked up worn wooden steps to get to the front door. Weathered wooden slats covered the outside, and white paint chips fell from the boards in a year-round, lead-based snow. Inside, it was just one room that held a child's dream of candy. All the pops were in hard glass bottles, and on the counter sat two obscenely large jars, one filled with giant pickles, the other with unnaturally pink pork franks. Birdie had white hair even when I was young. She seemed soft, like old age was treating her mercifully.

I still think of Birdie and that little store, and I long for the moments I remember in there, picking out candy cigarettes—the best ones had a bit of color at the end, which made it easier to pretend you were really smoking.

Everything was dark and closed, but Dad wanted a pop from the machine on the front porch of the store. Mom drove, and Dad grabbed the steering wheel over and over, pulling our long yellow Buick toward the creek, into the other lane, everywhere, as Junior and I sat silent in the back seat, at a time before children wore seat belts. There was the creek that bordered our one-lane gravel road, and then there was another creek across from Birdie's. I don't know how Mom kept us out of either one. Somehow, we did not die, and Dad got the Grape Crush he wanted. The next day, we waited until the afternoon to open our presents. From his bed, we heard him: *Tell those little motherfuckers to be quiet out there. My head hurts, and I don't want to hear a fucking sound.* I was still young enough to be surprised, at that point. Still young enough to think, *Surely he doesn't mean that.*

~

The holiday I looked forward to the most was the Fourth of July. My dad's cousin would bring his family from Tennessee, including a daughter close to my age and a son close to my brother's age. Their middle child, a girl, had the hard lot of trying to fit in somewhere, anywhere. They would show up with a trunk load of fireworks that were illegal in Kentucky, and we would grill hamburgers and hot dogs and fry potatoes in aluminum foil, waiting for the sun to set. The adults would drink their cheap drinks, and my dad would give us liberal sips of beer or hard liquor while his cousin wasn't looking. Then they would slip off to smoke a joint or maybe snort some pills while we caught lightning bugs, impatiently passing the time until we could watch the jumping jacks burn up the grass and experience the pure novelty of the Roman candle. The next day, we'd all go camping on the other side of Cave Run Lake, the biggest tourist attraction from there to Winchester.

The lake was built by flooding part of the Daniel Boone National Forest, but it happens that my great-grandmother—Granny's mother—owned land down there, too. The Army Corps of Engineers dammed the Licking River after paying, I'm sure, a terribly fair price for her land. By the 1960s, when the project began, the US government had watched while speculators bought the lumber and mineral rights from Appalachians, and those robber barons left the region polluted and broken. Even as a child, I knew we weren't supposed to trust politicians.

I grew up knowing that fact in the same way we knew not to pick up a snake—not because someone told me, but because it was necessary to survival. Listening to the news that Papaw Conn sometimes watched, I heard about promises of a brighter future, good jobs, better pay—but those things just didn't seem to make it to the poor people around me. How would someone like my father get a good job anyway, without a high school diploma?

The politicians who made these promises didn't look like us or talk like us. They always seemed to be talking out of both sides of their mouths—saying whatever they thought their audience wanted to hear and changing the message accordingly. Besides all that, it would have taken sacrifice to truly address the reality of poverty and the many kinds of despair in this country. Despair takes on a different look, depending on where you go, but those who have lived it can see it in others. No, the kind of sacrifice it takes to make real change isn't glamorous, and it's not a sure bet you'll get reelected or even recognized. Why would anybody want to stick their neck out for some ungrateful rednecks? At some point in my childhood, it seemed like the long-standing cultural disdain toward Appalachia became mutual.

None of that bothered us kids, of course, as we swam in the lake that drowned my great-grandmother's home, as we ran through the tame forest, picking up sticks for the grown-ups to build a fire. In retrospect, those vacations seemed to always go so well because the adults had plenty of beer, weed, and pills on hand. If it could have been that simple all the time, I would have loved to have seen my dad drunk and high. At home, though, he wasn't prone to being jovial unless someone else was around, and if he just couldn't get what he was looking for—well, we all suffered with him.

One particular year—1987?—something went wrong as we waited for our cousins to arrive for what was usually a whole week of Dad being mostly bearable. Junior and I were playing in the front yard when he yelled for us to come to the living room, and right away we recognized that as a bad sign. Sitting in his recliner, he was holding a tape recorder, one that my brother and I used to make recordings of ourselves telling stories and talking in funny voices, and sometimes my brother would record the sounds of our parents having sex. I thought we were going to be in trouble for something my dad had found recorded, but instead, the battery cover was missing from the back of the tape recorder, and the batteries along with it. He started out asking us, with unusual calm, *Who did this? You're not in trouble, just tell me.* Neither of us said anything. *Was it you?* He asked us both, and we each denied removing the battery cover. *Who was it then?* One of us offered that maybe it was our cousin, the daring one, the one who got whipped a lot. Dad didn't think it was him.

The more he asked, the more his voice betrayed an agitation that told me we were, in fact, getting closer to trouble. Still, we both denied removing the battery cover until he was calm again and said, *Fine, I'll whip you both and send you to bed, and there will be no fireworks for either one of you.* I knew he would follow through on the threat, and I looked at my brother, my one confidante and fellow prisoner there. I always felt like Junior was nicer than I was, and maybe more fragile, for some reason. He grew up to be nearly a foot taller than me and by no means a scrawny man, but back then, I wanted to protect him and thought I could maybe take a whipping better than he could, maybe it hurt him more since he was smaller. It also seemed terribly unjust that neither of us would get to see the fireworks, when both of us were innocent.

I took a small step forward and told our father, *I did it.* His calm gave way to rage, and he demanded over and over to know why I did it, but I couldn't answer him and didn't know what to say, so I stood there saying, *I don't know,* which might have been his least favorite thing. After a few more minutes of demanding that I explain myself, he finally got to the whipping, bringing his belt across my bottom and wherever else it landed. Was it three times? Four? More? It was excruciating. I knew the Bible said it was good for me, but I wasn't sure my father did it out of love. Could he save my soul even if he didn't mean to?

The worst part about my father's whippings was that afterward, we were not allowed to cry in his presence. If we cried, he said, *Dry it up, or I'll give you something to cry about.* And my brother and I would suck it all back in—the tears, the cries, the yelps—so he would not be further enraged. I held in my cries until he sent me to my room, where I threw myself on my bed and sobbed into my pillow as quietly as I could.

When my mother came to check on me, I told her I hadn't done it. She said she knew, so I asked her why she let him whip me. *You know how your father is,* she said. At that moment, I began to understand how each of us—my brother, my mother, and myself—were very much alone in that house. In my child's mind, I felt the most alone of all.

I didn't know why I wanted to protect my brother, and why no one could protect me. I didn't understand what happens to people when they are just trying to survive. I couldn't have told you that, as a girl, I felt like I had a duty to my family, a responsibility that was God given or something close to it. As if I was the only one who could save us.

CHAPTER 7

What We Can Fix

On our one-lane gravel road, my brother and I had more freedom with cars than most. From the time we were three or four, we were often allowed to sit on our parents' laps and steer the car as they drove from our house to Granny and Papaw Conn's, since it was such a short distance and there was so little traffic on our road. Of course, there were no police patrols and no neighbors close enough to see anything that happened at our house. The best treat was when our father would let us sit on the hood of the car, which he started letting us do when I was about six, and we would press ourselves against the hood or windshield, hanging on to nothing as he drove.

Those adventures usually seemed safe enough, as even our dad must have decided it was best not to lose a kid off the hood of a car. Sometimes, though, when there was a dog around, the dog would somehow get in front of the car, and suddenly Dad would accelerate. The car would be right on top of the dog, who was by then running as fast as he could. Junior and I would scream and yell for our dad to slow down and be careful, and Dad would just laugh and gun it a little, bringing us even closer, I was certain, to the dog's demise. We never ran over a dog, though, and we never fell off the car. On those days, it was a relief to reach our driveway and see the dog run safely into the yard, away from Dad's laughter and our racing hearts.

Other than the beagle named Daisy that one of Dad's friends gave us, dogs never lasted long enough at our house for me to remember their names, so I did not grow attached to them. Most of the time, strays showed up out of nowhere, and we fed them table scraps when we had them to spare. I'm certain we never bought a bag of dog food. They wandered up the gravel road or out of the woods like some unfortunate fairy-tale child who stumbles upon a suspicious gingerbread house.

I didn't realize people took animals to vets until I was much older, and later in life, it was still difficult to understand why people bought lamb-and-rice dog food or spent money on medicine for dogs or booties for their paws. Those are the kinds of things you buy when you have so much money, you don't have to worry anymore about how many times your children have eaten hot dogs this week, or how they're behind on their shots, or whether their clothes are looking too small or too stained so maybe someone's going to call social services on you.

Even after growing up and getting a job and being able to buy organic food and the name-brand clothes for my kids that I wore only as hand-me-downs from friends, I struggle to imagine how we could take care of a dog like a family member. It seems that my guilt and worry about all the dogs I saw mistreated come out in subtle cues to them now, as they sniff me and I tense up, suddenly filled with the same fear I had as a child, wondering what awful thing is going to happen next.

When I was about eight years old, we had a dog around for a while—whether it was one my dad chased down the road with us on the car, I couldn't say. Looking back, I can tell you it was about the size of a Lab and completely black. I don't think we gave it a name. Once, it followed me to Granny's house when I walked there to get some onions and tomatoes for my dad on a sunny afternoon. Granny and Papaw Conn were not home, but the chickens were out, pecking away at the dirt and grass, minding their own business. The dog got excited about the chickens and lunged for them, and my shouts could not stop him from chasing them in earnest. He finally caught a baby chick and crushed it in his jaws, dropped it and sniffed, then walked away. I was devastated by the chick's death and walked back to our house sobbing, tears rolling down my face.

My father was standing outside, and when he saw me approaching, he demanded to know what was wrong. He already seemed angry, and my sorrow gave way to another feeling, a caution. I tried to catch my breath and, through choked sobs, told him that the dog had killed one of Granny's baby chickens. I thought I might get in trouble, and some little part of me wondered whether he might tell me everything was okay, but he just grew angrier, and it seemed he was impatient, or unhappy that I interrupted him, or some other undefinable emotion. He unbuckled his belt and slid it out of his belt loops.

I thought I was going to be whipped for not controlling the dog, but he grabbed the dog by the scruff of the neck and yanked it into the air—all fifty or so pounds. The dog yelped at being jerked off the ground, but when my father whipped it over and over with the belt, the dog's cries shocked me into silence. I could not cry for myself anymore and just stood there watching, wishing I had known to protect it. When he dropped the dog, my father turned to me and told me to stop crying, or he'd give me something to cry about. But my tears had already stopped.

When I was older, I found that some of my friends would laughingly recall their mothers coming after them with a wooden spoon. They spoke of things like being *spanked*, which I didn't quite understand—it didn't seem to have any impact on them, and it was more like a joke shared between the children and parents, an act of authority and submission that was almost a charade.

My father's leather belt, though, fell on us without mercy, without reason. I was a Girl Scout for some of my grade school years, and one late fall, as winter darkened toward us, we picked paper angels from a plastic tree somewhere in town. The angels bore the names of children whose parents declared themselves unable to buy a doll or underwear or shoes for their children that year. Each of us Girl Scouts picked an angel from the tree and vowed to buy a gift or two for the unlucky child. Mine wanted a doll, and one afternoon, while my mother worked, my uncle came to get me, my brother, and our father to go to the dollar store and buy the doll. I think that was around the time that Dad no longer managed the gas station, but Mom still went there to do the bookkeeping. Dad had a pretty steady flow of people in and out of the house, and he was always *wheeling and dealing*, as he put it. Selling pills or the weed he grew meant we didn't have to put our own names on an angel tree.

As we started to pull out of the driveway, my father noticed that my brother had chocolate around the corners of his mouth. Dad told my uncle to stop the truck just as we were pulling away, and he sent us back inside. I wasn't quite sure what was going to happen until my dad started whipping Junior in the living room. After a few hits, he sent Junior to his room and turned toward me. I realized that he was about to make a mistake—his frustration had been with Junior, not with me, and I had done nothing to anger him. I thought he must have forgotten what upset him, and in a moment that stands out as the first and only time I tried to defend myself, I started to speak: *Wait*— But before I could explain, the belt hit my back, my ass, my legs, and my words were gone. What was I going to tell him? In that moment of clarity, I saw his unhinged rage and thought I could make him see it for what it was. For a moment, I knew I was innocent.

When my mother came home that evening, she went into the bathroom with me as I showed her the bruises on my body—somehow asking her, perhaps because of something I had heard at school, whether this was abuse. She murmured a dismissal, and I asked her whether he had told her what happened. She said *yes*, he told her we refused to clean our rooms, so we were punished. And that was all.

It was especially ironic that he told her we wouldn't clean our rooms. I cleaned constantly, always thinking that with a little more effort, everything would be perfect, and Dad would have nothing to be angry about. By the time I was seven, if we children were left alone for a few hours, I often set out to get the laundry folded, the floors vacuumed, the coal stove cleaned, and the coal buckets filled. I washed dishes, I organized my books alphabetically, I made my bed. I swept the coal-dust-covered cobwebs from the corners of our living room. Nothing worked, but I kept trying. I brought home report cards filled with As and teachers' praises, but Dad always pointed out with a laugh that while it was good, any A should have been an A+.

Looking back now, I can see that anxiety fueled my feeble attempts to fix the broken world around me, and that anxiety didn't go any damn where as I grew older and grew up. I would have to have children of my own and see their messy bedrooms and the toothpaste on the bathroom sink and some crumbs forgotten on the kitchen table. I would have to find myself back at the edge of panic and fear, not knowing what was happening inside me but knowing something bad would happen because of the mess, finding myself angry that someone else was sending me back to my childhood hell. I would have to see the hurt or anger in my children's eyes to slowly understand that no one was going to punish me anymore. To understand that if I didn't fix myself, I would pass my brokenness on to them—the burden of my anxiety and fear and heartache would somehow become theirs, no matter how hard I wished and prayed otherwise.

My brother didn't respond to all that fear and anxiety like I did. Instead, he would shove everything under his bed when he was supposed to clean his room. I told Mom once, thinking they were fooled, and she explained that he was younger and not as good at cleaning as I was. Junior made terrible grades, so when he brought home Cs and the occasional B, he was rewarded. One time, I mentioned how unfair it was that I got rewarded for only the highest grades, and Mom said since

I was capable of making the higher grades, that was what I should do. I was disappointed that I couldn't seem to win my parents' love that way, but making good grades was easy for me, and getting positive feedback from teachers was enough to keep me motivated to do well in school. That turned out to be very lucky for me, since it's a lot easier to claw your way out of poverty with scholarships and a college degree.

But I kept searching for ways to convince my dad to love me, and I finally thought I had figured something out—I could make him laugh. I began imitating one of the radio DJs we heard on the station our radio was always tuned to, the only station that reached us so deep into the holler. I tried to learn jokes so I could come home and tell them to him, and I thought for a short time that I had made myself good enough, that he finally loved me. It wasn't long, though, until he no longer laughed at my jokes. The happiness I felt lasted for such a brief time, and I was desperate to earn it again, to deserve his affection once more.

I began seeing my ugliness in the mirror. The more I looked at it, the more repulsive I found the face looking back at me, until it felt like torture to be in my own body. I already knew how to punish myself for everything that was wrong with me—I learned it from the adults—and so my self-loathing ate at me. I was certain my father didn't love me because I was unlovable, undeserving, unworthy. I could feel it in my body, which longed for safety.

But no matter what he did, I kept wanting life to be better for my father. I felt his rage and pain as if they were my own, and sometimes it seemed like I alone could fix it all. I never thought it was his fault that he was cruel or unloving—I thought it was the rest of the world, I thought it was the pills he had to take for his back, his back that got hurt at work, and he tried to get workers' compensation for it, but they screwed him over, and he was left with a bad back and nothing to show for all his hard work. And there he was, with a taste for painkillers and all that pain, and disks in his back that always needed surgeries he didn't get and some of those disks having just disappeared altogether. It was this sad mess, this chain of events that led him down the path of self-destruction, and it was the doctors and the lawyers and the banks, and it was not being able to make a living and support his family—that's what drove him to the point of no return.

I spent most of my life believing that, until I was twenty-seven. That's when I asked my mother what had happened to his back while managing the gas station, what injury had caused the pain that spread from him through our family and into the world, and she said it was something minor, something inconsequential. That he didn't get screwed by the workers' compensation office—he just didn't turn the paperwork in on time. That he came home with his minor hurt and tried to make it worse by bench-pressing their bed. So he could go to the doctor and get some good pills.

I knew then that I would never get him back, that maybe he was never there to lose in the first place. I had been dreaming of the man I knew he could be, that I just *knew* he wanted to be and surely would *choose* to be someday. For the first time, I was struck with the understanding that as hard as I had tried to make sense of the whole mess, it was time to give that up.

is much wider now than it seems it should be, considering how fine a line the razor drew.

Thoughts of suicide were nothing new to me, but I was not always interested in killing myself when I wanted to hurt myself. The first time I pretended to cut myself, I was about five years old and found a tube of Halloween vampire blood in my brother's bedroom. I squeezed a line of it across my wrist—how I knew that was the right spot, I have no idea—and ran into the kitchen, clutching my arm and dragging my leg a little, for effect. My mom was distracted, but when she saw my wrist, she started screaming and rushed me into the bathroom, thrust my wrist into the sink, and began running cold water over it. Concerned by how upset she seemed, I told her, *Mom, it's not real. It's fake.* She fairly exploded because I had fooled her in such a way, and that began a new favorite pastime for me that lasted through my teen years, though I never went quite that far with it again.

As a fourteen-year-old, when I was thinking about death, I was seriously contemplating the repercussions of various approaches. My favorite fantasy was one in which I would somehow procure a handgun, bring it to school, and make a small speech before shooting myself in front of my geometry class. Some very publicized school shootings occurred around that time, and it was the first time I saw the video for Pearl Jam's *Jeremy*, in which a young boy does much the same as I imagined doing. But whenever I asked myself whether I wanted vengeance, I quickly realized that I did not wish my classmates any harm, other than to know my pain for one moment.

By that point, I was overwhelmed by their ridicule, which had gone on for more than five years. It was hardly anything by the time I was a freshman in high school, but the looks on their faces said everything to me. I had stopped trying to perform well on the Speech and Drama team—during middle school, I had occasionally won awards, but when I did, the popular guys on the team would ask with disdain, *You won something?*

My father took me shopping at a clothing store in eighth grade—he somehow had plenty of money on hand, so he insisted on taking me to a real clothing store and told me to get whatever I wanted. I was so excited to have a silk shirt before they went out of style, and I wore it to one of the Speech and Drama competitions. When we were getting on the bus, one of the kids asked me where I got it, and I think they complimented me on it. For some reason—whether they asked or I volunteered the information, I don't remember—I told them how much it cost. Soon after, someone else told me it was a nice shirt and asked how much it cost. Then another, and another, and another.

I realized they were mocking me, and I finally wished that I wasn't wearing my new silk shirt and that I had never gotten it at all. I was afraid to wear it to school after that, thinking they might pour their derision on me without mercy, but it was the most expensive thing I had ever owned, and I felt obligated to wear it, although I assumed my father had probably stolen the money or sold drugs to get it.

I had sat with some of the popular girls in one class in eighth grade, but another kid brought me down a peg when I joined the other girls in making fun of him. *You're just their errand monkey,* he said with contempt. He was right—when everyone finished their papers, I would take them to the teacher's desk at the front of the room, happy to be so visibly part of their group, pushing away the nagging thought that I, in fact, did not belong.

I just wanted to tell them what my life at home had been like that whole time. Distraught over the nasty words and looks they seemed to take such pleasure in, I did not know how to stand up for myself. I could not understand what I had done to deserve it, but most of the time, I believed it was my fault—after all, I did not look like them, I did not own the things they owned. I realized I did not know how it felt to *be* them. In my isolation, I wanted them to have to listen to me, and I wanted them to wonder how it felt to be *me*, trying to bear their cruelty while I was trying so hard to survive my home, to endure being in my body.

But I said nothing, did nothing.

When I look back on those years, I try to make sense of how I kept going. All the things that had felt possibly *safe* and *good* were suddenly gone—church, my mother, my stepmother. The scraps of approval and affection were no longer, and I was further away from everything, and everyone, than I had ever been before.

CHAPTER 14

Happy Now

The summer after my freshman year, I ended up going to a movie with an older boy from school. Shawn flirted with me a lot wherever I had run into him—at the city pool, perhaps, but he was a rougher sort and not the kind of teenage boy who spent his time by the pool. Since Mom worked for the city, we got discounted passes. Shawn was the type who started smoking cigarettes when he was fourteen or fifteen, and he went on to join a motorcycle gang, though what that meant in our little town, I was never sure.

Shawn told me to meet him at a movie, and I was excited to go on my first date—it seemed like this was what normal people did. I didn't have to wonder for long whether he would make a move—he spent most of the time kissing me too hard, to the point where my lips were bruised a light purple the next day. He also put his hand down the front of my pants and into my vagina. A few minutes after that, he pulled his hand out and looked at it in the light of the movie, then laughed a little and wiped it on my jeans. I saw later that it was blood he wiped on me, and he left my breasts sore from squeezing them so hard. I was just happy that someone finally liked me, and it didn't occur to me it was a problem that nothing he did felt good. I was excited afterward at the thought he was interested in me, but he didn't call me or otherwise show any inclination toward seeing me again. We may have talked again at some point, but I had no idea what to expect and so expected nothing.

James, a boy from health class, called me a couple of weeks later and came over to go for a walk together. I told him I had gone to the movies with Shawn and wondered whether I should date him—as if I was asking for advice, since the two boys knew each other. As if Shawn wanted to date me and I had a choice in the matter. After a minute of silence, he responded that he didn't think I should date Shawn, but he thought I should date him instead. I was shocked he asked me to date him like that—it was the very first time a boy ever asked me to be his girlfriend, and he became my very first boyfriend. He met my mom and stepfather, who weren't impressed, but I guess they didn't think it would last long enough to be of any consequence.

That summer, James decided he wanted to be a hippie, and he asked me whether I wanted to be a hippie with him. I turned fifteen, and he was sixteen; he would turn seventeen in the winter. All I knew of hippies came from listening to my mother's one Janis Joplin album while we were still in the holler and from having a vague notion of what Woodstock was. James listened to the Grateful Dead and made me a mixtape of their songs, which to this day is the best mixtape I have ever heard. After giving up on pop music, I had turned to Chuck Berry and Sam Cooke, along with the Johnny Horton tape that my stepfather brought with him from Nevada—I had the least relatable music taste of anyone I knew. I was happy to give up on pop culture altogether, and James introduced me to another culture that made much more sense at the time—a *counterculture* that itself rejected the entire world I felt so rejected and battered by.

James also wanted to become a vegetarian that summer. At first, we went on a lot of hikes and took turkey sandwiches and apples from his mother's house, but then we began eschewing the meat for grilled cheese sandwiches. His mother had salad all the time, and whole wheat bread—stuff that tasted and felt good to me but that my mom and stepdad didn't buy. When he asked me whether I wanted to be a vegetarian, too, I said yes right away and ate whatever I could that didn't clearly involve meat. How nice it was to have someone to be *something* with.

My mother refused to support my new diet and wouldn't make any dish meat-free, or even a portion of the dish. Since she and my stepdad ate meat at every meal, I learned to cook fifteen-bean soup and potato soup. I taught myself to make bread so I could have whole wheat bread. She didn't want to buy me soy milk, which I wanted to try, so I spent my own money to buy all the health foods I had never heard of until then. I didn't get an allowance, though, so I ended up mostly eating the nonmeat side dishes they cooked—mashed potatoes, canned green beans, and the like.

That same summer, I had my first job, working for the United States Forest Service. They had an office right outside Morehead, by Cave Run Lake. I earned minimum wage—something close to five dollars an hour—and spent forty hours each week doing some sort of work with another girl from school who had also signed up for the employment program for high school sophomores.

By that time, James had reintroduced me to smoking weed. I had smoked with my father when I was thirteen or so, camping for the last time with our cousins from Tennessee. The weed had made me feel irritable, but not too long after, I asked my dad to teach me to roll a joint, hoping it would make me feel good that time. He did, but I still didn't feel a high. I persisted with James, though, and finally developed a liking for it. After a few more tries, I was thoroughly enjoying it. I had intense hallucinations just riding in James's mother's car, listening to Jefferson Airplane or Pink Floyd. Sometimes I would ask my dad to get us weed, and sometimes he bought it from my boyfriend.

I lost my virginity that year. Didn't lose it, really—I set it aside quite willingly.

Some of the older men at the Forest Service knew my dad, and some of them liked to smoke weed, so they would buy it from me, too. One guy took Mini Thin pills all day long *for his asthma*. I did other things out in the woods as we spread lime and seeds and fertilizer and straw to build ponds. I took off my shirt one day, wearing no bra, since it was as hot as hell and the older boy I was working with had his shirt off. I asked him whether he minded, and he said no—that seemed good enough for me. I didn't think of myself as a girl in this boy's eyes—just as a flat-chested, unattractive female he wouldn't want to see anyway. Later it would occur to me that boys like to tell stories about such things and that I just didn't have a good sense of what people expected of me or how much they could really accept. Much later, I realized that when it comes to taking off shirts, most boys his age do not differentiate between girls like me and other girls.

James spent most of that summer with his grandparents in Ashland. My mother wouldn't let me call him from our house, even if I paid her back for the long-distance charges. That summer, I put almost all the money I earned toward phone cards and walked to a pay phone in town to call him, though occasionally I would try calling from our house if my mother and stepfather were in bed but I thought maybe I wouldn't wake up his grandparents. Phone cards were terribly expensive at the time, and I managed to blow my entire salary on calling him and buying a few CDs.

When he came back and school started once again, we spent a lot of time at his mother's house after school. Frank and my mother decided to crack down on that, so they had me come straight home after school to do chores—namely, loading the dishwasher and washing all the dirty pots and pans by hand. I would then walk to meet James, and we either went to his mother's house until shortly before she would come home, or we went up into the woods behind the university's radio station tower, where we had stashed a gravity bong for smoking weed.

We would often smoke a little and then go down to the university library and into the basement, where they kept the bound periodicals. We did our homework completely stoned, and one night, after doing a lot of Algebra II homework, I ended up hallucinating the quadratic formula. We would also have sex in the basement, in the woods, in his mother's house, and wherever else we thought we could get away with it. I knew how pregnancy worked but never thought about condoms or birth control.

I loved the sex, but I also learned that I shouldn't enjoy it to the fullest—I had to rein myself in a bit and not enjoy it *too much*. He didn't like it when I orgasmed, so I learned to hold my orgasms back. I wanted to have sex all the time, and he called me a *nympho*. One time, he didn't want to have sex at all, and I rubbed myself lying next to him in bed. When I was finished, he looked at me and asked with disdain, *Happy now?*

Even as a very young girl, I somehow knew that sex was a problem all around me. It was when my father rubbed calamine lotion on my poison ivy–covered legs and said, *You know I'm not doing anything wrong, don't you?* and when I was five and slept in the bed close to him one night and tried to put my foot on his leg, and he moved away. I didn't understand why he didn't want his daughter's affection. It was every moment in which an older man looked into my eyes and smiled knowingly, the moments in which my father would lose it and call me a whore or a slut or whatever else. It was like I wore a flashing sign that said, *Take what you want!* and it took many years for me to remember who the first really was, who really took my virginity, to whom I *lost* something. But we never really forget—we just tuck things away, and they quietly creep into each of our actions, our thoughts, our words, our principles, and our fears.

I learned so much the year I was fifteen. I lied to my mother and told her I was spending the week with my father so I could go to my first rock concert—all the way to Providence, Rhode Island. There, I took

LSD for the first time—not a large dose, just enough to feel something different happening with my senses. Over the next two years, I tried opium, mushrooms, a few more doses of LSD (with a little more *oomph* to them), and DMT. It was a mother's nightmare. I stopped wearing deodorant and smeared patchouli oil on my armpits instead. I smelled like body odor all the time and did not care. I wore bell-bottoms that had actually been around since the 1970s and huge tie-dye shirts with Grateful Dead logos or mushrooms on them.

Although James and his older friends helped me feel like I finally belonged somewhere, I was still angry with the world, and now I had a language to help me articulate that feeling, however imprecise. I didn't think I was rebelling against my parents—I still came home after school to do my chores, and I was never more than a couple of minutes late for curfew, which was whenever the sun set, regardless of how early that could be in the winter. Thinking that I was rejecting some system or broken culture allowed me to say, *I can't do this anymore,* and *I do not belong here.* I found a reason for my not feeling *okay* that made my environment, my society, the problem—not me, not something inside me.

And that helped. It helped me to say there was something wrong with hierarchy, something wrong with societal norms, something dreadfully wrong with our culture of exploitation. It let me practice saying, *I don't belong here,* before I had to face the family and community who still claimed me. I learned to say, *I can't be a part of this,* to an audience that wasn't listening, and that experience helped me eventually say it when it counted.

While I was finally excited about my not belonging, I still felt compelled to achieve academically, though it felt a bit like a game at that point. I didn't take my classes seriously, and I didn't take my teachers seriously, but I enjoyed having mastery over the work they assigned me. I was a smart-ass in class and often still stoned from the weed we smoked in a cemetery on our way to the bus stop. Still, several of my teachers managed to have an impact on my thinking, whether they knew it or not.

In my sophomore Algebra II class, my teacher one day suggested that we take a practice test at home to prepare for an upcoming test. I raised my hand and asked him whether we would receive points for the practice test, and he said no. In typical fifteen-year-old fashion, I asked with a smirk, *Why would I do it, then?* He stopped in his tracks and stared straight at me to respond, *To learn.*

That was the first time a teacher had ever really made me think there was an intrinsic value to my learning. I had always thought of my good grades in school as being for others—to please my teachers, to please my parents. It was one of the few ways I received positive attention, when I did: *She's a smart little thing.*

I went home and took the practice test that night, then checked my answers and made sure I knew how to do all the problems. I scored higher than anyone in the class for the rest of the year, and since I earned almost every single bonus point our teacher offered, I ended the semester with a grade of 105 percent. The other *smart kids* who were in the accelerated classes with me wanted to pair up anytime we got to work together. They wanted something *I* had at that time, and though I did not like them, I would partner up with them and proceed to do most of the work.

The best part about dating an older boy and smoking lots of weed with him was that I found myself once again in the woods much of the time—smoking at our hidden spot or hiking the trails behind the university lake, walking in the woods around my house, or climbing the cliffs that sat above my granny's house and marked the border between her property and the Daniel Boone National Forest, along the ridgeline of the hills that cradled her fields and garden and home. We would often smoke and sit quietly, or my boyfriend would talk to a friend while I watched the leaves and noticed their perfect arrangement along the branches. I discovered that flocks of birds flew in perfect synchrony with one another and in time with heartbeats. That the wind loved the trees and that the forest floor loved the leaves, that the heat and the cold and the sun and its setting were all singing a love song. That the wordless joy of the forest was not lost in my past.

And I felt hope.

CHAPTER 15

Love and Marriage

I cheated on James shortly after we started dating. It wasn't that I particularly wanted to cheat on him—it was just that one of his friends made advances, and it didn't occur to me that I should say no, that I could say no. I told James but wouldn't tell him who it was. He broke up with me but decided to forgive me not too long afterward. There was a lot of forgiving yet to come, between the two of us.

James started college at the university in Morehead the same semester I started my junior year of high school. He made new friends, older college students who lived in houses they rented and had parties in. James moved in with them for a portion of the semester. I was part of his night life sometimes, on the rare occasion I was allowed to stay out past dark.

My stepdad went through my purse around that time and found the clay pipe I had made in art class—a ceramics project I had hidden in a bigger clay pot and fired in the kiln. I was grounded for a while, and then my mom sat me down at a fast-food restaurant and laid out some new ground rules: I would start shaving my legs. I would start eating meat. I would stop smoking pot. These things I was doing, they made her look bad. Everyone knew about it.

I quickly told her I would stop smoking pot, since it was illegal and I was living in her house. I thought that was fair. But I figured what I shaved and what I ate didn't really affect anyone but me. When I did find myself around someone telling me, *It's okay to smoke a little—she'll never know,* I just said, *No, I gave her my word.* Somehow, that still meant something.

Sometimes, when I couldn't go where James was going, I asked him to stay with me, to skip the party. He didn't, though, and I had a nagging sense that something was changing, that he was further away from me than it seemed. I was scared of losing the one person I thought would ever love me, so I just quietly worried and waited to feel good again.

One of his older friends decided to tell me one day that James was spending an awful lot of time with one of the college girls who sometimes came to their parties. I didn't believe he would cheat on me, but I was filled with jealousy and a new kind of anxiety I had never felt before. Each time I came to their house, I scanned the room for the blond girl whom I never really met, whose name made my stomach hurt.

Then James failed out of the university. After Christmas break, he transferred to Eastern Kentucky University, all the way in Richmond. I was working at Arby's, and once again, I spent all the money I made on phone cards to call his dorm room. Sometimes I left messages with his roommate. Mostly, the phone just rang. I would stand at the pay phone closest to my house and listen to the endless ringing, another taunt I could not fit into my mind. I wrote him letters and waited for his responses. My intuition told me something was wrong, but I desperately wanted everything to be okay, so instead I hoped that *I* was wrong, that my gut was wrong, that there was just something wrong with me.

There seemed to be an impenetrable wall between me and whoever was near. Then I fell in love with a friend's younger brother. We shared one kiss—in my excitement at finding him and his wit, his mind, and his love for music that I had never heard and that became the soundtrack for those months of my life, I kissed him lightly in one of the sweet groves of trees near my trailer, though he was not enthusiastic in the way I thought he would be. His face seemed to be made like a painting, eyes that narrowed just a bit, lips always on the verge of a smile.

He wanted me to break up with James, who was so far away by now, but I wouldn't. And yet, I couldn't pretend I wasn't in love with the younger boy, in love with his whole family. On school mornings, I walked to their house just to be around their laughter and their apparent understanding of one another, which seemed to extend even to me. I visited the sister after school sometimes—she was a year older and mostly seemed to tolerate me. She wrote me a letter one day, telling me to choose between her and her brother, as I couldn't be friends with both of them. I chose him, the one who had not given me an ultimatum.

I thought she would understand, just as I expected him to understand why I couldn't choose him over James. I showed up with a loaf of homemade bread once, and only the parents spoke to me, the kids all busy in their rooms, and it slowly dawned on me that something had changed. I'd walk to the bus stop near their house for a while longer, but there would be no laughter for me, no belonging with their family, and finally, I caught on.

James returned from school just as I ran out of other people to love me, and he hadn't made good-enough grades to go back the next semester. I had just turned seventeen that summer, and my mother and stepfather told me we were moving to Elliott County, which offered even less to entertain a teenager than where we were living. They said I could finish my senior year at my current high school and continue working at Long John Silver's—Arby's didn't last all that long—but I would have to drive straight home every day unless I was working, and no socializing. I knew what that meant—no more seeing James unless he could find a way to drive the thirty minutes to our new house, which would sit along a high ridge near the narrow, winding road that he and I often drove to our pot dealer's house as we meandered along the country roads, listening to Pink Floyd and Led Zeppelin and the Grateful Dead, me sometimes writing poetry. I was devastated. I didn't have a lot of friends, but this move would mean that I only experienced the worst of school and work, and none of the good things—hikes with James, going to his friends' houses, trying to be friends with the few people who still talked to me.

When I told him, James and I decided we should try to live together. I knew that my mom and stepdad wouldn't let me see him if they managed to take me to Elliott County, and I was certain I would lose him. I was sure he was the only man who would ever love me, and I clung to what we had, no matter how unhealthy or unhappy I sometimes knew it to be.

James didn't have a job but could probably come up with something, and I could finish my senior year living in town, closer to school. I thought it was a pretty reasonable idea with clear benefits that my mother would appreciate—less driving, saving gas money, and . . . probably some other things, too. But as soon as I started talking, she blew up and yelled that I wasn't going to embarrass her by living with a boyfriend when I wasn't married. I didn't understand her old-fashioned morals in the context of our history—they didn't fit.

She yelled herself into a frenzy, though James and I were sitting there quietly, and I was fully unprepared for her to respond with anger. Finally, she said, *You want to live with him? You marry him. I'll sign the papers today if you want to marry him. If you really want to live with him so bad, you do that!* James and I left a short time later and sat in his mother's car. *What do you think?* I asked. He paused, then said, *I think we should do it.*

Do what?

Get married.

And so we did. We went back inside and told my mother, who immediately started crying and asking me whether I was sure I wanted to. My stepfather just said that now she had to let me, since she had offered to sign the papers. I didn't know what to say except yes, I was sure, we were sure.

I don't know that she wanted me to get married. Historically, it is an easy way to be rid of a daughter, and I was probably giving her some gray hairs by that point, with my refusal to shave my legs or eat meat. Even though she didn't go to church, my mother would occasionally refer to God as if that was something she believed in, so I thought she might have been concerned about me *living in sin*. Or maybe with what everyone else would think about me living in sin. At the time, I didn't understand how she might have struggled to raise a girl. I couldn't fathom the difficulty of mothering a girl, with so much unhealed trauma around the experience of being a woman.

Two days later, we managed to get a preacher we had never met to marry us in a church we had never attended. I could only think, *This isn't right*. I briefly considered saying no, that I didn't want to, that I had just turned seventeen and didn't know the first damn thing about being somebody's wife, and if I were the betting kind, I would bet I was going to have a hard time figuring it out. But like everything else I had ever identified as *not right* in my life, I decided that what I thought didn't really matter. And anyway, wasn't James the only man who would ever love me? I thought it was my one chance to get married. One of my only friends at school soon told me, *You've clipped your wings,* and it took me twenty years to figure out what he meant.

Just like that, I joined a demographic I knew nothing about. Technically, I was a child bride, though I would have told you it was my choice and I knew what I was doing. I wasn't marrying my rapist. I wasn't marrying a man decades older—James was just a couple of years older than I was. Compared to my mom, who had run off to Jellico,

Tennessee, to marry my father when she was still seventeen, I was doing pretty good.

I didn't know how difficult it would be to finish high school, to heat our house, to keep my sense of hope alive. I didn't expect that I would lose all respect for my new husband, that our life together would never feel light or exciting or free. Having no preparation for adulthood, still reeling from all the nightmares of childhood and praying for the return of the indescribable magic I had found in nature, I took on the responsibility of caring for myself, thinking the work of raising me was already done. Many people could have told me—though none did—things were going to get worse before they could possibly get better. I wouldn't have listened anyway. I wouldn't have believed them.

CHAPTER 16

A Pretty Smile

We moved into the same house that James's college friends had rented, and each day I walked into the same entryway where his friend had told me James was probably sleeping with one of the college girls who was always around. At first, James got a job with the sawmill where Dry Branch Road met the highway. The highway was KY 519, just a two-lane road. My old church sits right off the road—the church where I learned about Jesus and was molested, saved, baptized, and finally told to leave.

James didn't work at that job for long but got another job at the sawmill a little farther down 519, closer to the road that would take you out to Amburgy Rocks, those five cliffs that sat partially on my granny's land and just a bit on United States Forest Service property. I didn't understand what happened to keep that job from lasting long, but next he got a job at a sawmill in Carter County, which took about forty-five minutes to get to each day.

I started my senior year in high school a couple of weeks after we got married, and everyone was surprised when I told them no, I wasn't pregnant, which filled me with a certain pride, though I knew I hadn't been careful enough in avoiding pregnancy to really be all that proud. We had one car, the 1986 Dodge Aries that Mom and Frank bought me for $600 after I turned sixteen. In their wisdom, they told me I could have a car or braces for my teeth, and in my wisdom, I chose the car.

Why was that the one time I was allowed to make a choice for myself? I didn't have the experience or insight to understand the relative value of braces at that time. I had no idea that it would just get harder and more expensive to fix my teeth, that there would be times I would resolve to do it, and other, more important things would come up that I would have to spend the money on instead. I couldn't predict the amount of shame I would endure as I looked in the mirror or how I would try to hide my teeth every time someone insisted I *smile for the camera*. The one time I was given control of my own body was the time I needed an adult to make the best decision for me.

James had to be at work at six in the morning, so I got up at four thirty to cook his breakfast and lunch, drive him to the sawmill, and then drive myself to school. Thankfully, the job didn't last that long.

We had roommates, God bless them—another couple. Now that I was no longer under my mother's roof, I saw no reason not to smoke all the weed I could, though I found that it was no longer an adventure but that I felt confined and anxious getting stoned in our house. There was always a party there, whether the living room was crowded or there were just two of us up all night, fully immersed in a chess game with a level of concentration made possible by the potent acid I generally had on hand. Since James couldn't hold a job and my paycheck from Long John Silver's didn't go far, we started buying sheets of acid to resell.

I don't know how the bills got paid, if they got paid. I may have met our landlord once. He was the father of a girl I went to school with, a girl who seemed poor and somehow more sexually advanced than the rest of us by middle school. She had a cute boyfriend from middle school onward, and last I heard, she married him and they moved into that house next to her father's several years after our heyday had ended.

The people at our house were almost always smoking weed or tripping on psychedelics. For the longest time, it seemed like a continuation of the scene that had unfolded when James's college friend and his roommates lived there. Back then, the house had felt light and comforting, airy and peaceful. I don't know whether it happened slowly or quickly, but somehow the feeling inside the house changed, and everything began feeling dark and dirty. Strange people eventually started coming around, and things were stolen off our porch when we left them overnight for a yard sale. Things were stolen from inside the house, too, and I couldn't begin to guess whether it was someone we counted as a friend who had done that.

Since I always had it on hand, I began taking LSD pretty regularly, though I found it had no effect the day after I had just taken it. For a while, I took it every other day, which gave my system just enough time to reestablish sensitivity to it. I loved nothing more than to play chess with a couple of different people while I was high on LSD, and we watched the Woodstock movie over and over that year. Since staying up all night and tripping had become habitual, I often missed entire days of school, showing up as soon as I could drive myself there safely. Now, I could laugh—or cry—thinking about my ability to judge what was safe back then. The truancy officer finally called me in and asked for directions to my house. I asked her what she needed that for, and when she told me, I understood I had to have a doctor's note to miss any more school. From then on, I went to the health department constantly, getting an excuse for whatever malady seemed to sound best at the time.

When I did make it to school, I was a sight to behold, with my unwashed and tangled hair, bathing once a week or so, pupils as big as dimes. We had a couple of pot plants growing in a closet, and James insisted we couldn't turn on the closet light to look at them—it would mess with their growing cycle or something like that. I didn't understand much of what he said about what we should and shouldn't do. It made me feel like a child again, struggling to comprehend what my father's rules were and what I had to do to keep him happy. I tried to just memorize everything and obey.

One afternoon, I lit a candle to carry into the closet with me—candlelight not being strong enough to disrupt our delicate plants and their growth hormones—and looked at the plants to see whether I saw anything of interest. I peered over the candle with my long, unwashed hair hanging above it, and soon my hair was on fire. I ran out of the closet to James, not knowing what to say, but he quickly grabbed a pillow or blanket and smothered the fire. My hair was singed all over on one side, but when I brushed it, the burnt pieces fell out, and I had no gaping bald spots, *praise the Lord.* The next day, when I walked into the school atrium, a girl greeted me by telling me that my hair looked good.

She brushed it, another girl pointed out, rolling her eyes. She was right—otherwise, I couldn't tell you how many times I brushed my hair that year. But you could get the number by counting on one hand.

My senior year, I had an English teacher who had us read *The Catcher in the Rye* and *Lord of the Flies.* While a lot of our rooms in the school were too cold during the warm months, hers was always mercifully comfortable because she stuffed the air-conditioning vent with paper towels to block the air. I sat right below the vent, and one day, I noticed I was terribly cold and someone had removed the paper towels. Several days later, I asked her after class why she had done that, and she hardly tried to suppress her laughter as she explained that other students were complaining of a particular student's body odor, so she removed the paper towels to combat the unpleasant smell. I found something about her explanation discomforting, and it took me a while to fully realize that the student with the offensive odor was most assuredly me.

Still, one day this teacher handed back a paper we had written, a personal narrative, which I had turned in but then requested that she let me revise, even though I had gotten an A, just to get it right. On my final draft she wrote, "Very beautiful. Your revision turned this into a jewel." She took me into the hallway to tell me that I shouldn't be hanging out with the people I was associating with, that they were bad news and would drag me down. She said that I was able to do something my peers could not do, that my writing was not at all average but beyond that. *Do you understand that?* she demanded to know.

Did I understand? I understood writing was the only thing that felt natural to me, the only time I felt I could make sense of the world around me. I understood I couldn't play the guitar or be confident like James, and I wasn't pretty enough to be a contender for the prom queen, and I apparently stank to high heaven. I understood that the only way I could stop hating myself and my life and everyone around me was to be a different person—not the girl who lived in the holler and who was afraid of the world, but maybe this girl who smoked a lot of weed and wore tie-dyes and had older friends anyway, so I didn't need the kids around me to like me. That I could have a husband—one person in the world who liked me as I was, or at least thought I was good enough for now. All I really understood was that I needed to survive, but I had no idea how to. I didn't understand that this wasn't what life should look like.

So I told her that I loved to write, that I wanted to write, and in her characteristic exasperated way, she told me that I should, that I had to do something with it, and *Don't just screw around.* But of course I did, until I didn't.

I also had a sociology class that year, and the teacher was funny and comfortable with all the students, for whom I had utter contempt at that point. I missed class so much that, one day, he told me I would come out of there with a C. I argued with him: *You know I have learned more than anyone else here. You know I understand more than anyone else here. You know that my work is A work, that when I have been here, I earned an A.* And *Yes,* he said, *all those things are true. But you weren't here. So you get a C.* After pleading my case for a few more minutes, he offered me a deal: if I read *Night Comes to the Cumberlands* and wrote him a paper on it, he would give me an A in the class.

I got the book immediately and started reading, wondering what it was about it that made him think it was worth me reading in exchange for the grade I wanted. Soon, it began to make sense as I read Harry Caudill's account of the history of Appalachia. I read as little as it took to complete my assignment and wouldn't learn until years later how and why that book was incomplete and, to many, an insulting perspective. But for me, reading it at the age of seventeen was a turning point, a moment of self-realization.

As the book unfolded, it seemed to illuminate the history of the region, the history of my people, in such a way as to account for the desperation that pervaded the water we drank, the air we polluted, the mountains we plundered, the love we longed for and withheld from one another. It made me see my father, for the first time, not just as my father, but as a descendant of sharecroppers, of thieves, of Irishmen, of desperate immigrants, of settlers who could not read or write and had never seen gold and so traded vast swaths of land for single, shiny gold dollars. The heartbreaking history my father told me through his stories, bits and pieces both recent and distant, now had a context—we suddenly fit into a narrative, and that brought us a little closer to making sense. For the first time, I saw myself as a great-granddaughter, a descendant—not just a *self*. But it made my self more complicated than I ever had conceived of it being.

How do we define a *self*? As the differentiator: *I can't understand you people.* As the reference point: *I didn't see anything.* The victim: *Why did this happen to me?* The perpetrator: *I didn't mean to . . .* The self, of course, is the main character of each of our stories—the hero, the martyr, the one whose suffering really matters and whose goodness is remarkable, whose shortcomings are both comprehensible and forgivable. The Bible tells us that the body is a temple, a sanctuary for the soul, a home for the *I* of every thought.

In my house, there are many mansions.

CHAPTER 17

The Walking Wounded

Granny was terribly worried about my health from the moment I told her I was a vegetarian. She could not fathom that a person could be healthy without hamburgers, sausage, bacon, and Christmas hams. My entire life, she had fed me in a way only a hardworking country grand-mother could do, making biscuits from scratch and gathering the eggs herself, growing and canning tomatoes and green beans all summer long, peeling potatoes with a paring knife that she stopped with her bare thumb as I watched, amazed she did not cut herself.

Granny's religious views seemed to complicate her morals in response to my meat-free diet. On one hand, she told me it was the Lord's will that we eat animals because the Bible said we had dominion over them. On the other hand, she had no qualms about slipping some ground beef into the vegetable soup she brought me in quart Mason jars, the soup she cooked up and canned for those cold winters. She promised there was no meat in the soup but seemed flustered at the question. Of course I could see the little clumps of fried hamburger, but even as an arguably book-smart teenager, I thought there had to be some kind of explanation beyond my comprehension—maybe it was a flavoring I knew nothing about, or a mystery vegetable.

I used to ask her to lie—*pretend*—that I hadn't called or wasn't visiting so my father wouldn't know I was close by when I saw her, but she would never agree to that dishonesty. And yet, she felt justified in her ground-beef deception because she was convinced that feeding me meat was part of her maternal duty, directed by the will of God himself. I could not make sense of it when I was a teenager, and I didn't want to make her feel bad, so we both ended up pretending that the ground beef in her soup was a vegetable.

She offered to give me her camper if I would eat meat, and another time, she offered me $300. With a sense of valiance, I declined both. I had stayed in that camper often as a child, "camping" in her backyard, next to the henhouse. My brother and our various cousins and I would listen to the country station whose signal somehow found its way into our holler. We would play cards and games for hours, laughing and enjoying the time that could be uncomplicated by the adults in our lives.

Though I refused Granny's offer at the time, I soon ended up living in that camper. At some point, my husband and I decided we could no longer afford to pay half the rent for the house we were living in, and we gave our roommates unceremonious notice before moving out. We decided to live in Granny's camper, which was then parked in her cow field, closer to my father's house than hers. My father ran a simple wire to it so we had enough electricity for a light at night and perhaps a radio. There was no water to connect to, so I brought it from the creek in a bucket to wash dishes, and we went to my father's to use the bathroom and shower.

It almost seemed like it would work for a while, though my dad often pressured us to come to his house. My husband was intimidated by him and, as my first boyfriend, had caught the full force of my father's threatening, domineering attempt to be protective.

On the other hand, before we were married, we were always allowed to spend the night at my father's house and sleep in the same room—sometimes on the floor, sometimes in the bed, according to my father's whims. He told me, *You better not be having sex in there,* and I said, *Oh no, of course not.* And he gave us weed sometimes, let us smoke our own anytime. Once, he went clambering up one of the hills near the house, searching for a pot plant that he had neglected for a while. He brought it back to us, all purple-green and strong smelling, but lacking any real substance, once you got down to it.

One night, my father beckoned us out of the camper. He *needed* my husband to go somewhere with him, he said. They would be back soon, he said. I was grouchy. I do not remember any particular frustration, other than the fact that my dad was taking my companion away to go on some dubious mission, and neither my husband nor I seemed able to deny my father. So they left, and I sat in his house while his new wife and children slept—he hadn't stayed single for long after his previous girlfriend moved out and finally broke it off for good. As the hours passed, I grew more and more irritated. I knew I couldn't express any anger toward my father, so when they finally returned, I tried to blame my husband for staying out so late.

He didn't want to talk until we returned to our camper. When we got there, he told me where they had gone—to a friend of my father's. That friend had light-blue eyes and made knives as a hobby. He had a little workshop filled with handles and blades that he fitted and sharpened to sell or trade. At least, that's what my father told me. I was always left to sit in the cab of his truck while my father went into the workshop. There could have been anything in there.

Earlier in the year, before we moved into the camper, a college student with a funny nickname, who came to our house a lot, had mentioned the mushroom mines in Carter County. In the 1920s and '30s, a 186-acre mountain was turned into an underground limestone mine, with 2.6 million square feet of tunnels honeycombed deep into the rock. From the mid-'50s to the late '70s or early '80s, a commercial mushroom business began operations, went under, tried again, and finally closed.

In 1995, before James and I married, my father told me that his friend the knife maker owned the mines. He urged me to go there with James and Junior, so we could camp while my dad's friend slept in the cab of his semi, which was parked just inside the mines. The entrance to the mines was littered with broken bottles, and the walls were covered in graffiti. A few years later, a young man and his girlfriend killed his parents and brought their bodies there. There were stories of satanic rituals, occult worship, drug deals, and ghosts in the mines—but we did not know that yet.

Why my dad had encouraged us to go there, I did not know. The entrance was framed with thick walls, and some sort of metal skeleton of a roof loomed above us. It was a chilly day, but the sun glinted off the shards of glass that lay everywhere. My brother and boyfriend walked around, exploring the outside of the cave. I stood in the abandoned entrance, wondering why my dad's friend always looked into my eyes so deeply, why he always smiled at me, why it felt like he knew a secret about me.

The cave was fairly warm, and we slept close to the entrance. Still, the stagnant air made us sick, and in the morning, I woke up feeling suffocated. A year later, when the college boy with a funny nickname mentioned the mines, he told us he had heard that someone burned the semi cab that was in there. We mentioned that to my father, and he and his friend wanted to know who did it.

So when my father took my young husband to his friend's house, it was because he and his friend wanted to question him. They took him into the workshop and showed him the knives, asking him questions about our acquaintance and the story we had heard. Finally, one of those two middle-aged men said he would love to get ahold of whoever had burned that semi—*Wouldn't you love to get ahold of him?*—with one of those sharp knives in hand. He held the knife to my husband's throat—*Just like this. Feel how sharp that is? It would cut right through somebody.*

And after my husband stood there with a knife held to his throat by two crazy, drugged men and somehow convinced my father and his friend he could be of no further use to them, after he told me what had happened and how those men did not believe that we did not have the information they wanted, that *he* did not have the information they wanted, and after he said he couldn't live next to my dad's house anymore, we packed our few belongings and drove off in the middle of the night.

I don't know what people thought when I went back to high school for my senior year, married and clearly high most of the time. Even when I was there, I wasn't there. It was the perfect ending to all those years of feeling completely, painfully alienated from my peers. If it takes a village to raise a child, I was the warning sign that our village had failed, or that there was no village after all.

I didn't talk to James about how I felt, and how I suspected he felt, regarding our attempt at a relationship. I had learned to listen and be quiet, to not make any noise. I never responded to people who were cruel or condescending, but I wrote words down. My voice became adept at self-protection, as I said one thing and meant another, as I remained silent and thought everything. My silence had at once kept me safe and made me vulnerable in childhood. That silence was a large part of my self-sabotage as an adult.

So many people who endure poverty as children end up making unhealthy choices or accepting their lots. Those around us don't realize that some of us never feel like we have a choice, never know we have a voice or a right to speak. Some children are taught they deserve and have such power, but for those of us who weren't given the privilege of that knowledge, we go on doing the things we saw adults around us do, we subconsciously choose the lives that were modeled for us. For most of us, there is no flash of understanding when we turn eighteen, no sudden self-awareness that transforms our child selves into responsible, world-savvy adults. We fight the demons that embedded themselves into the fabric of our consciousness, not knowing why we always feel like we're in a fight. We walk through the world as if we are part of it, but our anguish constantly reminds us that the world neither loves nor wants things that are broken.

CHAPTER 18

Holding On

In the spring of my senior year, James and I went to a music festival in Berea, the home of a college my art teacher had recommended I attend, and we decided we would move there after I graduated high school. A lot of the people around us were tripping on acid at the festival, though I was sober at the time. It took place in the forest that I didn't yet know belonged to the college. There was a Grateful Dead cover band, and young college students gave talks about being vegan and saving the world by recycling.

I fell in love with this new forest, which looked like the one I had grown up in. But instead of men like my father and the darkness that seemed to grow around him, the young men wore tie-dyes and played instruments or danced without fear. Young women stood onstage at the amphitheater and made impassioned speeches. I thought it was the perfect place for me—the best of where I had come from, with plenty of room for a culture I believed in.

We went back a couple of weeks later and found an apartment for rent and put our deposit down with the money I had received as graduation gifts. One day, my mother gave me a message that I needed to contact the college—they had called her phone since I didn't have one. I reached them from a pay phone, and they said they had six spots left and one of them was mine if I wanted it. They asked whether I was serious about coming there. Standing in the Save-A-Lot parking lot, I told the admissions officer yes, I was moving there next week, one way or another.

When we got there, James spent a bit of time submitting applications and working here and there. For a while, he worked at a factory, putting in long hours. We hardly had any food or money. I cooked soups and spread the ingredients as far as I could, sometimes eating one meal a day, figuring that since my husband was working, he needed to eat more than I did—I was always giving away what I needed. I spent a lot of time reading, going to the library and picking out anything I could find to stave off the boredom and loneliness while he was gone. At that time, I had never been alone for very long and was afraid of what being by myself meant. I probably feared I would be left alone forever, and in my mind, losing the *possibility* of being loved by a man had to be worse than all the suffering that comes with a relationship not truly defined by love.

After a few weeks, he came home early one night, and my immediate happiness to see him quickly gave way to dread. He had walked out of the factory over something his supervisor said, and that was the end of that job.

Soon, I started working in a Laundromat. The old man who ran it showed me around and put me to work cleaning the machines, sweeping, mopping, and doing laundry. I would call James during my lunch break, and sometimes he was home, sometimes not. The old man liked to sit in a plastic chair between the rows of washing machines and watch me while I mopped, and soon I decided I could no longer take that for just over five dollars an hour.

I called the college and asked whether there was any way I could work for them. Since I hadn't officially begun my first semester, I wasn't considered a student yet and wasn't eligible to work as such. Someone pulled some strings, though, and soon I was on the housekeeping crew at the college. It was long, hot work. Once, we cleaned out maggot-infested trash that had sat in an empty dorm kitchen for months, but I had people my age to talk to, and a steady paycheck.

One day, I came home and James said he hoped I didn't mind, but he had run into some traveling hippies in town, and they asked for spare change. The alarm on my face must have been clear, because he reassured me he didn't give them any change but instead had invited them to eat a homemade vegan dinner with us. We had no money to spare and often dug around for loose change to buy gas—once, I bought thirty-seven cents' worth at the gas station down the street from us. But I felt comfortable with feeding people, and I was sure we could do something kind through food.

A black guy and a white girl showed up at our apartment that night—they were probably my age or close to it. They were traveling with a Rainbow tribe—young, wandering hippies—and they stayed with us for a few weeks, and then the young man ended up staying with us for several months at different times over the next couple of years. He was a lanky thing, over six feet tall, and his body was so stiff, he couldn't get cross-legged when he sat on the floor. Sit on my floor he did, though, and it seemed like he took up most of the room when he sat there beating on a drum, often while I was trying to read Plato or Aristotle for my freshman philosophy class.

During my senior year of high school, I had tried to teach myself yoga from a book, but I have never been good at learning physical skills by reading about them. I gave that yoga book to the young hippie, hoping he would gain enough flexibility so he could cross his legs. He started doing yoga from the book and became interested in Eastern philosophies, meditation, Buddhism, and so forth, to the point where he soon went to the same college I was attending and then moved to India to teach English and study Buddhism and Buddhist dialectics.

My freshman year of college was, in some ways, an extension of high school, though I was thrilled to find that I could reinvent myself and that no one knew me from before. No one I met had ever known me to cry or be humiliated by my peers, and there were far more liberal, hippie types at the college than there had been in high school. I almost felt like I belonged.

After the philosophy class I took as an elective my first semester, I felt my mind changing, expanding as I struggled with the logic exercises and analytical reading. I loved it. I would go to my professor's office and ask him questions after class, which he urged me to ask during class, but I was too self-conscious, at least at first.

I also took a course on argumentation and debate, and James started complaining that I liked to argue too much because of it, and picked apart every little discussion. I almost felt bad about it, but he spent most of his days playing guitar and smoking weed with my college friends, so I think it evened out, our ways of frustrating one another.

During the spring leading up to the first break in our marriage, I worked at a Denny's, waitressing in the small college town with the women and young girls who were not college students, not vegetarians or vegans, and who tried to convince me to let them put makeup on me and fix my hair. James protested me getting a job at first, not because I was also a full-time student or because the college required me to work ten hours on campus as well, but because he said I would complain about him not working. Desperate to pay our bills, I assured him I would not complain, and I didn't.

While I was working or doing homework one night, James went to a party at a friend's house and came home with crystal meth. He had tried it in the bathroom at our friend's house and thought I would like it, he explained. By the time summer began, I was snorting crystal meth almost daily, and I somehow became a relatively successful waitress, making more in tips than any of the other women, but my body rebelled constantly, hardly able to take in food. When I did try to eat, my body reminded me it did not want any food at that time. By the end of the school year, my professors had started telling me I wasn't looking well.

There was a guy at work, though, who thought I looked well enough to flirt with. He was cute and had a great smile, though he was a lazy waiter. He talked to me a lot, and outside one night, during a smoke break, he told me his girlfriend didn't mind him being with other people. He pulled me to him at some point, and it was more than I could stand. I told James that night, lying in bed, that I wanted to have an open relationship. He didn't say much. I asked him whether he wanted to talk about it, and he said no, he would say something he regretted. So we didn't talk about it.

A few days later, I made my way to the party house affectionately known as *the crack house*, where this coworker was hanging out with some of my sort-of friends. The cute, young flirt had actually gotten fired or quit his job, so I had gone out of my way to stop by the crack house a couple of times, hoping to see him there. When I finally did, there was no fire, no spark. I knew right away that my excitement over being flirted with, being wanted by such an attractive guy, was indeed not going to have any long-term benefit. I felt dirty and ashamed before we even started. After a few minutes of chatter around the other friends, he led me into someone's bedroom and sat me on the edge of the bed, where I waited for him to do what he wanted and be done. It was only then that I wondered about his girlfriend and realized I had most likely fallen for a trick, and I probably wasn't the only one.

The worst part was knowing I had gone out of my way to see him. I never went to that house to party, and it had a feeling about it that made me uncomfortable, like the darkness I had left behind in Morehead. That boy knew how to use his smile to make a girl feel special, and as I followed him into the bedroom, I tried to ignore the dawning realization that I was anything but special. My shame at wanting to feel pretty and wanted and worthy of his lovely face and lovely smile was endlessly multiplied as I saw the truth of myself, how I had come to him like a starved animal. A married woman pretending this fit into my relationship or my own map of desire. Knowing it was a lie that his girlfriend was okay with this. Having my friends-acquaintances watch me walk into the bedroom, come back out, and leave shortly thereafter because I had no other reason to be there. Because I wanted that scrap of affection, there was no lie that was too big to tell myself. And though I forgot his name not too long after that happened, I still can't forget any other detail.

CHAPTER 19

Letting Go

My college classes, though, were incredible. The college itself was the first interracial college in the South, as well as the first to educate men and women together. The most important aspect of it for me was that it was completely free, and I could therefore afford it without going into debt—a rarity I didn't appreciate at the time. But I also didn't understand then that I could have gotten scholarships and taken out loans to attend other schools. When I took the ACT test, the paper forms we filled out already had Morehead State University listed as a college that would receive our scores. I added Berea College to that list because of what my art teacher had said. Despite my constant defiance of teachers and school rules, I was still listening.

I went to college because I wasn't sure what else I could do. I didn't have sense enough to understand what college meant or to understand student loans and terms. I knew that the little college town had people who seemed like me—they liked to take LSD and kick a Hacky Sack and listen to the Grateful Dead. College seemed a safe way forward as I moved toward an uncertain future. There had been so many times I wanted to die, to finally be done with the difficulty of surviving. But dying never seemed to be an option. Maybe I never lost my childhood fear that if I couldn't figure out how to survive my life, someone else would have to be me. School was the only thing that had come easy for me growing up, which set me apart from the majority of people who grew up as I did. Unlike them, when I didn't know what to do with myself, my ability and desire to perform well at school could easily serve me. It was probably the only aspect of my unconscious thinking that did so.

I had signed up for a philosophy class as an elective but thought I would be an English major. I found myself surrounded by people who knew words I did not know, which I wrote down and looked up in a dictionary after class, so I would never be in the dark about that particular word again. My professors didn't mind my questions, and I never ran out of them. Finally, I felt free to ask questions, to argue, to say what I thought. Finally, I was allowed to have a voice.

I ended up with what I thought was a large group of friends. For the first time, a lot of people knew me and seemed to like me. I had a best friend who looked similar to me—long hair, unshaved, and we were both vegan by that time. Many of my friends were hippies and looked it, to varying degrees. I smoked weed, but I usually just did that when I was also going to take psychedelics—otherwise, by the time I was eighteen, smoking weed brought that familiar anxiety rushing back. I drank a little more than I had before—though not much, still. My best friend didn't mind doing just about anything, like me. When I offered her crystal meth, she snorted it with me, though I was the one who always went just a little *too far*, who wanted more than anyone around me wanted, whether it was LSD or meth or the conversations my professors offered, which I sought at every turn. All that childhood hunger had left me insatiable.

On one of the last few days before school ended for the year, a friend had a keg party, and I decided to go. I didn't take James because I liked talking to this friend so much, an older guy who I thought was the smartest person I had ever met. I may have had a small crush on him. I would ask him his thoughts about various topics or get his opinions on James's ideas. The more I did that, the less confident I felt that James was as smart as I had once thought he was. The more I talked to my guy friend, the more I felt that my own beliefs had been naïve and not entirely logical. I didn't know it at the time, but he often told his girlfriend that he didn't know why I was with James, that I was so much smarter than my husband.

At the party, I started drinking right away, and while I wasn't keeping track of time, I'm pretty sure it didn't take long for me to feel the effects. A girl I knew from school started drinking with me, while a cute boy who was clearly hoping to win her over drank a little with us. Julie and I rummaged around our friend's house until we found a bottle of vodka and some orange juice, which we claimed all for ourselves. Soon, she and I started making out in the kitchen, standing in the middle of the floor. I forgot about the party that was still going on until our host cleared his throat loudly and said with a grin, *I hope you all brought enough for everyone.* We hadn't, so we went outside and continued our make-out session sitting on the grass.

Eventually, my friend Iris asked whether I wanted her to drive me home, which sounded like a terrible idea. It was clear, though, that the make-out session could continue in the back seat of my car, so Iris drove, with the long-legged, dreadlocked hippie who sometimes lived with me in front, Julie and I in the back. We took Julie to campus to drop her off at her dorm, but at the last traffic light, Iris—who had only had one cup of beer hours earlier—turned left even though the arrow was red. Red-and-blue lights flashed immediately, and she pulled over on campus property.

The police officer asked some questions about where we were coming from and whether my friend had been drinking, which Iris answered truthfully. The police officer asked whether he could search the car, and Iris told him it wasn't hers. When he asked whose it was, I leaned forward with a drunk, happy grin and said it was mine, and I would prefer he didn't. He asked our ages—none of us were twenty-one—then looked at the other officer with a smile and said, *Well, since this is a zero-tolerance state, we'll arrest them all and then search the car.*

That was also when I found out Julie was seventeen. *You're seventeen?* I asked, shocked. I felt as if kissing an underage girl was the most immoral part of my evening. He sent her to her dorm, and Iris and I went into one cruiser, my dreadlocked friend into another.

At the station where we were booked, I was still drunk enough to give the female officer a grin when she patted me down. She asked whether I had anything in my pockets, and I told her I had a Mini Thin, which she pulled out and told me wasn't good for me. We had to be driven to the county jail for holding, which was in Richmond, where Eastern Kentucky University had been designated the third-ranked party school in the nation around that time—the same university James had failed out of. There were two mattresses on the floor, and Iris was the only person in there with me. Wearing nothing but my jail jumpsuit and still too drunk to care, I quickly fell asleep.

The next morning, they gave me my phone call, and I called my house phone number. Nobody answered, which seemed strange, so I left a message. I was released on my own recognizance, and they sent me out the back of the jail, where my dreadlocked friend was waiting.

We scrounged some change for a nearby pay phone, and I called a couple's house whose number I had memorized, explained where I was and how I couldn't get ahold of James. They came to pick us up a while later, and I finally got home.

I walked into my unlocked living room with nothing on me except what I had taken to the party, no doubt looking like I had spent the night in jail on a dirty mattress. My mother-in-law, sister-in-law, and James's grandparents were sitting inside.

Where's James? they asked, clearly irritated.

I told them I didn't know and had spent the night at a friend's house.

He knew we were coming. I can't believe he did this to us. We have been waiting here for two hours.

They got tired of waiting and eventually left. They were angry at him, and like everything else, I was sure it was somehow my fault. I made a couple of calls, but no one had seen James. I walked up to campus, to the dining area, where I was relieved to find him sitting at a table alone, not eating. I thought he would be relieved to see me, or maybe upset because I had stayed out all night. He was neither. Instead, he told me he wanted a divorce. I begged him to reconsider and told him I no longer wanted an open relationship and we could go to counseling, but his mind was made up.

Since I was still working, and paying for the apartment, we decided I would be the one to keep it. Since he wasn't working or paying for anything, we decided he would continue to sleep and eat there for as long as he needed to. We would have an amicable breakup, mature and conscious of our underlying friendship.

I asked him once to hold me at night as he slept beside me. *No,* he told me, *you make me feel dirty.*

Another time, I asked him whether we could spend some time together before he moved out—work on our friendship. *Sure,* he said.

Tonight?

Sure. But when I got home, he wasn't there. He wasn't there a couple of hours later, either, so I called a friend's house, and he was there, enjoying an impromptu party. It was raining a little, so I asked whether he needed a ride, but he didn't. I wondered when he would be getting home to spend that time with me, but he didn't know.

It dawned on me that he didn't care about *our friendship* and that, in fact, he was done with me and I had been a fool. I was angry then. Angry at him, angry at myself. I found a razor blade—it wasn't hiding, I always knew where they were—and dragged it upward along my right thigh six or seven times, moving through the flat moles on my leg without notice. I pulled the blade along my left arm but realized it would be too visible—*always put the marks where no one will see.* It suddenly occurred to me that there could be *too much* blood, that I could go *too far,* so I took a cold shower to encourage the wounds to close, quietly begging my skin to knit itself back together. James saw them a day or two later and snorted his disgust before turning away.

But something had changed as I watched the blood stream down my legs and wash away into the shower drain. I whispered a promise and a prayer, asking God to *Please make it stop, and I will never cut myself again.* I knew I didn't want to die this way, in my efficiency apartment or even at the hospital, covered in gashes that no one could sew or couldn't sew quickly enough. I also knew I wasn't sure where that fine line was set, where all the most important veins and arteries lay pulsing beneath my skin. And I suddenly understood that there were enough other people in the world who were willing to do me harm and that I couldn't do this to myself anymore. It wasn't exactly self-love, and I didn't turn my life around and stop doing things that filled me with shame or go out and choose better relationships. I just promised not to cut myself anymore, and so I didn't.

I wore long shorts in the summer heat, and pants if I wanted to be sure no one would see the cuts. But their starting points stuck out below my shorts, and my father saw them once. He demanded to know where they came from, and I told him I had been hiking and got into someone's barbed-wire fence. There was anger in his voice—it didn't feel like he cared that I was hurting myself but that he was going to punish me further. He didn't believe me, and he asked me more than once, but he finally stopped asking, and the cuts became long, unnaturally straight scars. They stand out more prominently when I get a tan, and any carefree time on a beach or in shorts is always tempered with the reminder of what I have inside me—an anguish that seeks an outlet. A wound that marks me as both victim and perpetrator. A pain that my children will notice in some form, no matter how well I hide it or how deeply it is buried beneath my love for them.

anytime. The house came with a woodstove that got way too hot some-times, and that's where we heated water for baths or washing dishes, until a friend from another eastern-Kentucky holler insisted on giving us a gas hot plate to use for the summer. We moved into the house in a chilly spring but still didn't have wood cut for the fall and winter, so when it got cold, neighbors sold or gave us wood sometimes, and my dad brought loads down a couple of times, too—mostly pine, which filled the pipe with creosote and smoked up the house, or half-rotten wood that also filled the house with smoke. I would learn how to make a fire out of damn near anything after my son was born.

The road was almost impassable without four-wheel drive, but some folks tried anyway. Several vehicles were ruined by the bouncing, and the road itself was as much chunks of conglomerate rock as it was dirt and gravel. You had to know where to put your tires, and due to rain or snow, that kept changing. For a while, I still had my little Volkswagen Fox, the first car I bought by myself, with a standard transmission. It couldn't make the trip down into the holler, so I had to park it at the top of the mile-long driveway and walk down to the house.

I didn't know it when Jacob bought the house, but the couple who sold it to him did so in part because one of the rednecks who lived around there told the husband he had seen the wife naked through his gun scope one day, so the wife was no longer willing to live there. During my pregnancy, that redneck and several others would periodi-cally ride their four-wheelers through our property, sometimes when I was alone, and I would wonder whether I could fight them off with nothing but the ax I kept next to the futon mattress on the floor while I slept.

There was electric at the barn, so Granny gave me a minifridge to keep food there after the big refrigerator that came with the farm died. She told me not to lift it, but I was stubborn and unloaded it anyway, alone in that empty holler after I drove it back. There was a solar-electric system at the house, but it wasn't set up well, or the batteries were too old or had gotten too cold—I never really understood why it wouldn't work. We couldn't have more than one thing on at a time, so if you wanted to listen to the radio during the summer, you had to turn the fan off. And at night, if you wanted to use a lamp, you couldn't have the fan or the television on.

Rainwater fell from the roof into a gutter and then into the plastic water-storage tank. Sometimes the water turned green, so we added bleach to it and went on with our bathing and teeth brushing. We carried water from the spring in five-gallon jugs, even after we found a six-inch parasitic worm whipping about in one of the jugs we drank from when I was just a month or two pregnant.

~

When I was fifteen, I started thinking I wouldn't live past the age of nineteen—at the time, nineteen seemed like an old age, and I thought I would be through with all this living by that time. I spent a lot of time with my new little brother, who was about two years old when I moved away from Morehead. My dad had married a woman just eight years older than me, and he started over as a father. I hoped that, somehow, he would be gentler with the younger kids than he was with Junior and me. Two-year-old William would spend the night with me, sometimes up to a week at a time. People thought he was my child, and though I loved him and changed his diapers and it felt right to take care of him, I was horrified at the idea of being a mother.

By the time I was seventeen, I told my family I would never have children of my own. I did not want the responsibility of having a child, but I also thought I was incapable of loving someone enough to be a mother. In my young wisdom, I thought that the universe, or God, or anyone else who might have a say in the matter, would not allow me to get pregnant, that I was as good as barren.

So when my period was late for the first time, I thought it was because I had abandoned my vegan diet, and the dairy I was consuming had somehow altered my hormones. I thought that my body was readjusting to the new food, even though I only consumed dairy from cows who didn't receive extra hormones. When I mentioned my theory to a friend, she looked at me with raised eyebrows and asked whether I could be pregnant. I had always been so convinced that I couldn't be a mother, the thought had truly never occurred to me, though I was not on birth control.

Jacob and I went to a Rite Aid in Lexington and got a pregnancy test. As soon as the results showed up positive, he said I needed to decide whether to keep it or not, which I thought was surprising because, although I had debated about abortion in my philosophy classes, I knew it to be a thing good girls don't do. We drove to the Henry Clay Estate and sat on a bench in the garden, surrounded by hedges and looking out at an array of rosebushes. It was beautiful, unlike anything I had ever seen. We talked, and with little thought, I decided I wanted to have the baby.

We had to get married, Jacob said. His family was Catholic and would consider our child a bastard if I didn't marry him. They were true southerners, with the accents and money and not-sweet corn bread to prove it. They approved of me somewhat because I had gotten into a good college with no help from my family. I decided to marry him even though I had told him, when we started dating, that I didn't want to get remarried anytime soon. When I was little, one of my aunts had read my palm and told me I would be married and divorced three times. I was determined never to let that happen, since three failed marriages sounded like a hard way to live. But more than that, I didn't want my child to be scorned by his father's family, so I agreed to it.

We were riding through town in his little red pickup truck one day, my feet propped up against the dashboard. He reached over and grabbed one of my toes and pulled it toward him, bending it the wrong way, smiling at me. I told him to stop, *That really hurts,* and he did it for a moment longer before letting go. I reached over and gave him a push, checking my anger at the last second to be sure I was playful and not aggressive. He didn't like that, though. He pulled the truck into a parking lot and, with visible anger, ordered, *Never touch me like that again.* I tried to explain that it was playful, whereas he had really hurt me. I felt like a fool for trying to make a joke out of the anger I had rightfully felt, giving him this ammunition against me. He told me that he wasn't sure he wanted to marry me and that he would leave me in the parking lot if I weren't pregnant. Eventually, he decided to forgive me, and we drove away.

I should have known it was a bad sign when Jacob accused me of being selfish like his mother in the first few months of dating. He hated that they had raised him next to a golf course and had shoved a golf club into his hands. They were materialistic, especially his mom, and he was determined not to be. When we officially lived together—when I moved into the house he bought—we disagreed over money, but I lost all those arguments since his money was not mine to spend, and the little I received for school needed to go toward our family.

We visited some of Jacob's friends in Tennessee, who ran a specialized greenhouse and nursery, and he later told me they lived on five thousand dollars a year, and he wanted to get to that point. *I grew up so poor,* I told him, panic rising inside me. *I don't want to be poor again—I want a better life.* But Jacob said he knew what it was like to be poor, too. He had lived on fifty dollars a month and had lived under bridges with the young girlfriend.

Who bought you that truck? I asked.

He had bought it himself with money from selling his car.

Who bought you the car?

His parents.

And where did you get that fifty dollars a month?

His parents.

Where did you go when you didn't want to live under a bridge anymore?
To his parents.

I tried to explain that being poor means there is no car to sell, no certainty in any income. And most of all, there is nowhere to go when things get too hard or you get too tired. There is no one to call, no saving grace. Just the fear of losing your children or your home, the fear of freezing or starving. Dignity is far from important, and in the throes of poverty, the need to survive outweighs all else except the need to forget your misery.

Over the next few months, doubts about motherhood crept into my mind without rest. Morning sickness had kicked in a couple of days after the pregnancy test, immediately after I drank a shot of wheatgrass juice and walked around the health-food store, dazed, for hours. I researched herbs and home birth and read everything I could find about women's bodies, unborn babies, vitamins, and breastfeeding. In the back of my mind, though, was the thought that I did not have to have the baby, that maybe I wasn't ready after all. I wondered how my body would change, whether I would be big forever afterward, when I was used to being small. I wondered whether my breasts would sag, whether I would suddenly look like mothers appeared to me, with their unflattering clothes and tired bodies.

One morning, Jacob sat up in bed and turned to me as I awoke. He said the spirits had told him that I had to decide whether I wanted the baby or not, that if I did not decide, the baby was not going to come.

I know, I said. I thought about it all day. I thought about it while swinging in my hammock chair, in the hot, damp air of that summer. I thought about it while reading. I thought about the alternative, and that scared me more than the thought of giving up all the control I had over my body at that time. I decided to brave the stretch marks, to brave gravity, and to brave the great breaking open I knew would happen when the baby finally came. And I said, *Yes, I choose this baby, I want this baby, please let him come,* though I knew I did not know what that meant.

~

After that, I was certain I would have a son with blond hair and blue eyes. I picked out a boy name, and as soon as I saw it, I knew the meaning was for him. His father came to agree, and although we gave a girl's name a little thought, I did not want a daughter, and I secretly prayed I would not have one. I was not ready, I thought, to have a girl—I was not ready to love a girl, not sure what that meant. I felt like I could take care of a boy, having spent so much of my life trying to earn my father's love and trying to protect my brother. I knew I could serve my son in a way that I could not serve a daughter.

Throughout my pregnancy, I gained seventeen pounds, though technically I probably lost some muscle weight and gained weight in fat, so the baby had more to work with than what it seemed. On a bright and cold February day, eight days after the estimated due date, I was awoken by a sharp contraction at about six in the morning. I told Jacob, and he encouraged me to go back to sleep. I woke up again around nine and had contractions steadily throughout the day. It was the first stage of labor, all very bearable and somewhat pleasant. I called my mother and told her my labor had started, and she tried to convince me one last time to go to a hospital, but I dismissed her concern. She was afraid, she said, for me to experience so much pain and not have any relief from it.

I wasn't afraid, because I didn't think any physical pain could rival the emotional pain I had known to that point.

Natural childbirth would mark my first memorable experience with physical pain, and it would surely establish a new reference point that I would use from then on.

My midwife showed up that evening, when the contractions were no longer somewhat pleasant. She brought an assistant with her, who was the same woman she had apprenticed under and who had attended over six hundred births. That woman had retired, but my midwife asked her for this favor, knowing we were an hour's drive from a hospital and no ambulance could reach us.

By eleven o'clock that night, it was clear the baby was nowhere near ready to make his entrance. My midwife had me take a bath to try to relax and ease the contractions. When that didn't work, she had me drink half of a home-brewed beer, again hoping it would slow the contractions and allow me to sleep for a little while that evening.

Everyone else went to sleep—the midwives and my friends who came to help found places to sleep downstairs near the woodstove, and the father of my child in our bed in the loft. One friend was a massage therapist, the other a student and friend of mine who majored in art and photography and would photograph the birth. I sat in a rocking chair next to an enormous window in the loft and rocked silently through my contractions all night. I labored in the dreamland of maternal solitude. I did not count contractions or minutes or anything else, and we did not have a clock to watch anyway. There were no lights on anywhere, inside or out, and no noises except the occasional creak of wood beneath me, the sound of someone moving in their sleep next to me, worlds away. In the darkness, I watched the moon travel in its arc over the sky as my child and body worked together toward a new life for us both. When the sun rose, I decided it was time to vocalize my suffering.

I let myself moan with each contraction throughout the morning. I wanted to be left alone in the ocean of pain that kept pulling me further away from the world.

My midwife checked me around noon and found I was ready, though my water had not broken. I asked her to rupture the membranes artificially—to break the caul that surrounded my unborn son and that held him in blissful suspension, in sublime safety. She did, using a tool that looked like a crochet needle, but to my surprise, it did not hurt. After that, things got interesting.

My irritation with the people around me was completely obliterated. I had felt distracted when I heard their talking downstairs, and though I wanted to be comforted, I did not want to have to speak or hear any voices. After the water poured out of me, I entered a new world, the kind of world that sets your body and your mind adrift and shows you why the Crucifixion of Christ is also called *the Passion*. My midwife reached inside me to push my bones apart and allow my son's head to descend. The indentations we all have in our lower backs—the two dimples that sit several inches apart—mark the width of the ischial spines, where yet-unborn heads must first arrive before coming to the light of day. My ischial spines, it turns out, were quite narrow, and though we did not know it yet, my son's head was relatively large.

If I had bellowed through my contractions as the sun rose, I could only scream when my bones were forced outward. The midwife was gentle, careful, respectful—but the goal was to move something farther than it wished to move, and resistance like that, of course, is a force to be reckoned with.

When my son's head was finally visible, it was a small, wrinkled bit that my midwife encouraged me to view with a mirror. I found it alarming, though, and failed to see the beauty in that first glimpse. After reading books about natural childbirth, unassisted childbirth, water births, and everything in between, I had thought I would give birth in a squatting position, aided by gravity and with a nod to my tribal ancestors, who understood the efficiency of such an irresistible force. I found myself instead lying on my back, my photographer friend behind me to help me arch my spine into a *C*. My husband held my right leg, and my massage-therapist friend held my left leg in the air. My midwife kneeled between my legs, trying to coax my son out, once and for all.

My son's head crowned for an hour, on the verge of slipping into this world and giving him his first breath of air, his first view of his mother, his first opportunity to cry. But he stayed inside, so my midwife reached for her scissors. It had to be done.

By this point, the other midwife was kneeling beside me, her hands on the top of my still-pregnant belly, pushing downward to help force the baby out. Finally, my son's head emerged and he cried out.

Another moment later, his body followed, and my son was born. Sometime later, Jacob would bury the placenta in a hole where he planted a tree for our son.

I got my first tattoo about a year later. One morning, while I was lying in bed with my son and enjoying the first few weeks of his life, dazed and soaked with the various essences of human life, I thought that my stretch marks looked like lightning bolts, and I considered it an apt symbol for my son's birth, as well as for my experience of birth, though the man who did my tattoo executed an image that was markedly different from what he had sketched for me.

Pain is a place, a substance, a state of being: *I am in pain.* We say *hurt*, and we mean *like that baseball that hit me in the face when I was twelve.* Or we say *excruciating*, and we mean *like giving birth and the stitches that follow.* We say *broken* and mean *my arm* or *my heart* or *something else I clearly need to be whole.*

Suffer enough, and if we are lucky, you and I decide *something has to change*, and somehow, sooner or later, it does.

CHAPTER 28

Cyclical

I spent my first six weeks with the baby down in the holler, leaving only to have him examined by a local doctor who was sympathetic to home birth—there was a fairly large Mennonite community nearby who took their babies to him. The rest of that time, I held and nursed my baby and discovered my capacity for love in a new, sacred dreamworld. I couldn't fathom leaving the protective hills then—I carried my son at my chest when he wasn't eating or sleeping, and there was nothing else in the world for me that mattered. It seemed all I did was nurse him and change his cloth diapers while my body slowly healed from the tearing apart.

That holler was so much like the one where I came from, with its breathtaking beauty, its carpets of wildflowers, the furled fronds of the ferns taking invisible breaths as they revealed themselves to a waiting forest. But for all the beauty such places hide, they hide everything else as well. Those hills are hallowed, the terrain unyielding, like a church whose walls write secrets upon the hearts of the trembling.

And that holler was equally severe. We boiled the rainwater from the roof in five-gallon pots on the woodstove, fifteen minutes for each pot—one pot at a time, usually—so I could bathe in clean water. Somehow, that didn't prove clean enough, and within a few weeks of giving birth, my postbirth blood turned rancid. For a couple of days, I wondered what was wrong and finally asked Jacob to bring me the thermometer from the bathroom.

You're fine, you don't have a fever.

He refused, so I walked gingerly down the loft stairs, rough-cut boards with no railing. I made my way to the bathroom, mindful of the stitches that must not come apart, and took my temperature. It was 102.5. Jacob went outside and came back with an echinacea root that he rinsed off and handed to me.

Chew this and swallow the juices.

I did what he said, and the juice was bitter and burning all at once. But I chewed the entire root, and a couple of days later, the infection cleared. When I felt well enough to walk outside, I used my cell phone on the one spot it worked in the holler—standing on the corner of the porch, facing the barn. I called my midwife, and with evident frustration, she told me I had had a uterine infection and, if it happened again, to make him take me to the doctor. I looked it up and found that a uterine infection is the same as *childbed fever*, the malady that has taken so many women without clean water, without proper care. I was more careful then and took no more sitting baths until I healed, though I was almost always covered in sour milk and spit-up.

Jacob worked on weekends and was gone the entire weekend, coming back on Monday afternoon with our weekly groceries. I think he stayed home with us for two weeks or so before going back to work. I slept with an ax between me and the loft stairs and kept my baby close. Winter gave way to spring, and my enchantment was punctured only by the reality of how cold the house could be. I learned to build a fire out of anything—we occasionally had a nice load of red oak, but at other times, it was wet and rotten wood that I coaxed into burning while the baby lay safely nearby. I wondered whether it was possible to freeze in that house, like our eggs and lettuce had done in the cabinet on the porch—a ramshackle, makeshift icebox that spared us from walking to the barn several times a day.

Thankfully, the chilly spring gave way to warmth and a hot summer. The failed passive-solar design ensured that the house was always hot, and we kept a box fan running when we could, moving the damp, heavy air through the living room space. There were few walls within the house, so the fan did what little it could to provide some relief. The baby and I were always covered in milk and sweat, and I did what little I could to keep him cool and dry. We often walked to the waterfalls before they dried up for the season, and I relished the cool, trickling streams.

I had taken off the spring semester from college and had the summer off as well, and would then have just my senior year to finish before I graduated. As the summer wore on, though, I worried about how I would make it to class. The trip out of the holler took time and care, and it was another thirty minutes or so to get to campus after reaching the road. With his unflagging criticism of the idea of college, I began to suspect that Jacob wouldn't make it easy for me to leave the holler and do the work I needed to do to finish.

One afternoon, I realized I hadn't brushed my hair in a few days, and I was suddenly frustrated with how little time I had to take care of myself. I asked Jacob to watch the baby while I went downstairs—I wanted to brush my teeth as well. He lay next to the baby on our mattress and rubbed the baby's back as he started fussing. Standing beneath the loft, I knew what the baby's cries meant as they intensified: *Pick me up. Hold me. Let's walk around.*

I stepped out of the bathroom and looked up and said something like, *Can you calm him down?*

I've got this, we're fine, Jacob replied.

I brushed my teeth, and the baby began to cry in earnest. I again stepped out and looked up, and this time, I did not hide my irritation. *Can you take care of him?*

Jacob stood up and came downstairs, leaving the baby on the mattress. I don't remember whether he said anything, but he was clearly angry, and I went upstairs to pick up the baby and then brought him back down. Jacob kicked the baby's walker, and it flew across the floor before hitting something else that stopped it. I grabbed my little zippered purse, the phone and charger, and the diaper bag and hurried to the old Toyota 4Runner we had bought with some of the wedding gift money Jacob's parents had given us.

I buckled the baby into his car seat in the front passenger seat—why it wasn't in the back seat, I can't say. I locked the door as I always did, a measure of precaution in a time when most car doors—especially the older cars—didn't have automatic locks. As I buckled myself into the driver's seat, Jacob came to the passenger door, tried to open it, and then just stood looking at the baby. I thought he wanted to give the baby a kiss or say a little goodbye, because clearly I needed to leave him alone for a while, and this was no time to talk about what had just happened.

But when I unlocked the door, he immediately began unbuckling the baby, and I reached out in horror—*What are you doing? You can't take him, you can't keep him here.* I held on to the baby as gently as I could, suddenly afraid in a way that I had never been before.

Please let me go, I said. *Please don't do this. I won't take anything, you can have everything. Just let me leave.*

Finally, saying nothing, he stepped back, and I shut and locked the door again, my heart racing. I started the engine and looked in the rearview mirror, ready to back up and turn around near the old shed at the corner of the dirt driveway. Jacob stood at the back of the vehicle, reaching his arms to the top of it. A couple of times, I asked him to move; he finally did, and I could see him walking into the house as I drove away.

Then I was seized by a new fear. Would he follow me? Try to stop me again? He had the white pickup that I had clutch-started during my pregnancy. Of course I would not leave him without a vehicle. There was no way to drive up the hill quickly—you had to be so careful as you negotiated the chunks of rock that jutted this way and that from the dirt of the driveway. To be careless or drive too fast meant that something would be knocked loose under the hood, as several people came to find out. Part of the way, someone could walk faster than driving up.

I reached the top of the hill, breathless with fear, but he never appeared in my rearview mirror. I made it to a friend's house and stayed for a night or two. Jacob called me and said he wanted to talk, and I met him in a parking lot, hoping it was a safe and smart thing to do.

When we argued, Jacob would tell me I was like my father. I had told him some of the stories about my childhood, and early in our relationship, I related every story of my shame and mistakes—I thought that's what it meant to be honest, to be vulnerable and trusting within a relationship. When the first signs of his disapproval surfaced, he compared me to his mother: selfish, materialistic. But after a while, it was my father he saw in me—at least, the version of my father I had shared with him: *violent, full of anger, fucked up.* I believed him, already so convinced of my flaws, so certain that any anger I ever felt was a sign I had failed to escape fate. I feared becoming like my father, and comparing me to him was a keen weapon.

In the parking lot where we met, Jacob told me it was my fault he had acted like he did. Somehow, it was a drama he felt forced to play, and the role of my father had been forced upon him. But he wanted me to come back. *You belong at home, and so does our son,* he told me.

I took another day or two to think about what he said. I couldn't wrap my mind around what had happened, it seemed so surreal. Just after he kicked the walker, part of me wanted to stop and talk to Jacob, to say, *Okay, this is ridiculous, we don't have to do this, this is not who you are.* Like the time I thought I could stop my father from whipping me, when I realized that I had done nothing wrong and that it was unfair. I had thought better of my father than he thought of himself—I believed his reckless violence was beneath him and not his true nature.

None of it made sense to me, but maybe I had subconsciously provoked Jacob. I was always filled with so much guilt, I accepted that I had magically orchestrated everything he ever disliked about his life. I was lost inside myself, certain of nothing good about me other than the fierce and selfless love I felt for my baby. To my friend's dismay, I went back.

CHAPTER 29

The Whore

Within a few weeks of the fall semester starting, I found that I was right to be concerned about getting to my classes. My childhood fear returned, that of being trapped and not allowed to leave, isolated from the rest of the world in a beautiful prison. One day we were in town, and I had someone watch the baby while Jacob and I ate at the Mexican restaurant. We walked down the street afterward, holding hands, and things felt so pleasant, I thought he might understand what I told him next.

I had used some of my student grant money to put down a deposit on an apartment in town, within walking distance of the college. Jacob dropped my hand and stopped walking as I explained—I wouldn't be able to get to classes from the holler, and it was so important to me to finish my degree. No, I wasn't sure what I would do with a bachelor's degree in philosophy. Yes, it was just a piece of paper. But for whatever reason, I felt like it was necessary that I finish, that I prove myself.

I told Jacob he could live in the apartment with us if he wanted, and we could just go back to Rockcastle County as we pleased, and after I graduated, we would be there for good. Or he could come and go as he wished, as my husband, staying in town sometimes and in the holler whenever he felt like it. He could take care of the baby while I went to class, or I would pay a babysitter—he didn't have to do anything. Eventually, he seemed to accept the arrangement, though he was not happy about it.

One of his best friends, Greg, was living near me with his wife and their child, who was born just before ours. Jacob arranged for them to watch the baby sometimes, and I would drop him off on my way to class. I brought the baby's food already cut into pieces so no one would accidentally give him too big of a bite. When I could, I came back between classes to nurse him, and I pumped milk so he would have bottles when I couldn't be there. Jacob showed up to watch the baby less and less, so when I didn't have anything else arranged, I often ended up taking him to class with me in a baby backpack. He grew so big, people constantly remarked that he was bigger than me.

My professors were as understanding as possible. I brought him to my weight-lifting class one day when Jacob didn't show up, and the coach sent me outside to walk laps around the track with my son pulling my hair and drooling on me. He was quickly bored, so I bounced around the track, trying to keep him entertained, wondering how I was going to make it work. I brought him to my senior-seminar class another time, and he fussed so much, I ended up nursing him to keep him quiet and to not have to leave the room. There were two other students in the seminar—both male—and our professor was male. I was well covered while I nursed, but they kept their eyes fixed to mine, and they took everything I said about Wittgenstein seriously, which almost kept me from being embarrassed. I was a research assistant for another philosophy professor that year and once nursed the baby in his office during a meeting—the baby only nursed briefly but then spat it all back up onto the professor's carpet. The professor refused to let me clean it, and I didn't cry until I was outside his office again.

Jacob still came over and spent the night, usually a couple of days a week. During one of the many arguments that seemed to always happen, I looked at our son's face and saw he was still playing happily, unaware and unaffected. I just kept washing the dishes. I decided in that moment that I wouldn't fight with Jacob and that I would never again let our son hear us arguing.

I wanted to go out on Halloween that year—I hadn't spent much time with friends in a long while, especially without the baby. He agreed to watch the baby so I could go to a Halloween party, but when I returned, he was back at it, telling me how I was a terrible person, a horrible mother. I told him if I was such a negative person in his life, he should leave me. By that point, I couldn't think of any reason he would want to be with me. I knew he wanted to hurt my feelings, but I didn't understand how he could hate me so much. I had done everything I knew to be a good wife.

He stood up and told me he would leave me. For a moment, I thought about everything that meant and then said, *Okay.* He walked out and came right back, pleading with me to *work this out.* I told him that he deserved better, that I was making him miserable. I wasn't sure I was so bad, but he had been so insistent just moments earlier, I figured agreeing with him and apologizing would be the quickest way to end the painful evening. I was emotionally and mentally exhausted and didn't feel like I could do any more mental gymnastics to determine who was the worst of us, where all the blame for our lost love should be placed. And yet, we talked into the night.

I moved to a one-bedroom apartment soon after—I couldn't quite afford the two-bedroom apartment I was living in, and the downstairs neighbors were young men who loved heavy-metal music and who didn't care how many times I banged on the floor or went to their door, asking them to be quiet. Jacob kept a few things at my new apartment until I finally told him to take them home—his nice kitchen knives, a cookbook, that sort of thing.

He was over one day before work, and I began vomiting—I was too weak to walk to the bedroom, so I slept on the couch in between vomiting. He put the baby to sleep in the playpen in my bedroom—the playpen served as a crib—and started to leave. *Please don't leave me, call in to work—I can't take care of the baby like this.*

But he would not miss work. When the baby woke up, I was too weak to stand, and I crawled to his playpen, trying to comfort him. My downstairs neighbors knocked on the door at the top of the stairs between their apartment and mine—we shared a washer and dryer that sat on their floor, at the bottom of those stairs. I crawled to the door, the baby crying in earnest now.

Do you need help with your baby? They had never heard him cry so much. I told them, *Yes, please—he just wants to be held,* and the woman came in and picked him up and soothed him, then took him to the far end of the living room, which I had set up as a play area with toys and bright pictures to counter the dark wood paneling of the apartment. I don't remember her name, but I wish I could find her and thank her for that. I could often hear her boyfriend's booming voice—he always seemed to be yelling at her—but she came into my house that evening and wasn't a bit worried about getting sick herself.

Jacob and I were no longer together, but he came to my apartment one day and found another young man there—he was a friend, and we had been intimate once, but that's not why he was there. Still, Jacob was mad at me and asked, *So this is who you leave me for? That boy?* He also read my journal when he got a chance and had nothing but disdain for me.

During the first year after I moved out of Jacob's house—he was always clear that it was his house, his money—the people around me seemed to change. I had lived in Berea for almost four years and had my college friends who were mostly my age, but I also had a group of older, hippieish friends who were involved in sustainable living. I had met most of them when I was a freshman and had always been welcome to go swimming with them in their private ponds, and to attend their potlucks and parties.

But after I first moved out, before we really split up, Jacob told me that he and his lesbian friends had discussed my leaving him, and they all decided I must be a lesbian. These were women I knew, a couple that I had thought of as matriarchs in the community, though they weren't that much older than me. I had not told anyone but my closest friends what he had done, the things he had said to me, but he apparently told all kinds of stories about me to anyone who would listen.

About a year later, one of those women happened to see me at a mutual friend's on a summer day. I brought my son with me to this older couple's house, quite a ways from town. They had a large, deep pond—more like a lake—and I was allowed to come there and swim whenever I wanted. When I arrived that Sunday afternoon, I found there were a lot of cars parked along the gravel driveway and quite a few people swimming. Some were naked, some were clothed, but I didn't own a bathing suit at the time and always swam in my friends' ponds naked, as did the owners. After we swam around for a little while, someone mentioned the trampoline that sat in the field and how much we would enjoy it, so I wrapped myself and my son in towels and went to the trampoline alone. I didn't bother with shoes—I loved feeling like I was part of nature again, and the path was mostly soft. I let him jump for a few minutes, and we were quickly dry, so I wrapped us both up and headed back toward the pond.

I had never been out to that field before and, until I was walking on gravel, didn't realize I had taken the path to the left, which led to the rest of the driveway and another small house, rather than the path on the right, which headed back to the pond. I suddenly found myself walking on sharp gravel, carrying my son, surrounded by a lot of people I knew and a few I did not. The house owners had thrown their annual party that weekend, and most of these people had spent the entire weekend there. The mood was relaxed and cheerful as people chatted, and some drank beers and smoked. The wife of the couple soon came up to me as I tried to walk down the gravel road and return to the pond.

Are you naked under there? she asked me.

Yes, I'm really sorry. I took the wrong way back from the trampoline. I'm trying to get back to my clothes, I told her.

Oh no, honey—we don't mind that kind of thing a bit here. You look like Eve in the Garden of Eden. Go sit down—I'll get your clothes and shoes for you.

And with that, she walked off, and I was free to put my son down, a one-year-old who was big for his age. The guys on the porch offered me a chair, and I sat, relieved and embarrassed, but also heartened to hear the owner's compliment. After a few minutes of sitting and drinking a beer, I thought it was reasonable to take my towel off and sit naked, rather than pretending I wasn't basically naked already. I chatted with some of the guys, and plenty of people wandered about. My son played in the dirt, and for a moment, I thought I was in some kind of heaven—where being *natural* was not just accepted but encouraged. The men kept their eyes aimed toward my face, and since I thought I was so ugly, it never occurred to me that anyone would think anything about me other than I was a tomboy who happened to be naked, but so were a bunch of other people at the pond, and most of those people had seen each other swimming around naked anyway.

I was wrong. Jacob's lesbian friend showed up at the party and was all of a sudden walking down the same road that I had come up, heading to the field with a few other people. She turned and looked at me, said hi, and turned back around without stopping. A couple of days later, Jacob said, *She told me she saw you out there, naked and sprawled out for all the men to see what they could have if they wanted it.* I didn't know how to defend myself, didn't have the words to say, *I was like Eve in the Garden, not a whore. I thought that was freedom. And didn't you all decide I was a lesbian anyway?*

Some months later, I was buying a couple of groceries in the health-food store—the same one I had worked in for a time—and I ran into Jacob's friend Greg, whose wife had babysat for me. Greg walked up to me, and my stomach knotted with dread, but he told me he owed me an apology.

For what? I asked.

Jacob told us that you were such a bitch, and we believed him. He said you wanted to sleep with other men but didn't want him to sleep with other women, and that's why you split up. He said that you were a terrible mother and that you didn't care at all about the baby. Soon after, Greg's wife echoed what he had said and told me, *I believed him for a while, but you were always there for the baby, bringing his food already cut up*—she laughed—*I told my husband that this is not a woman who doesn't love her child.*

I called Jacob and asked him whether he had said all those things, and he said yes. I told him he knew that wasn't true—I had never wanted to be with anyone else when we were together. He reminded me that I had told him I thought an open relationship was a good idea.

I told you I believed that when I was seventeen, and it didn't work for me.

Well, I can't help what people say about you, he responded.

Yes you can, if you stop telling them lies and tell them what you said isn't true.

But of course, that was not going to happen. For that first year or two, I lost one round of friends. *That's okay, they weren't my friends anyway,* I told myself. But I missed being able to go to the potlucks and the outdoor parties with the other hippies and homesteaders.

There would be another wave of loss later, when I tried to fight for my son in court. When I was ready to file for divorce, Jacob told me he wanted to keep the baby half the time and not pay child support. I didn't know then that he had gotten that idea from another man, someone I would end up dating. Jacob had been giving me a couple hundred dollars each month, which I had thought was really good. But he had insisted that I couldn't keep either of the vehicles that we bought with the five thousand dollars from his parents' wedding gift—that money was going into the land and would stay there. He agreed to give me seven hundred dollars, and other than some fancy CorningWare baking dishes, that's all I got of the property we owned together.

I signed up for legal aid, a free attorney who would represent me in court, and refused to take my granny's money when she begged me to go hire a good lawyer. I felt like I had taken so much, it didn't make sense to spend her money on a lawyer when I could get a perfectly good one for free. I didn't want Jacob to take our son back to the ramshackle house in Rockcastle County overnight, so far away, but he insisted. When he brought him back, I asked how it went, and with an edge to his voice he told me they were fine but would say no more. When Jacob first mentioned keeping our son half the time, I insisted he couldn't because the baby was still nursing, but after spending some nights away from me, he quickly weaned himself.

Soon after the baby turned one, Jacob told me that his dad had advised him to just take the baby and move back down to Atlanta, where they were from. I asked him what his mother thought of that idea, and he said she didn't approve of taking the baby away from me—I was glad, since I had spent that past Christmas with them just so Jacob wouldn't be away from his son for *his* first Christmas—but I got the message loud and clear that I was in no position to fight Jacob, who had his parents' money at his disposal. I met with a couple of lawyers for consultations—not the free lawyer, because there was a long waiting list—and they told me that in Kentucky, since we were still married and there was no custody agreement, Jacob could take the baby whenever he wanted, wherever he wanted, and not give him back to me. And if he did that, it could be a year or more before I saw my child again. So I agreed to the equal time sharing and began drinking when my son was away, trying to drown my grief.

CHAPTER 30

Pretending

The day I graduated from Berea College, Jacob held the baby while I sat through the ceremony. My mother and stepfather came, and my granny came with my dad. After it was over, I got my son and looked for the rest of my family. I found Granny and Dad, and they told me they were leaving—though it was early afternoon, Granny didn't want it to get any later before they drove the hour and a half home. I never found my mother, but when I called her later, she said they left immediately after the ceremony ended, so she wouldn't run into my father. I walked out of the gym, where my friends and classmates were hugging their families and taking pictures, and went home with my baby.

I was scared after I graduated—I realized I needed to find work immediately but had no idea what I could do or how to land a real job besides waitressing. My stepdad told me I should go to a temp agency in Lexington, so I did, and I was able to work a couple of short-term jobs through them and made enough money to pay the bills. One of those short-term jobs led to a long-term, but still temporary, position as an administrative assistant in Lexington.

I felt like I didn't know how to do anything, so I worked as hard and fast as I could at everything. The director of the department found out that I liked to write, so she had me help edit the newsletters the company sent out to customers, and soon I was drafting articles and learned to do the layout as well. I picked up on how to write macros in Excel, and anytime someone asked whether I could do something I couldn't do, I said yes, then learned how to do it. Eventually, they offered me a full-time job.

I constantly worried about how to make ends meet and wondered what would happen to me and my son if I failed to make it in this new world—the world of working and babysitters and commuting and flat tires on the interstate. Since the time I had moved out when I was seventeen, my mother had given me money only once—when one of the struts broke on my car. I was surprised—she usually wouldn't even lend me money, but she and my stepdad paid the garage that fixed it, so I could drive my car to work. At other times I asked for help, and if they lent me money, I had to tell them the exact date I would pay it all back. When another of my cars spewed oil everywhere right before I started a new job, they wouldn't lend me their extra vehicle—*neither a lender nor a borrower be,* my stepfather reminded me.

I knew I couldn't move back in with them if I couldn't survive as an adult—now a parent myself, with someone else to care for. I tried to hide my fear at work, and I kept my face as expressionless as possible—an essential key to survival, as I had learned when my dad whipped me for crying, and at other times for smiling, or when, all those years ago, I saw Granny talk to my dad like her grandchildren and our mother weren't crouched on the floorboard of Papaw's truck, holding our breaths.

Eventually, I became friends with another woman there, who told me she had thought I was *haughty* due to how disinterested I looked all the time. I hadn't thought I was better than my coworkers, but as in the past, I found that I couldn't relate to them, that what I did to survive somehow made me wrong in their eyes. They talked about watching *The Bachelor,* losing weight, and giving their husbands blow jobs. When I brought Indian food for lunch, they made faces, and the director asked me not to eat it at my desk. I didn't understand why they were content with fast-food cheeseburgers and fries, or how it mattered if one woman didn't like another.

Once I left Morehead, a lot of the people I met told me I didn't have an accent after they found out I was from eastern Kentucky, but anyone who heard me on the phone with my family commented on how my accent came right back. I had worked hard in college to say words the right way, enunciating the endings like we never did back home and quickly scanning my brain for different words when I wanted to say *wallering around* or *up in the holler* or *I reckon*. I didn't know anything about linguistics, and even when I did take a linguistics class in graduate school, it didn't dawn on me that my people had their own grammar. Like all cultures everywhere, there are unspoken rules for how certain sounds are pronounced, and for arranging those words, but it all follows a structure and has nothing to do with being ignorant or lazy—we were just country people talking like people from the country. Every group of people, everywhere, has a way of talking.

The mockery of Appalachia has evolved from *The Beverly Hillbillies* to concerts where musicians who've gotten rich off Appalachian music traditions don't mind making fun of toothless Kentuckians right here in Kentucky. Quiznos featured a "hillbilly hot tub" in one of their commercials, which was met with some disdain for the homoerotic undertones, but I never found any backlash at the ad's depiction of hillbillies as ignorant and mentally slow. Maybe I was the only person who boycotted Quiznos from then on. And I was horrified when I recently watched *The Simpsons*, and it featured a woman from Kentucky—she was a hopeless heroin addict who made beautiful music but who ultimately disappointed everyone by turning back to drugs and alcohol after Lisa tried to save her from herself. I knew when we were supposed to laugh, but all I could think of was the people I have loved and the mounting losses between us. The punchlines we're so good for.

Sometimes, when I was around my family, they would turn to each other when I used a word they didn't understand—*a five-dollar word, too rich for our blood*—and I would look away, knowing my new way of speaking marked me as an outsider. No matter what I did, I couldn't do good enough in someone's eyes. But I couldn't take back the education and years of reading poets and philosophers and history. And I couldn't tell them, *I am still one of you,* because in so many ways, I wasn't able to be. For a while, I thought I could show them what was so good about the education I had received, show them that the *going away and having your head filled with nonsense* our people had looked down on for so long was just wrong thinking, that there was so much good in those books and classrooms.

The years wore on, and each time Jacob was angry with me, another group of friends and acquaintances turned their scorn toward me. One friend who had told me, *He doesn't help at all with the baby,* later described him as one of her favorite people. Another friend, a man who had been as good as a brother to me, ended up telling me, *Jacob isn't so bad these days.* When Jacob told a story about me, no one ever asked me my side of what had happened, and I didn't volunteer it. If there's one thing you learn growing up as a girl in the country, it's not to air your dirty laundry in public.

I started to wonder, though, what would have happened if I had told all my stories to these people. Would they have believed me, would they have cared? Would they have turned their backs on Jacob in line at a restaurant, or have stopped inviting him to their parties? Would he have seen so many friendly faces close themselves to him, shut him out from the small-town social life of the farmers' market and elementary school events? And would Jacob have wondered what he had done wrong, how I had single-handedly taken a town—a chosen home— away from him? Or does that just happen to girls like me?

The answers don't actually matter. I didn't want him to feel lonely or abandoned, so I didn't tell the stories that would have led to him being judged by those people. The loneliness I carried for so much of my life, though, was deepened and sharpened, somehow a vast hollowness that left me bleeding and aching and wishing for comfort. And though I shared my stories with my closest friends, some of those people chose him, in the end. It took me years to realize that they couldn't love me and still celebrate the man who had belittled me. And even longer to realize that those people, with their talk about community and female empowerment and protecting children, could not see the disconnect between their theories and the world we live in. They did not want to see people like me, who *needed* the world they claimed to want.

I wasn't great at being an employee, as hard as I worked. Sometimes it was because I had bad luck—two flat tires in one month, a boyfriend living with me had a seizure and I *had* to stay home with him. Sometimes it was because I drank so much while my son was at his dad's, I drove in late or I had to sleep during my lunch break. Other times, I was clearly just sabotaging myself, and my boss had the kindness and good sense to point that out, but I didn't know how to fix it.

Because of my absences and lateness—you could have only five occurrences in a twelve-month period—they sent me to the employee assistance program. I soon found myself in a therapist's office, trying to figure out why I had a hard time enjoying my job and getting to work on time, and he asked me whether I believed in God. He seemed like a nice guy, but nice in the way that I felt like he couldn't understand a word I said, or he could be a really crazy person who would shock me with his own darkness. Either way, I didn't trust him. When he asked me to close my eyes and pretend I was telling Jesus why I was angry with him, I was even more concerned. It didn't seem worth it to try to explain that I didn't blame a god or Jesus for anything I had experienced but that I wasn't very happy with the people in the churches I knew.

I couldn't keep my eyes closed for long. I took about fifteen minutes to tell him what I thought had been most traumatic to me. Then I suggested I needed a female therapist, someone I could open up to a little more comfortably. He sent me to the in-house psychiatrist, who was, indeed, a woman, so I could get some medication for what he thought was post-traumatic stress disorder. That made sense to me—I could imagine what it meant to have PTSD but not due to war or famine. I hadn't thought about it before, but it made sense that enough scary experiences might have impacted me in ways I didn't understand, that I might be carrying some of that with me still.

It took a long time for me to feel safe enough to let go of my church-induced hellfire-and-damnation, born-into-sin fears. For a long time, I cast a glance upward and asked to be enlightened—either gently prodded or firmly reprimanded—if I was sorely mistaken in my views. But ultimately, no matter how afraid I felt of my own sinful nature, I saw God as a smiling benefactor, someone like Papaw Wright, who was quick to give us kids a quarter or a dollar, who always offered us his exotic cans of pineapple juice, and who never seemed drunk even though he always had a beer in hand after his workday was finished.

I found the Sufi notion of God more poetic and enjoyable—God as the Lover and the Friend, the ultimate companion. I found the Hindu gods particularly attractive—especially the trickster and seducer Krishna. I imagined myself in the woods, happening upon the beautiful, blue-skinned god as he played his flute. I could see myself going to him, disarmed by his gaze and enchanted by his music. I always thought that whatever consequences there would be in losing myself with one such as he, the ecstasy would surely be worth it.

I read and consumed whatever I could find in religion and philosophy, searching for a cohesive map to lay on top of the story of my life. I felt I could stitch discordant fragments of spiritual truth together or convert to Judaism, so long as it gave me the magic missing piece, like the prize from a cereal box that you set upon the jumbled picture, and it suddenly becomes clear, it suddenly makes sense.

After a twenty-minute question-and-answer session with the psychiatrist revealed I was prone to making bad decisions, they prescribed two different medications and scheduled my first appointment with the psychologist. I liked him—he wanted to sit outside and smoke cigarettes with me while we talked, and when I told him I had been praying for clarity, he told me how he had prayed for the same thing. And when I told him I was afraid of being alone, he said there would always be a man who would love me and my fine little body. The next time I expressed that fear, he said, *With that tight little ass? You'll be fine.* He had set me up with family medical leave due to my *condition*, and when I stopped using one of the medicines, he told me he would have to take away the benefits.

But I didn't want a therapist talking about my tight ass, and I didn't want a prescription to help me stop making bad decisions, so I stopped taking both medications and bid my family medical leave farewell. I decided to try to make better decisions more or less on my own. I broke up with my boyfriend and stopped drinking bourbon all the time, too. I had my birth control removed—the one that had kept me from having a period for years, by that point.

After three and a half years of working in the corporate world, I decided to go to graduate school. Now and then, I had fleeting thoughts that maybe my desire to be a writer would dwindle away, but instead, it seemed to eat at me, like a wolf that wouldn't leave its prey alone. I called my mother and stepfather to tell them the news.

What will you do with an English degree?

Maybe I'll be an English teacher.

The world has enough English teachers. You should move to Vegas and deal blackjack—that's where the real money is.

I loved graduate school, though—especially literary theory class. We looked at so many different theories—*lenses of perception*, I thought— and each one made sense, each was so valuable and good. One day in class, our professor asked me how old I was. *Twenty-eight*, I told her.

You're gonna be all right, she said.

For one of my comprehensive exams, I decided to explore Walt Whitman's *Leaves of Grass* through feminist theory—it seemed easy, really, but fun. Years later, I found myself standing in the coffee shop where I had bought coffee and brownies and sandwiches for twenty years. Our local prominent feminist stood beside me, a woman who had written plenty of books and essays on all aspects of what it means to be female and how race intersects. She was one of Jacob's best friends. To that point, she had been friendly with me, though I never got to talk to her in a real conversation, as I had asked Jacob to introduce us, but he had not. She loved my son, though, and made that clear, doting on him anytime she saw him. She had chatted with me and introduced me to her sister, and I was glad to finally be able to form my own connection with her.

This time, though, was just after Jacob had grown angry with me again—our son wanted to live with me full time and wasn't happy with Jacob's home. We had *blindsided* Jacob by asking to meet at a restaurant to talk, and he didn't even want to know what schedule our son was suggesting. He told our fifteen-year-old that if the schedule involved less time at their house, he didn't even need to hear it.

In the coffee shop, the prominent feminist author turned away, instead of acknowledging me, and gave my son a cold *hello* instead of her usual affection—she had told me more than once how wonderful he was. I stood in line behind another friend a few days later—a woman I had known for nearly twenty years—and she and her husband looked at me before turning away, silent.

It was then that I understood the difference between theory and life. It was then that I realized I could never go home to the women like my mother—like me—and tell them feminists were working for them by writing essays or books or songs. I finally understood that the same people who sign petitions for laborers across the world don't always love the laborers next to them. And that *health care for all* sometimes means *not the ones who smoke*. I realized that the feminists around me would still ask, *Why didn't you kick him in the balls?* because a woman should be able to fight off two men twice her size. A feminist can still say, *She was sprawled out for the men,* and an entire community will shut out a young woman who is trying to figure out how to survive and be a mother if her decisions don't meet their standards, if she doesn't control the story told about her. I finally understood that so much of what I did looked *ugly* to the people around me, and they were happy to accept whatever a man decided was ugly.

I had never asked myself what I thought feminism *should be.* I try not to worry too much about what people call themselves, or what nuances separate their ideas from mine. There are so many of us trying, striving through our imperfections to be *good.* But what would I tell a daughter who calls me one night, excited about the young man she has met, who knows so much about *everything* and is a *feminist who really cares about women's rights, Mom?*

I think I would tell her to see how he reacts when she doesn't please him, when she doesn't follow his unspoken rules. When she is too loud or accidentally breaks his favorite cup. When she wears something he doesn't like or gets excited about something he doesn't care about. *Does he talk out both sides of his mouth?* I'd ask. She'd know what I mean— does he find a way to make himself right when he's wrong? Does he charm people with his endless wit and wisdom, and where does he want her to sit while he does it?

And then there's the other women, so good at deciding when a woman's sexuality is her empowerment or her sluttiness. So wrapped up in keeping women in their place—whatever that place may look like— they forget that the rules they embrace are also their own bondage.

In my small world, I found myself more alone than ever and wondered whether any of these other worlds would ever truly want me, whether I could belong anywhere. I couldn't return to the holler where I grew up—my father lives there still, shut in my granny's house, all the old magic gone from a place now filled with the sorrow and torment of a man shooting up heroin that is somehow affordable to the hillbillies that once had to rely on Lortabs for such a high. The new home and family I thought I had—the family I chose, the ones who care about social justice and the environment—have abandoned me each time a man told them to, and I never know who is gone until I meet them in the grocery store or at a restaurant and they look at me, full of knowing, then turn away.

CHAPTER 31

Handwritten

After I graduated from college, one time I went to a party in Elliott County—the same county in which I had gone to court as a girl but never testified. The party was thrown by one of my college friends who was living on someone's lovely, rambling wooded property. When I first arrived, I went to the deck adjoined to the house and introduced myself to the owner. I knew he was an attorney in this godforsaken county, and I asked him what kind of law he practiced. He said he was a criminal-defense attorney, and I grinned.

Criminal defense? You must know my father, then!

I laughed a little at my joke, and he asked me my father's name. When I told him, his eyes widened, and he looked at me in disbelief. I stopped laughing and asked, *Do you know him?*

It turned out that not only did he know my father, but, as he said, he had kept my father out of prison.

Which time? I asked breezily.

It was the time my dad got caught stealing copper from railroads, when I was about six years old. I remember the fires he had by the creek, stacks of coiled wire burning and melting away the protective rubber casings. I don't know how he got caught, but like every other illegal thing he has done, he managed to stay out of prison—and here I was, looking at the man who kept him out of it that time, getting ready to eat a hamburger on his deck. As he stared at me, I grew nervous and wondered what he was thinking of me, this man who knew where I came from, who may have even seen me in his office fifteen or so years before that.

My mind raced through the same thought I've so often entertained, trying to understand how the hell my father has been in a courtroom and even in a jail cell so many times, and yet it was never for anything he did to me, my brother, or our mother. Like many poor people, I grew up learning not to trust the police, and nobody had to sit me down to tell me why. I knew that poor people had a good chance of getting into more trouble if they called the police—you might have a warrant for unpaid traffic fines, or maybe the baby has a bruise and the police call Social Services. Maybe you had a drink or something to calm the nerves, and now your husband's come home to knock you into the wall a little. Call the cops—maybe you'll go to jail, maybe he will. Maybe both. It's harder to pretend when you're poor—harder to keep up the shiny veneer that tells the rest of the world that you're harmless and innocent, that you deserve protection.

I faked what I hoped was humble confidence and said, *I guess sometimes the apple does fall far from the tree.* I think I was hoping to reassure him that I was nothing like my father, that I wasn't going to steal from him or start a fight or kill any dogs while I camped on his property over the weekend.

Looks like the apple rolled down a hill and into a creek and washed up on another bank, in this case. He kept staring, but reassured me that he could perceive, even in that small amount of time, that I was, indeed, not my father. I was shaken, though, and spent the next few weeks wondering what would have happened if my father hadn't gotten such a competent lawyer. Who paid for the lawyer anyway? It was probably Granny, whose allegiance to her children always came first, right after

God but before the Law. And then us grandchildren—we took a place ahead of our parents, who she often had to protect us from.

I imagined what it would have been like if he had gone to prison, if my mother had raised us alone. Would she have stayed in that holler? Would she have worked, or would we have lived off welfare? Would she have divorced him sooner, or later, and would she have replaced him with someone else to dominate every facet of our lives? Or would we have found freedom, living in the midst of so much forest, and would there suddenly have been so much space in our lives to be loud, to be happy, to be children? Would the nightmares have ended sooner? Would we have visited him in prison? Would he have died there, knifed by someone he robbed or refused?

But there is no use in daydreaming about such things. His prison was always internal, and we were always right there with him—captor and captives, king and slaves.

Though I grew up reading everything I could get my hands on, our family didn't tell regular fairy tales. Our stories were of real people, with real villains and casualties—never the happy or meaningful endings of fiction. When I was about twenty-three years old, my dad told me how he ended up in rehab. He told me that he and his second wife were convicted for prescription-pill fraud. His wife went to prison, but he was allowed to stay in the county jail because his father was a Freemason, his brother was a Freemason, and the judge was a Freemason. He was even made the trustee in the county jail and carried keys to get in and out of various rooms; he mopped the floors and was able to stay well supplied with his pills. After being in the county jail for a bit, he went to the Hope Center in Lexington.

He had written me a letter or two while he was in the county jail—the only times he had ever written me, at that point. He would write me more letters from the same county jail years later, but they are all the same. His sprawling handwriting can't be contained within the lines. I can tell he presses the pencil down hard, as if he is struggling to put the words on the paper. He always says he wants to see me, he loves me. And he'll call me when he can—sometimes a collect call from jail and sometimes from a new cell phone number when he's out—and wonder aloud why I won't come see him, then tell me about the latest person to steal from him, or who he stole from last, or how he got a little money and wants to send me some, wants to send birthday money and Christmas money, but the cards never come, that money never arrives, and he doesn't call back.

But this was the first time he had gone to rehab, and I thought there was a chance that something was different this time. I wanted to see him and see what had changed, whether he had finally *hit bottom*, as many people have to, or whether he had been inspired to make a new life for himself. Maybe he just wanted to be a dad now—a real dad who could love us and see his grandkids, and we could meet for lunch on Saturdays like I saw other grown daughters doing. It had been fifteen years since I dreamt I had saved him, and I thought fifteen years wasn't too long to wait to see my father finally be *okay*. I arrived at the Hope Center with my son and went inside to the front desk. He showed up a few minutes later, grumbling about something and talking a little to the men around us, who opened and closed their lockers and looked at us with blank faces.

We went outside so he could smoke a cigarette, and I sat down next to him, ready to hear how he was getting his life straight and turning over a new leaf and that sort of thing. Instead, he told me another story. He told me about his buddy at the Hope Center and how he and his buddy went out one night, over to the edge of the field, and got the knife that another guy dropped there for him. Then he told me about the man who had tried to take his change when he bought something from the vending machine. But he and his buddy convinced that guy to walk to the train tracks with them a few days later, and that's when my dad pulled out the knife, and his buddy knocked the guy out—*a big ol' boy*, my dad said, with a laugh—and they put him in a train car and shut the door. It was June and hot. He'd wake up in Chicago or even farther, if he woke up at all, my dad mused, still laughing. I sat there quietly, grateful my son would not remember the conversation.

After that, I wondered whether my dad had ever killed anyone. Maybe he killed the man he put on the train—where would *he* be now? There was another story I remember from when I was very young, but the details were always murky to me. It seemed that a man was bothering my dad at the gas station he managed, where he worked for several years. I heard him talk several times about breaking an Ale-8 bottle and threatening the guy with it, but he also mentioned his brother being there to help him, and I don't know—maybe they cut the guy, maybe they didn't.

On one hand, my dad's stories instilled in me a sense of vigilante justice, of people taking care of each other in families and communities, not waiting for police to arrive and not settling matters in court. I loved watching *Bonnie and Clyde* and westerns with Clint Eastwood, stories about Jesse James and even the cartoon version of *Robin Hood*, where Robin Hood and Maid Marian are foxes.

On the other hand, it became clear over the years that Dad's black-market dealings, his law-of-the-land justice, his defiance of the system, none of that really translated into loyalty to family or protection of his children—to love. He even managed to sever his relationships with the men he traded guns and knives and old coins with, grew weed with, and sold pills to or snorted them with in the barn. Sooner or later, it seemed like everyone who knew him held a grudge against him. The last time he went to jail, I realized that he had a growing group of enemies, and people told my brother there was a price on Dad's head. I wondered how, in his state, he could manage to survive being in jail any longer, and particularly how he could still get the drugs he needed to survive at that point. That line of thinking quickly goes where I am not ready to go, so I leave it, not yet at the end point—not ready to lose that which has caused me so much harm.

While he and his wife were both in jail during one of those times, their kids in foster care, I visited his house. There was a dog there, worse off than any of the ones we watched come and go when I was little. This one, like all the dogs my father and his wife somehow ended up with, was tethered to a ramshackle doghouse by the creek, fed for a while, and then forgotten. The dog whined and strained at its chain, its cry broken for lack of water. I wanted to ignore its ribs and the parasites that must have feasted on it in the dusty, shadeless circle it inhabited, no more than thirty feet in diameter. I was scared to get close to it, but I felt implicated in its torment, as if eventually some day of reckoning might come, and I might be required to define *compassion: How much do you wish for? How much did you show?*

There was no dog food, of course, so I looked through the kitchen cabinets for acceptable substitutes. The refrigerator held nothing edible. Finally, I opened a can of baked beans. Looking at it, I tried to guess how long the dog had gone without food. Granny had little sympathy for the animals at this house, but she claimed she had fed it once or twice. I pulled another can of beans out of the cabinet and paused. Would my youngest brother and my sister return to this house? Would the beans be replaced? Was I taking food that might feed them, and if so, would there be other food for them? Was this a *choice*?

I opened the second can and muttered, *Fuck.* The dog went into hysterics as I approached, and I saw that he had an empty stainless steel bowl. I poured the beans onto the ground in as neat a pile as I could, and he lapped them up as if they were filet mignon, as if they were anything designed for his body. I laid the cans out of reach and quickly grabbed his bowl. The creek looked like it always had, but smaller. I dipped a bowlful of the clear water and watched a crawdad zip underneath a rock. I took the water up to the dog, and he rushed for it, lapping furiously until it was gone.

Okay, okay. I picked up the bowl, avoiding his paws, and refilled it while he returned to the spot where the beans had been, licking hopefully at the dirt. Standing by the creek for a moment, I wondered at the countless hours I had spent there. I had seen copperheads and a rabid fox; I had played in the barn where rats prowled the abandoned corncrib; I had crossed the swollen creek once during a flood, walking over a rotten log that hung suspended above it, holding on to the rusty barbed wire that formed the rest of the strange fence. Would anyone ever again love that place as I did?

I carried the bowl to the dog and set it before him. I turned away as quickly as I could, grabbed the cans, and took them to the garbage pile by the creek, a mound of trash bags and refuse that only the desperate seem to be able to produce. As I drove away, I realized that I could have freed the dog, and wondered what it was that kept me from doing so.

CHAPTER 32

Silver Dollars

Around that time, Dad finally lost the house I grew up in. He couldn't hustle for the payments while he was in jail, so the bank finally got what it had hovered over for twenty years. As he promised all my life, though, the house burned down before anybody else could live in it. Granny and I had gone in there not long beforehand. Someone had moved nearly everything somewhere else, most of it never to be seen again. I found a paper grocery bag full of weed under his bed and shoved it back under when Granny noticed it. We both pretended we didn't know what it was.

I got a few things that day—my dad's knife and coin collections and an antique railroad lantern—that were the fixtures of my childhood. I would often ask him to show me his knives and coins, fascinated by the history they represented. The railroad lantern came from my great-grandfather who sold moonshine in Chicago during the Depression. He was a drunk and a murderer and mostly in prison, but there are fascinating stories about him, some of which make my father look like an upright citizen. That lantern was my night-light when I was very young; it hung in my bedroom and cast a strange blue-green light from two of the glass lenses, a harsh red light from the other two. It was never a comforting, soft kind of night-light, but it was the light I had, so I treasured it. Why didn't the person who took everything else also take those things? They were set carefully in what used to be my father's closet, not forgotten or overlooked. Maybe someone knew I would want them, somehow knew I would come.

My father was my first storyteller, and though his stories never reflected what might be called "traditional values," they still comforted me, and I could sense the magic with which they were infused, like all other icons of childhood. There wasn't a lot that I could thank my father for, but there was a tenderness in his desire to tell me stories, which were so much more like the original *Grimm's Fairy Tales* than the *happily ever afters* I could have heard. I didn't grow up believing he loved me, but he did think I was worth giving these histories to, and I cherished them.

He kept boxes full of newspapers and newspaper clippings, preserving the news of an arrest, a death, or a scandal. He showed me one clipping of my great-grandfather, for whom my papaw and brother were named, standing in a prison next to Al Capone. The men stood in their boxer shorts, arms slung over one another's shoulders. My great-grandfather, Dad said, became friends with Capone while running moonshine to Chicago. Because the prison warden was one of his customers, my great-grandfather spent most of his time doing as he pleased, enjoying the fruits of corruption while paying the price for his lawlessness.

There was the story about the sheriff of Carter County, who tried to find my great-grandfather and his moonshine still one too many times and ended up shot and dead at the end of my great-grandfather's gun. My dad laughed at the end of all his stories, including the one about my great-grandmother's father, whom my great-grandfather shot during dinner, after they argued over who made better moonshine. I didn't find that one as amusing, and I wondered afterward how my great-grandmother must have felt, having her father killed by her husband while sitting down for a dinner she must have cooked.

She favored her youngest son, my father said, who was conceived while her husband was in prison. In the end, he got everything she left to her children, and my father said that youngest son swindled Papaw Conn out of his inheritance. My papaw would hardly talk about it when I asked, but expressed his conviction that the money and the property were not worth bearing a grudge.

Papaw was particularly good at not holding a grudge. He had worked for a dairy for about twenty-five years and was ready to retire when they suddenly let him go. He used to take us in his milk truck sometimes, riding around in those dark, early mornings, and we would get a little chocolate milk if we could stay awake long enough to drink it. I asked why they had let him go, and someone told me it was so they didn't have to pay his retirement. An enormous clock from the dairy hung above the bureau in Granny and Papaw's dining room, and Granny took it down after that happened. I asked Papaw about it one day, expecting his righteous indignation—like my father so often expressed. Instead, he looked away. *There's no use in dwelling on these things.* But I grieved for how unfair they had been to him. Instead of resenting it himself, Papaw just worked at the county roads department for another fifteen or twenty years, tirelessly.

My great-grandfather died the year before I was born. I wonder whether he ever imagined that he would become the hero of my father's stories and the legend of my childhood. I wonder whether he realized at some point that my father idolized him, and whether he ever recognized the influence he had in shaping my father. I wonder whether he loved his wife, or regretted his absence from his children's lives, or regretted killing his father-in-law, or the sheriff, or whether he thought much at all about such things.

My great-grandmother outlived him by many years, and we would go visit her in Bath County. She lived in a light-yellow house that some of her sons built for her and that sat immediately next to the house where she had raised those sons—the two doorways were about twenty feet apart from one another, facing each other diagonally. She had short white-gray hair and was very large in my memory, always sitting in her chair and watching the small television that sat high on a shelf in the living room. The living room was filled with stacks of newspapers and other strange collections. She had dolls everywhere, and several of the largest ones stood as sentries next to her chair, their lifeless eyes staring always, their hair perfectly colored and cut, their clothes nicer than anything I owned.

Her house had a funny smell, and it wasn't until I bought mothballs some twenty years later that I recognized the familiar scent. It filled each room—the cramped and cluttered kitchen, the spare bedroom that housed most of the dolls, the strange bathroom with a soft toilet seat. When we visited, I would go directly to hug Great-Grandma in her chair and stand around for a few minutes, waiting to see whether she would give me a two-dollar bill, a half dollar, or, rarest of all, a silver dollar from her collection.

Outside her house was an exotic array of plants that grew around the perimeter. There were grapevines in a corner, touch-me-nots that I touched over and over, watching the little seed pods explode, and lush islands of color scattered around. My brother and I explored the vines and the gardens through overgrown grass, stepping away from snakes whenever we found them curling and sliding through their paradise.

My favorite place at her home—and perhaps anywhere else—was the abandoned house of her childbearing years. It sat two stories high and was a slate-gray color, weathered and worn. It smelled even older than the house she lived in, and must have been home to many creatures by that time, but it was filled to the brim with the objects from her past and from her children's pasts. My father and grandparents would sit inside the yellow house with my great-grandmother, visiting for hours, while I moved through the old house, searching for treasures.

At the end of each visit, I would go to Great-Grandma with whatever I had found, asking her whether I could keep the items. She let me take the 1905 *Sears, Roebuck & Co. Catalogue* that was about three inches thick. I was seven or eight years old when I acquired the catalog, and I would sit on my bed, turning through the pages carefully so as to preserve them. The catalog reminded me of the books I read by John D. Fitzgerald, the Great Brain series. I longed for things like Radio Flyer wagons and Tinkertoys, though I did not know what they were. I thought about how it would feel to get an apple and an orange in my Christmas stocking, and somehow, that seemed much better than the toys I received. I imagined simple holidays with a rare Christmas bird—perhaps even a goose, like in the stories—and savoring treats like roasted nuts. I didn't know why, but I was fully enamored with my conception of the past and longed to experience it. Maybe, like so many people, I thought all the terrible things I had seen and felt and heard only existed due to inventions—in our case, pharmaceuticals. Maybe guns, every now and then. As if no one was beating or raping women before that. As if every adult had behaved before gunpowder came along.

The floorboards in the old house were rotten or broken in places, and I would climb the stairs with some fear, knowing I had been warned not to go up them. Upstairs would have been a room for a child—or two or three children—and it seemed that the objects there had been abandoned for even longer. I picked up fewer things, afraid I would find a snake or worse in the hot darkness. I felt the presence of the children who had grown up there, though—their games, their arguments, their hiding beneath hand-sewn quilts. I felt like they were still there, all around me—not the adult siblings of my papaw, and not quite ghosts—and it was vital to leave their things undisturbed, so they could return someday and find everything where it belonged, waiting for them in an endless childhood.

I felt comfortable throughout the downstairs and ventured around as even my father hesitated to do. The rooms held dishes, newspapers, clothes, and furniture; it seemed as if Great-Grandma had simply stepped out of the house and walked into her new one at some point, leaving everything behind and accumulating a new houseful of things. I was an explorer, and I sometimes brought her things that she had long forgotten but was glad to have moved into her new house. Once, I found a collection of coins, all organized in books with labels. I immediately recognized their value, as my father's coin collections had instilled in me a great awe for the uncommon currency.

She kept those coins, and I wonder now what happened to them when she died. Perhaps another relative asked for them before that point, and she gave them away. Maybe they went to another great-grandchild, someone not in my papaw's line. Who went through her things, parceling out the riches I had longed for in childhood?

Another time, I thought to look behind the door that always stood open, the one between the dining room and the living room. Behind it, I found a vodka bottle that was about one-third full. When my dad came into the house to look for me and perhaps find something for himself, I showed him the bottle where it sat, hoping he would be impressed by my grown-up discovery.

Look, Dad, I found a bottle of vodka. He picked up the bottle and unscrewed the lid, then smelled the alcohol inside.

That's not vodka, he said. *That's your great-grandfather's moonshine. Don't tell Great-Grandma you found this.* He tucked the bottle inside the jacket he was wearing and managed to save it for several years, until one day shortly after my mother left him for the last time. I was spending the night at his house, and he was particularly happy and cheerful. He bought us a pizza and gave me and Junior permission to watch movies, then disappeared for hours. Later, he told me he had gone into the woods with that bottle and drank every bit of the twenty-year-old moonshine inside it, roving around the forest in the dark, missing my mother terribly.

I must have inherited some of my sentimentality from my father. Every chance I got, I took our family pictures from his house, telling myself that they would someday be lost and squandered like everything else. One of the pictures I rescued/stole is a reprint dated 1953, of a black-and-white picture that was probably taken in the early 1900s. My father once told me that the youngest boy in the picture, who is almost lying down in someone's lap, is my great-grandfather. On the back of the picture are names I do not recognize, though, so I wonder now whether he was right. Either way, they are my ancestors—men with handlebar mustaches and sharp jawbones; women with their hair pulled back into buns, even the young ones looking haunted; the younger people almost indistinguishable from their parents; nobody smiling— the image of all I've inherited.

I've never known anything about my great-grandfather's father, about his story and how he became an outlaw. He was the only real hero I ever heard of as a child, and his legacy still haunts us. I wonder whether any of our men were ever good, whether any of them ever loved their children or touched their wives with tenderness. I wonder whether the women were gentle, or whether their hollow expressions accurately reflect their despair, their loneliness, their sense of futility. I wonder what they passed down to me—my blurred vision, my thin frame, my long fingers, my penchant for superstition, my longing for green hills and cliff faces?

I want their stories, so I can write my backstory. I want their names, their loves, their longings, their addictions, and their brutalities. I want them to whisper to me their heroic moments, their indiscretions, their final regrets, and the recognitions that filled their eyes in the moments before death.

But the storyteller was always my father, the original unreliable narrator. Drunk, drugged, lost.

described—one with sharp corners that the jeweler, God himself, must carve away. I saw myself as the gold that must be purified by burning away the impurities. For once, I thought of myself as a child of God. I saw all my past suffering and all that I carried, all I had seen and felt and heard in the long night of my childhood.

~

My daughter was born right after my son turned seven. Rose is a leap-year baby, and every bit deserves the rarity of that day. Her birth took not quite as long as Orion's, but it was unexpectedly lengthy, given that I was in a hospital and hooked up to an IV full of Pitocin for a little more than twenty-four hours. She had stopped growing at around eight months, and my midwife told me that home birth was no longer an option. I was low in iron, too, so at a greater risk of hemorrhaging—and I had already hemorrhaged enough the first time for her to be concerned. Not being able to have my daughter at home seemed to fit—nothing was making sense at that time. I knew I wasn't bringing her into a good situation, but I couldn't sort out what fell on me and what fell elsewhere.

We had started the Pitocin drip at five o'clock the night before. It slowly took hold, and I knew from reading journals for doctors at college, and then at work, that Pitocin was contraindicated for pregnant women. Still, I understood what it was meant to do—set my uterus in motion, start the contractions, *get the baby out.* At noon the next day, I started worrying about what it meant to be here, in a hospital. I had an ultrasound before they admitted me—they were concerned, they said, and if I was their patient, they would give me twenty-four hours before inducing labor. But I could have forty-eight, and then I needed to come back if I wanted to have the baby there. I had thought I still had a couple of weeks left to get everything together but made sure to return within their time frame. I realized I wasn't progressing well, though— I asked the nurse to check me at noon, and she said I was about two centimeters dilated. I asked her to break my water. *Are you sure?* she asked. *Yes, I'm sure.* I knew I had been lucky not to have a C-section with Orion. I knew I couldn't labor with this baby for too long.

The nurse broke my water, and the serious contractions set in—the *real* contractions. These came on top of the medication-induced contractions from the Pitocin, so there was no relief, no break between them, and my body had not had time to prepare itself for this level of labor. Suddenly, my mother and stepfather arrived. Thankfully, I still had my hospital gown on. I greeted them and tolerated them for a bit, but then had someone ask them to leave—or maybe I did it myself. I couldn't really say.

My labor to bring Orion into the world had been filled with moans, but I was quiet through so much of it. Not this time. The nurse walked in at one point, and instead of my earlier smiling *yes, please,* and *yes, thank you,* she found me naked on my hands and knees, howling every obscenity I could think of. The nurse said, *Oh, how things change,* and even in my anguish, I could appreciate the wry truth of her remark.

I knew that the odds of pushing my baby out naturally would dwindle soon, and every muscle in my body was tensed with these contractions—there was no way to breathe through them. I wanted to climb outside myself, escape this unnatural pain, but instead I was crawling on a tiny hospital bed with an IV still in my arm, hooked to a pole. I asked the nurse what my options were for pain relief, and she offered an epidural or Stadol. I remember her quickly telling me that they could give Stadol only when there was at least another hour of labor left, because they didn't want the baby born with the drug in its bloodstream. She checked me—three centimeters—and said that I could have it if I wanted it, that it would make me feel drunk and give me about an hour of relief, but that I would still have contractions. My massage-therapist friend was there and reminded me, *You wanted a natural birth,* and I didn't bother telling her that at that point, I was just waiting for my midwife to arrive before asking for an epidural— I wanted to give my midwife a chance to give me any reason not to.

Though she couldn't assist in the birth, she had agreed to come to the hospital to support me.

They added the opioid to my IV, and almost immediately, I was able to sleep. I still had contractions that shook me from my slumber, but I moaned through those, and the anguish was gone. I dreamt during a lull between them: *I am walking through a forest, next to a tall man with brown, curly hair. There is a lovely cabin nearby. I tell him,* I can't do this, *and he says,* Yes you can, it's almost over.

I woke up and felt like I needed to shit, so I asked someone in the room—who, I don't remember—to help me to the toilet chair that sat beside my bed. The same nurse as before walked in at that moment and urged me back onto the bed while I insisted I had to shit, and she gently told me, *That's fine, just do it on the bed, I'll put something under you, just please get back on the bed.* The last thing I wanted was to lie in a bed and relieve myself when I was fully capable of sitting up, but I eased back onto it. I still had sense enough to cooperate.

It turns out the nurse knew her stuff, because in fact I didn't need to shit—it was time for the baby to come out.

I lay there pushing with each contraction, and someone told me, *Don't do that, wait until the doctor comes,* and I thought, *Fuck that,* and kept pushing. Soon, perched between my legs, there was a grouchy doctor I had never met—I found out later she was sick. Earlier, they had asked whether I would allow students to observe, and I said yes, but I didn't realize that when it was time for the baby to come, they would turn on spotlights aimed at my naked body and desperate face. I didn't expect the students to watch without expression, as if they had no idea that when we give birth, we flirt with the edge of death. I searched the room frantically for eyes to lock onto and finally found my midwife, present and full of care and love. I focused only on her eyes, and about forty-five minutes after I started pushing, my daughter was born.

She was so small, no one had to cut me, and she slipped out with so much less effort than Orion had taken. I was still feeling drunk from the Stadol when she was born, and she came so soon after the drug was injected into my IV, she was probably born with it in her bloodstream. What can I do but mourn that?

It was not the birth I wanted to have, nor what I wanted for my girl. I knew she was a girl when I felt the first difference in my body: my mouth watered too much one day. My herbalist said, *That's not a symptom,* but I knew. The pregnancy test came back negative that day, a Friday, so I drank as much beer as I could that night and sat alone, crying, knowing I would have a girl. I took another pregnancy test on Monday, and it was positive.

But looking at my daughter's face over the next days and weeks and years, I understood why people compare cheeks to apples. She doubled her birth weight in the first six weeks. I carried her everywhere, just as I had my son. I fell in love with her as I had never loved any other girl.

I didn't even love myself at that point. I still struggled with the guilt and shame of what I had experienced, what I had done in response. And there was so much I had been told about women—how catty we are, how manipulative—that I didn't acknowledge but believed to be true. I still carried the idea that everything that had happened to me was somehow my fault.

Rose was always sweet, but she was also fiery and wild. I found that I had to discipline her differently. I quickly saw that the tone of voice I sometimes used with Orion—to convey *I mean it* and *you'd better do what I say*—would crush her, and I knew what happened when a girl was crushed. I learned how difficult it is to take care of a wild and free girl, not to squelch her into obedience and silent resentment or, worse yet, self-loathing. I found that when I cared for her, though, it changed how I felt inside. I started thinking it was okay that my parents didn't love and adore me—I could love and adore *this girl,* and that was enough for the both of us. And when it was time to fight for her, I fought with everything I had and then some. I prayed to anyone who would listen to show me how to protect her and help her, and I think they answered.

CHAPTER 38

Defiance

Still, I stumbled as a parent. I used to spank Orion—my mother saw him act out once, when he was still in diapers. *You'd better start spanking him, or one day, he'll be bigger than you, and you won't be able to control him.* I knew what she meant, but I didn't want to believe it. I read everything I could find about raising children and discipline, knowing I needed a new model, an example that had never been shown to me and that I would have to patchwork together myself. I already loved him with such ferocity and knew our bond defied description. I was sure I could find the right care to give so he would be neither spoiled nor broken.

I flicked him on the hand when he was little, teaching him that my simple, calm *no* was something to listen to. He was exceedingly easy to teach, and I taught him *please* and *thank you*, and when he was difficult, I was the benevolent dictator of our household—authoritative, without being authoritarian. Loving, without being permissive.

I spanked him for a while. Once, he threw a handful of gravel at our neighbor's back as the neighbor and I chatted beneath a weeping willow tree. I told Orion to pick up a switch and go sit on the porch and wait for me. When I was pregnant with his sister, I found myself spanking him with anger that I knew had nothing to do with him. He started telling me the spankings didn't hurt, no matter how hard I smacked his bottom. That was when I decided I had to find a new way. I apologized to him when he was about sixteen, and I couldn't help but cry. *I'm sorry I ever spanked you, I didn't know what else to do. I did my best, but it wasn't good enough.* In his usual kind way, he said, *Oh, it's okay, Mom. I'm glad you spanked me. I needed it.* I told him no, he didn't, and no one did.

On the cusp of adulthood, he asked me what I really would have done if he had disobeyed me as a teenager—he didn't ask out of defiance, but with curiosity. And I told him that the most important thing we had was the love and trust between us, and though I could threaten him with any number of things, the loss of trust is worse than anything else. He agreed.

By the time my daughter was one and I was a single mother again, I moved my small family into an old, dark rental house that I could hardly afford. I had graduated from my master's program seven months pregnant. When Rose was six months old, I started teaching at the same university, as an adjunct professor, but didn't realize I would only have two classes in the spring, not three. I moved us into that dark house thinking I would have a third more income than I ended up with. But I took on extra work, and after getting the kids in bed, I would start again on whatever project I had scrounged for, working until midnight or one in the morning.

The house looked like I felt. An old fireplace dropped soot and god knows what else when the wind blew outside. A huge roach crawled into the living room once, prompting Orion to name our home *the Roach House* and prompting me to pay for an exterminator for the first time in my life. The light switches were not switches at all, but old-fashioned buttons you pressed to turn the lights on or off. There were no overhead lights in the living room or kitchen, ensuring that shadows flew through the spaces I most enjoyed—those rooms where my children and I communed together.

The house was heated by an old, stand-alone heater that glowed red, a few thin metal rods sitting in front of the elements, and there was nothing to protect a child's fingers or face from touching any of it. Rose was learning to walk and almost fell into it one day—how she never touched it I do not know, other than my constant watching and carrying her and maybe a guardian angel or two. Orion caught her from falling into it one day and then wrote a few paragraphs about it at school, and I worried that someone would see it as a reason to take my baby from me.

That's what happens when your house is unsafe and you can't afford anything better—you're called unfit, and nobody asks how you got to this place. That's why someone who used to be poor will, if they have it, lend money to a poor person to pay a bill—they know the stakes. That's why I eventually paid a friend's utility bill with a credit card. A broken water pipe in the yard had put the power bill too far out of reach for her. If just one of her kids had mentioned the lights being off, she could have lost all her children.

Spring came quickly, though, and my bedroom filled with roly-poly bugs that surrounded the head of my mattress and died there. The washer and dryer were in the basement, which was perpetually flooded. I had to put my daughter in a baby backpack and carry the laundry out the kitchen door, down the wooden stairs to the yard, and down the concrete steps into the basement, then make my way across some old wooden pallets someone had placed on the floor to keep feet dry on laundry day. A single, bare lightbulb illuminated the basement, and rickety shelves lined the sides, filled with dust and other forgotten things.

I worried over the baby touching the paint that flaked around the low windowsills—it probably had lead in it. Someone had come to fix a short in the wiring one day and looked at the ceiling in the third bedroom. *Don't put the baby in here—that ceiling probably has asbestos, and you don't want the dust falling onto her.* I put my computer in there instead, and when someone gave me a crib, I put the crib in my bedroom. I wouldn't realize until she started sleeping through the night that I hadn't slept through an entire night for three years, but you don't always see those things while they are happening.

Orion played soccer—I wanted him to do something active, and I knew that running would be good for him. It might even build his self-esteem, provide some measure of protection. I went to his practices and games, which were often in Richmond—around fifteen miles away—so that meant sometimes I drove up there twice a day. It didn't really matter where they were. Everywhere I went, I felt like I was coming apart. Every *thing* felt hard—driving to a soccer game, comforting the children, cooking meals, preparing for my classes. Opening the mail was torture—if I didn't recognize the sender but it looked like it could be a bill, I left it unopened, knowing I had no way to pay anything but the basics. I didn't know who else might be sending me bills, but I believed it was a very real possibility that there was always something else I owed, some other debt I couldn't manage. I just opened what it took to keep the lights and water on and a roof overhead—if you don't have those things, someone very likely *will* take your baby away from you.

Nearly all the time, I felt like my insides were on fire, and there was no relief.

I had moved to Lexington toward the end of my pregnancy, and when I came back to Berea with Rose and Orion, I thought my old friends would want to spend time together, hang out like we had always done. But many of them were getting married and settling into careers and not yet having babies. I tried to be friends with some of the other women living nearby—a couple of them were also single mothers—but it seemed as if they never really liked me. The support I had felt when Orion was a toddler disappeared, and the group of friends who welcomed him to every event and doted on him no longer wanted to see me so much. The people I had come to regard as my chosen family, with my usual stubborn and fierce devotion, were all but gone.

I walked around those days with my mind occupied by anger and fear, relieved only in the moments when my children reminded me of their sweetness. One day, as my mind ground away, asking *Why are things like this,* I had a new thought: every terrible relationship I ever had, had one thing in common—me. *Well shit,* I thought. I considered my last ex-boyfriend and how he didn't even try to convince me he loved me. It was I who did that. I thought of all the boyfriends and the couple of husbands over the previous fifteen years and suddenly understood that while they didn't look like my father, or talk like him, or try to scam the system like he did, they all *felt* like him, to me. I knew then that I couldn't trust myself to love a man, that something inside me drew me to the kind of men who wouldn't really love me but whose love I would desperately try to earn.

After that unpleasant realization, I wrestled for a while with the guilt I felt for making the same bad choice over and over—always in new packaging, because I tried so damn hard, but I couldn't escape the jailer within who kept me locked in a cage. I realized that no matter what else I accomplished, my cage wasn't so different from my mother's.

But I kept struggling with those feelings. I kept asking myself *why* and *how,* and as frustrated as I was with myself, I knew there had to be something better. I had seen beauty and felt joy. I was determined to claim some of it—if not for me, then for my children, who surely couldn't go through this, too. One day, a new thought hit me: although my life had not been my *fault,* I had reached the point at which I wanted my life to be wholly mine and not a constant reaction to the trauma I had known. There was no knight in shining armor coming to rescue me, to protect me from my father or any other man. I knew I had every right to be angry about the things I had experienced, but I also had to find a way to undo the damage that had been done, so I would never again choose the things that were bad for me. So I could stop being haunted by nightmares that belonged in the past.

I went to a financial counselor soon after that, knowing I had to figure out how to manage money if I was going to survive. It was a free service in Richmond, offered by the same people who ran the free bus. The financial counselor seemed much too normal to understand me, but she set me up with a spreadsheet, and we walked through all my bills, the due dates, and my spending. It turned out that I had no idea what I was spending—it usually seemed like there was no money at all, and then enough, and then none again. I wasn't buying anything extravagant, but it was the first time I thought about knowing *when* to spend. At the end of our session, the financial counselor suggested I find a one-bedroom apartment or someone's basement to live in. *Give the bedroom to your son. You can sleep in the living room with your daughter.*

I politely thanked her and thought, *No way in hell.* I decided to buy a house instead—I was paying $375 in rent, so I was certain I could find a mortgage I could afford. The mortgage officer at the first bank I went to told me about a government-subsidized mortgage program—she said she would be doing me a disservice not to tell me. Looking back, I know she was under some pressure to get me into a mortgage with the bank but chose to send me to that program instead. And I know that it was a dream to imagine I could buy a house at that point. There was no reason for me to succeed, on paper.

But around five months later, I bought a house that was nicer than anywhere I had ever lived, and though we hardly had any furniture, it felt like a palace. Just before we moved in, I started a new job—one day an old friend from my first job forwarded me an email and wondered whether I was interested. She was being asked to apply but had moved to another state. I applied and suddenly was making a middle-class income for the first time in my life. I lost the little bit of food stamps I was getting, and the kids' medical cards, and asked myself, *Can I really do this?*

There were so many things I knew were still broken inside me. *Orion filled the Jacuzzi tub with bubbles, and I yelled at him. I'm afraid I*

won't be able to keep the house clean, and it will turn into a nasty place with
soap scum and dirty bathrooms, and I will fail my children, and they will
feel like white trash, just like I did. I cussed at my two-year-old daughter
today. I hate myself for it. I'm just exhausted by how much she needs, how
much she demands. At the end of the day, I feel like a cigarette is the only
comfort I have.

I had romanticized self-awareness when I read *Be Here Now* by Ram
Dass and smoked lots of weed and took all the LSD I could get my
hands on. Back then, the idea of being self-aware was so romantic, so
wrapped up in the feelings of magic and excitement I experienced with
all those altered states. The goodness I felt and saw during my chemical
escapes made me think I was really getting somewhere in my growth as
a person. And maybe I did—I'm not sure what my outlook for survival
would have been if I had not found some relief from my inner hell,
some temporary respite. But by the time I grew up—*really grew up*—I
realized I had just barely survived childhood and young adulthood. The
only reason I survived motherhood was because I was so stubborn, I
poured every bit of myself into it, unwilling to fail my children in the
ways I had been failed.

But looking at myself as a thirty-year-old, knowing how much I
had squandered, how little I had accomplished, was its own fresh hell.
I gained a lot of empathy for the people around me who didn't seem at
all interested in thinking about their lives and the choices they made.
Taking an honest look at myself and what I had become was the most
painful thing I ever experienced. I couldn't wait for my parents to love
me, or for my granny to come back from her deathbed and remind me
that I was lovable. The world I wanted would not pull me into it, not
with me so accustomed to the hell I had come to think of as normal. I
wanted something beautiful and magical to swoop down and save me,
to show that it recognized how *special* I was, how *worth saving*. I was not
excited or inspired when I discovered I had to be the one to save me.

After years of conscious work, I eventually realized my life had become different, that *I* had become different. Not perfect, of course. I still get upset when the kids leave things in our front yard, but I don't tell them it makes us look trashy and I'm afraid the neighbors will see me for what I really am. I don't let them eat on the couch, but I don't yell as I used to when I felt like every mess, every broken thing, every dollar wasted, was going to drag me back into childhood, where I would forever be helpless and afraid and poor and dirty. I tell them I love them and why I love them, and I listen to their made-up songs or the music they discovered and want me to hear. I go to their plays and concerts and games—I still don't feel at ease, but I don't always feel like something is clawing at my insides now, as I sit among so many people who might be enemies. To my surprise, I mean it when I smile and applaud.

In graduate school, I had written a story about my father and how he had sent me to my granny's house to call her a whore. I didn't think it would ever amount to much—there are so many people who want to write, and so many who have better stories or better luck. But it felt important, for some reason. The story had come as a surprise to me as I was earning a master's degree in English—I wanted to write poetry, but I didn't think I could fit all my words into a poem. After grad school, I kept working on my story and revising it, adding what needed to be said, finding God in the details along the way. I wrote it and rewrote it over the years to come, each time seeing more clearly that I had become the storyteller, that it was *my story* and that *I had to tell it*. With each revision, I understood that although many people had quieted me, even whipped me into silence, I still had words they could not take away from me. And while my words were in part the defiance and anger I had always been too afraid to voice, they were more than that, too.

As I wrote, I discovered words for what I felt in the forest, the sweet stillness that endures from countless hours in that holy place. I discovered that the words of the King James Bible that were sometimes used to frighten me still contain their own mystery and magic, and I can see what might have comforted and ignited my granny's inimitable heart. I beheld my granny and the poetry of her life, a life lived in quiet strength and selflessness—the life of a mountain woman whose power suffuses the kingdom within. I saw that every word I had to speak was the honoring of my history, the history of everyone I had ever loved, and the landscapes in which I had sought refuge, time and time again: first, the streams and forests of Kentucky, and then, every book I could get my hands on. And even when my story isn't pretty, or I wasn't, the living itself is. After all is said and done, I can't help but see the beauty we belong to.

I wrote from the time I was in middle school, even though my classmates ridiculed my imitation of the *Odyssey*. As an adult, I wrote and sent my work to professors and literary agents, asking over and over for their approval and affirmation, to be let into their world. Perhaps I just wanted someone to listen to all the words I had finally found the courage to bring to the light of day.

As I wrote, I understood myself as a character, as a person in a grand and vast story that endures far beyond me. I wrote and saw myself in a context beyond my family or place or time. I wrote my story again and again, until I came to love the little girl who survived it. I wrote to free her, to vindicate her, to give her justice. Writing was my best rebellion, my silent outcry, my ravaged testament to how much a person can love a world that does not suffer her. Writing my story became my duty, too—a duty to the grown and still-young children who stumble in the darkness, knowing there is something *good* but not believing that goodness is for them.

I wrote myself and found myself. I wrote nearly all the words I had swallowed for decades, passion transmuted.

CHAPTER 39

Out of Line

I grew up thinking there was something wrong with my family and especially with me. But I realize that, for the most part, the adults around me then felt like I feel now—childhood slips away without warning, and we find ourselves pretending to be grown, pretending we want to be part of this world with jobs and bills, but numbing ourselves with television or another glass of wine. We have our own children and see ourselves in them—we relive our teen years (*the best years of your life*), or we play out our unresolved conflicts while our own parents become grandparents and suddenly aren't so awful anymore.

For so many years—has it been decades?—I've felt misunderstood, and every time I thought someone truly saw me for who I was, for the *good girl* still inside me, I lapped up their attention like my father's dog devoured beans and dirt alike. I tried so hard to avoid dating or becoming my father. I didn't date anyone who did hard drugs (at least after my first marriage ended). I congratulated myself that no man ever hit me (*the bruises on my neck were more than ten years ago now, and that was only once*), though I never stopped being afraid of it, never stopped wondering whether it would happen if I dared say too much, if I let my face betray my true feelings. In the end, though, there was never a good set of rules to follow to protect myself.

My first husband and a later boyfriend were talented musicians, so I vowed not to date any guitar players. After my second husband and the guitarist boyfriend, I swore I wouldn't date a man who was a Cancer. After that, it was no guys who worked at bars. Then, no Capricorns. But the kind of men who will hurt women—especially women who have been deprived of love—are everywhere, and they look like everyone. In some ways, it's disappointing to know that bad men aren't just the ones who look like my father—raised in a holler, shooting guns, and making moonshine or dropping out of high school. For the longest time, that made it much more difficult to figure out who was *safe*.

It's more complicated, too, knowing that people who call them-selves *feminists* and *social-rights activists* might turn their backs on the ones who need them: Women who are desperate to be loved, so they sleep with too many men. Men who are snorting pills or shooting up heroin or some mysterious opiate concoction, because being alive hurts so much, it is worth it to risk overdose and disease and losing everything you have, everyone who loves you, to escape the hell inside you, even for just a few hours. Poor people without the wherewithal to stop smoking or stop burning their trash by the creek, who would rather die in a coal mine than get free health care. How do you love people who look like this, who live like this? People like me, like my father, my brother, and my mother.

My brother—he is the one who was with me through it all, who saw and heard and felt everything alongside me. Did he not *feel like me*, too? What does he feel now, if he lets himself feel anything? I don't know, because we were never close again after he left prison and the halfway house. I wonder why he is somewhere else, not beside me as I write a new life for myself, not rejoicing in the freedom we gain from leaving behind the sins of our father.

I was so envious of him growing up. Everything seemed better for him, and I assumed it was because he was more lovable than I was. He had a cherubic face, and even though his baby teeth rotted at the same time mine did, he still had a beautiful, easy smile. It seemed like everyone wanted to take care of him—except our father, of course—and even I was willing to take a whipping to protect him from the pain our father subjected us to. Later, I was willing to wear the shoes I knew my classmates might mock, so I could protect my brother from the torment our peers subjected us to.

One time when we had both reached adulthood, I asked Junior what he remembered of our growing up. He had blocked some things out, he said—like our mother had—but he told me about the time he went to a cave with our father and how our father climbed onto a higher ledge while they were inside the cave, and he stepped on Junior's fingers. Junior yelped in pain, and Dad looked down at him with an empty expression, said nothing, and continued climbing or walking to wherever he was going. When Junior told me this story, he was still in wonder that a parent could hurt their child, even accidentally, and not feel remorse. Like me, Junior found it almost impossible to believe our father could really do the things he did, feel the way he felt toward us, over the years.

Unlike me, Junior had to *be a man* about these things. He learned on the school bus that the quickest way to escape abuse from other boys was to show them he could hurt them back. I'm not sure I ever really escaped, until my tormentors found more interesting things to do. I turned inward to seek a safe haven, and immersed myself in all the beauty I could find in books and nature and psychedelia. And in Granny, of course, and in what I could claim of church. I turned my anger inward, too, since I wasn't allowed to express it.

Junior didn't love reading like I did, and didn't do particularly well in school. He didn't seem to care about it, while I relished every bit of praise my teachers gave me. My love of reading and ability to perform well academically reinforced the positive feedback I received from adults at school. I came to want and need affirmation that I was smart, while Junior was rewarded for achieving less than I did. My achievements, though, gave me an easy route to a college degree without debt, and I had to leave my hometown in order to get it—the most vital step in escaping one's childhood hell, it seems.

And while I was subject to the whims and tempers of men who did not deserve the power they held, I sometimes wonder whether it would have been better or worse to be a boy, expected to *act like a man* in places where men are unpredictable, dangerous, forbidden to feel pain or fear. As a girl, I was yoked with the desire to please. As a boy, my brother was saddled with the command to dominate. For either of us, stepping out of line was met with brutality.

CHAPTER 40

In the Holler

When I hear people musing over the contradictions and sorrows that plague this region—Appalachia, with its unparalleled beauty—I want to remind them that it's always easy to see someone else's flaws, especially when the *other* doesn't have pretty clothes to hide behind. Whether it's addiction or racism or cycles of abuse, I want to tell them how *these are not just Appalachian problems*. We didn't invent fentanyl or Lortabs or OxyContin. It's not hillbillies who are getting rich off opioids—but just like this land's lumber and coal that fueled the economy for the rest of the country, someone is getting rich off our desperate and dying people, our last expendable resource.

And I cannot say what kind of hate is in anyone else's heart, but I know it is easy to turn a man to hate if you can convince him that the outsider is the cause of his problems. In a place like this, outsiders have taken away everything the people had—the very minerals from under their feet—time and time again. But just like the coal bosses brought in *scabs* to break the strikes, it is always someone at a higher pay grade who convinces workers to blame immigrants, people of color, and other poor people when the owner won't pay fair wages. In a land like this, people have *actually* been fighting for their lives—not figuratively or metaphorically—since they first decided to take their chances in this unforgiving Eden.

I've discovered that people of all classes fail their children—sometimes they abuse them, sometimes they neglect them. But if you can afford a good lawyer, you might not go to prison, and your kids probably won't be going to foster care. Sometimes judges even decide, *He's not well suited for prison,* so victims watch while abusers walk free because they themselves are too fragile to suffer the consequences of their choices.

These are rotten fruits we are reaping from conquerors who planted their flags in other people's homes and holy lands long ago.

When people ask, *What's wrong with eastern Kentucky?* all I know is *it's the same thing that's wrong with all of us.* My father was not the first man to hurt his children or his wife or his parents. My brother won't be the last to watch his children go into foster care while he—full of love as he is—chooses pills and prison. If we trace these heartbreaks back to some comprehensible root, we would probably find that somewhere along the way, some vital trust was broken.

It is bittersweet, finally knowing that I can't save my father—whether he's too far gone or had nothing to save in the first place, I may never know. I can't save any other men, either, no matter how lovable I see they are, and how I know they would be okay if they could feel the depth of my love for just one moment. I can't save my siblings, can't undo the things that broke inside them while our father filled them with fear and loss and pain. While their mothers watched.

I can't change anything that happened to my mother or take away any fear or loss that has haunted her. I can't give her vibrant youth back to her, nor the beauty in her high cheekbones and smooth skin. Without knowing it, I spent much of my young life longing for a new story with her, one in which we are close and she helps me understand motherhood, or how to be a strong woman. Maybe we get lunch together, just the two of us, or slip away for the weekend.

But perhaps like me, my mother wasn't ready to have a girl in her early twenties. And maybe my father loves me as much as he could ever love anyone, and loves himself least of all. There's nothing to be done with what happened. All I can do is write the future.

People tell me that my children look just like me. They were both born with almond eyes; my daughter's were deep and dreamlike for weeks, as if she were sent from another world that held part of her until they knew I was ready. My children's faces are symmetrical, their teeth straight. A babbling brook of confusion obscured my thoughts for most of their childhoods, but I still read books to them and sang songs and listened when they were sad or angry. I taught myself to apologize when I had wronged them. I taught them to apologize when they had wronged someone else. I know there is nothing I can tell them for certain, other than how I love them.

I tell my daughter bedtime stories about a certain girl who was sent down from Heaven because her mother wanted her so much. I tell my son stories about being wild and free in the woods, just like he got to be at times. I tell them both stories about Papaw and Granny, about meals and prayers that took place for generations at our kitchen table, about growing up in the holler. They ask for those stories over and over again—*my* stories, *our* stories—the threads of a story they will tell their children and grandchildren, who will someday savor those words.

When Papaw Conn was on his deathbed, I begged him to tell me some of his stories. *They don't matter now,* he told me. And I let it go, already mourning what I could never know of him and his life. But I discovered that our stories *do* matter—they tell us who we are, give us history and context that help us define ourselves. Some stories serve as a warning, while others are an endless source of hope. And there is always more to be written.

I look into my children's faces and see the best of myself, a reminder of how important it is to choose my best every day. I see life that springs forth and defies the cruelty we so often inflict. That I can give my children something better, give my *self* something better. That I must, come hell or high water. I feel the magic of childhood and the whispering strength of forests waiting for us. I see miracles incarnate. I hear the stories I tell my children, the stories of their births and how their lives are gifts to us all. I see myself and my parents, grandparents, generations I never knew but whose love and loss are bound into each thread of my being. I see the holler I was born to, as much as I was born to any person—a place and a symbol filled with power and knowledge, comfort and paradox.

I see my granny. We're sitting in the white glider on her front porch, a bucket of beans in front of us. She strings them with knowing hands, snapping off the ends without hesitation, breaking them into perfect pieces. I try to mimic her, carefully pulling the strings from each pod, knowing how they feel in your teeth once they're canned. She does not speak, and I do not need her to. I have watched her carry split wood from this porch—the fire never died in her house. I've watched her wring the chickens' necks and make pie out of just about anything you could ever want. I've watched her cry and pray and love when surely there was no reason to.

Not far from us is the creek I grew up playing in, full of pinching crawdads and the occasional copperhead. There's the forest with its guardians, oaks and maples who watched me as a child. Granny and I can hear the sound of the leaves moving in the distance. It's like a prayer she has taught me.

EPILOGUE
Endless Revision

At his high school graduation, Orion walked across the same stage I had crossed seventeen years earlier, when I received my college degree—his little school's gymnasium couldn't accommodate the ceremony. Orion earned the highest honors and received scholarships to various universities. Going to college was never even a question in his mind.

I took him to get his wisdom teeth out earlier in the week. We got home after that appointment, and I picked up his medicines a little later—an antibiotic and something for the pain, in case he needed it. I set them on the kitchen counter and didn't think about them until he picked them up.

What's this?

We looked at the labels.

Oxycodone? I'm not taking this shit. Why would they prescribe that to me?

You're right, I told him. *You don't need that. We'll use ibuprofen and Tylenol.* I wondered whether he remembered the time we went to my father's house and I cried in the car afterward, pleading with him not to ever take pills. Later, he said he didn't remember that specifically, but he knew how badly pills had affected so many people—he wasn't willing to take that chance.

I think about my own prescriptions—an opiate for pain from having teeth extracted so I could get my own teeth straightened after my kids both had braces. A muscle relaxer I was given following a car accident. They sit in a container high on a shelf, unopened.

During a thunderstorm, my daughter, now eleven, calls to me: *Come snuggle with me and the dog, Mama. You were made for comforting—we need you.* She doesn't share my love of thunderstorms, which cooled the thick heat in my childhood bedroom.

I look for every chance to show her I love her, though I sometimes feel so stretched for time, patience, energy. We go on mommy-daughter dates—usually just a simple meal. We go shopping sometimes, but we stick to what we really need and what she can buy with her small allowance.

Like Granny before me, I have largely hidden my emotional work and struggles from my children. All their lives, I have thought about how my choices will affect them, how they will remember all this, and what stories they might tell themselves about the life we are sharing. I force myself to speak gently when I just want everyone to be quiet. We say grace at the table to remind us all that there is always something to be grateful for. I try to find the balance between giving them everything and saving something for myself.

I put my arms around my daughter and pull her close.

I wish everyone could have what we have, she says. *I wish every family was like ours.*

When I sit alone at the end of the night, I realize this is my greatest triumph—to give my children the love and comfort I longed for, but which were not to be found in my childhood home. To give them a new world—one where they can thrive—without having first seen that world myself. What greater magic is there? Every day, I try to give my children the kind of life I know Granny wanted for me. And I do it without knowing quite how, writing a new story for us, revising until I get it right.

I think of my little-girl self, who is surely still inside me, and know I could tell her that she is good and that everything is going to be okay. I would tell her there are angels and spirits who have loved her since before she was born, and they have filled the forest with treasures that only she can find. I would tell her that everything she longs for is also looking for her, yearning to be found. Some of it is in the creek behind her house, hidden in the fossils and the sound the water makes as it caresses each stone. Some is at Granny's house and at her holy table, where love and sacrifice are made manifest. Some is in the books she loves to read, with characters whose lives she feels as if they were her own. Mostly, it is concealed within her own hopeful heart, just waiting for her to write her story.

ACKNOWLEDGMENTS

I would like to thank Young Smith, my creative writing mentor, for being the first person to encourage me to write my story and for convincing me it was a story worth telling. I am forever grateful to Lois Giancola, who believed in me before I could believe in myself, and who has endlessly supported and encouraged me. Thanks to Adriann Ranta Zurhellen, Bianca Spriggs, and Hafizah Geter—three amazing women who helped this book be the best it could be and saw the value in bringing it to life. I thank my children for loving and accepting me throughout this project and during all our time together—to both of you, I love you most.